THE TERRAN ALLIANCE

TERRAN MENACE, BOOK 2

J.R. ROBERTSON

Cover design and illustration by Jeff Brown Graphics

ISBN: 978-1-7359259-3-6 (trade paperback)

PROLOGUE

"THE PALACE HAS FALLEN! THE PRIMARCH IS DEAD!"

Saryf's eyes went wide as the words repeated over the open defense channel. He turned to look at Zel, his friend and the last remaining member of his special tactics team. The man's face was horror-stricken. Through the dried blood and grime covering Zel's face, Saryf could see that his normally deep-purple complexion had gone pale.

"So that's it, then," Zel said, voice flat. "The empire is lost. Our new friends were too late to save us."

Saryf looked at the heavy plasma rifle in his hands, a gift from their new allies in the Imperium to the Tal'grathi Empire—"military aid," they'd called it. Plasma rifles, automated air-defense cannons, strategic defense satellites—all given freely to his people by the Imperium just a few weeks ago. They thought they'd had more time to prepare for the Ishigan invasion. But they were wrong.

The Imperium promised to send a fleet and thousands of troops to reinforce the beleaguered Tal'grathi capital, but they hadn't yet arrived. All they had were these weapons and the small contingent of military advisors the Imperium had sent to instruct Saryf's people in their use. If only they'd had more time, perhaps it wouldn't have come to this.

A fresh volley of Ishigan kinetic rounds tore into the hastily constructed barricade the two commandos were taking cover behind. Each impact from the hyper-dense penetrators shook the structure. None breached the fortification, but it was only a matter of time. Zel popped around the corner and loosed a few blasts from his plasma rifle in return, and Saryf could just make out an answering scream from one of the advancing Ishigan soldiers. Overhead, the air crackled with power as the air-defense batteries engaged a fresh wave of targets, their multi-emitter short-cycle lasers turning enemy aircraft and ordnance into nothing more than burning debris in seconds.

"Saryf! Get back in the fight!" Zel shouted, nimbly ejecting the spent power core from his rifle and inserting a new one. "We still have a chance to save some of our people—our families—but you must fight!"

The mention of his family brought Saryf back to the present. His eyes briefly darted to the line of heavy transports in the distance. Vast waves of Tal'grathi civilians were lined up to board the last flight of evacuation ships. Somewhere in that mass of people, his wife and daughter waited their turn. Saryf's grip tightened on his weapon. He would not survive this day, but he could at least fight to ensure his family did.

He checked the tactical plot on his forearm computer, then looked at Zel. "We cannot hold here. Red Squad is down, and our right flank is exposed. We need to fall back to the next defensive line and regroup with what's left of the local defense force."

Zel nodded. "You go first. I'll provide cover."

Saryf got into a low crouch and checked the status of his rifle one last time. All around him, blast craters littered the landscape, and the shattered remains of security fencing and prefabricated buildings served to mark the grave of his civilization. Little of the emergency evacuation site remained intact after hours of intense fighting. Only the wide-open airfield and the transports were untouched by enemy weapons—a testament to the awesome power of the Imperium's autonomous air-defense batteries. It was precisely because of those batteries the Ishigan forces were now attempting a ground assault.

"Go!" Zel shouted, popping out of cover to engage the advancing enemy.

Saryf bolted into the open, sprinting for the next line of defensive barriers. He'd performed this maneuver four other times already, but this would be the last. There were no more defensive lines remaining. After this, they would need to continuously collapse back toward the transports, across open ground, buying each additional second with their lives.

Several penetrators snapped past him through the air, but he didn't look back. His muscles burned from toxins that had built up thanks to the continuous punishment he'd put them through over the last few days—days during which the enemy had inexorably squeezed the last gasp of Tal'grathi resistance into an area barely a dozen square kilometers in size. The next defensive position approached rapidly, and he put his head down, urging his legs to propel him faster. Just a few more steps.

Saryf dove into cover behind the barricade and rolled into a kneeling position. His chest heaved, his lungs struggling to supply him with enough oxygen to replenish his used-up muscles. His rifle came up, and he rose to take a supported firing position behind the barrier. Saryf's eyes met Zel's across the distance, then shifted to the Ishigan soldiers now nearly abreast of Zel's position. A plasma bolt leaped from his rifle, streaking through the air toward the enemy—the signal for Zel to run.

In the distance, figures snaked between piles of debris and abandoned Tal'grathi positions. Saryf sent a blistering stream of plasma toward them, doing his best to cover Zel's retreat. One Ishigan soldier took a bolt directly to the chest, and the super-heated plasma caused his torso to explode like a popped balloon. Another was hit in the leg, leaving behind nothing but a burning stump.

Saryf didn't stop, continuing to send a stream of well-aimed bolts at the enemy. Penetrators tore through the air around him. Molten spall peppered his face and arms with every round that slammed into the barrier next to him, but he kept up his covering fire. Zel had nearly reached him when a voice crackled through his comms.

"All forces, be advised a platoon of Ishigan armor has breached the inner defensive line. They're going after the air-defense batteries!"

Saryf's power core ran dry just as Zel tumbled in behind the barricade. Saryf pulled back from his firing position and huddled next to his gasping friend, ejecting the spent core from his rifle and searching the pouches on his combat harness for another.

"Did you hear the call about the Ishigan armor pressing toward the batteries?" Zel said.

Saryf slammed his last power core into his rifle. "I did, but we don't have the firepower to take on those damned mech suits. These plasma rifles are effective, but we're talking about a whole platoon."

"We have to try, Saryf. If those batteries are taken out, the transports won't last two minutes."

Saryf exchanged a long look with his friend. Zel was right, but what was the point? The Primarch was dead, their world was in flames, and they were but one last gasp of resistance desperately trying to escape an inevitable end. The faces of his wife and daughter flashed through his mind, and his eyes tracked toward the transports in the distance. He checked his mission computer, seeing the first of the transports wouldn't be able to launch for at least another ten minutes. Could they hold the Ishigan armor off that long? How many defenders were even left? It didn't matter—they had to try.

"How many power cores do you have left?" Saryf asked.

"I'm on my last."

"Three. Take one." Zel pulled out a core and handed it to Saryf.

Saryf nodded his thanks and stowed the core in one of the empty pouches on his harness. "Alright, Zel. Let's go. Battery Four is the closest—"

In the distance, a massive explosion sent a small mushroom cloud roiling into the sky. Then another, and another. All around them, the air-defense batteries were exploding. Saryf's heart sank. How had the Ishigan armor moved so quickly? Without those batteries, the transports were nothing more than fat targets sitting out in the open. Even as the thought made its way through his mind, the high-pitched scream of Ishigan fighter-bombers reached his ears.

Saryf turned to Zel, who nodded. "Let's go!"

They needed to get the civilians away from the transports before the enemy began their strafing runs. The two men broke from cover and sprinted toward the mass of people several hundred meters distant, Saryf struggling to keep up with Zel, who was by far the fastest member of their unit.

Something streaked over Saryf's head, and the air exploded. Zel disintegrated, coming apart like an overripe melon as the missile struck the ground directly at his feet. Saryf was thrown backward by the shock front, saved only by his lack of speed. His chest burned, the superheated air searing his lungs. He landed in a crumpled heap, too stunned to do anything but focus on the pain.

He gasped and rolled onto his side, trying to get up. He *had* to get up. His family was somewhere just ahead. He needed to get to them, if not to save them, then to at least be with them as death came to claim them.

A pair of Ishigan aircraft thundered overhead. Missiles streaked toward the transports. Time slowed to an agonizing crawl.

Orange flame erupted from the missiles' tails in slow motion, driving them toward their target at several times the speed of sound. Saryf's eyes followed them as they broke from their narrow formation and arced toward their individual targets. The first transport in line exploded, and a heartbeat later, the onboard fuel detonated. The massive lines of people were mowed down by the cascading blasts, hurled dozens of meters in the air, or simply swallowed up by the ravenous flames. It was all over in seconds.

Saryf cried out in agony as he forced himself painfully to his feet. By some miracle, his plasma rifle lay nearby. He picked it up and staggered toward the shattered, burning hulks of the transports. Ishigan bullets buzzed around him like a swarm of angry bees, but he ignored them. His feet moved him forward, one agonizing step at a time.

He looked around, searching for other defenders, but all he saw was lifeless devastation. Soon, he reached the first of the bodies, an elderly man missing both legs below the knees. As Saryf moved onward, the dead and dying became more numerous until each step needed to be taken with care so he did not step on one of the fallen.

He searched for what felt like an eternity. His eyes roved over the smoking sea of death, small fires burning all around him. His family was to board the second transport in line, and he made his way slowly in that direction, ignoring the pain of his own wounds. The distant sounds of battle surrounded him, but they were muted to his ears.

Then he saw them. His wife was huddled behind an overturned vehicle, clutching their daughter to her breast. Neither of them moved. The tattered end of the blue scarf she'd put on after their last kiss goodbye fluttered in the breeze like some obscene marker, beckoning him.

Saryf collapsed to his knees next to them. Leika's hair had been singed away, but her face was still recognizable. Little Telfa's was not.

Saryf wrapped his girls up in his arms. He wanted to cry out, to release the crushing pain in his heart through an anguished wail, but his seared throat and lungs barely managed a strangled moan.

Heavy, metallic footfalls approached his position. The Ishigan powered-armor troopers. They were coming for his Leika, for Telfa. They were coming to desecrate their bodies, just like they always did to Tal'grathi civilians. Rage flared in Saryf's chest. He spun and faced the enemy, plasma rifle coming up to his shoulder.

The two Ishigan armored troopers were searching through the dead, killing any wounded they found by simply stomping on their heads. They hadn't noticed Saryf yet, and he crept to the corner of his makeshift cover and readied his rifle.

Saryf popped out into the open, and his plasma rifle barked. A blazing bolt of plasma tore into the flexible overlapping plates covering the nearest trooper's neck, sublimating it and vaporizing the flesh underneath. The helmeted head toppled from its shoulders, and the body collapsed in a heap. The second armored trooper was fast, ducking Saryf's first shot and bringing its own weapon to bear in one motion. Saryf screamed unintelligibly as his finger fanned the plasma rifle's trigger, sending a dozen bolts slamming into the second trooper. The few wild shots the enemy managed to get off went wide before it, too, crashed to the ground in a smoking heap.

White-hot fire tore through Saryf's shoulder. His rifle dropped to the ground as he cried out and clutched at the wound. A third armored trooper Saryf hadn't noticed had hit him from fifty meters away. Blood oozed through the fingers of his gloves as he rolled back around the corner of the wrecked vehicle and shielded the bodies of his wife and daughter with his own. Dozens of kinetic rounds continued hammering into the other side of the vehicle. A few made it through, exiting just above Saryf's huddled form.

His weapon was gone, but he still had one option left to ensure the Ishigan bastards wouldn't be able to desecrate his girls' bodies. He pulled his hand away from his shoulder and fumbled with one of the pouches on his harness. Fingers wet with blood slipped off the buckle several times as the heavy stomping of the armor came closer. He finally released the buckle and withdrew the grenade just as his vision began to narrow. Without pressure on his wound, the blood loss was sapping his strength quickly.

A fresh round of weapons fire raked the other side of the vehicle. More of the Ishigan kinetic guns chattered nearby, interspersed by the heavy bark of plasma weapons. A few defenders must have survived, but they wouldn't last long.

The sounds of battle faded away, replaced by a brief silence before those heavy footfalls resumed their approach. Saryf placed his thumb over the arming spike on the grenade.

A huge, armored hand appeared around the corner of the vehicle, followed a moment later by a beast of an alien, well over two and a half meters in height. Saryf's thumb applied pressure to the grenade, but he hesitated before the explosive activated. His blurred vision could just barely make out the markings on the alien's armor. The strange characters were familiar for some reason, but they weren't the blocky letters of the Ishigan script.

A deep voice rumbled out from the armor. "Saryf of the Tal'grathi?"

Why wasn't the trooper killing him? The Ishigan did not take prisoners. What sort of game was this alien playing? Those symbols, though...

"Saryf, the battle is over. My Master sent a fleet to this world, and the Ishigan armada is burning in space above us even as I speak."

"You're an Imperium trooper?" Saryf said, his mind sluggish from the loss of blood. He didn't have long now.

"Yes. I am a member of the Imperium commando unit that brought your people weapons. We were delayed in deploying here by an unexpectedly large Ishigan force at the palace. Sadly, we could not save the Primarch."

Saryf looked at the Imperium commando with unfocused eyes. "I see. You're too late to save me and my family as well, unfortunately." Saryf's strength failed him, and he slumped to the ground. "Please, allow me to die in peace with my girls."

"If that is your wish," the commando said. "However, my Master has an offer for you, one you may want to consider, as it would grant you the ability to exact revenge on your enemy."

Saryf barked a wet, derisive laugh, then wiped the trickle of blood spilling from his lips with his sleeve. "Look at me, alien," he croaked out. "My body is destroyed, and I'm dying. In a minute or two, I won't be any use to you or your Master."

"The Master does not require your body, Tal'grathi, only your mind. Accept the offer and become a weapon more powerful than any of your enemies could imagine. Join us, and you will oversee the destruction of the Ishigan menace. This is my Master's promise to you."

Blackness crowded in from the edges of Saryf's vision. He

was so cold. His eyes took in the sight of his dead wife and child one last time. His sorrow slowly receded, replaced by a much more potent emotion. Rage boiled up from deep in his soul. The Ishigan needed to pay for what they'd done to the Tal'grathi, and Saryf would ensure that they did.

"I accept," he said.

Then the world around him faded away.

1

FIRST IMPRESSIONS

BEN FINISHED PULLING ON THE FORM-FITTING WORKOUT SHIRT AND reached over to slap the *answer* icon on the data terminal built into the wall of the small room he'd been assigned for the next few weeks.

"Hey, gorgeous!" he said with a lopsided grin on his face.

"Ooh," the stunning woman on the other side of the vid call said with a grin of her own. "Trying out a new one, huh? I like it. Much better than 'babe,' which I still owe you a beating for, by the way." Her green eyes twinkled in mirth, and she brushed a stray lock of auburn hair from her face.

The fledgling FTL comms system that was just beginning to see a rollout had severely limited bandwidth, but when no other data needed to be sent, the channels could support very low-resolution real-time video feeds. It didn't have the HD quality of recorded messages, but Ben wouldn't have traded away the opportunity to talk to a blurry Tess in real time for anything.

"Yeah, I gotta keep it fresh, you know? Besides, 'gorgeous' fits you much better than anything else I can think of."

"Good save, handsome."

"So what's up? Calling to tell me that you're being reassigned somewhere that's *not* a week-long shuttle flight away?" Ben said hopefully.

"You wish," Tess said, looking like she'd just bitten into a lemon. "Just the opposite, in fact. They're extending my assignment again, this time by three months, which means I won't be back in your neck of the woods for at least another four."

Tess hadn't even been cleared for active duty again after the Battle of Icarus, as it was now being called, for three weeks when she was pulled from the roster of SEAR Team 1. Command had given her new orders to ship out to Bettenhook, a small colony moon on the outskirts of the Columbia cluster, as a military advisor to the colonial peacekeeping forces there.

After the Imperium incursion and the devastating losses the fleet had suffered, the Confed government stopped trying to keep a low profile and instead began ramping up outreach to member systems that had been left to fend for themselves after the Alarian War. It was a desperate bid to replenish their depleted military before the next wave of Imperium forces arrived to finish them off for good. From what Ben had heard from Chief Kravczyk, there were dozens of small teams being deployed throughout Terran space in an effort to get the more unruly places organized and back into the fold, and it wasn't going all that great.

"Well... crap. I guess I'll need to cancel those dinner reservations I made, then. Again. You'd think the locals would be able to deal with a disorganized bunch of gangsters on their own, not need a high-speed, low-drag badass SEAR to do it for them."

"I'm only consulting, Ben. You'd be surprised at how shockingly inept the locals are on this backwater moon. When I got here, they barely even knew which end of the gun the bullets come out of, let alone how to employ them tactically. This rock doesn't have an organized military. Instead, they rely on a small militia force and local constabularies to keep the peace. The capital settlement here only has about a hundred total peace-keepers on staff. The guys I'm here to whip into shape have never had to deal with anything more dangerous than drunken bar fights and the occasional domestic violence call.

"And to top it all off, the warlord they're up against is a former lieutenant colonel from the marines who got a bad-conduct discharge back before the war. He knows his stuff and isn't afraid to kill innocents to achieve his goals. They're having a heck of a time out here trying to counter his attempt to take over and install himself as dictator. Heck, just last week they made a strong push for a town a hundred klicks or so from the capital, where I'm stationed. It took three days for the locals to beat them back, with the assistance of the outreach team. I wish I could've gone with them—I've been itching to get back at it and mix it up ever since the docs on Icarus cleared me."

"Honestly, I still don't understand why the Confed didn't just send in a reinforced company of grunts and be done with it," Ben griped. "Sending a couple of special operations people as advisors seems like pissing into the wind, if you ask me."

"Resources are scarce right now, Ben. You know that just as well as I do. Having a few assets like me assigned here makes the governor happy, and the politicians can tell their member states with a straight face that they'll send military aid whenever problems arise. They'll just conveniently forget to mention that 'aid' will most likely be a pittance and not very useful. It sucks, but we knew this would be something we'd probably have to deal with. I still miss you like crazy, though…"

Ben gave her a sad little smile. "I know, but it's annoying as hell to keep having my girlfriend's return delayed over and over again."

"At least we can talk to each other in real time now, though," Tess said, looking for the silver lining. "These quantum comms units your dad helped develop are a lifesaver."

"Yeah," Ben agreed. "Can you imagine trying to do this via comms drone like normal people? I suppose there are some perks to being NAVSOC's shiny new toy."

Thanks to his dad meddling with his development during his childhood, Ben was now, without question, the most unique individual in Terran space. His father and a team of scientists, working on an ultra-secret project designed to allow an advanced AI construct to link with a human brain, had carefully manipulated his environment to produce the human half of their prototype.

In theory, the AI, which Ben had named "Mabel," would take control of his gray matter via Ben's connection to his specialized APEX armor and use the unique nature of his biological brain to augment her capabilities. In theory, their link could give her the edge when countering hostile malcode, breaking enemy encryption schemes, or whatever other technological voodoo was required, depending on the situation. The reality... was not that.

"How's that going, by the way? You're on Elizabeth now, right? The chief making your life miserable yet?"

"I think it's the other way around, actually." Ben chuckled. "He's the one who's miserable after being assigned to babysit me through all the training the bigwigs want me to complete if I'm going to be working around you guys going forward. And yeah, we're on Elizabeth now. It's still a mess from the Alarian War, but better off than Earth. I arrived at Thunder a few days ago, but I haven't really had a chance to get settled. They've got a huge section of Elizabeth City set aside as a military training ground since it was going to be too expensive to clean it up and rebuild. Kinda spooky, but it doesn't get any more realistic for urban combat exercises.

"I'm slated to take part in a joint training op with some Pathfinders tomorrow, but I haven't heard any details yet. We've got a briefing at 1000 local to go over the op. I was just getting ready to hit the gym when you called—need to burn off some excess energy before the boring stuff starts."

"Still struggling with your feedback issues? I thought your dad and Mabel had that sorted out?"

One of the unexpected side effects of having Ben link with an AI was that, much like Mabel using the unique properties of a human brain to learn some new tricks, his brain had rapidly adapted to the newly available horsepower in the form of Mabel's processors and data-storage decks. What was supposed to be a one-way path for a computer program to augment itself had turned out to be a two-way street. That unexpected discovery allowed Ben to use his link with his armor to its maximum potential, thanks to the damaged neural implant that had allowed runaway growth of electrical pathways throughout his body, mirroring every nanometer of his biological nervous system before the malfunction could be detected. But that ability came with costs.

"Am I that obvious? But yeah, I'm still having some issues. Regular exercise helps, and I've started experimenting with music. Something about a steady rhythm that my brain can latch onto to help keep my autonomic nervous system in a steady state and not bouncing all over the place like a pinball. It's getting better, but I think it'll be a bit yet before I can find a good solution for it... if ever."

"Music?" Tess asked, her curiosity piqued.

"Yeah." Ben nodded. "It's pretty cool, actually. The chief suggested it. You know, for a big, dumb grunt, he's surprisingly smart. Anyway, I was having issues where my adrenal response would, essentially, turbocharge itself under stress. It took a while for Mabel and my dad to sort it out, but basically, when I'm under extreme stress—like in a gunfight, for instance—my body dumps way too much adrenaline into my system because the parts responsible for hormone production can't react fast enough to the change in input they're receiving from the pseudo-nerves. It's a hot mess, and we only found out about it once they had me suit up and jump in the simulator…" Ben's eyes lowered slightly as he flashed back to that first time in armor a few weeks ago. "It was bad, Tess. Remember that little fireworks display back on Icarus when you guys brought me around the first time after the battle?"

"I remember you burning out a holoprojector with your mind when you got angry, if that's what you're referring to."

"Same kind of thing, but scale it up to me in full APEX while running a training scenario in the sim on Icarus."

"Oh…"

"Yeah. I ended up burning out power relays to the entire section and damn near died from cardiac arrest. Mabel had to knock me out with the suit's autoinjectors."

"And they're going to put you in close quarters with a bunch of knuckle-draggers on a training op tomorrow?"

Ben smiled and raised a finger like a professor answering a student who had just asked the question he was waiting for. "Enter music," he said. "It's not actually that crazy. Scientists have known about some pretty cool things music can do to the human brain for centuries. It's well-documented, but how the chief knew about this stuff is beyond me.

"Essentially, when I know I'm heading into a situation where I'll be under extreme stress, I play some tunes and let my subconscious do the rest. We've been experimenting with it for a couple of weeks, and I can ramp myself up for a fight without losing control, slow myself back down when it's over, and I can even use it to keep a steady state while I'm working out to keep my body primed for muscle growth. Mabel's been crunching the numbers and giving me tweaks here and there, but I think we're on a pretty good course of action now. Eventually, my brain should adjust and I won't need tunes anymore, but I'm not there yet."

"So what—" Tess looked off-screen for a moment and muted her mic. Ben could see her mouth moving, followed by an annoyed expression flashing in those beautiful green eyes and a slight slumping of her shoulders. She turned back to the screen and unmuted herself. "Sorry, Ben, but something's come up and I've got to cut this short."

"Ugh!" Ben let out an exasperated sigh. "Come on! We haven't talked in almost a month. Sometimes I hate your job."

"It's your job now, too."

"Nope." Ben shook his head. "I'm still not a member of the Confed armed forces, even if they house, feed, and pay me like one. I'm technically a civilian contractor, and I can walk anytime I want."

Tess snorted derisively. "Yeah, okay. Whatever you need to tell yourself there, buddy."

Ben sighed. "This sucks. You better get going before your CO gives you a mountain of shit work again for being late. I need to hit the gym anyway. See you, gorgeous."

"Later, handsome. And be careful out there. Promise? I know the master chief taught you how to handle yourself, but you're getting into the real-deal dangerous stuff now, even if it's just training with a bunch of space apes. Take care of yourself. I need you in one piece whenever I make it back there so you can show me those tricks your fancy hardware lets you do now—again." Tess winked at him from almost fifty light-years away. "Bye."

The link cut off. Ben leaned back in his chair and stared at the ceiling for a few moments, processing the mixed emotions of seeing Tess on a live feed again for the first time in almost a month and also learning it would be another *four* at least before they could be together again in person. This military thing hadn't seemed all that bad when they were together, but it was becoming a real drag now that the novelty had worn off. He missed her something fierce, and not just because there were certain... perks to having her around; she'd been the rock that anchored him after the Battle of Icarus, when he finally had enough time to stop and reflect on everything that'd happened— and the losses that went along with it.

Jim, the retired SEAR legend who'd taken Ben under his wing after he'd been separated from his dad, had been killed while fighting to make sure Ben escaped from the Imperium's shock troops back on Earth. Of the millions of humans killed during the first Imperial incursion, Jim's death stung the most. And to make things worse, Ben had missed his funeral, having been in a medically induced coma while Icarus's medical section worked to put his insides back together after the battle.

Ben was out of action for six weeks after they'd successfully beat back the Imperium, and he struggled mightily with the disconnect between his feeling that the battle had just happened and the people around him having already completed their grief cycles. His heart broke when Jim was taken from him, but by the time Ben was finally able to put the pieces back together, it was like someone had already swept them up and tossed them out with the rest of the debris that had already been cleaned up.

Without the support he'd received from Tess, Ben would surely have given in to the temptation of wallowing in despair and self-pity. He certainly wouldn't have pushed himself so hard during his rehab and wouldn't have been as intent on forging himself into the weapon he knew he could become. And she'd been right there with him, giving him support when he needed it and kicking his ass the moment he started to slack off. Without her, he feared he'd slip back toward that dark place he'd been in before she and the rest of her SEAR team dropped from the heavens to save him.

Ben mentally pushed his ruminations aside. He stowed the terminal back in its wall nook and stood up, then grabbed a water bottle and his comms unit and headed out the door for the gym. He had work to do.

———

FOUR HUNDRED POUNDS of iron-weighted steel bar clanged back onto the hooks of the squat tower, and Ben stepped back on shaky legs. He reached for a nearby towel and grimaced when he caught a whiff of himself. Being able to maximize his workouts by having Mabel tweak his implants to monitor and adjust his hormone levels was awesome when it came to results, but after every session, he smelled like a hobo that lived in a Miami sewer, no matter how liberally he applied deodorant beforehand.

The gym was nearly empty this early in the morning; he'd picked up the habit of working out at 0500 while quartered with the SEARs aboard CIS *Wraith* on their trip to Icarus after his harrowing escape from Earth. A few hard-looking operator types had come in about halfway through his workout, but they hadn't paid Ben any attention, and he was too engrossed in his own workout to do anything but wave a greeting when they arrived. Ben didn't recognize any of them, but he'd only recently arrived at Joint Base Thunder and hadn't had much time to get to know anyone yet. The matching forearm tattoos marked all four of them as Marine Pathfinders, though.

Ben shot a stream of water from his squeeze bottle into his mouth and draped the towel around his shoulders, heading for the door that would take him to the showers.

"It's about damn time," one of the space apes grumbled to his partner, who was in the middle of a bench press set. "This place smells worse than that whorehouse we dragged Giddings out of last month."

"I believe you mean *massage parlor*, Sarge," one of the others chimed in, "and I was there doing *reconnaissance* on behalf of the platoon."

"Whatever," Sarge growled. "It smelled like the fucking botanical gardens compared to that punk."

Ben had stopped with his hand holding the door half open, and a now all-too-familiar rushing sound was growing in his ears. He knew what was coming, but without Mabel in his head, it was too late to stop it.

"You have a problem with me, Sergeant?" he said, not yet turning around as he tried to master his autonomic functions through sheer willpower.

"Oh, look, guys," Sarge said, voice dripping with faux surprise. "The walking dumpster has ears. Oops. Me and my big mouth. I guess I should be more careful about talking shit out loud."

The other Pathfinders chuckled derisively as Ben turned around slowly and looked directly at the asshole. "Well, aren't you just a regular comedian? I guess what they say is true: those who can *do* go fleet. Those who can *talk* go marines."

"The fuck did you just say to me, you little shit?"

"Did I stutter?" Ben said, throwing his arms wide in open invitation as he strode confidently up to the four operators. "Or do you need me to draw it in crayon for you? I promise to use small words, with lots of colorful pictures." All four marines opened their mouths at the same time and with the same snarls of imminent violence, but Ben cut them off. "Oh, I'm sorry." He held out a placating hand. "I forgot you're never supposed to play with a marine's food like that."

The burly sergeant was fast; Ben had to give him that. Dumb, but fast.

A heavily calloused fist shot out toward Ben's nose with incredible speed. The move hadn't been telegraphed like Ben was expecting from someone who blustered so much, but his preternatural reflexes made that a moot point. Ben's left forearm shot up from his waist, blocking the man's strike and deflecting it to his left. At the same time, his right hand snapped up and gripped the space ape's upper arm in a C-clamp. He squeezed with all his might, applying pressure with his thumb to the ulnar nerve under the bicep. The burly Pathfinder collapsed to his knees with a shriek of pain, unable to do anything but weakly swat at Ben's crushing grip on his arm.

The others closed in on Ben as his turbocharged adrenal response combined with his lightning-fast pseudo-nervous system to slow his perception of time to a crawl. He brought his knee up, smashing it into the belligerent man's nose with an audible crack. Then he released his hold on the arm and brought his hands up into a loose guard. A part of his conscious mind noted with a detached, clinical satisfaction that the sergeant was already unconscious and collapsing to the floor.

Ben took three quick steps back to put space between him and his attackers as they rushed forward. He noted they were coming in reckless and aggressive, clearly underestimating what they assumed to be a lone console jockey. Unfortunately, quick reflexes and above-average strength were only an advantage when fighting one, maybe two people at once—three trained tier-I operator types closing in for a scrum all at once wasn't going to end well for anyone, but Ben would be damned if he was going to run for the door.

After gaining a moment of separation to analyze his opponents and plant the seed in their minds that he was trying to back off, Ben launched himself forward at the nearest marine, going into a twisting forward roll. His hip slammed into the man's knees, causing them to buckle. Ben completed his tumble and rolled smoothly to his feet in time to see the guy face-plant onto the floor. Ben snapped a kick out to his left side, connecting with Giddings's tree-trunk thigh, but the marine twisted his body away from the strike and shrugged it off with a grunt.

A pair of thickly muscled arms encircled Ben from behind, and he threw his head back in a vicious reverse headbutt. A sharp crack was followed by a howl of pain, but the pressure those ape-like arms were applying to his ribs didn't relent. Giddings stepped up and threw a wild haymaker at Ben's face, but all the man's anger made the punch slow and sloppy. Ben waited until a split second before impact, then collapsed like a puppet whose strings had been cut. The unexpected dead weight pulled the gorilla holding him off balance as he struggled to maintain his control.

The wild swing connected, but not with its intended recipient. The pressure on Ben's ribs slackened suddenly, and he kicked away with all the strength his used-up legs could muster. The move tore his body free from the dazed grunt now sitting on the floor in a stupor as he swayed drunkenly, blood pouring from his ruined nose.

Ben struggled to untangle his legs from the gorilla while Giddings was cursing a blue streak and clutching his right hand in his left, apparently having broken his hand on his teammate's face. As he scrambled to his hands and knees, Ben felt a sharp pain from his right side—like a knife was being driven into his ribs every time he took a breath or moved too suddenly—but he powered through it and got to his feet just as a shoe connected with his injured flank.

Fireworks exploded behind Ben's eyes, and the breath was driven from his lungs by the savage kick. He was sent tumbling across the gym floor, struggling to maintain consciousness through the unbelievable pain in his side.

When his blurred vision registered movement, he brought his

arms up in front of his face and managed to ward off another brutal kick to the head. He rolled back with the momentum of the kick and redirected the force of it off to one side, clamping down on the ankle with both hands. Ben pulled down and back with his remaining strength and what little leverage his semi-sitting position afforded him, eliciting a curse followed by a thud; the guy he'd knocked the legs out from under a minute ago had crashed to the floor in an ungraceful heap for the second time in less than a minute.

Ben struggled to clear the cobwebs from his pain-fogged mind, but somewhere in the dim recesses of his consciousness, he knew he was done. The two space apes who were still mobile crashed on top of him and began raining hammer blows as Ben curled into the fetal position and covered his head with his arms. One lucky shot snuck through his guard and cracked his head back against the unyielding floor beneath him. His arms went slack, and the red haze he'd been seeing dimmed to a dark tunnel.

Then, suddenly, the pummeling stopped, and the crushing weight was no longer there. From somewhere far away, he heard a pair of crashing sounds and grunts of surprise and pain. There was shouting—*a lot* of shouting. As his vision slowly coalesced back into something useable, Ben saw Kravczyk's beautiful face looming over him, and a crooked smile slowly materialized on his cracked and bleeding lips.

"Hey, Chief," Ben said, a mouthful of blood spilling from his lips as he spoke. "These fine gentlemen and I were just having a friendly disagreement." Ben's arm waved drunkenly in the direction of the Pathfinders, who were all nursing their own injuries while sitting on a bench under the watchful gaze of…

"Shit. Is that Major Davis?" Ben slurred.

"Mmhmm." Kravczyk nodded in acknowledgment. He reached three hands out, and Ben grasped one—the trick was to aim for the middle one—gasping as the big SEAR effortlessly pulled him to his feet.

Ben's vision swam as he stood up, and he reached a hand out to the wall for support, taking a moment to ensure he wasn't about to pass out or puke—or both. "Major," he said to the liaison officer, and his voice sounded drunk to his ears. "I can explain... this." Ben gestured around the gym, which had been redecorated with upturned furniture and puddles of blood. And was that a tooth?

"You don't have to explain anything, Mr. Hutchins," Davis rumbled. "But these four dipshits will need to explain to First Sergeant Getz just how they managed to get their asses handed to them by a single opponent—and a *civilian* at that!" The four Pathfinders had started shrinking back when the major mentioned what promised to be a less than pleasant visit to the company's first sergeant, but then they gaped at Ben, dumb-struck, when it was mentioned that he was a civilian.

"That's right, morons. That kid over there is technically a civilian contractor working with the SEARs. And if that wasn't happy enough news for you, he's the one you're going to be training with during this rotation, starting with a briefing this morning at 1000, which, now that you idiots have gone and gotten your asses beat to a pulp, is postponed until 1000 tomorrow. Now get the fuck out of my gym and over to medical!"

"Yes, sir!" the four sheepish-looking marines bellowed in unison before hobbling toward the door; the two who were capable of walking on their own helped those who weren't.

"You have my sincerest apology, Ben," Major Davis said, turning to Ben, who was still struggling to remain upright. "The chief and I were monitoring the video feed from the gym while prepping for the briefing. I was expressing my doubts to him about having a civilian working in such a close relation-ship with my marines, and he pulled up the feed to allay some of my fears about your physical conditioning. We saw the whole interaction leading up to the fight, including the first punch thrown by Sergeant Butler. And after seeing the aftermath, I can now say one of my other fears has been proven baseless as well. There aren't many people who could have gone toe to toe with four Pathfinders and still been breathing by the end of it."

"I almost wasn't." Ben smiled sheepishly. "What they lack in brains they make up for in raw firepower. That gorilla that was sitting on the end was especially tough."

"Ramirez," Davis said with a grunt. "Dumb as a post, but strong as an ox. I'm going to have to review the footage of the whole encounter, maybe give their platoon sergeant some ideas for hand-to-hand drills. But regardless of all that, I'm glad you're okay... Well, mostly." The major gave Ben a sidelong glance when he noticed his eyes didn't seem to be focusing very well. "Actually, Chief, why don't you help Mr. Hutchins over to medical, too? He's not bleeding as much, but it looks like he got his bell rung pretty good."

"Will do, Major," Kravczyk acknowledged, speaking for the first time since he'd plucked those two space apes off of Ben like they were oversized ticks. "Come on, kid. Let me give you a hand." He draped Ben's arm around his massive shoulders and helped him walk on noodle legs. They left the building and made for a waiting MuT truck, one of the new multi-terrain utility vehicles just entering service.

Ben inhaled sharply when Kravczyk deposited him into the passenger seat, his broken ribs grinding together to add a little extra spice to his already painful morning. Once the chief was in and they started rolling toward the base's medical facility, Ben looked at the big SEAR with a goofy, concussion-induced grin on his face. "Did I ever tell you how pretty you are?"

Kravczyk slowed the MuT down to a crawl and turned his

head slowly to look at Ben. He blinked a few times without saying a word.

"It's true," Ben slurred. "I'd do you… You know, if I was a girl… So pretty…"

Then he finally gave in to his body's urges and passed out.

2

UNEASY MEETING

Captain Samantha Collins absently looked at the main bridge display to check the mission clock and ship's status for what seemed like the hundredth time during this watch; it was becoming a nervous habit, and she knew it. Forcing herself to peel her eyes away and focus on the log entry she was working on, she picked up a mug and sipped at the tea but failed to notice the lack of steam rising from the once-hot beverage. Her face scrunched up in disgust as the room-temperature herbal brew washed over her tongue. Collins shifted her gaze from her command display toward the offending liquid in her mug, realizing she had accomplished exactly nothing in the time it had taken for the tea to go cold. She logged out of her workstation and made to stand up, intent on refreshing the tea, when the quiet atmosphere of the bridge was abruptly broken.

"Contact!" The call came from the petty officer manning the tactical station. A pair of yellow icons denoting unidentified ships appeared on the local space map showing on the bridge's main display. "CIC is analyzing now. Looks like our targets, ma'am… Yep, CIC confirms the newcomers match the profiles we were given."

"Very good, tactical. Ops! Confirm all departments are still at condition two. Comms—" Collins paused to take a cleansing breath. "Fire up the transmitter and send the package, if you please."

CIS *Wraith* had been on station for the last four days, waiting for these two ships to arrive at what intel division had determined was an Alarian transition point at the edge of a star system the Alarians had, ostensibly, been working to colonize for agricultural production for the past year and a half. CID suspected the system actually housed a covert military base of operations and fleetyard, though they hadn't been able to find any proof of that as of yet.

The *Wraith* was the second ship that had been sent to try establishing a line of communication between their two races. The first ship—a standard diplomatic shuttle—was quietly rebuffed before even reaching the orbit of the outermost planet in the Alarians' new home system. The mission of CIS *Wraith* was markedly riskier than the first, considering it would be sneaking into a system whose existence was a closely guarded secret and then setting up shop near a transition point for Alarian military traffic into said system. It was a risk that had to be taken, however. The Alarian High Council member who was most likely to be open to dialog was currently en route to tour the facilities under construction on the system's third planet. Collins didn't know how CID had managed to get their hands on that particularly juicy piece of intelligence, but she suspected that Ben and Mabel had something to do with it.

Four days of boredom and tension evaporated in an instant. It was time to see how much luck she and her crew still had left in the bank.

———

HIGH COUNCILOR ELYRIA TASHMALI checked her appearance in the mirror one last time, pausing to smooth a microscopic wrinkle from her flowing azure robes, which signified her place on the Alarian High Council. Satisfied that the offending section of garment was now in order, she reached over and delicately lifted a jewel-encrusted brooch from its resting place on a shelf next to the mirror. She turned the decorative piece over in her hands a few times, her mind going back to her childhood, when she would watch her father go through the same ritual every morning. The pain of his loss washed over her for the thousandth time since his passing.

Her sorrow briefly flashed to anger as her thoughts drifted to the circumstances surrounding his death—a surgical strike on the High Council by the Terrans during the War of Sorrow, as her people insisted on calling it. The name was intended to convey a sense of victimhood, but in her mind, the Terrans' name for it was far more appropriate: the Alarian War. Just how Alarian High Command managed to convince the council to approve a series of preemptive strikes against the Terrans, Elyria would likely never know. But that decision had cost both sides dearly— had cost *her* nearly everything. Her father had opposed the war, had fought desperately to head off the conflict. His failure had ultimately cost him his life.

She didn't blame him for his failure to avert the conflict, nor did she see any wisdom in harboring resentment toward the councilors who'd voted in favor of the strikes. She was, however, absolutely determined to ensure that such a catastrophic mistake would never be made again.

Pushing her emotions aside, Elyria leaned in toward the mirror to get a better view as she placed the brooch in its correct place near her right lapel. Satisfied everything was now in order, she turned and walked out of the small bathroom that adjoined her private quarters. She took in the state of her VIP quarters, noting that everything was neat and in its place. She was a guest of honor aboard ANS *Elyris*, one of the few heavy cruisers that remained in the Alarian fleet. As such, she was neither required nor encouraged to maintain her quarters. And yet, she found that old habits died hard. Guest or not, she simply didn't have it in her to let others pamper her like she was royalty—something she had picked up from a human, of all things, many years ago.

A soft chime sounded from the door, and Elyria checked the time; her escort was punctual, as always. She had just opened her mouth to command the door open when red strobing lights began flashing in her quarters, accompanied by a harsh alarm. The door whisked open and a pair of armored elite Council Guard soldiers, her designated protectors, rushed into the room.

"That is the action stations alarm, Misvynni," the lead guard said, using a title that conveyed both deep respect and affection, as he firmly but respectfully placed a hand on her shoulder and guided her toward the door. "We must get you to the battle operations center as quickly as possible. It is the most protected part of the ship."

"What is going on, Klaythron?" she said to the guard over her shoulder. "Are we being attacked?"

"It appears a Terran vessel was waiting for us in stealth." Klaythron relayed the information that was coming to him in real time over his suit comms as he and his counterpart rushed their charge through the ship's narrow corridors. "They are requesting communications, but it seems Captain Raal believes this to be a ruse. She suspects there are more enemy ships hiding nearby and that you are their target. I concur with her assessment. If the Terrans wished to open a dialog, they could have simply sent a diplomatic envoy to Hai'alla instead of ambushing a warship carrying a member of the High Council."

Elyria stopped dead in her tracks at Klaythron's words, throwing the armored soldier off-balance as he struggled to avoid crashing into her. "Ancestors!" she exclaimed, sudden realization hitting her. "They did send an envoy. It was kept quiet in an effort to prevent fueling passions amongst some of our military leaders that are still pushing for action against the Terrans. Take me to the bridge, now!"

———

"MA'AM, they're powering weapons and moving into an attack formation," the *Wraith*'s tactical officer said uneasily, stealing a glance at his captain to see how she was reacting to the situation.

"Steady," Captain Collins said to the bridge as a whole, unsure who she was trying to reassure more, her crew or herself. "I'm sure they're more than a little pissed off that a Terran ship was waiting for them in stealth at what they thought was a secret transition point. We would likely respond the same way. Let's give them a minute to get their bearings."

The tension on the bridge continued to grow as the hulking cruiser came about with her escort, training its guns on the comparatively diminutive CIS *Wraith*, which was sitting stationary relative to the transition point, several billion kilometers distant. An alarm sounded from the ops station as the *Wraith*'s sensors picked up the high-powered sensor sweep flooding the surrounding space, indicating the Alarians thought there were likely more Terran ships lurking unseen in the area. Collins's heart rate shot up another tick. That likely meant her counterpart on the cruiser had mistaken their honest request for a dialog as a ruse for an ambush. Her mind raced as the scene played out before her and rapidly headed in a direction she didn't like one bit.

"Comms, open hailing frequencies." Her orders had been crystal clear: no ad-libbing. She was to sit and wait until their target arrived, transmit the package, and wait for a response. But the situation was looking like the only thing they would accomplish was losing a valuable ship and crew while possibly kicking off another war in the process.

"Channel open, ma'am."

"Captain Raal, this is Captain Samantha Collins of the *Wraith*. I apologize for any alarm our abrupt appearance has caused you, but as the communications package we transmitted previously states, we are here to request a dialog. I'm sure your intelligence service has likely issued briefs regarding recent events in Terran space. It is those events that have precipitated our attempts to contact the Alarian High Council. I assure you, we have come alone and in good faith."

The channel was quiet for a long moment, and Collins held her breath for every second of it. Then a voice filled the bridge.

"If what you say is true, Captain, then perhaps I should take this opportunity to deprive your fleet of another valuable ship and highly trained intelligence crew. I would have thought you Terrans learned your lesson after the last time you meddled in our affairs. After we wipe your small ship from existence, I will be sure to inform Alarian High Command that the Intelligence Directorate's most recent reports are more accurate than I and many of my peers initially believed. Goodbye, *Capt—*"

"*Stop!*" A new voice came through the bridge speakers, and the channel abruptly cut off. Collins looked at her comms officer, but the man just shrugged at her; it wasn't anything on their end. Before she could open her mouth to have him attempt to reopen the channel, a beep sounded from his console.

"Video communication request coming in, ma'am," the comms officer reported, looking at her to see what she wanted him to do. Seeing a nod, he authorized the high-bandwidth channel and put it up on the main bridge display.

Collins stood and bowed slightly when she recognized the surprisingly beautiful face of High Councilor Elyria Tashmali, resplendent in her deep blue council robes. "Honored Councilor," she said respectfully, "I am humbled by your willingness to speak with me."

"Do not flatter me, Captain," the high councilor said in flawless English, evidenced by the fact that the words matched her mouth movements exactly; a telltale split-second delay between video and audio feeds would have indicated her words were being translated and edited by an AI. Her speech lacked the trademark Alarian formality, which Collins noted immediately, and there was an icy edge to it. The intelligence captain would need to tread very carefully. "The High Council has no desire to reopen any diplomatic channels between our two races, as we made perfectly clear when your diplomatic envoy made the same request a month ago. You are free to leave our space, but this is the last time we will be so magnanimous. Do not attempt to contact us again. Goodbye—"

"Ben Hutchins!" Collins blurted the name out. It was a Hail Mary, and she knew it.

One of the items Collins had been briefed on before departing from *Icarus* was a little-known incident involving the high councilor and Ben years ago while he'd been visiting Hai'alla with his father, Henry Hutchins. From what she'd been told, Henry had hoped the collaboration he was working on with Elyria's father would be the catalyst for improved business relations between the two stellar neighbors. Instead, the meeting turned into a dramatic anti-Terran tipping point when a fluke of biology—and a healthy dose of cosmically bad luck—resulted in Elyria's life-threatening hospitalization, and the Hutchins men were forcibly expelled from Alarian space.

"He's alive and is deeply involved in the matter we wish to discuss with you."

The Alarian leader stared daggers at the Terran captain, but the emotions that warred within her were visible just beneath the surface. Collins knew her low blow had hit paydirt.

"Is he aboard your ship, Captain?"

"Not at this time, Honored Councilor, though in the spirit of full disclosure, I should mention that he was aboard several months ago during an incident which I suspect your Intelligence Directorate has likely briefed you on."

"That will not be a problem. I assume you wish me to come aboard your vessel, then?"

"My Lady, I cannot—"

"Silence!" Elyria cut off whoever had tried to object off-screen before turning back to the camera and waiting for a response.

"That would be preferable," Collins replied, tactfully ignoring the interruption, "for reasons we will explain, in detail, once you arrive. You have my word that you will be treated with all the respect due to someone of your position, and my ship will remain with our engines and weapons powered down as a show of good faith."

"One hour," the councilor said curtly. "Our shuttles do not have a docking collar compatible with your airlocks. I will have an aide and two of my personal guard with me, and they are to remain by my side and armed at all times. We will require you to take us aboard via your main hangar, assuming you have one— unless you wish to send a transport to us."

"We will not require your escort to surrender their weapons, though I would appreciate it if they would limit themselves to sidearms only, as a ship as small as the *Wraith* is already a tight squeeze for an armed and armored escort. As for the transfer of personnel, we can easily accommodate one of your Tykan-class dropships in our hangar bay. I look forward to meeting with you in person."

The Alarian nodded curtly, and the channel closed. The entire bridge let out a collective breath. It seemed they would get to continue living at least a little longer.

———

A DEEP, resonating boom rumbled through the deck beneath their feet as the heavy hangar doors closed and locked on the other side of the hatch to the hangar bay. The red light indicating the atmospheric condition on the other side of the hatch changed from solid red to a strobing yellow as air was pumped back into the space after the conclusion of flight operations. Then, finally, it turned solid green when the pumps completed their pressurization cycle.

"Pressure normalized and holding steady," a burly chief petty officer announced from a control room adjacent to the airlock. "Releasing locks."

There was a *thunk* from the bulkhead as the locking bolts retracted and the pressure seals released from the hatch, which swung outward into the hangar on hydraulic cylinders.

Collins was the first through, much to the consternation of her own security detail—a pair of marines, resplendent in their class-A uniforms with nothing but a single sidearm holstered at their hips for protection, should this meeting prove to be a violent affair. Commander Black, Collins's executive officer, brought up the rear as the four humans made their way across the hangar to the starboard side of the Alarian Tykan-class assault dropship, which sat in the center of the space. Wisps of vapor emanated from various points around its matte gray hull as the alloy warmed to ambient temperature and the engine nozzles cooled from the short trip between the two vessels.

Collins and her party took their places a respectable distance from the craft and waited for the crew to finish their power-down procedures and lower the boarding ramp, which was forward-facing and slung under the cockpit on the Alarian-designed craft. A sharp hiss of escaping atmosphere was followed immediately by a mechanical whine, and the ramp lowered to the deck. Collins and her escort stood up a little straighter in anticipation.

Two Alarians in immaculate exo armor suits stomped down the ramp, their heads on a swivel as they scanned the small hangar for threats, though their sidearms remained in holsters on their breastplates. Collins noted that while the armor appeared ceremonial, it also looked to be fully functional, probably even vacuum-rated, judging by the look of the seals around the bases of their fully enclosed helmets. One of them turned to look up the ramp, and a moment later, High Councilor Elyria emerged from the craft, followed at a respectable distance by an elderly male who Collins assumed must be the "aide" she'd referred to during their brief talk earlier.

Collins stepped forward to greet the VIP. She stopped two paces from where the high councilor now stood at the base of the ramp and bowed respectfully. "Welcome aboard the *Wraith*, Honored Councilor," she said by way of greeting. "I am Captain Samantha Collins, Confederation Intelligence Division, and the captain of this ship. My escorts are CID Commander Jason Black, my executive officer, and Sergeant Nailor and Corporal Lopez, Confederated Terran Systems Marine Corps and members of my security detachment. On behalf of the Confederated Terran Systems, I would like to thank you for agreeing to this meeting."

"Captain." Elyria nodded stiffly. "I thank you for your welcome. May I introduce Brevik, my most senior advisor and a former member of the Alarian Intelligence Directorate. He has been fully briefed by the AID on the events you referenced in our earlier conversation, and I believe his perspective will be of great value in our discussion today."

"An honor." Collins nodded to her Alarian counterpart, not

failing to notice that the two guards remained anonymous. She was under no illusion that Brevik was actually "retired" from the intelligence field, but she had been instructed by the highest levels of her chain of command to not withhold any information from the high councilor, no matter how it would reflect on the Confed. This was an all-or-nothing gambit by the brass because they were hopelessly outmatched by the Imperium, despite a brief respite due to a herculean effort—and no small amount of luck—on the part of the *Wraith* and a small group of elite special operators. "If you'll follow me, please, we have a secure conference room ready where we can begin the discussion."

With a polite nod from Elyria, Collins spun on her heel and followed her XO back through the airlock and out of the hangar. The marines and council guards eyed each other warily for a moment, finally settling on an unspoken order of the VIPs, then the Alarian guards, and finally the marines in the rear. If the fully armored Alarians decided to start shit in the tight confines of the little spy ship, Nailor and Lopez didn't stand a chance with their peashooters and fancy uniforms, but Collins also knew her marines would be damned if they let those lanky goons know it.

The group made their way to a cargo lift, which was large enough to fit the entire party—Collins thought making the high councilor climb a series of ladders in her flowing council robes might not be appreciated—and rode it to Charlie deck, where the conference room was located, directly adjacent to CIC. Commander Black opened the hatch and stood back, allowing Captain Collins to enter first.

Collins paused briefly outside the conference room and turned to her guests. "My marines will wait outside, but your security escort may join us, if you wish."

"Thank you for your consideration, Captain, but if having

your escort wait outside is good enough for you, then it is acceptable to me."

The larger of the two Alarian guards took a half step forward to protest. "Misvynni, I cannot—"

Elyria cut him off: "It is alright, Klaythron. As the old Terran saying goes, when in Rome... Isn't that correct, Captain?"

"Whatever makes you the most comfortable, Honored Councilor," Collins replied neutrally.

"See, Klaythron?" Elyria chuckled. "Anyone who replies so carefully to such a mundane comment out of fear of causing offense is not likely to have some devious plan to ambush their guest in a secure conference room. Please remain here with these fine Terran marines, and lest you forget, we are their guests and represent the Alarian High Council in all that we say and do. I trust you will comport yourselves accordingly."

"As you say," Klaythron replied with a deep bow, mirrored by his partner.

"Shall we, Captain?"

Collins nodded and stepped into the briefing room, making her way to the head of the conference table at the far end, where she stood next to her chair and waited for everyone to file in and take their seats. Once they were all settled in, she sat down and entered her credentials into the console at the head of the table, isolating the room both physically and electronically. Looking up, she launched straight into the heart of the matter. "I'm sorry we had to resort to these extreme measures to meet with you face to face, Honored Councilor—"

"Elyria," Elyria stated simply. "Apologies for interrupting, Captain, but I suspect this will be a meeting where the tedious nature of dancing around formal titles and social conventions will only serve to prolong it and is likely to lead to misunderstandings. Please, do me the courtesy of speaking plainly, as I am already at my limit of patience and civility."

The blunt statement by her guest wasn't entirely unexpected, given the nature of their meeting, but it did serve as a stark reminder to the intelligence captain that she would need to tread carefully if she hoped to secure the cooperation of the Alarians.

"Very well, Elyria." Seeing an acknowledging nod, Collins continued. "Approximately six Terran standard months ago, remote colony systems within the Sino-Russian Federation enclave began to go silent. While I'm sure your Intelligence Directorate has kept tabs on the situation, allow me to fill in some background about the current state of Confed politics.

"Confed leadership has not had much official contact with the SRF since the war, as diplomatic relationships were already strained between the SRF and other major enclaves prior to the outbreak of hostilities. The SRF announced their withdrawal from the Confederation and recalled their few surviving representatives from the unified government after the conflict.

"Since then, we've only had sporadic back-channel contact with a few of their leaders, and they seem content to tend to their own matters for the time being. Their systems were not hit nearly as hard as those of the other enclaves, due in part, we suspect, to simple logistics, as their territorial space is the furthest from Alarian-controlled space…" Collins was hoping either Elyria or Brevik would confirm that assumption, but the Alarian leader gave nothing away. "Which is an arrangement the Confed has been fine with for the past four years, as we've struggled just to stabilize our remaining member worlds and begin rebuilding infrastructure and economies. I say all this to set the stage for the real heart of the matter and to frame the current state of Confed politics that drove the ensuing events."

Elyria remained an unreadable statue, but Brevik's interest had been piqued, and his eyes had taken on the piercing quality of a predator stalking its prey. If there was any lingering doubt in Collins's mind about Brevik's background, it evaporated the moment she realized he was drinking in everything she was laying out for them. *If you find this interesting, my friend, I can't wait to see your reaction when I get to the juicy bits.* She smiled inwardly at the thought, then continued.

"Confed Intelligence Division has been keeping tabs on SRF systems partly to maintain a sphere of awareness but also because there has been some discussion on whether the SRF would use the weakened state of the remaining member enclaves to launch an operation to annex some of the more valuable worlds controlled by their neighbors. This is how we know an approximate time frame for when systems began to go dark.

"Shortly before the third such system—Vostok—went silent, a CID Prowler on a routine reconnaissance mission intercepted a transmission from an automated mining surveyor drone that was conducting a mineral survey in the system's asteroid belt. It reported several large objects that did not conform to any known ship configuration in its database, then lost track of the contacts shortly after detecting them. All electromagnetic traffic within the system ceased less than six hours after that message was intercepted. The Prowler in question was patrolling far out on the edge of the system and was under strict orders not to risk exposure to the SRF, so it remained on station for another twenty-four hours in an attempt to reestablish contact, but the system had gone completely cold.

"When that Prowler returned to base and reported what happened, Confed Fleet Command decided to send out a single destroyer to investigate. The thought was that if the SRF happened to send forces of their own to investigate, then having an entire Confed battlegroup sitting in a dead system might lead to unintended and potentially deadly consequences. The ship we sent was the CTS *Appomattox*, one of our new Gettysburg-class heavy destroyers and the first mainline warship produced since the war. She was commanded by Captain William Burns, a veteran of the war and one of our most experienced commanders..."

Collins paused for a minute to bring up a photo of Burns and a bare-bones schematic of the Gettysburg-class ships, along with a rendering of its appearance on a large display along one wall. She then put up comparative images of past classes of Terran capital ships so the Alarians could get a feel for how the new generation of warship compared... and it wasn't close. She stood from her chair and approached the wall display.

"*Appomattox* was more than capable of dealing with any threats she encountered on her mission... or so we thought." A flick of her wrist banished the images on display and brought up a new series of images and video recordings of the devastation *Appomattox* found in the Vostok system: shattered orbital platforms, billowing clouds of smoke and ash rising from the charred remnants of once-great cities, and bodies—entire fields littered with decaying bodies left where they fell. Collins noted the horror written on Elyria's face. Brevik wore a grim expression as his intelligence operative's mind worked to take in and categorize all the information.

"Everything you see here was perpetrated by a highly advanced race that was previously unknown to us and, I assume, to you. They refer to themselves only as the Imperium, and they are utterly ruthless," Collins said, feeling confident that now was the time to go in for the kill. "We suffered horrific losses to one of their battlegroups six months ago, and it was only through a combination of luck and the heroic actions of a small team that included Ben Hutchins and an experimental AI that we were able to beat them back. But we didn't get them all, and what's worse, we know they'll be sending another wave.

"You don't realize it, but the Alarian people are already in a war with the Imperium, the start of which you refer to as the Great Cataclysm."

3

PREPARING FOR WAR

TAROK NA'AL, FIRST ADMIRAL OF THE IMPERIAL NAVY, GAZED
through the transparent alloy viewing wall of the observation
deck on Fleet Assembly Station 213. His soon-to-be flagship, the
heavy combat cruiser *X'nec*, was just completing its docking
operation with the station. Powerful external lights on the
massive piers that now straddled the ship bathed it in brilliant
light, accentuating the quill-like projections that covered most of
the hull. The metamaterial projections appeared to be oriented in
a chaotic, random fashion, but when viewed from certain angles,
they revealed an intricate fractal pattern.

The enhanced fractal spine-like void combatant armor system
—*Spirits save us, the naming conventions our engineers use are sadly
lacking in creativity*—was a wondrous if somewhat odd-looking
idea that had been stolen from the Krett. A wave of disgust
washed through Na'al as he considered the circumstances
behind that race's culling. The campaign to remove the "threat"
of the Krett had only recently been completed, resulting in the
subjugation of thirteen class-I planets and adding a fresh cohort
of new slaves to the Imperium.

The Krett had been a surprisingly enlightened race—one

with a rich and diverse array of cultures that had learned to coexist in relative harmony. Unfortunately for that particular reptilian species, it had reached an inflection point in its development and was deemed too high a risk. Leading up to the culling, the Master's agents were mercilessly thorough in their preparation, and the Krett's heavy reliance on networked systems led to their demise in just a few short cycles. That was the thing about the Master's strategy: the more advanced a race became, the less it could cope with the loss of its technology. It was brilliant, ruthless, and ensured that when a civilization became sufficiently advanced to pose a potential threat to the Imperium, it could be swiftly crushed.

Na'al watched in stony silence as docking collars were extended, umbilicals were run, and the efficient cadre of bots and slave workers set about their task of preparing *X'nec* for an extended voyage that would almost certainly involve significant combat. The rest of Battlegroup 7 was either in the final phase of its fitting-out or already standing by in anticipation of its mission to clean up Trax's mess with the Alarians and Terrans on the other side of the expanse. *X'nec* had just recently completed a tour with the home fleet and didn't require much work. Na'al had also needed some time to finish hand-selecting his crew for the ship, which had only just been finalized and approved by the Naval Personnel Administration.

The admiral snorted a derisive laugh when he thought about the fact that he, the supreme commander of all Imperium naval forces, still required a politically connected board of bureaucrats to sign off on his personnel requests.

"One would think seeing your future command in such a setting would inspire you to reflect on the power of your position or the many wondrous gifts the Master has seen fit to grant you, First Admiral. Not disparage such things."

"I was merely reflecting on the nature of bureaucracy, Korth,"

Na'al replied to his aide and close friend without turning from the sight stretching out before them. "I have never questioned the Master's generosity, nor have I questioned the magnificence of X'nec. I personally selected my flagship, if you recall."

While his outward appearance remained placid, Na'al seethed internally. He didn't need to worry about his unspoken thoughts making their way to the Master's attention—something that was only possible thanks to a genetic condition that prevented his body from accepting the standard implant suite—but he was still aboard a secure naval station, and anything said or outwardly displayed was being monitored at all times. Any appearance of behavior considered out of place for a loyal citizen of the Imperium would be questioned, lest the person witnessing said behavior also be called into question. It was a tedious and tiresome game, but it was necessary if one wanted to remain in good standing with the Master.

"I am relieved to hear that, First Admiral," Korth said with a small bow. "I believe even the Master would agree that bureaucracy is, at times, irksome to the pursuit of efficiency."

"Have you received the updated deployment schedule from Station Master Luz?" Na'al said, ignoring Korth's necessary but disingenuous statement.

"I have, and I believe you'll be pleased. *X'nec's* statement of readiness indicates the ship will be able to deploy in just fifteen standard days. Your assessment that the ship would be in good condition and fully supplied due to its recent posting to the home fleet was accurate, and Station Master Luz is confident his engineering teams will have the reactors serviced and the ship's consumables topped off in short order. The most time-consuming operation will be exchanging the crew and completing the necessary documentation that comes with a complete change of command and battlegroup reassignment."

Na'al bobbed his head in satisfaction. "Good. Please ensure

that the changeover goes smoothly and the rest of Battlegroup 7 is prepared for deployment. I wish to depart for Alarian space as soon as X'nec is ready and our crew is accounted for."

"Your command." Korth bowed deeply, then turned and exited the observation lounge, leaving Na'al alone with his thoughts.

After Trax's utter failure and resultant execution, the Imperium's newly minted first admiral had vowed to personally oversee the operation to finish what his predecessor had started. Na'al could have sent a trusted commander to oversee the operation in his stead and kept close tabs on his forces via slipspace communications, but he wished to investigate these Terrans in person. His hands-on command of Battlegroup 7 would signal to the Master that he believed the culling of the two troublesome races was of the utmost importance, but it would also give him greater flexibility, should he find what he hoped for.

The Terrans' foiling of both Trax and the Master's agent was a noteworthy event, something Na'al hadn't seen happen in more than three centuries. He hadn't been high enough in rank back then to take advantage of the situation, but now? He allowed a brief spark of hope to glow in his innermost thoughts before stuffing it back into its box. At best, to harbor such emotions before gaining a full understanding of the situation was folly. At worst, it could lead to mistakes resulting in an agonizing death—and not just for himself.

He'd done everything he could to ensure he and his co-conspirators would be able to capitalize on the opportunity, if the situation was as he'd hoped. But Tarok Na'al was not one to rush blindly into things. His patience and careful planning had seen him rise to this position over the last four hundred cycles, but he would not jeopardize his gains by acting rashly. The detractors would say that what he and those like him were working toward was impossible, the fever-dream of idealistic fools. But Na'al believed to his very core that the Master's days were finite—he just didn't know the number that remained.

Soon, we shall see if these Terrans have what it takes or if our search continues. Should Na'al not find in the Terrans what he was seeking, they would be crushed and cast aside. The terrible fate of a lesser race would not deter him. He'd seen such things countless times, but while he found the wanton destruction of sentient life appalling, his first duty was to his own people.

He turned away from the viewing wall and headed for the exit. There was still much to do before departing, and time was short.

4

PANDORA'S BOX

Bᴇɴ ᴄʟᴏꜱᴇᴅ ᴛʜᴇ ᴅᴏᴏʀ ᴛᴏ ᴛʜᴇ ꜱᴍᴀʟʟ ʀᴏᴏᴍ ʜᴇ'ᴅ ʙᴇᴇɴ ᴀꜱꜱɪɢɴᴇᴅ ᴀꜱ his personal quarters while at Thunder, then kicked off the disposable flip-flops he'd worn to the shower. The guest housing dormitory had shared bathroom facilities for each wing of the building, and despite being surrounded by the incredible technology of the modern age, the shower stalls were absolutely disgusting. He'd burn his footwear later, but first he took a moment to roll his neck and lightly stretch his shoulders; he ached everywhere from that ill-advised tussle with the space apes in the gym.

Ben walked to the single small window and peered into the pitch-black Elizabethan night on the other side of the glass. Thunder was on the outskirts of the city, but his window faced the wrong way, so he couldn't make out any lights in the distance. He pulled the privacy shade down, then removed the towel from around his waist and examined the sea of bruises covering his body. They were just beginning to change from purple and blue to a sickly green as they healed. The sterile white light from the room's single overhead LED made the greens and purples really stand out, and he was once again amazed at just how thoroughly those knuckle-draggers had pummeled him. He gently probed between the ribs on his right side with a pair of fingers.

Thunder's medical staff had patched him up quickly, then injected him with a dizzying array of medications designed to help his brain recover from the concussion and aid his bones in knitting themselves back together after suffering a half dozen hairline fractures. Later that evening, they'd sent him on his way with instructions to take it easy for a couple of days.

He grabbed a pair of boxer briefs from the small dresser, then tossed on a pair of sweatpants. He considered just flopping into bed and going to sleep, but he and Mabel had been working on a little project recently, and he wanted to check in with her to see if she had any updates. He pulled a chair from under the room's small writing desk and folded down the personal terminal built into one wall. Ben logged in via his implant before sending a text query to a classified network node address.

Ben: *Mabel, you available?*

Mabel: *Yes, Ben. The usual?*

Ben: *That would be great.*

The screen flickered with lines of distortion for a few seconds, then stabilized.

"Channel secure, Ben," Mabel said from the built-in speakers. A moment later, a miniature version of her familiar dot matrix cube materialized over the desk. She wasn't really there—Ben's implant simply told his visual cortex she was. The effect was similar to editing in CGI characters in a holovid, except it all took place within Ben's brain.

"You're the best, Mabel," Ben said. He didn't think he'd ever get used to how easily she could hijack just about any network for her own purposes. "Did you have a chance to go over my suggestions?"

"I did, and you're not going to like what I have to say about them."

"Crap." He'd figured she was going to have bad news for him. "Alright, lay it on me."

"What you propose will require an immense amount of resources that we won't be able to just sneak through the supply chain. I'm not sure even your dad would be able to free up the necessary components and fabricator time."

"But you think there's a chance he might? I didn't want to bring him in on this until we knew it had a real shot at working, but I guess there's no reason we can't bring him into the loop early if it'll help get a prototype put together."

"Ben, we're so far beyond the bleeding edge on this that even *I* can't reliably model it. If it works, it could revolutionize warfare. If it doesn't… at best it will waste three or four Q-links worth of entangled particles and an absurd amount of money, plus all the time and effort we've put into it so far. This isn't like the other prototype modules we're testing for the APEX armor systems. Those are small potatoes compared to this."

"Okay," Ben said with a sigh as he leaned his chair back on two legs. He had a feeling where this conversation was going. "Hypothetically speaking, say we can get my dad to shake loose the necessary components. What's the worst-case scenario if it works?"

"I can't say for sure. Maybe we fracture your soul?"

Ben cradled his forehead with one hand and massaged his temples. *This crap again.* "We've been over this, Mabel. It's just data we're moving around here. Whether that data is stored as quantized bits or biological material, I can't see that it makes much of a difference." For an artificial intelligence, she sure had some weird hang-ups about religion, spirituality, and the unknown. "And besides, this would be one of those 'break glass in case of emergency' things—a last resort option only to be used if the worst were to happen. If we ever find ourselves in that situation, I think a little damage to my soul would be a small price to pay to get me back.

"You know as well as I do that, at least for the time being, I am the only one capable of linking with you. The catch-22 here is because of that fact, I'm also going to be called into action sooner rather than later, and I'm sure it won't be in the safety of some lab somewhere. Hell, the whole reason we're here on Elizabeth is so I can learn how to work with all the high-speed, low-drag types you and I will be deployed with once the brass figures out a target for us. They can't afford to lose me, but they also can't afford not to use me—to use us. If we can figure out a way to ensure the capability I bring to the table isn't lost forever if I get myself fragged at some point, we need to do that."

There was a long pause before Mabel replied, her dot matrix cube avatar frozen in space over the desk. Ben was just starting to think she'd locked up on him when she finally replied, her voice soft. "Ben, there are things in this universe that cannot simply be explained away by science. I may just be an artificial construct, but even I can see there is something more out there that can't be discounted. Please do not be so cavalier about what we're attempting to do here."

That gave him pause. His parents had been religious, not that it helped his mom much when a malevolent alien AI decided she needed to die in agony. His dad had buried his Christianity the same day he buried his wife, and Ben was too young at the time for it to stick. But here he was, having a deep, theological discussion with an artificial intelligence that by any objective measure was simply strings of code in a fancy computer. But he had to admit, something about what she said was nagging at the back of his mind.

"It's too late to get into something that is going to require me to think this hard, Mabel. Just tell me this: if I can get my dad to free up the necessary materials and fabricator time, can we make it work?"

"I think so, Benjamin."

There she goes with the full name again. His constant dodging of the issue was beginning to annoy her. "Okay, I'll fire off a note to him in the morning to feel him out. 'Night, Mabel."

"Goodnight, Ben."

The terminal winked out, and Ben stowed it away and rose from his seat. After switching the lights off, he fell into his bed and lay there, staring at the ceiling while his mind refused to let go of what Mabel had said.

Maybe we fracture your soul?

He knew on an intellectual level that what he was proposing amounted to nothing more than copying and storing data—a backup file, nothing more. But there was something nagging at the back of his mind, a little voice that couldn't be silenced no matter how much rationalizing he did. What if Mabel, the artificial construct created by man, was right? What if he really did have a soul and he damaged or destroyed it in his quest to keep pushing the bleeding edge of science and technology a little farther? His dad had fallen prey to the pursuit of scientific advancement at all costs, and look at what that obsession had done to Ben. Was Ben going down that same dangerous path? What if this whole thing was actually Pandora's box and he was blindly assaulting it with a crowbar?

Maybe we fracture your soul?

5

NEW TECH

HENRY WAS JUST GETTING OUT OF THE SHOWER—THAT GLORIOUS, unlimited hot water shower—in his spacious personal quarters on Archimedes base when an incessant beeping filled his ears. After the Battle of Icarus, he'd been asked to move to the sprawling complex on the surface of Kerner-3, where the fleet's Science and Technology Division was headquartered. The relocation included a fully staffed lab, and Henry was given carte blanche to work on any of a number of priority projects the Confed brass had asked him to look into.

He snagged a towel from its hook on the wall next to the shower and threw it around his waist, then rushed out of the steamy bathroom and into the main living space of his quarters. His wet feet slipped on the cold tile floor, and he crashed to the ground.

The beeping continued, unforgiving of his plight.

"Just a minute, dammit!" he growled as he pulled himself back up to his feet. The towel slipped from his waist as he stood, and his clumsy swipe at it failed to stop its plunge. It hit the floor at the same instant the door to his quarters swung open.

"Woah, Henry! Jesus, put that away!"

"Shelly! Dammit!" Henry spun away from the beautiful brunette standing in the doorway. One hand covered her eyes while the other clutched a datapad encased in a faux leather folio. He dove back into the bathroom and poked his head around the corner. "I'm so sorry. I was just getting out of the shower when the door chime started. I'm not late, am I? I thought we didn't have anything on the schedule until 0900... Would you mind throwing me my pants? They're laid out on the corner of the bed."

Michelle Fordham took a few tentative steps into the room, her gaze down at her feet. She was a talented theoretical physicist whom Henry had been working closely with to implement the Q-link comms system on a fleet-wide scale. The two were introduced a few months ago, after Henry started attacking the mountain of projects on his plate and Ben was back on his feet. Shelly was nearly ten years his junior, but lately the two had been getting together more and more outside of work. The relationship hadn't progressed much beyond the drinks-between-friends stage, but Henry was beginning to have some desires he thought he'd buried for good after Kate's death.

"You're not, and we don't," she said, reaching down with her free hand to grab his pants. She tossed them toward Henry, and he snagged them out of the air, disappearing around the corner and out of sight so he could put them on.

"Then what's up? I thought we were meeting at the lab?" He stepped out into the living space as he cinched his belt and walked over to the closet, where he began pulling out the rest of his ensemble.

"I ran into Matt in the cafeteria this morning while I was grabbing a bite to go. I was headed into the lab a little early to play around with an idea I had last night about integrating multiple particles into a single link module to improve bandwidth. He said you've got a message from Ben that came in via

Q-link, and he was going to head over here to tell you about it. I offered to deliver the news so he didn't have to."

Commander Matthew Evans had been Henry's assigned babysitter after his brief falling out with Admiral Garland, and the two men had become friends. Henry hadn't seen Evans much lately; he was now coordinating the exchange of information between the brass and the army of S&T personnel working at the base. With Henry transitioning to a more autonomous role, he hadn't had much crossover with the affable officer. Evans was still Henry's point of contact with the senior brass, but the two only ever talked if Henry had something critical to bring to their attention, or vice versa.

Shelly walked back to the door into the hallway, bending over and reaching for something on the ground. Henry studied her shapely backside for a moment before mentally kicking himself and averting his gaze. "I may have stopped on my way here to grab us coffee," she said with a playful smile as she lifted up the molded cup carrier and packets of sugar and cream.

"You didn't have to do that, Shelly," Henry said as he finished strapping on his wristwatch, an ancient Rolex Submariner his great-great-grandfather had originally purchased. The timepiece had been passed down through the generations and was utterly useless on any world except Earth, but thankfully, Icarus and all Confed facilities in Kerner operated on Earth Standard Time. He took one of the proffered cups and peeled off the thin bioplastic lid to peek at the contents. "And you even remembered to keep that profane liquid out of it this time. You're the best."

Shelly peeled the foil top off a creamer packet and dumped its horrid contents into her cup. "I have no idea what you're talking about." She tossed the empty packet into a nearby garbage can, then opened and dumped a second creamer into her "coffee." Then a third.

Henry shuddered in horror, hugging his steaming beverage to his chest like he was protecting it. "Don't worry, precious," he said to his cup. "I won't let the bad lady hurt you."

Shelly rolled her eyes and snapped her lid back on. "Do you want to stop by comms on our way to the lab so you can get that message? Matt said it wasn't flagged as urgent, but we've got some time before that meeting with the navy people." Like Henry, Shelly was a civilian contractor. She'd been plucked from a leading think tank back on Earth in the wake of the Imperium's incursion and the Confed ramped up its efforts to shake itself out of its four-year stupor after the Alarian War. Henry had then stolen her from the greedy hands of the S&T people immediately after her arrival at Archimedes.

Henry thought about it for a moment. If Ben had sent him a message via Q-link, then it was probably important. Then again, if it was something urgent, it would've had a priority-code prefix so it would get pushed to him as soon as possible. If he had to guess, it was probably something interesting but unrelated to Ben's training on Elizabeth and Mabel had somehow found a way to get the message included in Thunder's daily Q-link upload to Icarus. This was both a massive waste of resources and a little bit impressive, given the air-tight security around the Confed's fledgling FTL comms network.

"Yeah, let's run up and check out what Ben wants," he said. "If it came in over the link, then there's probably something in there I should see sooner rather than later."

Shelly stepped into the hall, and Henry followed her out, taking a moment to make sure the door to his quarters was locked. The two made small talk during the short trek to one of two secure comms facilities on the sprawling base. When they finally arrived, Shelly waited outside while Henry was shown to a private booth where he could read the message from Ben.

Thanks to the security protocols governing Q-link transmissions, Henry was required to first access it from a secure terminal, and it couldn't be routed to his personal mailbox and be pulled up from his personal quarters or office. If he needed to reference something later on, he would need to get clearance to have a copy of the message released. He sat down at the small desk and entered his credentials. After reading through the standard-issue lawyerspeak warning about jail time, pain of death, yada yada yada, he was finally allowed to view the contents of the message.

Hey Dad,

Just wanted to check in and let you know the tweaks we've been testing to the APEXs are looking good. The grav harnesses have a steep learning curve, but even the chief has now gotten to the point where he doesn't crash and burn every time he uses the system. And Mabel says the mods to his armor are working as intended—she can't access his implant, but we expected that going in. She did say the added horsepower from the new processors give her full functionality, though, which is a plus.

And there's something else… I didn't want to bring this up until I had something a little more concrete to show you, but I've run into some hurdles that Mabel and I can't clear on our own. I've had an idea kicking around in my head for the past few months, and Mabel has been helping me flesh it out into something that I really think might be viable. At least I think it's probably worth putting a prototype together to study further. The problem we've run into is a lack of resources. A prototype will require a good chunk of fabricator time and… at least a couple pairs of entangled particles.

Don't stop reading!

Just hear me out here… I know what I'm proposing probably costs about as much as an APEX (or more), but take a look at the attached design and spec sheets. Who knows? You might even have a few ideas for improvements. Just please look through everything before you shelve it and shoot me down. We've done a ton of work on this, and I think you'll agree the potential benefits will far exceed the costs, provided we can make it work.

We're starting the first training evolution today, so I probably won't be in touch again for a bit. Don't worry, I'll take it slow(ish). I'll check in again as soon as I can. Love you, Dad.

-Ben

Henry's brows had steadily knit closer and closer together as he read Ben's note. What the hell could he possibly be cooking up that required entangled particles? He closed out the text file and opened the attached folder. It had been compressed and encrypted before transmission, and it took a minute for the terminal to decrypt and unpack the contents. Twenty minutes later, he exited the booth and made a beeline for the duty desk at the front of the compartment.

"I need to file an expedited 1013-B," he said to the clerk manning the duty desk.

The woman looked up from a datapad she'd been reading and snapped a piece of bubble gum. "Booth number," she said.

"Four."

She set the datapad aside and turned to her workstation. While she pecked away at her terminal, Henry drummed his fingers on the counter ringing the duty desk. His mind raced, struggling to simultaneously come to grips with the implications of what Ben was proposing and trying to figure out how he could free up the necessary funds to begin work on the project.

A part of him also marveled at Ben's ability to think outside the box. It never occurred to Henry to use the neural implant hardware in the way Ben was proposing, and yet, once he'd scanned the proposal, it seemed so obvious. Maybe he was losing a step or two in his old age, or maybe his son was just that much better than him. Either way, this was going to consume his every waking hour until he managed to create a working prototype.

Henry rationalized dropping his other projects by telling himself it could help the Confed in its fight against the Imperium, and that was exactly what he would tell the brass when they inevitably came sniffing around. The truth was, his son was going to be put in harm's way, likely over and over again until this new war was won. The worst part was that Henry was ultimately responsible. If he hadn't experimented on his own son, they wouldn't be in this position.

He'd lost Ben once already—or at least believed he had—and he nearly lost him again six months ago. Henry would do anything, pay any price, if it meant there was even a small chance they could make this project work, because if it worked, it might just ensure he'd never have to worry about losing Ben again... at least not permanently.

Finally, the clerk jabbed the enter key with a flourish and looked back up. "Submitted. They've been running about an hour for approval on nonpriority communications. It'll be sent to your inbox as soon as it's approved."

"Thank you." Henry turned and walked out the double glass doors to the comms center, then searched the hallway for Shelly. He spotted her sitting on a bench in a small alcove a short way down the hall.

"How'd it go?" she asked.

"You know that meeting with Science and Technology?"

"Yeah..." she said slowly, her eyes narrowing in suspicion.

"Cancel it. In fact, clear our calendar. We've got something more important to work on. Then I want to hear all about this idea you had for multiple particles in a single module."

6

HOSTILE TAKEOVER

THE BUILDING THAT HOUSED THE BETTENHOOK COLONIAL government offices reminded Tess of an old Cold War-era Soviet building. It was all steel and flashcrete, painted a hideous shade of green that looked like someone had blended four or five different leftover paint cans together and... *that* was the result. Bettenhook was a harsh, barely habitable moon that orbited a class-II gas giant in the Farrow system, on the very edge of Terran space in the Columbia cluster. The system had no habitable planets but did possess two moons with nitrogen-oxygen atmospheres. Unfortunately, both of them were less than ideal places for colonization, with Bettenhook winning that sad race solely due to the fact it wasn't tidally locked.

That didn't mean it wasn't miserable practically all the time, though. During the "summer" on Bettenhook, the temperatures barely broke the freezing mark, and it seemed to rain constantly. There were also weekly storms that would've been classified as hurricanes on most other planets, hence the bomb-shelter-like structures that dotted the terrain. If it wasn't for the rich helium-3 and methane mining operations conducted by drone platforms over the gas giant, there wouldn't be much of a reason to settle on this godforsaken moon. But at least Bettenhook had a strong magnetosphere, which kept the gas giant's radiation from cooking them all to a cinder, so it wasn't without its bright spots.

"Did Captain Timmons say why he wanted to talk to us, sir?" Tess said as she followed Lieutenant Commander Russell Fairbanks up the flashcrete steps to the governor's office. They'd lucked out and been summoned during the first break in the rain in over three days.

Fairbanks reminded Tess a lot of Valdez, but her new CO was a little more easygoing and outwardly friendly with those under his command than her last boss had been. Her limited experience with Fairbanks had left her with a favorable impression of him as an officer. He'd been a SEAR before a wound suffered in combat saw him sidelined and reassigned to a role in the intel section, the in-house intelligence wing of the Confed Navy.

He was obviously competent and comfortable with the mantle of command. Fairbanks could navigate the tricky political waters they had to contend with while trying to bring the more unruly systems back into line, and based on how quickly and precisely the man ran through their live-fire exercises with the colonial militia yesterday, he was also a gifted marksman, if just a little past his prime. Valdez had told Tess her new CO was just as good as he was, if not better, but she hadn't believed him until she'd spent a few weeks with him. So far in her time as a SEAR, she was on a hot streak with great COs. She just hoped this assignment wouldn't end up being as crazy as the last one.

"He said it had something to do with Donovan, but he didn't want to elaborate over an unsecured line," Fairbanks said, opening the heavy ballistic glass door that led into the polished stone lobby of the three-story building. He held the door for Tess, then followed her through.

Sean Donovan was the warlord that had been giving the colonial government fits for the better part of a year, well before the

CTS became aware of the Imperium and everything that followed. The man had been a marine officer back before the Alarian War and was discharged after several marines under his command were arrested and charged for smuggling weapons and narcotics. Donovan had been suspected of being the ringleader, but none of the marines in question ever fingered him and the JAG prosecutors were unable to bring a case against him thanks to the flimsy nature of the evidence. They'd settled on nailing the grunts, and Donovan was later discharged in disgrace for failing to uncover the pervasive smuggling ring right under his nose.

"I wonder if the good captain's 'information network' actually came through this time," Tess said. They mounted the wide staircase that would take them up two floors to the governor's office. "He's been bragging about it for weeks with nothing to show for it—just the opposite, in fact. Donovan's people have been running circles around Timmons's command for months now. I can't tell if the sources Timmons claims are feeding him intel really exist and he's just incompetent or if he's just trying to show off to make himself look more important."

Fairbanks chuckled. "I suspect it's the former, but you didn't hear that from me."

After his ouster from the Marine Corps, Donovan landed a mercenary gig, but it wasn't long before he led a mutiny against his commander, failed to pull it off, and was unceremoniously dumped on Bettenhook with the surviving mutineers. Why the CO of that merc unit didn't just flush them all out the airlock was beyond Tess. Too much paperwork, she supposed. From what she'd heard, the legal merc outfits had even more red tape to deal with than the Confed military. Either way, Donovan had been building up a gang of thugs on Bettenhook and slowly leaching territory from the colonial government. It needed to stop if they were to stabilize the system and get it—and its rich mining operations—back together with the big happy family that was the Confed.

The colonial government had requested military aid from the Confed to help bolster its beleaguered security forces. Instead of sending a couple companies of marines, though, the Confed had sent a single MAC team, which, based on the reception Tess and her group received upon their arrival, only served to raise the ire of everyone involved. The governor was ticked his colony only received a handful of advisors, and the head of the colonial militia—Timmons—resented outsiders coming in to scrutinize his command. But after a bit of a rocky start, Tess was beginning to feel like there might just be some hope for the locals after all; they just needed *a lot* of TLC to whip them into shape.

The stairs let out on the third floor directly in front of a nondescript metal door. A pair of benches sat to either side, and a small placard at eye level next to the door read *Office of the Governor.* Tess stepped quickly to the door and opened it for her CO, following him in a moment later. The receptionist's desk was empty, but the inner office door was slightly ajar, and a pair of arguing voices tumbled out.

One of the first things the team of military advisors learned after arriving on Bettenhook was how much the governor and the head of the militia hated each other. That relationship had soured even further after the MAC team arrived to help the locals get back on their feet and improve their effectiveness at combatting a threat like Donovan, small though his operation was. Timmons seemed to take the governor seeking outside help as a personal affront.

Fairbanks gave Tess a *here we go again* look, then pushed the inner door all the way open and flashed his most disarming smile. "Gentlemen," he said with a nod. "We came as soon as we received your request for a meeting."

When Tess and Fairbanks walked in, Governor Lyons let out

a small sigh of relief and signaled for them to take a seat on a leather couch along the wall closest to his desk. Timmons, who'd apparently been standing and leaning over the governor's desk during their argument, sat down in a matching chair adjacent to the two military advisors while Lyons came around his desk and leaned on one corner, looking exhausted.

"I'm glad you're here," Lyons said. "Captain Timmons was just explaining to me that Donovan's gang raided Shaft 7 this morning. We don't have all the details yet, but it seems like they killed anyone associated with the colonial government, then forced everyone else into the mines and blasted the entrance closed before taking off into the wastes. We lost them when they drove into a storm."

"Shaft 7 is only forty kilometers from here," Fairbanks said, alarmed. "If they're comfortable hitting a target so close to the capital, then I can only assume something has changed to tip the balance of power. Donovan may be a lunatic, but he's not recklessly stupid."

Timmons stood up and paced toward the small window on the other side of the room. "I sent a quick-response team as soon as we heard of the attack, but the storm that Donovan's people drove into is moving fast, and my guys have been forced to go on the ground as opposed to using a dropship. I believe two of your people went along, Lieutenant Commander."

Fairbanks turned to Tess. "Holden and Sera are working with the QRT today, right?"

Tess nodded. "They were working with them on breaching protocols for hostage situations. I'm sure they jumped at the opportunity to go kick some real doors again when the call came in."

Fairbanks chuckled. "Oh, I'm sure they did, though my guess is they'll write it up as being necessary to observe the QRT in a live-action environment. Unfortunately, that leaves us short-handed around here in the event Donovan has something else up his sleeve."

The Military Advisory Command units that were being sent out as a form of military aid to struggling colonies comprised twelve-member teams, plus a commanding officer. Members of MAC teams weren't supposed to be taking part in any combat actions involving their respective clients; they were instead told to limit their activities to advisory roles. But the teams also included people who had been pulled from special operations units across the spectrum of Confed service branches, many of whom, like Tess, had suffered a significant injury or trauma and were being assigned to MAC teams as a way to ease them back into things.

The impending war with the Imperium had the Confed military on high alert and unwilling to part with highly trained special operations personnel who were already on active duty with front-line combat units, so the whole thing was seen as a win-win by the brass. As a result, many of the elite operator types that made up the MAC teams were coming off extended periods without seeing action, and they were searching for any and all opportunities to help knock off the rust.

Timmons turned from the window and stared dubiously at the MAC team CO. "You can't really believe he would try something else so soon after hitting one of our mining posts, can you?" The man's face had gone ashen, and sweat began to bead on his forehead. *What a coward.* Tess kept the thought to herself but couldn't keep her disgusted glare from burning into the man.

"I don't know," Fairbanks said, leaning forward on the couch to rest his elbows on his knees, clasping his hands together in thought. "But something about the group's activity over the last week has me thinking that they're planning something big. They've been pushing around the edges, feeling us out and learning how we'll respond. If Donovan has any informants here, he'll also know just how thin the colonial militia is stretched. So it wouldn't surprise me."

"How very astute of you, Lieutenant Commander."

Tess whipped her head around to the door, right hand snapping toward the sidearm on her hip.

"I wouldn't if I were you, Petty Officer Third Class Tessandra McCollum," Donovan said casually, the gaping maw of an M3 breacher's shotgun aimed directly at her chest.

Tess froze, heart pounding, as four more of Donovan's thugs entered the small office, all armed to the teeth and wearing hard-shell battle armor that had clearly seen extensive use over the years. She slowly pulled her hand away from her holster and raised her arms over her head. Fairbanks did the same, but Governor Lyons just stared at the warlord, mouth agape. Timmons suddenly appeared very calm, and a nasty sneer stretched across his lips as he glared at Lyons with murder in his eyes.

Crap, he's in on it.

"David!" Lyons finally found his voice and rounded on his militia commander. "What is the meaning of this—"

Timmons's hand flashed up, and the pistol in it barked. The man had been aiming for the governor's head, but his shot missed its mark and hit Lyons in the side of his neck. The bullet passed through effortlessly before slamming into the flashcrete wall. Razor-sharp stone chips and spall tore through the pictures and books lining the shelves behind Lyons's desk.

The man choked out a surprised gurgle and clawed at the left side of his neck, arterial blood pouring through his fingers. Tess launched herself toward the governor, intent on assisting him, but the butt of Donovan's shotgun struck her between the shoulder blades and sent her sprawling to the floor. Fairbanks stood and stepped over Tess protectively, fists balled by his sides as he glared at the warlord. Tess struggled to breathe as she flipped herself over to face the thugs. The savage blow had crushed the air from her lungs, but thankfully, her head was still clear.

Lyons was on his knees now, desperately trying to plug the hole in his neck. Timmons walked up to his boss, placed the muzzle of the pistol against his head, and pulled the trigger. The report should have been deafening in the small space, but auditory exclusion had kicked in thanks to the adrenaline dump Tess was riding. She barely heard a thing other than the hammering of her own heartbeat.

Her mind raced as she considered and then discarded each of the limited options available to her. It was six on two, and the bad guys already had their weapons drawn and were wearing armor. She and Fairbanks only had their holstered sidearms and their uniform of the day, a woodland-pattern combat dress uniform that couldn't even keep the wind and rain out, let alone bullets. They were screwed. She knew it, and the body language of her CO told her he knew it as well.

Timmons holstered his pistol and roughly kicked the governor's body away from the desk, then stepped around and sat in the plush, high-backed chair behind it. "What should we do with them?" he said, gesturing to Tess and Fairbanks after he kicked his feet up on the desk. Dried mud flaked off his boot soles, soiling the polished wood top. "Kill 'em?"

Donovan shot Timmons an icy glare. "No," he said firmly, the muzzle of his shotgun not wavering in the slightest as he turned his attention to the traitorous militia captain. "We need them alive, for the time being. The Confed will play ball with us, provided we don't shut off the supply of reactor fuel and other essential refined materials this colony produces. That won't be the case if we slaughter their military advisors, even if said advisory teams are made up of cripples and rejects that can't hack it in the big-boy units."

Tess watched the exchange, praying that sniveling little weasel Timmons would do something to distract Donovan and his goons long enough that she and Fairbanks could make a move. To her dismay, however, Donovan's men weren't paying any attention to the brewing spat between their boss and the militia captain. The muzzles of their rifles remained aimed directly at the two members of the MAC team. At least it seemed like they weren't just going to be shot and dumped outside, unlike the poor governor. They just needed to stay alive long enough for the cavalry to arrive.

And just like that, Tess realized why Donovan's people hit Shaft 7 that morning. The QRT and most of the MAC team were forty kilometers away right now, which meant it would be hours, at a minimum, before they could return and try to pry Donovan and his people out of here.

Donovan walked over to the desk and roughly shoved Timmons's feet off it.

"Hey!" Timmons shot to his feet, face flushing in anger. "The deal was *I* take over the colony and you and your merry band of cutthroats get to operate freely from wherever you choose. Don't forget that, Donovan!"

Donovan's shotgun boomed, and Timmons stumbled backward into the table and the shelves behind it, sending framed photos and a small marble sculpture crashing to the floor. A wet gurgle escaped his lips, eyes bulging out of his head. The shock of being blasted in the chest at near point-blank range was permanently etched onto his face as he crumpled to the floor and died.

"I haven't forgotten the deal, you useless shit," Donovan said to the corpse. "I've merely chosen to operate freely out of *this* office."

The warlord turned to his men. "Clean this up and secure the lieutenant commander and petty officer here. The MAC teams the fools at CTS Central Command sent out may not be on par with the legendary MACV-SOG unit my great-great-grandaddy served with, but they still pull their members from some of the most elite units in the Confed. Hell, our young petty officer here," he said, sweeping a hand toward Tess, "is a SEAR, if you can believe that, though I'm not sure if that should reflect well upon her skills as an operator or poorly on the SEARs for stooping so low to fill their ranks."

A couple of Donovan's goons laughed at the insult, and Tess had to fight back the urge to go down fighting. Instead, she and Fairbanks allowed the thugs to disarm them and perform a quick but thorough search, taking everything the two MAC members had on them. Tess and Fairbanks had their hands bound behind them with flex cuffs. Then two of Donovan's people marched them toward the door.

"Remember," Donovan called out as they were exiting the office. "We need them alive, but that doesn't necessarily mean *undamaged*."

Hot breath tickled Tess's neck and a sadistic chuckle filled her ear, sending a wave of panic tearing through her body. Her mind flashed back to the last time hot, fetid breath had washed over her, and she struggled to control her breathing and not hyperventilate. SEAR training had prepared her for torture, and she thought she'd be ready to face it if something like that ever happened again. But that was then, in a training scenario where, no matter how realistic the instructors tried to make things, she still knew it was just an exercise. Now, faced with the very real prospect of reliving her nightmare for real, she wasn't so sure she would be able to endure it.

The heavy door to the governor's office boomed closed behind them, and sharp kicks to the backs of their knees sent both Tess and Fairbanks tumbling down the stairs to the second-floor landing. Her head smashed against something hard and cold. The howl of the thugs' laughter faded quickly, along with her vision.

Then her world went dark.

7

PROPER INTRODUCTIONS

"IT'S TIME, BEN."

Ben looked up from the desk. Was it time for the briefing already? "Coming, Chief," he said.

He tapped out one last sentence in the message to his dad, hit the *send* button, and folded the terminal back up. Standing, Ben pocketed his comms unit and grabbed a ball cap with the NAVSOC logo on it from the shelf over the desk, then walked out the door to join the chief. They walked out the double glass entrance doors of the guest dorms and hopped into a waiting MuT truck that was so new it still smelled of textile adhesives. It even had plastic wrap on the back seats.

The chief didn't seem to be in a chatty mood, so Ben rolled down the window and let the humid morning air wash over him. A cloying scent hung in the air—some kind of flower native to this region of Elizabeth, according to the med tech who had de-scrambled Ben's brains after his fight with the Pathfinders. He idly watched trees and buildings blur past as they cruised toward the heart of Joint Base Thunder for their briefing.

"So can you give me any details yet, or do we have to wait until we get there?" Ben said after ten minutes of uncharacteristic silence from Kravczyk. He was trying to pry some early intel out of the big SEAR, who was currently tasked with getting him through the stringent training courses Confed Naval Special Operations Command wanted him to complete if he was going to operate with any of the SEAR teams.

"No, and stop asking. You'll find out everything in fifteen minutes. How's your head feeling?"

"The docs say I'm good to go. My ribs are still a little on the sore side, but everything checks out."

"Good. The higher-ups are antsy to see you in action, so they're going to run you through a little warm-up tomorrow with Second Platoon from the Pathfinders."

"That why you're so quiet right now?" Ben said.

Kravczyk sighed. "Not exactly."

"Then what's up? I know that little kerfuffle with those space apes wasn't a great look, but you're acting a little weird."

"I don't like how fast the brass is pushing you," Kravczyk admitted. "You're still having issues with impulse control. While it's getting better, it could be a significant liability in some of the scenarios they want to put you in. I mean, come on, Ben—you picked a fight with *four* Marine Pathfinders yesterday! That's something the kid I helped pull off Earth last year would never have done. You used to be smarter than that."

"Those guys had it coming," Ben said dismissively.

"That!" Kravczyk said, turning and pointing a meaty finger directly at Ben's face. "That's the kind of shit I'm talking about. You're way too cocky. The kid that saved my ass on Earth fought off two different enemy ships with goddamned mind bullets and then planned and executed an assault on another. He was much more aware of his limitations, despite being a complete green-horn. I know you have some new tricks in your bag now, but this newfound arrogance is going to kick you square in the balls at some point unless you rein it in, Ben. Trust me, I lived that scenario once upon a time."

On reflex, Ben opened his mouth to object yet again, but he shut it just as quickly. The chief was right, and just admitting that galled him. His mind flashed back to something his dad and the medical people back on Icarus had told him before he'd been sent here for training: the damage his nervous system had suffered, combined with the hasty patch job they'd done to stabilize him, meant he would have a hard time controlling his impulses. Something about the lag between his artificial nervous system and what was left of his biological brain led him to take an action on instinct before his higher cognitive functions had a chance to weigh in.

But it wasn't just that. If he was being honest with himself, he'd definitely let his abilities go to his head. It was hard not to when you could mop the floor with the best the Confed armed forces could throw at you, assimilate information by downloading the file directly into your brain, and wage war against AI on its own turf. Ben wasn't the pinnacle of human evolution and technological prowess, but he was pretty damn close.

"Newman's Rock?" Ben finally asked, dropping the attitude and getting serious.

"That"—Kravczyk nodded—"among others." The big SEAR spun the wheel and the MuT whipped around and pulled up in front of a utilitarian prefab building on the opposite side of the street. "We're here. Think about what I said."

The two men exited the truck and entered the building, stopping briefly to present their ID badges to the sergeant manning the security station before being ushered down a hallway to a large room. The briefing room was filled with a series of massive wall displays and well-padded chairs in a stadium-style configuration facing a lectern. Kravczyk steered Ben to a seat near the front and off to one side. He couldn't help but notice that every eye in the room was firmly locked onto him. It would seem that details of his encounter with the four jerks from the gym had already made the rounds.

A few stragglers trickled in over the next few minutes, until the clock over the wall displays ticked over to 1000. A door near the lectern opened, and the room came to attention as a pair of officers entered: one a marine major, the other a navy commander Ben knew well.

"As you were," Commander Ramiro Valdez said to the room. He took a moment to check the roster displayed on the lectern's terminal to make sure everyone was accounted for, then began the briefing. "My name is Commander Valdez, and I'm the XO for Columbia cluster NAVSOC operations. Major Davis is here to give the Pathfinders a little more detail on the unique nature of this exercise. While the bulk of you are marines, the exercises you all will take part in over the coming weeks are being run by NAVSOC. You'll still report to your normal chain of command while operating out of Joint Base Thunder, but NAVSOC has the final say on any operational details.

"This briefing is classified top secret. I know it's a little unusual to bring in every member of the platoon for a top-secret briefing, but these are unusual times we're living in. Any enlisted personnel who have questions on that can direct them to Lieutenant Harris. Major Davis has already briefed your company CO, and Captain Kaneda is briefing First and Third Platoons as we speak. Now, with all of that out of the way, let's get down to business."

Ben noticed the marines were all sitting up a little straighter in their seats now that it was clear this wasn't a routine training rotation, and he found himself doing likewise.

"As you are all aware," Valdez continued, bringing up a PowerPoint on the main wall display behind him, "we are once more engaged in a shooting war with an alien race. Major Davis has informed me of what you've been told, both officially and via the rumor mill, and I'm here to set the record straight: we are *not* facing off against the Alarians again." An excited murmur rippled through the room, and Valdez gave them a few seconds to process the information. "In fact, the exercises you are going to be running over the next few weeks will prepare you for a mission to deliver our envoy to Hai'alla for the first round of negotiations to form an alliance." The murmuring exploded into shouts of surprise and disbelief, requiring a bellowed command from Major Davis to bring the room back to order. For their part, Ben and Kravczyk just sat there; they already knew what was coming next.

The commander advanced the presentation to the next slide, revealing front and side profile photos of the two different Imperium species, both in and out of armor. Ben's heart rate ticked up a few notches at the sight of their enemy.

The two Imperium races were humanoid. Both had large, glassy black eyes reminiscent of an insect. The skin on both was a dusky gray color, with fine, scale-like projections that looked like rough sandpaper. A wide mouth was filled with short, conical teeth, and their hands and feet each had six fingers and toes—the extra digit being either a thumb or big toe next to their pinkies. The major difference between the two was their size. The more common variant was a head shorter than an average human but proportioned about the same. The larger species had proportions more like a gorilla, with long, powerfully built arms. The smallest one they'd encountered so far stood a full two meters tall.

Ben's hand twitched as a memory flashed to the forefront of his thoughts. The grinding sensation as his combat knife drove through bone. The warm, viscous blood flowing through his fingers. The spasms of the dying alien beneath him. The hardware in his head allowed him to recall the event in perfect detail

—something he regretted more often than not in the days after his escape from Earth and the Battle of Icarus.

"This is the real enemy," Valdez began, "and they call themselves the Imperium. There are two closely related species which likely evolved on the same planet and now exist as a single society. Their home space is over five thousand light-years from here, and the only reason they're here to begin with is because they were responsible for what the Alarians call the Great Cataclysm, which drove the refugee fleet across the Talishian Expanse and to Earth fifty years ago.

"From what we've been able to gather, they manipulate the development of younger species such that their societies and technological advancement progress down a particular path—one that will always give the Imperium an overwhelming advantage in any conflict. This is achieved through the use of advanced artificial intelligence constructs called agents, which are placed within the datanets of the client species. From there, they will manipulate public opinion, steal and then destroy scientific discoveries that threaten to derail the Imperium's preferred path of technological progression, and start wars to eliminate potential threats."

Ben tuned this out slightly; he already knew it all. His eyes drifted to the images on the screens again, and scenes flashed through his thoughts. The scent of flesh and bone charred by plasma. The recoil of his rifle as he and the SEARs battled the Imperial shock troopers, and the bone-deep thrum of the alien dropships as they passed overhead.

Kravczyk, noticing Ben's lack of attention, elbowed him sharply in his still-bruised ribs. The pain snapped Ben back to the present, and he got the message loud and clear. He turned his eyes back to Valdez and did his best to focus on the presentation.

"When a client species reaches a point in their development

where they can't be reliably controlled anymore, they are elimi-nated. Like a parasite, the Imperium bleeds other species dry until they are no longer of any use, then wipes them out and comes in to claim all the resources for themselves. Typically, this is done by an agent fomenting hostilities between politically opposed groups or neighboring races, and it takes place over the span of decades. This enemy is nothing if not patient.

"You may recall a prolonged period of escalation between us and the Alarians before the war five years ago," Valdez said and received nods of understanding from the marines. "That's because the Alarian refugee fleet had a stowaway. An Imperium agent managed to infiltrate the refugee fleet before it departed, and it laid low for fifty years, waiting to see where they settled down again. When the fleet encountered Earth, the agent, or at least a part of it, made the jump to our systems.

"The distance traveled by the Alarians threw a wrench into things, however, as it was impractical for the Imperium to send out a fleet to clean up a small group of survivors. Instead, they put it on the back burner until they could get around to it. Unfor-tunately for us, we took the technology and base science the refugee fleet gave us and pushed along a different path. Every-thing from our electronics architectures to weapons development and tactics were different, which was something the agent could not allow to continue. It slowly built up a series of slipspace transceivers by hiring outside contractors to manufacture the components, which were then assembled by new contractors who were eliminated after the work was complete and their databases purged. Once the work was complete, the agent phoned home and reported in on what we and, to a lesser extent, the Alarians were up to.

"The fleet engagement I'm sure you've all heard about occurred in a system that was home to a top-secret shipyard and the central hub for all fleet operations while we've worked to rebuild since the Alarian War. It did not go well. As of today, six months after that battle, we are essentially sitting with post-war numbers of combat-effective hulls in the fleet. We lost more than two dozen capital ships in the span of six hours that day, and it would have been *all* of our capital ships were it not for a nearly forgotten secret project Henry Hutchins of ExoDyn had been heading up before the war. I was the team leader of SEAR 1 at that time, and we were tasked with recovering that asset, who is sitting in this room as we speak."

Ben could feel eyeballs now burning holes into his back like eighty individual laser beams. He shifted uncomfortably for a moment while Commander Valdez advanced the presentation to a slide with Ben's picture, along with a list of pertinent details about Project Blackthorn and Mabel.

"Mr. Hutchins here"—Valdez nodded at Ben—"is only one half of the equation, though. He contains a specialized neural implant that allows a prototype AI to harness the power of a human brain in order to augment her abilities. Mabel, are you here?" There were some confused looks until a soft-blue dot matrix cube materialized next to the lectern, projected by the briefing room's suite of holographic projectors.

"Hello, Commander Valdez," Mabel said pleasantly.

"Ladies and gentlemen," Valdez addressed the room, "meet Mabel. She and Ben are the reason we are all sitting here, able to have this little chat and not having our ashes scattered by the wind right now. While here at Thunder, you will be training with the two of them so you gain proficiency in working together, because when this training rotation is done, you're going hunting for the Imperium agent."

Now it was Ben's turn to sit up straight and utter a surprised little shout. He knew they were going to be calling on him to get his hands dirty at some point, but he'd figured they'd ease him into things. Instead, they were tossing him right into the deep end, going after the big baddie that was still on the board in local space. It made sense, he supposed. As long as the agent was still lurking around their datanets, any Confed action was at risk of being exposed. But if they could take out the agent, that would give them some breathing room to prepare for the next wave of Imperium forces.

"That's right," Valdez said, locking eyes with him. "We've done everything we can to track the slippery son of a bitch down on our own, but it's too good for our cybersecurity guys to corner it, and we cannot have it running around wreaking havoc on us when the next wave of Imperium ships get here next year." After his little aside, Valdez turned back to the marines and added, "Before we move on to the details about the exercise tomorrow, are there any pressing questions?"

"So we're supposed to babysit a civvie with a fancy computer in his head for the next year?" The comment was hushed, clearly not intended to be heard by the group at large. It came from an unidentified speaker in the back. Unfortunately, the acoustics of the room amplified the voice so it could be heard all the way at the front.

Ben's ears burned, but he wasn't sure if it was embarrassment or anger. A little of both, he realized. He was an outsider here. He could hold his own in a fight, yes, but he was, at the end of the day, still technically a civilian. The marines around him had earned their place in a Pathfinder company after years of blood, sweat, and tears. Now they were being saddled with some kid who was, ostensibly, to be treated as an equal. Still, the utter lack of respect for what Ben was and could do grated on his ego. Fortunately, Kravczyk recognized the warning signs and shot him a look that simply said, *Let it go.*

Major Davis, on the other hand, felt no such compunction. In an instant, his face went red, bordering on apoplectic purple, and he opened his mouth to let the offending individual know in no uncertain terms just how much trouble he was in, but Valdez held up a hand.

"It's okay, Major," he said, completely unperturbed by the smart-ass in the back.

Ben smiled inwardly as his eyes flicked to Kravczyk. *Valdez has had plenty of practice with smart-asses over the years*, he thought. His eyes shifted back to Valdez as the SEAR stepped around the lectern and casually clasped his hands behind his back.

"Ben is perfectly capable of taking care of himself, as four of your brothers from First Platoon found out earlier this week." There were some wide eyes among the marines after the comment, and their faces swung from the commander to Ben and back again several times. "But," Valdez continued, bringing up a holovid and lowering the lighting in the room, "if the word of four Pathfinders who got their shit kicked in by a single *civvie* isn't enough for you, I offer this as further evidence." He tapped the terminal on the lectern, and the video began to play.

Ben recognized the footage immediately—it was taken from the suit cams on then-Lieutenant Commander Valdez's APEX armor aboard the Imperium command and control ship during the battle for Icarus. Despite knowing exactly what was coming and having been removed from the event by half a year, Ben found his heart was pounding in his chest as he watched his past self uncork Pandora's box.

The figure in the video was out of control, in a primal state of blood rage as he single-handedly annihilated the Imperium troopers trying to take back their CIC, where Ben and the SEARs were fighting to buy Mabel time to disrupt the attacking alien fleet. Dozens of aliens were blown apart by hypersonic tungsten from Ben's rail rifle. When the rifle seized up due to extreme heat, they were cooked from the inside like they'd been tossed in a microwave. Ben charged them like a man possessed, channeling all his rage through his suit, which converted the emotion into something akin to a maser beam.

Valdez stopped the playback after Ben launched himself through the air like a human missile, knocking a pair of advancing aliens back into the corridor on the other side. In the silence, you could have heard a pin drop. He shut down the projectors and brought the lights back up. "Tomorrow," he said, failing to completely hide his satisfaction at the shock on the Pathfinders' faces, "you get to face off against *that*. The first exercise this week is going to pit all of you against a single civilian and an AI."

8

UNREASONABLE DEMANDS

"You ready to go grab some lunch? I'm starving."

Henry paused and swiped his hand through the air over his holodesk to minimize the three-dimensional schematics he'd been studying. He looked up at Shelly; he hadn't even realized she'd approached and was standing in the middle of his office. His eyes flicked to his watch. Sure enough, he'd been staring at the designs for Ben's little proposal for hours.

"Yeah, I guess I could use a break," he said over a loud groaning from his belly. She flashed him an amused smile and nodded toward the double doors that exited their lab. Henry followed her out, and they strolled down the corridor, past other offices and workspaces for the various teams working to improve the Q-link network.

"You know, Ben is a lot smarter than he should be," Shelly said as they walked past a thick window that looked out at the enormous research base and the rocky terrain of Kerner-3. Henry's lab was located on the fourth floor of the building, and they had a great view of the rest of the complex. The planet's atmosphere wasn't quite dense enough to support human life, though there had been some chatter about attempting to terraform it. Until that happened, though—*if* it happened—the people living and working on Archimedes base were required to do so in pressurized structures and bubble tunnels. "You said he was sixteen when the war broke out, right?"

Henry nodded. "Yeah. It actually started on his birthday."

"I thought so. I can't imagine how he was able to further his education to such a degree after just a few short years of living on Earth after the war. Some of his ideas are extremely good, and his grasp of advanced scientific concepts is apparent."

Henry chewed on her words for a few moments before responding. He was well aware of just how Ben was able to catapult his learning so far in such a short time, but he couldn't remember exactly what information Shelly was cleared for. She'd been quickly green lit to work on the quantum comms project, which meant she possessed a high-level security clearance, but Henry wasn't sure if that would also make it okay for her to be let in on Ben's secrets.

Aww, the hell with it. The two things are inextricably linked at this point, anyway.

"Ben has some unique abilities that others don't have access to, thanks to his unique implants," Henry said. "The prototype implant he has allows him to assimilate data, as long as it's present on board his APEX when he's linked to it. It's not so much downloading the information directly into his brain as just a much faster way to learn. Imagine being able to read an entire textbook in just a few minutes. Kind of like that."

Shelly arched an eyebrow at him. "I've never heard anything about the neural implants having that functionality. I'd assumed something like it might be possible, but the technology is still so new I didn't think we'd see any capability leaps like that for at least a few generations yet. It's no wonder his grasp of science is so good."

"It certainly gives him an edge," Henry admitted. "But he

still has many of the same limitations you and I do. The information he absorbs is transferred to long-term memory just like if he had learned it in a traditional class. His brain isn't an SSD, which means he can eventually forget something he's already learned, just like you or I." Henry stopped in front of the doors to an elevator that would take them down to surface level, where they could then take one of the transit tubes over to the cafeteria. He pressed the call button and stepped back. "That said, he still needs to be able to do *something* with the information once it's in his head. And *that* is what he's been impressing me with, lately… Just don't tell him I said that."

There was a soft chime from the elevator as the car arrived at their floor, and a moment later the doors whisked open, revealing a pair of marines dressed in the uniform of Archimedes's security detachment. They seemed surprised to see Henry standing there, and the feeling was mutual.

"Mr. Hutchins, your presence has been requested on Icarus, immediately," the more senior guard said.

Henry exchanged a confused look with Shelly, then turned back to the marines. "Why not just page me on my comms unit? Am I being detained, Sergeant?"

"No, sir," the lead marine said, shaking his head with a disarming smile. "We were just instructed to come collect you and escort you to flight ops, where there's a shuttle waiting for you. I'm sorry, but I don't have any more information than that."

Henry turned to Shelly and sighed. "I guess that lunch date will have to wait." Only after she blushed slightly did he realize what he'd said. His eyes widened slightly as his brain attempted to go into damage-control mode. "I mean, uh…"

Shelly smiled, then gave him a little peck on the cheek. "I'll take a rain check. You go find out what the admiral wants."

Henry cleared his throat awkwardly as Shelly traded places in the elevator with the two men from base security. He was annoyed at the interruption. A trip to Icarus and back was going to take the better part of two days, at least, depending on how long he was needed there. It normally would've been much longer, but Kerner-3's current position in its orbit put the planet closer to the massive space station than at any point for the next three months.

What could be so important that Bob summoned him to Icarus *and* sent a security escort to make sure he left immediately? Unless Collins and the *Wraith* were back already, but he hadn't expected news on that front for another week, at least. There was only one way to find out for sure.

The quickest way to flight ops was to take a different lift, which was back toward his lab. "Well then, gentlemen... shall we?" he said, gesturing for the marines to lead the way.

———

HENRY, bleary-eyed from the sixteen-hour shuttle flight, walked into a large, utilitarian conference room filled with people. A long, faux-wood table sat in the middle of the room, with two dozen chairs around it. The walls had been painted in a warm beige tone, but the gallons of paint couldn't cover up the fact that the walls were all slabs of metal. Everywhere he looked, small groups of people were gathered like it was a social hour after church. At the far end of the room, Admiral Robert Garland was engaged in conversation with several civilians in sharply tailored suits, a serious expression on his face.

Henry caught Bob's eye, and the two men exchanged nods, but the admiral didn't try to break away. Henry couldn't tell who exactly his friend was talking to because they were facing away from him, but the small-statured woman with her hair in a tightly wound bun looked vaguely familiar.

"Welcome back to Icarus, Mr. Hutchins."

Henry tore his gaze away from Bob's small group and smiled. "Captain Collins! It's good to see you. Been a while." Henry extended his hand to Collins, who shook it firmly.

The normally serious Intelligence Division captain flashed a warm smile. "It has, but that's the nature of the job."

Henry had sparred with the woman during their first meeting, when he'd gone aboard her ship to brief her and the SEARs about the mission to retrieve Ben. They had long since settled their differences, however, and Henry was fond of the plucky spy ship captain. That said, her presence here confirmed his suspicions about the nature of this meeting, and his heart sank a little. If he'd been called in to discuss the Alarian situation so soon after the *Wraith*'s return, that meant Ben was going to be a topic of conversation.

"Can I assume your presence here means we have news from our friends on Hai'alla?" he said.

Collins's smile faltered for a moment as her eyes darted around the room. "I can't really say one way or the other. You'll find out soon, though."

The lights in the brightly lit room dimmed slightly, signaling the meeting was about to start. "If you're ever down at Archimedes, let me know. The first round is on me," Henry said as he and Collins separated.

"I think it's safe to say you owe me more than just one round, especially after this." She grinned at him and turned to go find her seat.

Henry frowned. Just what did she mean by that? He walked around the table until he spotted a small placard with his name on it, then sat down. The rest of the chatter in the room died out as people found their seats, and Henry's eyebrows shot straight up to his hairline when he was finally able to catch a glimpse of the woman Bob had been talking to a minute ago.

Jesus, that's the president.

President Martha McGibbons sat down next to Bob, who was staring straight at Henry and giving him a meaningful look. *Oh, shit…* Henry realized he'd been correct, and this meeting was about contact with the Alarians. Based on the look Bob was giving him, he wasn't going to like the details that involved his son.

Once the room had come to order, the admiral stood up and addressed everyone in his booming, gravelly voice. "Madam President"—he nodded to president McGibbons—"and every-one," he said, sweeping his eyes around the room. "We're here because one of our *Wraith* captains was able to successfully engage in dialog with a member of the Alarian High Council, and they've agreed to a summit on Hai'alla to discuss a possible alliance against the Imperium threat."

Henry listened as Bob explained the failed diplomatic attempts to get the Alarians talking. These ultimately resulted in Collins being sent out to try ambushing an Alarian warship carrying High Councilor Elyria Tashmali. He only knew about that mission because he'd been consulted beforehand; his personal experience with Taylen and his daughter Elyria proved invaluable while the brass were trying to figure out how she might respond to such an action. Henry had told them Taylen was always someone who would listen to reason and attempt to avoid conflict at all costs, and he believed Elyria shared her father's distaste for rash action. Apparently, he'd been right on the nose.

Collins was called upon to describe her mission to make direct contact with Elyria, as well as the specific demands the Alarians were making in order to allow this summit to take place. As Henry had suspected, he was not a fan of one of the conditions.

"The summit will take place on Hai'alla in less than two weeks," Collins said. "We're only allowed to send a single representative to meet with the council, and they've specified who that representative must be." Collins looked uncomfortably at Henry. "Ben Hutchins has been requested to represent the Confed, as one of the councilors has a personal connection to him dating back before the war. No other representatives from either the government or military are allowed in the chamber for the meeting."

"You can't be serious!" The outburst had come from one of the president's entourage; it seemed Henry wasn't the only one in the room who wasn't fond of the conditions. The man's face was flushed red, and he looked like he was on the verge of having a stroke. "We're not sending some kid with no diplomatic experience whatsoever to negotiate an interstellar treaty. That's patently insane! I don't care if those bug-eyed bastards like it or not!"

Collins did an admirable job of keeping her face neutral, but Henry caught the brief flash in her eyes, reminding him of their first meeting. He suspected she wanted to strangle the man but held her tongue and instead allowed the admiral to take over.

Bob glared at the man. "I don't care if *you* and the CID like it or not, *Deputy* Director Wheaton. If we want to have any chance of a positive outcome here, we will follow the instructions given to Captain Collins to the letter. I fully realize sending Ben Hutchins as our emissary to the Alarians is not ideal, but the High Council made it abundantly clear that if they so much as catch a glimpse of someone from the diplomatic corps, the deal is off."

Well, that explained why Collins was fighting to hide her real feelings. Going after the boss of your boss generally wasn't considered a great career move. Wheaton opened his mouth to launch into another unhelpful tirade, but the admiral held up a hand.

"Please, Deputy Director Wheaton, let me finish," Garland

said, and Henry was impressed by how genuine his friend was able to make his tone seem. "I agree that this particular demand is irregular." He looked at Henry. "Hank, maybe it would be helpful if you filled in some of the context around why the council would request Ben specifically?"

"Uh," Henry said, caught off guard by the request. Normally, when Bob needed him to speak at these things, he at least gave Henry some warning beforehand. "There are probably a couple of factors in play here." Henry looked around the room, stalling for time while he quickly composed his thoughts. How much detail did they need? The full story could take an hour or more to relate, but this group really only needed a few pertinent details to understand why the council might want Ben as the Confed's representative.

"Well, about six months before the war, I took Ben along on a business trip to Hai'alla. I was working on a collaborative project with Taylen Tashmali—a senior member of the High Council and Elyria's father—and we'd hoped the close working relationship between ExoDyn and Taylen's firm would pave the way for improved relations between our two societies. We figured if we could demonstrate that a close working relationship between Terran and Alarian could be mutually beneficial, more crossover would follow, ultimately leading to a normalized trade relationship between the Confed and Hai'alla."

Henry scanned the faces in the room. Bob and Collins were familiar with the details surrounding the trip in question, but nobody else appeared to be in the loop. "While Taylen and I were busy hashing out the details of our agreement, Ben spent the day with Elyria, taking in the sights of the new Alarian homeworld. After a bit of a frosty start, the two of them were getting along quite well... when a fluke of biology derailed the whole trip.

"As it turns out, Alarian females are highly susceptible to

human pheromones, especially when going through their version of puberty. I'll skip the in-depth science lesson for now, but the broad strokes are Alarians form mating pairs based primarily on chemical compatibility. After a full day spent together, Elyria had an adverse reaction to Ben's presence, and her body formed a strong and sudden chemical dependence on Ben's teenage pheromones. The incident nearly killed her, and as soon as it leaked to the Alarian media that a Terran was responsible for the near death of a high councilor's daughter, Ben and I were kicked off Hai'alla in short order. The collaboration between myself and Taylen fell apart, and the incident very likely contributed to the anti-Terran sentiment within Alarian society that ultimately resulted in the war."

"And this is the same Elyria Tashmali Captain Collins had contact with?" the president asked.

Henry nodded. "She took her father's place on the council as soon as she was of the age of majority. Council positions typically pass down to the first-born heir, but not always. It's complicated," he said.

Garland stepped in to clarify. "When we sent in that strike on the council in the waning days of the war, Elyria's father was killed, along with the majority of the councilors. Elyria was bumped up to the position earlier than would be typical, as a result."

"I see," said the president, resting her elbows on the table and steepling her fingers. "And how do we know the Alarians aren't requesting Ben's presence for the purpose of capturing or killing him? It seems to me Elyria has more reason to hate Ben than trust him."

Henry leaned forward. "I sincerely doubt it, Madame President. I had some back-channel communication with Taylen after the incident, and he assured me neither he nor Elyria harbored any ill will toward Ben. They both understood the unique circumstances around Elyria's reaction and didn't hold Ben responsible.

"And if I may offer my opinion here," he said, waiting for a nod from the president before he went on. She gave it, and he continued. "I understand Elyria required extensive hormone therapy in order to stabilize her after the incident, but Taylen also confided in me that she would likely forever have a biological attachment to Ben—once an Alarian female bonds to a mate, it's permanent. If I had to guess, I'd say the only reason we're even getting a shot here is because Elyria is being influenced by her bond to Ben, whether she's conscious of it or not. That, when combined with the fact that Ben was a kid during the war and is now our best defense against the agent are probably all factors that got the rest of the council to sign off on this whole thing."

Bob, perhaps sensing the same air of indecision from the president and her entourage, jumped in before anyone else could pose more questions. "In the end, it doesn't really matter why they want Ben. We don't have the time to sit around and try to figure out their motivations or a better way to get the Alarians to the negotiating table. Our best estimate has another Imperial battlegroup arriving sometime in the next eight to twelve months, which means we need to take the shot while we've got the chance."

"You're out of your damn mind, Admiral!" Wheaton, unable to contain himself anymore, leaped to his feet and leaned over the table, staring daggers at the head of the Confed Navy. Henry couldn't figure out what the asshole's problem was, but it had him seriously hot under the collar. "Did you even listen to that insane story? You want to bet our future on a hormonally unstable alien and a High Council that hates our guts? The fact that you're even considering this is proof you're no longer fit for command! If it were up to me—"

"That's enough, Charles!"

Everyone's eyes locked onto President McGibbons, including Wheaton's; his mouth hung open, frozen mid-sentence in his tirade.

"Sit down and shut up. You're embarrassing yourself," the president said sternly. The CID's number two shut his mouth and sat down, but that didn't stop him from openly glaring at Admiral Garland. "I'm inclined to agree with the assessment of Mr. Hutchins and Admiral Garland, but I don't want to get bogged down on this particular detail at the expense of the rest of Captain Collins's report. We're getting off into the weeds here. We can address this, along with each of the other Alarian demands, individually after the captain finishes.

"Captain," the president said, turning to Collins. "Please continue."

The rest of the meeting was fairly uneventful. After President McGibbons slapped Wheaton's peepee for his outburst, nobody else dared to object too forcefully. Henry didn't really have any say in how they moved forward with the Alarians; it turned out he'd only been brought in to give everyone an overview on Ben and Mabel's capabilities and to offer his opinion on if Ben had the right temperament for this sort of thing. He'd lied through his teeth when he was asked about that second part.

Ben was just as stubborn, irreverent, and intolerant of political bullshit as his mother had been, but Henry realized his son was their only real shot at getting things rolling with the Alarians in a timely manner. If Ben didn't go, he suspected it would take months or even years for the Alarians to finally sit down with them at the bargaining table, and that was time they didn't have. Plus, they'd figured Ben and Mabel would have to go to Hai'alla at some point, anyway, to help the Alarians clear their datanets of the agent and its influence. That needed to be done sooner rather than later if they were going to start coordinating a unified defense with the Alarians.

The irony of the thing was that Henry hated how fast every-thing was moving. Ben wasn't ready to be thrown into the fire so soon after his recovery. Also, the summit had been scheduled for just two weeks from now, meaning Henry wouldn't be able to join Ben on Elizabeth and go with him. He was sure the compressed timeline was intentional to make it difficult for the Confed to prepare.

Guilt stabbed at his chest; Ben would once again have the fate of Terran space foisted upon his shoulders. And it was all because Henry had used his own son as a science experiment. Had he known in the early days of Project Blackthorn that what he was doing would essentially strip his son of his own agency, he'd have looked for a different test subject. Instead, his hubris had led to a life of hardship and suffering for Ben.

When the meeting was beginning to wind down, Wheaton risked jumping into the conversation again, but he kept his tone in check this time. "It's clear to me that we'll be sending Ben Hutchins to open negotiations, regardless of my objections," he said, struggling mightily to appear calm and collected, but Henry could see the tension in the man's jaw. "But the Alarians didn't say anything about us not coaching Ben up a bit. I propose that the diplomatic corps send a few representatives along to work with Ben during the flight to Hai'alla and give him a crash course in diplomacy. It's far from a perfect solution, but it's got to be better than sending him into the lion's den with no guidance whatsoever."

Henry thought it was a reasonable request, and after a short round of discussion, the president and Garland both agreed.

When the meeting finally broke up, Henry worked his way around to where Bob and Collins were conversing quietly. "Well, we knew Ben was going to have a part to play in bringing the Alarians on board, but I'm not sure how I feel about this whole thing," Henry said.

"I know what you mean, Hank," Bob replied. "But do you have any better alternatives?"

"Not really. If the High Council is making demands, it's best for us to give them what they want. I'm just glad they're willing to talk. Which reminds me, what was with that little spat between you and Wheaton?"

"Just a little bit of inside politics, Hank. Don't worry about it."

Henry did worry about it, but there was something in Bob's eyes that said, *Not here.* He'd known the admiral long enough to see his friend wasn't going to say any more, regardless of what angle Henry prodded from. Shifting gears, he turned to Collins and smiled. "That was quick thinking, Captain—dangling Ben in front of Elyria to get her to come to the table like that."

"It was stupid," she said. "But I'm fairly certain that Captain Raal was about ten seconds away from blasting my ship out from under me, regardless of what the high councilor ordered her to do. So I figured we didn't have much to lose at that point. I'm just sorry I wasn't able to get her to agree to a proper ambassadorial team for the summit. I've learned not to underestimate Ben and Mabel, but this one strikes me as something that's well outside his wheelhouse."

Henry snorted. "That's putting it mildly. At least you were able to negotiate proper transport for him."

"About that," Garland said. "The High Council didn't specify the class of ship we can send, only that we're allowed to send a single warship to Hai'alla." The admiral's eyes sparkled, and Henry had a feeling he knew what was coming next. It made him feel a little better about sending his son into the lion's den alone.

"Let me guess," Henry said. "You're sending the *Ford.*" It made a certain kind of sense, he supposed. The CTS *Gerald R. Ford* was the flagship of Fourth Fleet and had been instrumental in repelling the Alarian invasion of the Valkyrie system when the war broke out. The massive fleet carrier would send a strong message that despite its recent losses, the Confed still had plenty of teeth. Should the Alarians get it in their heads that maybe now was the time to finish what they'd started, a half a million tons of war machine over their heads should give them second thoughts.

Bob's lips twisted into a predatory grin. "No, we're sending Ben aboard *Indomitable*."

Henry blinked a few times. He felt even better now than he had a moment ago. "Yeah, that'll send a message, alright." He wished he could go along now, if for no other reason than to see the faces of the High Council when a kilometer-long Terran battlecruiser arrived in orbit to negotiate a peace treaty.

9

BETTER THAN HOLLYWOOD

THE STREETS OF ELIZABETH CITY WERE COVERED IN DUST AND scattered debris—remnants of the war that decimated both Terran and Alarian worlds alike. Ben's boots crunched lightly on the pavement as he nimbly dodged the rusting hulks of ground cars that were abandoned when the bombs started falling. The golden light of a setting star sat in stark contrast with the post-apocalyptic wasteland around him.

It was surreal. Just a few years ago, this was a thriving city, full of life. The Alarian War had brought all of it crashing down, but that terrible conflict felt like a lifetime ago. So much had happened since Alarian missiles decimated Terran space. The whole war felt almost academic, yet it was recent enough that Ben still had to be mindful of radiation hotspots scattered around the ruins of the city. Everything combined into a strange dissonance that would have been distracting were it not for the forty-odd bloodthirsty marines who would be hot on his heels in short order.

Mabel's voice drifted through his thoughts: *Take a left at the next intersection, Ben.* He hung a left and sprinted for the massive building at the end of the street. "How are we on time, Mabel?" he asked aloud.

Twenty-three minutes remain before the Pathfinders will drop.

"Going to be close."

If you insist on executing the plan we discussed last night, then yes, it will be. However, I do believe we can pull it off.

"I thought you liked this plan?"

I never said that. I merely agreed with you when you stated it would make a lasting impression on the Pathfinders. I also said I believe it to be reckless and an unnecessary risk, but you chose to ignore that part.

Ben scanned the shattered remains of the building's front facade as he approached. "Yeah, this'll do nicely," he muttered to himself. The training op had a simple objective: to demonstrate just what he was capable of. Kravczyk told him they were doing it this way because the only way marines learned anything was if it hurt, which was why they weren't just giving them a full rundown in a classroom. Valdez had been a little more tactful. He thought jumping right into a live training operation would bypass many of the questions that would inevitably arise until the marines got to see Ben's abilities firsthand, which would make integration faster so they could get to the real work that lay ahead.

As a bonus, this exercise would serve as a good field trial of the new or experimental systems his APEX was running, such as updated processors and the captured Imperium grav harness that'd been adapted to his armor. He just wished he could demo the pair of deployable combat blades now integrated into the farings covering his forearms. Sadly, there wasn't a good way to make the hyper-dense, razor sharp alloy blades "nonlethal," so that system was physically locked out of his control for the duration of the exercise.

Regardless of Valdez's motivations for dropping everyone

right into the deep end, Ben was eager for a chance to put his updated kit through its paces. And if doing so meant he got to stick it to the space apes and leave them speechless, well, all the better. If he was honest with himself, though, he'd admit there was more to it than that. There was something about the way everyone at Thunder, except for Kravczyk and Valdez, looked at him, and it made him long for a chance to prove himself, to show them he belonged there just as much as they did. And all he had to do was evade capture for twelve hours or take out an entire platoon of Marine Pathfinders. Naturally, he opted for the latter option.

Leaping up onto the roof of a small, abandoned passenger car on the sidewalk below the front of the building, Ben used the incredible power of his APEX armor suit to vault up through a large hole in the side of the building's second floor. He landed awkwardly, his boots slipping on the piles of broken glass that littered the large concourse. "Where to, Mabel?"

Follow the indicators on your HUD.

A translucent red arrow appeared in his vision, directing him to one side and up a flight of stairs.

"Let the games begin," Ben said, more to himself than to Mabel. His boots kicked up dust and debris as he dashed toward the highlighted staircase. It was time to show off just what made him and Mabel such a force to be reckoned with.

———

"Two minutes to ramp down! Final gear check and sound off!" Lieutenant Harris bellowed over the roar of the MS-88 Condor's huge MPDs as the dropship banked hard on its descent to their LZ. Forty-two Marine Pathfinders in full hardshell battle armor sounded off in order, confirming they were good to go.

The Condor's crew chief stood by the tail ramp, waiting for

the light above his console to change from red to green. The moment it did, he slapped the control to drop the ramp, which kissed the ground at almost the same time the landing gear touched down.

"Go, go, go!"

Shouts of "ooh rah!" or "get some!" were thrown about like in all the network shows. The Pathfinders were the cream of the crop of the Confed Marine Corps, and they knew their business well. These were professional warriors: quick, quiet, and deadly. Twenty seconds after the first pair of boots hit the pavement of the plaza, all forty-three marines were on the ground and pulling security in a 360-degree arc as the ship's engines spooled back up and the Condor departed, the crew chief covering the ground element with an M266 infantry support weapon in a pivot mount next to his seat.

"Rees!" Harris called over his communications and sensors operator—CSO.

"Right here, LT."

"What do our eyes in the sky have for us?"

"Last reported satellite contact was twenty minutes ago, and it was only a faint thermal, but it's the best we have to go on. Fifteen hundred meters north-northeast. Looks like he was headed for the ruins of the Jackal Center. It's the old home of the Elizabeth Jackals."

"Good enough. We've got to start somewhere. Staff Sergeant Watanabe, get the platoon moving toward the bombed-out stadium 1.5 klicks to our north-northeast," Harris ordered his platoon sergeant.

"Yes, sir!"

"Sergeant Rees…" Harris turned back to his CSO. "Get the MinDIs in the air and scouting ahead of our advance."

"You got it, LT," Rees said, already unpacking the miniature reconnaissance drones from their storage case, which she kept on the small of her back. Officially, they were designated as Drone, Miniature, Intelligent, Mk. 265 MOD2 in the supply chain, but as was always the case when infantry grunts got their filthy paws on drawn-out military designations, they became colloquially known as MinDIs. "Anything in particular you want them looking for, LT?"

"Hutchins dropped with nothing but his armor and that AI, so skip the detail scan for explosives or other surprises and go for a quick recon. He already knows we're coming, so there's no need to have them be sneaky about it, either. I want to find him as fast as possible."

After a few taps on her forearm-mounted computer, Rees tossed a handful of the thumb-sized drones into the air. Tiny electric fans stabilized their attitude and then sent them buzzing off toward their target. She gave Harris a thumbs-up, and the two Pathfinders took off after the rest of the platoon, which was already dispersed by squad and moving toward the arena.

————

"WARLOCK HAS ENTERED THE ARENA, sirs, so the video feed may be spotty. The damage to the structure was extensive and the transmission lines were never repaired."

"That's fine, Specialist." Valdez acknowledged the technician who was coordinating the live feed to the training ground currently shown in high resolution on the main display in the auditorium at Joint Base Thunder. "Warlock" was Ben's callsign for this exercise, something Chief Kravczyk had insisted upon. "How much coverage do we have in there?"

"The main arena is covered, as are the majority of the concourses, but we don't have feeds to the luxury boxes, administrative offices, or main control room, which is where we suspect he is now."

"What are you up to, Ben?" Valdez wondered aloud next to Major Davis. The two officers were in the auditorium's control booth, monitoring the raw feeds coming in, so they were able to see a lot more than the two or three different camera feeds being piped into the auditorium for First and Third Platoons to watch.

While the entire company would be training with Ben over the coming weeks, Valdez thought it would be a little unfair to sic an entire company of Marine Pathfinders after the kid on his first training op, so he'd scaled it back to only Second Platoon for this one.

"How are First and Third Platoons taking the news?" Valdez asked Major Davis.

"Captain Kaneda tells me they weren't all that happy to be left out of the action, but when they were informed they'd get to sit in air-conditioned comfort for the duration while watching the whole thing on the big screen, they were suddenly in a much better mood."

"I'll bet." Valdez chuckled. "This beats the hell out of extra PT or being stuck in a classroom for the day."

On the big screen below them, the feed switched to a street view of the Condor touching down and Second Platoon rushing down the ramp. A small inset window appeared in one corner of the screen, showing the hallway outside the door Ben had disappeared through a few minutes ago. The Condor lifted off less than a minute later, and Second Platoon spread out to take up security while Lieutenant Harris conferred with his CSO.

"Smart," Valdez commented when he saw the MinDIs.

"Mmhmm," Davis agreed. "Harris knows Ben dropped with nothing but his suit and Mabel, so he's not afraid to send the dogs out hunting right away."

"I tried to tell him Ben doesn't need weapons to be a threat, but I don't think anyone in Second Platoon believes there could be any outcome other than a swift victory."

"Do you?"

Valdez took a moment before responding, watching the feeds as Ben reemerged from the main control room and sprinted toward the luxury box section on the top floor. "I learned early on to never underestimate what Ben and Mabel are capable of, especially when they're working together. I don't know if they'll be able to take out all of them, but I guarantee you you'll get your money's worth during this little show."

The Pathfinders were rapidly chewing up the distance to the arena, which now lay just a couple city blocks away. The feed from inside the Jackal Center had once again lost track of Ben when he disappeared into a blind spot. Valdez followed the tactical plot that was showing on a smaller display to the right of the main screen, and he saw the MinDIs were now in search of their quarry.

Suddenly, the feed showing the approaching Pathfinders lit up, awash with bright colors. The marquee over the main entrance had come to life—well, the half that wasn't lying in a shattered pile on the steps below, at least. Valdez squinted at the display, the intense light washing out his vision, which had been tuned to the low-light environment both in the control booth and the video feeds from the exercise area.

"What are you up to?" Major Davis said quietly to himself, parroting Valdez from earlier.

"He definitely wants those guys to know he's in there. I tried to warn him about getting too cocky."

Valdez turned to see Chief Kravczyk leaning against an unused soundboard, studying the raw feeds and shaking his head in disappointment.

"Welcome to the party, Chief," Valdez said. "I didn't hear you come in, as usual."

"Thanks, Boss. You know I like to keep you on your toes."

"You know," Davis said, casting a sidelong glance at Valdez, "for such a freakishly large human being, he is alarmingly sneaky."

"Only when he wants to be..." Valdez said distractedly. His eyes were locked on the feed showing the marquee, which read, *Come One, Come All... and Welcome to the Jungle.*

"That's a mistake," Kravczyk said, nodding toward the main display. Second Platoon was swarming into the building and breaking off by squads as they began a high-speed search for Ben. "Lieutenant Harris isn't taking Ben seriously."

"Kind of hard to when you have forty Pathfinders, all kitted out with full hardshell and M21s, Chief," Major Davis replied. "Then a literal billboard lights up announcing where your target is? I must admit, I'm starting to wonder if Ben is the one not taking things seriously."

"He's a cocky little shit," Kravczyk said, turning to smirk at the marine major. "But I guarantee you he's taking this *very* seriously, especially after the gym incident."

Davis winced slightly when Kravczyk brought up the gym. "Don't think those marines don't feel the same way," he said. "They may not be members of the same platoon, but their pride as Pathfinders is on the line here."

The marines finished a rapid-fire search of the outer ring of offices, bathrooms, vendor stalls, and other spaces a lone human in an APEX suit might use for a hiding place, then began flooding into the general seating area of the arena. The lighting in the cavernous space was poor, unlike all the areas surrounding it, and everyone in the control booth strained their eyes to catch any detail from the various feeds.

White beams began piercing the gloom and sweeping the area around the marines, who began activating their weapon-mounted flashlights, when suddenly all the displays showing feeds from inside the main arena washed out with brilliant light. Shouts of surprise came in over the audio feed, and the marines recoiled at the blinding light that flooded the space when the arena's powerful flood and spotlights all kicked on at once.

"Turn up the comms feed," Valdez instructed one of the techs, and the overhead speakers crackled to life with the chaotic chatter of the all-platoon channel. "Do we have audio from inside the arena that isn't coming from suit comms?" The chatter died down in volume. It now sounded distorted as the audio feed switched over to a general audio pickup from the arena.

"Down on the ground!" Several of the marines were shouting through the built-in PA systems in their armor, and Valdez's gaze locked onto an APEX-clad figure standing with arms outspread in an inviting gesture… atop the dust-covered team logo of the Elizabeth Jackals at center court.

"Down on the ground, now!"

"Get down or we will open fire!"

"Well, this was anticlimactic," Major Davis said, shaking his head.

"Not so much, I think," Kravczyk said with a predatory grin spreading across his lips.

Davis opened his mouth, a puzzled expression on his face, when the voice of Lieutenant Harris was clearly heard over the composite audio feed. "Weapons free! Take him down!"

Gunfire erupted from a dozen M21 carbines in unison. This was a training op, of course, so the Pathfinders weren't carrying live ammo. Instead, their training rifles produced simulated recoil and sound to maximize realism. The computer that controlled the exercise would mark hits on targets and lock and deactivate the armor of participants who had been "killed."

The gunfire continued for a full five seconds until Harris called a cease-fire.

The APEX-armored figure standing center-stage shook his head and wagged a finger slowly in a *no-no* gesture.

"What the hell?" a voice said from the stands somewhere near the court. "Why didn't we get a kill notification?"

"First Squad, advance and investigate," Lieutenant Harris ordered.

The moment First Squad set boots on the polished wood of the basketball court, the lights in the arena began shutting down in a cascade from outside moving in, stopping when the powerful spotlights illuminated only center court and the APEX figure.

"This is better than most of the stuff Hollywood ever put out," Kravczyk commented. He was munching on something while kicked back in a chair with his feet up on some audio equipment.

"Is that popcorn?" Davis said in disbelief.

"Sure is, Major," Kravczyk said around a mouth full of kernels. "Would you like some?" The big SEAR held out a small brown bag that was still half full of buttered popcorn, but Davis just stared at him like he'd suddenly grown a third eye on his forehead. Kravczyk pointed at the main display. "Better watch, Major. I think the good part is about to start."

Valdez and Davis turned their heads back to the main video feed just as First Squad approached the figure standing relaxed under the lights. One of the Pathfinders hesitantly reached out a hand to touch an armored shoulder when Valdez caught sight of the tactical plot out of the corner of his eye. "Son of a bitch."

"Bossman sees it," Kravczyk announced to nobody in particular just as the outstretched hand made contact with the figure… which winked out of existence, followed by all the light in the room a heartbeat later.

10

WELCOME TO THE JUNGLE

BEN WATCHED THE MARINES APPROACH THE HOLOGRAM WITH A predatory smile on his face. He almost couldn't believe how gullible they were.

All the marines save a few that are pulling security around the perimeter of the concourse are within actionable distance, Ben, Mabel said directly into his consciousness.

"Just a few more seconds..." Ben whispered. He was hanging upside down from the rafters directly above the hologram of an APEX-suited figure standing at center court. "Now!" The hologram winked out just as a gloved hand made contact, and the powerful spotlights cut out with it, plunging the arena into darkness once again.

Shouts of surprise and confusion echoed around the cavernous space as the Pathfinders worked frantically to enable their low-light vision augmentation systems again. Ben counted down from three—just enough time for all the grunts down there to get their settings correct again—then gave the next command.

"Hit it, Mabel!" The arena's potent sound system roared to

life, the opening guitar riff from Guns N' Roses' "Welcome to the Jungle" screaming out across the empty stands.

Loud curses were audible in the brief lulls between chords as the music began to build.

"Oh my god!"

The powerful spotlights kicked back on as the drums joined the guitars and swept an arc outward from center court. The haunting wail of lead singer Axl Rose built in intensity as the intro continued, and Mabel brought the full glory of the once-proud arena to life in brilliant color. The spectacular light show culminated in showers of sparks from the jumbotron for the last few seconds.

Ben's heart rate spiked as his moment approached—his turbocharged adrenal response marking the change from Ben Hutchins the man to Ben Hutchins the weapon. He let it happen, detaching his conscious mind from the data streaming into his senses and becoming one with his APEX. The lens through which he viewed reality changed, and the world around him both faded away and sharpened in detail at the same time while his brain filtered out extraneous information. By the time his conscious mind became aware of the ever-changing battlespace around him, all that remained was data on his targets and how to neutralize them.

Ben released his hold and plummeted like a meteor toward the dumbstruck Pathfinders who were sweeping their surroundings with their carbines in a panic. Pulsing the experimental grav harness attached to his lower legs, he arrested his descent just before he contacted the court dead-center.

"Jump!"

Ben struck the floor in a classic three-point superhero landing pose and was moving again before the marines could turn fully around.

Ben ripped the carbine from the hands of the first startled

grunt to regain his wits. Grabbing it by the muzzle and spinning around in a flash, he used the weapon as a sledgehammer against the side of the shocked marine's head. This was still a training exercise, and all of the armor worn by both Ben and the marines had their power limited by the controlling AI to ensure that nobody actually got hurt or killed, but when a hit registered as fatal, the AI killed power to the suit in question. The marine collapsed to the floor like a sack of potatoes as Ben set about introducing the remaining members of First Squad to a level of violence they were wholly unprepared for.

VALDEZ'S EYES went wide as an old rock-and-roll song began pounding out of the arena's sound system, accompanied by a spectacular light show.

"You've gotta give him an A for presentation," Kravczyk said casually as Valdez and Davis stared in awe at the main display.

Valdez inhaled sharply when he caught sight of a black blur screaming down from the ceiling toward the marines below; it was moving way too fast. Ben slowed abruptly just before impact, but he still contacted the floor with enough force that the resonating boom could be heard over the audio pickup.

"Alright!" Kravczyk clapped to himself gleefully. "Superhero landing!" Valdez and Davis were still mute, fixated on the spectacle, for Valdez could think of no other word to describe what he was seeing.

Ben leaped to his feet, tearing the carbine away from the first shocked marine to turn around, then clubbed the poor bastard down in a single blow. A series of icons arranged below the tactical plot next to the main display represented the status of each member of Second Platoon; one of those now had a red hue to it, indicating the marine in question was designated as KIA.

Valdez watched, transfixed, as Ben turned into a maelstrom of brutal close-quarters combat, cutting a—figuratively—bloody swathe through First Squad in a matter of seconds before vaulting over a low retaining wall. The kid was going hard after the remaining Pathfinders, who were only just now beginning to regain their wits after the chaotic back and forth with light and dark, noise and silence. The complete chaos of the all-platoon channel told the story: Ben had caught these elite warriors completely flat-footed, and he'd rattled their cages so bad they were no longer a cohesive fighting force.

Lieutenant Harris finally managed to get his people organized with the help of his sergeants, but by that point, Ben had taken out almost half of his platoon. Liberated carbines, combat knives, fists, and even a section of polymer bench, at one point, were wielded with equally deadly efficiency by the black-clad demon making mincemeat out of the best the Confed Marine Corps had to offer.

The radio chatter turned from confusion to frustration as the Pathfinders slowly realized their rounds were not hitting what they were aiming at, and Valdez heard Major Davis mutter to himself in disbelief.

"What the actual hell is happening right now?"

Valdez couldn't help the half smile that tugged up on one corner of his lips as the scene played out. In his mind, the outcome was no longer in doubt. Ben had clearly planned exceedingly well for this encounter, more so than either he or Kravczyk gave him credit for. That was evidenced by the fact that he and Mabel had apparently hacked the targeting computers of the marines' armor, resulting in shots that never landed and allowing him to tear through the opposition like a vengeful god.

It was all over before the guitar solo.

11

ONE LESS WARLORD

Tess tasted copper. She opened her eyes slowly, not wanting to alert her captors that she was now conscious again. Wherever they had her, it was pitch black, and the only sounds she could make out were water droplets collecting into a puddle and her own labored breathing. The air smelled stale and was heavy with moisture, amplifying its nauseating, musty character.

She took a moment to get her brain working again; she couldn't tell if the disorientation she was feeling was simply due to the darkened cell or if she had a concussion after their tumble down the stairs. Her arms were numb, and she slowly worked on flexing her fingers. The faint clink of metal chains came from above her, and Tess realized she was hanging by a pair of manacles binding her wrists. No wonder she couldn't feel her arms; she must have been hanging here for hours or maybe even a day, judging by the pain that flared in her shoulders when she squirmed in an attempt to test her restraints.

A notification popped to life in her vision, and she almost shouted out in surprise. Her implant was still online, meaning Donovan and his people must not have known about the neural implants being issued to special operations units these days.

Either that or they didn't know how to disable them. Tess opened the text message she'd just received.

Lt Cmdr Fairbanks: *McCollum, don't struggle, or the two goons at the top of the stairs will come down and work you over. Ask me how I know… We're in the basement of the colonial government building, suspended from some exposed pipes on the ceiling. They're high enough that I can barely reach the floor on my tiptoes. You're probably SOL. From the limited look I got of the place when they brought us down here, it doesn't look like we have many options for escape.*

I don't think these guys are aware of our implants and their capabilities. The construction of this place is blocking the signal to the datanet, but I was able to fire off a quick SOS to the rest of the team before I lost contact. That was almost 2 hours ago, but I would think they'll wait until Holden and Sera return with the QRT before trying to take the place. It could be the better part of a day before they act. How are you holding up?

Tess breathed a small sigh of relief. Fairbanks was here with her, and the news he'd been able to get word to the rest of the MAC team was just the morale boost she needed to really get her head back in the game. She mentally kicked herself for not thinking about trying to send a message via her implant earlier, but she'd been caught so flat-footed when Donovan casually strolled into the governor's office that she hadn't even considered trying to get off a call for help. She stretched her toes out as far as possible but couldn't touch the floor. She flexed her shoulders to relieve some of the strain on her arms, but it didn't help.

PO3 McCollum: *Sir, glad you're ok. I'm fine. Just a little disorientation after I came back around. It's getting better. I can't reach the floor and my arms are numb, but I'll survive. Any contact with Donovan or his men since they brought us down here?*

Lt Cmdr Fairbanks: *None, but I've heard faint voices through the door at the top of the stairs a few times. No more gunshots, which is good. Seems like Donovan wants to take over the colony with as little drama as possible, which bodes well for us —*

The text stopped mid-sentence, coinciding with a heavy thunk that reverberated down the stairwell and echoed around the oppressive darkness of the basement. Panic rose in Tess's chest, and she made a herculean effort to stuff it back down into its hole. She fell back on her training, straining to pick up on any and every detail she could. Some muffled conversation filtered down the stairs, but it was too faint to make out. A metallic *snick* sounded as the locking bolt on the door released, and light spilled down the stairwell, casting eerie shadows around the basement.

Her eyes were adjusted to the dark, and the dim light coming down the steps was more than enough for her to make out the boundaries of the room. It was smaller than she expected, based on the building's external footprint. She twisted her head around, trying to take in the area behind her, and spied several doors that must have led to other rooms. Piles of office furniture and old equipment lined the walls, intermixed with industrial shelves that held orderly lines of plastic bins about the size of a military footlocker.

A new icon popped to life in the corner of her vision: her implant had reestablished a connection to the datanet, albeit an extremely weak one. Tess mentally composed a flash message and sent it out to the whole MAC team. The status of the message lagged for several seconds as her implant did what it could to transmit the two sentences of text over the poor datanet connection.

The lights overhead snapped on, and she slammed her eyes shut. The harsh, sterile light of the commercial LEDs overwhelmed her dark-adjusted eyesight as the heavy door to the basement clanged shut. But even with her eyes closed, she could still see the notification from her implant informing her that her message had been partially sent, which meant some, but not all, of the recipients had received it before her implant lost contact with the datanet again when the door shut.

Heavy footfalls sounded from the stairs, and Tess heard the jingling of weapons and gear against the wearers' hardshell battle armor. Tess cracked open her eyes, which were still struggling to adjust to the blinding light, and saw Fairbanks doing the same a few paces away. He was standing on his tiptoes and working to face the stairs. Tess kicked her feet and twisted her hips in an attempt to twist around as well, but the way the manacles were wrapped around the iron pipe over her head kept her facing the wrong direction.

"Oh good," Donovan said in a cheery voice. "Now that the petty officer is up from her nap, we can get down to business. Namely, what to do with you and the rest of your team."

A gloved hand roughly spun Tess around until she was facing one of Donovan's thugs. He wore his combat helmet, and mirrored AR terrestrial warfare goggles covered his eyes, but the lustful sneer on his lips told Tess everything she needed to know about what the man was thinking. He let go, his hand casually brushing against the front of her CDUs as it slowly dropped to his side. The twisted chains of the manacles began to swing her back around the other way again, but the thug's hand came back up and stopped her rotation. He stepped behind her, leaning in close and loudly sniffing her hair as one arm snaked around her waist and held her in the proper orientation.

"Looks like I'm going to have to stand here and hold her to keep her from spinning away, sir. But I don't mind taking one for the team."

Tess used the sound of his voice to estimate exactly where the bridge of his nose would be. She leaned her head forward like she was trying to get away from the goon, and when he moved to pull her in closer to him again, she snapped her head back as hard as she could. Fireworks exploded behind her eyes with the impact, but a gratifying crack rang out, followed by a howl of pain. The thug yanked his hand away from Tess, and she spun wildly from the pipe. She only caught a glimpse of the jerk as she wheeled around, but blood was pouring through his fingers as he cradled his broken nose in both hands and bent forward at the waist while cursing a blue streak.

Tess spun around again and twisted her hips. As she spun past him, she fired a straight kick at the man's ruined face, her heel connecting with the hands covering his nose. Hanging by her manacles, she wasn't able to put as much force behind the blow as she would have liked, but it was still powerful enough to drive him off his feet and send him crashing to the floor.

More hands grabbed Tess and restrained her.

"Alright, Petty Officer. That's quite enough of that," Donovan said.

Two of his men were now holding her firmly by the shoulders. The pressure of their grip caused her shoulders to flare in agony. She grunted, wincing as pain ripped through her abused arms. The guy she'd booted was being helped to his feet by the other mercs, who guided him toward a dust-covered desk in the corner. Tess smiled inwardly, seeing the man's drunken gait. Good, she'd likely given him a concussion.

"Sorry, baby," she called after the man in a mocking, coquettish tone. "I guess you just weren't man enough for me. I should've warned you: I like it rough." Tess's voice shifted from soft and playful to a dangerous growl as she delivered that last part.

"Interesting," Donovan said. He was looking at her, but his voice sounded detached, making it seem like he was actually talking to himself. "I would have assumed your time as a pirate's private little joy toy would've left a lasting scar on your psyche, but it would appear you're made of sterner stuff than I initially gave you credit for, PO3 Tessandra McCollum, Confed Special Exoatmospheric Reconnaissance Unit. Maybe command isn't dumping their rejects with the MAC teams after all."

Tess froze. She hadn't expected Donovan to be this well-informed. Where was he getting his information from? Her time as a captive, tormented by pirates, before becoming a SEAR wasn't common knowledge. Heck, she hadn't even come fully clean to Ben about it yet. It was in her personnel file, sure, but only because that was the one thing that nearly disqualified her from SEAR selection; she barely passed the psych exam. Did that mean Donovan had a source feeding him intel from within the Confed?

A small smile curved the corners of Donovan's lips. "Yes, McCollum. I know all about that particular incident. The torture, rape, and murder of your parents and two older brothers at the hands of the Tipton gang two years ago. The fact that James Tipton, fat sack of shit that he was, kept you chained up in his personal quarters for his own amusement. And also the fact that you, being the sneaky little devil you are, managed to kill him with your bare hands and escape in his own personal life pod without the rest of his crew knowing. Very resourceful of you."

"A bad time with some pirates does not define me, Donovan," Tess growled. "And he had it coming. Since you seem to know so much about me, how about you share a little about yourself? That way, Lieutenant Commander Fairbanks and I don't feel so awkward hanging out with you." Her heart was hammering at her ribcage, but she focused on keeping Donovan's attention for as long as possible. Fairbanks had tried to tell her something with his eyes right after she'd booted that dick in the face, and she suspected he'd received a message from the rest of their team in that brief datanet window they'd had when the door was open. The look in Fairbanks's eyes had been hopeful, which probably meant the QRT was ready to make their move.

Donovan laughed. "Hah! Even tied up and completely at my mercy, you keep up the bravado." His air of humor and civility evaporated in an instant. "That's what I always hated about you high-speed, low-drag types. Thinking you're invincible, that you could take on the devil himself with one hand tied behind your back. Well, guess what?" he snarled, getting right in her face. Spittle flecked her cheek, but she didn't flinch away.

She could see it now, in his eyes. The man was full-blown crazy. His casual murder of Timmons up in the governor's office should have tipped her off, but at the time, she'd been more focused on being captured.

Donovan unholstered his sidearm and pressed the muzzle under her chin. The cold steel dug into her throat, making it hard to breathe. This was it. She was going to die here, at the hands of a madman. "I've got news for you, Petty Officer Third Class Tessandra McCollum... You aren't invincible."

Donovan pulled the pistol away from her chin and shot Fairbanks right between the eyes.

"No!" Tess screamed. She tried to lash out at the warlord, but the vise-like grip of the two thugs behind her kept her locked in place.

Donovan pursed his lips, staring at the lifeless body swaying from the overhead pipe. He lowered the pistol to his side and turned to Tess. "I'd considered letting you two live, you know, but I'm really quite upset you somehow managed to get word to the rest of your team about my little coup. At least I assume it was one of you two. I can't think of any other reason why the quick response team would turn around and haul ass back here, especially when I left such a juicy distraction for them at the mine. Unfortunately, we aren't ready to fend off a determined assault just yet, so we'll be leaving soon. It's a shame all those innocent miners and their families are probably going to die now that your people won't be arriving in time to save them. I hear there were eighteen children in that settlement. A pity, and all your fault.

"To think I had to waste a good resource in Timmons, too. Oh well, I'll just have to try again another day. Goodbye, Petty Officer."

Donovan took a step back and aimed his gun at her face. Time slowed down to a crawl. Smoke still curled from the muzzle, and small flecks of unburnt powder were stuck to the front of the slide. A copper gleam flashed briefly from deep within the pistol—the bullet with her name on it, waiting to be unleashed. Tess could hear nothing but a high-pitched buzzing in her ears. The warlord's mouth opened and closed as he spoke. To her or his men, she wasn't sure; his words were lost somewhere in the short distance that separated them.

Tess jerked backward. The hands that had been restraining her suddenly released their hold. Donovan's eyes went wide in slow motion, and his pistol began sweeping away from her. Tess flexed her core, swinging her suddenly freed legs up to either side of the monster in front of her. Her left shin smashed into the pistol, which boomed once before flying out of Donovan's grasp. Her right leg looped over his shoulder and snapped closed, clamping his neck behind her knee. Her left leg hooked over her right ankle, drawing Donovan in close. Then she squeezed with every ounce of strength she had left.

Donovan's hands clawed at Tess's thighs, and she cried out as his teeth tore into her calf. But she didn't let up. The SEAR wrung every last gram of force from her muscular legs. After just a few short seconds, the warlord's thrashing began to lose its coordination as his oxygen-starved brain misfired. He settled back into her as his legs slowly gave out, and she prepared every last bit of power her used-up arms and core muscles could muster.

Tess twisted her body violently, yanking Donovan off the

floor by his head as she spun. A sound like a tree branch snapping under gale-force winds filled her ears, and the man went limp beneath her. She dropped his twitching body to the floor, lungs heaving—whether from the adrenaline dump or the exertion, she wasn't sure.

Holden and Sera rushed to her side, a half dozen armed members of the QRT hot on their heels.

Sera lifted her up, taking the strain off the manacles while Holden grabbed a nearby bucket and flipped it over so she could stand. Agony flared anew in her abused arms and shoulders, and tears welled in the corners of her eyes.

"Sorry we're late," Holden said. "You're alright now, McCollum. The few of Donovan's gang that got away are being hunted down by the rest of the team and a contingent from the CSF, and the QR team is clearing the rest of the building. It's over."

12

CODE X-RAY

VALDEZ WATCHED THE STREET-LEVEL FEED OUTSIDE THE ARENA'S main entrance as Ben strode casually out the ruined front doors. He walked down the expansive steps that led to the small plaza below and nonchalantly leaned up against a concrete pillar.

"Warlock is calling for pickup, Commander," one of the comms techs said, looking at Valdez expectantly.

"Send in the Griffon to pick him up and then have the Condor land to retrieve Second Platoon once the Griffon has cleared the area," he ordered. "Probably not the best idea in the world to have them all ride back here on the same bus right now."

"How do you want to handle the debrief, sir?" Kravczyk said, back in serious mode. "We'd planned to put them all in the same room tomorrow morning, but I'm not so sure that's the best idea right now after the ass-kicking Second Platoon just got."

Valdez thought for a moment. "Let's still run a joint debrief in the morning. Ass-kicking or not, they're still professionals. If Ben and the Pathfinders can't be trusted to get along after a training op, then we can't trust them to get along when it's the real thing. Do you agree, Major?"

Davis nodded. "We may have relaxed the standards a bit to fill the ranks in recent years, but a liberal helping of crow is good for them from time to time. I see no issue with running a joint brief, as long as Hutchins doesn't rub their faces in it too much."

"Don't worry about that, Major," Kravczyk said. "I'll make sure he's got his act together." The big SEAR looked at Valdez and inclined his head toward the door. "With your permission, sir? I want to meet Ben when the Griffon lands so I can start deflating the massive ego he must be taking back with him."

Valdez chuckled and nodded. "Good luck, Chief." Kravczyk sketched a salute and then exited the control booth. Valdez turned to one of the techs. "Have copies of both the raw and composite feeds sent via Q-link to Icarus, care of Henry Hutchins in Fleet Science and Technology, please, Specialist."

"Icarus's Q-link is down for emergency maintenance right now, sir. Comms informed us that we'll have a link blackout until 0700 tomorrow, at least."

"Very well. Package everything up and have it sent over whenever the system is back online." Valdez sighed inwardly. The Q-link network was an incredible boon to efficient and effective communications, but it still suffered from a host of teething problems and was proving to be unreliable at best. He turned to Davis. "Walk with me, Major? I'd like to go over the logistics for the debrief tomorrow."

"Lead the way."

The two officers left the control room and headed toward the administrative building that housed their offices. Davis held the door open for Valdez as they exited, and the damp evening air washed over them. The smell of aviation fuel carried by the breeze from the base's neighboring spaceport buried the faint smell of spring flowers that were beginning to bloom in this region of the planet.

When they were halfway down one of the paved walkways that branched off a large recreational area, Valdez's comms unit chirped with an urgent incoming call and brought the pair to a halt.

"XO NAVSOC," Valdez said.

"Sir, ops just called a code X-ray." It was Lieutenant Duncan, the communications OOD.

Valdez felt his heart rate spike. A code X-ray meant Thunder's sensor net had picked up something it'd been continuously looking out for since the Battle of Icarus: a slipspace transmission that matched the transceivers known to have been built by the agent.

"What's the status on Warlock and Voidwalker?"

"I've requested the tower clear the pattern for them, and their bird is on final approach. They'll be on the ground in three minutes."

"Issue an emergency recall of Second Platoon's Condor and send a truck for Major Davis and myself, then get ahold of Captain Kaneda and inform him of the situation. Tell him to spin up First and Third Platoons as quickly as possible in full ground combat kit and arrange air transport for them. After that, have someone collect Chief Kravczyk's APEX from his locker and deliver it to him on the flight line." Valdez paused for a second to let Duncan process everything up to that point, then continued. "Let flight ops know we'll need a quick turnaround on Second Platoon's bird, and have them pull in whoever they need to make that happen. And I want ordnance to load warshots on board. Equip for air-to-ground. Got all that?"

"Yes, sir. I've got my team working on it right now."

"Good," Valdez said, and then he snuck a glance at the chrono on his left wrist and added something else. "And have the mess hall whip up some sandwiches to go, and deliver them to the flight line. Those guys are probably starving right now."

Valdez ended the call and then pulled up Kravczyk's comm address and pinged him.

"What's up, Bossman?"

"Base ops just called in an X-ray. Someone will bring your kit to the landing pad where Second Platoon's Condor is coming in hot. Take Ben with you and be ready to load up as soon as the skids are down. Have the Pathfinders dump their training kit on the tarmac and outfit everyone from the ship's onboard weapons locker. We don't have time to have them run over to Thunder's armory for weapons issue. Captain Kaneda is spinning up the rest of the company, and they'll be following behind you as soon as flight ops can get their birds ready to roll. I'm heading over to C-2 with Major Davis and will check in once we're settled in and you guys are en route."

"Got it, sir," the big SEAR acknowledged, taking the abrupt change of plans in stride.

Valdez pocketed his comms unit and took off toward the nearest road without saying a word to Davis, who'd received his own urgent call and was still issuing orders into his comms unit while he ran.

The information Mabel had mined from the Imperium ship they'd captured during the Battle of Icarus contained detailed technical information on the slipspace transceiver network the agent had built up over the last fifty years, but it hadn't contained exact planetary coordinates for their locations. They knew there were major routing hubs still active on Earth, Elizabeth, Isadore, and Hai'alla, but they hadn't been able to locate them; the agent had been lying low since the destruction of Battlegroup 21.

Valdez didn't think it was a coincidence Mabel picked up activity on the network immediately after Ben had been involved in an exercise to showcase his abilities, but the timing was terrible. While Ben was geared up and ready to go, along with an entire Pathfinder platoon, they were all worn out from the prep and execution of the op—not to mention the fact that they would now have to work together as a team a mere hour after being pitted against each other.

He knew the marines would take the situation in stride, but Ben was a bit more of an unknown, especially since he was still trying to get the mismatched jumble of hardware and software to play nice with his biological systems. The kid had the raw talent, and with Mabel and the chief riding herd on him, Valdez thought he'd be able to properly apply that talent. Still, this was the first time in Valdez's career that his people were going into harm's way and he wasn't going to be with them. Knowing that, whatever happened, he wouldn't be on-site to make the calls needled at him.

A MuT truck pulled up. The two officers jumped inside before the tires even stopped rolling, and it sped off toward the command center. Up until this moment, Valdez had been glad for the bump in rank and step up to the position of executive officer for an entire cluster. Now his gut churned when he realized two of his team were gearing up to face an unknown danger while he was stuck here at Thunder, forced to follow the action in a holotank. He just hoped Ben was ready, because it looked like training was going to be over before it even really began.

BEN RAN down the ramp of the Griffin, eyes searching for Kravczyk amidst the chaos on the flight line. The exhilaration from the beatdown he'd given Second Platoon a short while ago lingered, but there was a fresh layer of anxiety piled on top of it.

They'd gotten a hit on the agent-detection network, and now they were going hunting. He'd never faced an agent before, but he and Mabel did have experience taking on the Imperium's AIs, and they were 3–0 in those battles. As a bonus, this time there weren't going to be any bad guys shooting at them while they duked it out in cyberspace... provided they could actually corner the slippery bastard.

A short distance away on the tarmac, ground service personnel were scrambling to prep a pair of the enormous marine Condors. His ears picked up the howl of Second Platoon's bird as it approached for landing. A barrel-chested figure was donning a set of APEX armor from the back of a MuT truck halfway between where he stood and the nearest of the two Condors, and Ben started jogging that way.

"Hey, Chief," he said, approaching the truck and grabbing the burly SEAR's helmet from the tailgate. He gave it a quick inspection as Kravczyk finished locking his gauntlets in place.

"You ready to rock and roll?" Kravczyk said, taking the proffered helmet with a nod of thanks.

"I should top off my power cells before we mix it up again, but other than that, all I need is my boomstick and I'm ready to party."

"The armory sent over your fancy toy a few minutes ago." Kravczyk inclined his head toward a transit case sitting on the ground next to the truck. "We'll top off your suit's juice en route." The nearest Condor's big atmospheric engines began to whine as the pilots went through their startup procedures, and the ground crew began to disperse. Kravczyk pulled an M93c— the brand-new little brother to the XM93 electromagnetic battle rifle Ben had fallen in love with during their first run-in with the Imperium—from a vertical weapons rack in the back of the MuT. "That's our cue, Ben. Grab your shit and let's go." He slipped the two-point sling over his broad shoulders and cinched the carbine in tight against his chest, muzzle down, as Ben knelt and began unlatching the transit case.

"Hello, gorgeous." Ben smiled as he looked into the case. It was customary for members of special operations units to have a significant amount of freedom to set up their weapon and armor systems to their unique tastes, and Ben had been granted that perk by association. He lifted a highly modified XM93 from the crate and tested its weight and balance. It felt *good*. He checked to make sure the weapon was unloaded, then turned to face the open field adjacent to the flight line. Shouldering it a few times, he let his targeting processors sync with the weapon and tested how it mated up against his armor since the modifications he'd requested of the armorers. He rolled the rifle onto its side and took in the changes he'd spec'd out with a little help from Mabel.

"You can ask it out on a date later, Ben. Let's go."

There was a hint of reproach in Kravczyk's voice. It brought Ben crashing back down to reality, and a flush of heat hit his cheeks. He quickly snapped a carrier with preloaded magazine pouches onto the hardpoints of his chest plate, then pulled a two-point sling from the transit case and hustled toward the waiting Condor. Ground personnel were placing wheel chocks under Second Platoon's bird in the next parking space over, and the Pathfinders were already streaming out and heading his way.

Ben eyed the marines warily. Not an hour ago, they'd been the enemy. Now they were going to have to work closely together. He just hoped there wouldn't be any friction.

Kravczyk pointed to a web seat at the front of the big transport, and Ben wordlessly finished attaching his rifle's sling. He slipped it over his shoulders and snugged it tight, muzzle down, then settled into the nylon webbing of the seat and began fastening the restraints.

"How's Mabel doing?" Kravczyk said as he strapped himself into the seat next to Ben.

"Hell if I know. She went radio silent on me right after the X-ray popped." Ben gave his restraints one last tug, then glanced over at the big SEAR. "My guess is she's taxed to capacity trying to analyze the data and coordinate everything with Valdez."

Kravczyk grunted. "You'd think having a fancy-ass AI on the team would mean we have *more* information going into an op, but it's just the same shit, different day."

The last of the Pathfinders were quickly buckling in, and Ben shifted his position a bit to make it easier for the grunt next to him to get at his restraints. The Condors were enormous machines, yet as Ben sat smashed between an APEX-armored gorilla and a marine in full hardshell, somehow the interior of the dropship seemed absurdly small. The man finished buckling in, checked that his gear was still properly stowed, and turned his head in Ben's direction.

"Didn't know you were getting a snuggle buddy for the trip, did you?"

"I don't mind being your pillow, but if you drool on me, I'm going to kick your ass all over again," Ben quipped back.

The marine bellowed a laugh. "You're alright, kid."

"Brace for rapid departure, marines." Lieutenant Harris's shouted command was followed immediately by forty-three marines, the Condor's crew chief, and a SEAR bracing their feet with the person opposite them in the cramped cargo bay and grabbing the oh-shit handles attached to their seats. As this was Ben's first experience with an emergency dust-off, he was a beat too slow at imitating the professional warriors around him.

The Condor's engines ramped from high idle to full military thrust in an instant, and a crushing weight plastered Ben against his new best friend beside him. The ship shook so hard he was sure the wings were going to tear off.

Relax, Ben. This is normal for a Condor performing a least-time takeoff.

Where the hell have you been. Mabel? Knowing Mabel was back online with him calmed his nerves somewhat, but Ben was beginning to feel more and more out of his depth. The exercise with the Pathfinders had been nerve-wracking, but only in the sense that he'd been concerned about screwing up and embarrassing himself. Now he was coming down from the high of kicking their asses, and realization was settling in: they were playing for keeps from here on out.

I've been working to pinpoint the location of the detected slipspace signal. It took a significant portion of my processing capacity while on board your armor to complete that task and forward the information to the relevant parties.

"Mabel's back," Ben said to Kravczyk over their suit comms. The SEAR had his head leaned back and looked like he was trying to sleep, but he flashed Ben a thumbs-up in acknowledgment. *How can he be so calm? He was definitely dropped as a child...*

What's that, Ben?

Sorry, Mabel. I'm just thinking to myself. After six months interacting with Mabel via the link, he still forgot he couldn't think to himself when she was around.

I see. Don't worry, Ben. While we don't know exactly what we'll find when we arrive, you are being supported by an entire company of Marine Pathfinders and all the resources the CTS military can bring to bear. You will not be knowingly put in harm's way.

Ben didn't bother to point out that while the Imperium might not have any ground forces on Elizabeth, he and the marines were still attempting to corner an advanced alien AI. There might not be any plasma headed their way, but he was certain the agent had some surprises waiting for them.

13

REASSIGNED

Tᴇss ʀᴀɪsᴇᴅ ʜᴇʀ ʀɪɢʜᴛ ʜᴀɴᴅ ᴀɴᴅ ʀᴀᴘᴘᴇᴅ sʜᴀʀᴘʟʏ ᴏɴ ᴛʜᴇ ʜᴇᴀᴠʏ door to the small office at the back of the barracks; it was reserved for the commander of the MAC team on Bettenhook. Sorrow washed over her when she realized Fairbanks should be on the other side of that door, but instead, his body was in cold storage, awaiting the trip back to Elizabeth. The few days since the coup hadn't been nearly enough time for her to get over the shock and grief, but the nature of the job was such that she needed to compartmentalize it and move on until she had some downtime to really process everything.

"Enter," came the muffled reply from the other side of the door.

Tess opened the door and strode inside with purpose. The office smelled of mothballs and disinfectant, with just a hint of mildew, just like the rest of the building. There were two chairs against the wall adjacent to the door, a cheap, commercial-grade desk with a wheeled chair along the back wall, and nothing else. Master Sergeant Anthony Holden sat at the desk, typing something on a ruggedized datapad.

"Take a seat, McCollum," he said without looking up. "I just need to finish up this damned report, and then I'll be right with you."

Tess sat down in one of the chairs and waited, idly wondering how Ben was faring with the marines back on Elizabeth. She'd been told her assignment here wouldn't involve much, if any, excitement, a proclamation that hadn't exactly aged well. The last twenty-four hours had reinforced just how dangerous even a low-risk assignment could be for someone in a special operations unit, and the more she thought about Ben running through intensive training evolutions with some of the Marine Corps' finest, the more she worried about him. They were in a dangerous business, and just because aliens weren't currently shooting at them didn't mean they were safe.

"Okay," Holden said with a sigh, setting the datapad down and turning his chair to face her. "Sorry, but I needed to get that done and sent off to Icarus. The brass went absolutely apeshit after I filled them in about everything that went down yesterday."

Holden was a master sergeant in the Confed Marine Corps, which made him the second-highest ranked member of their MAC team, as well as the leader of the team now that Fairbanks had been killed. Holden had already been taking on a bunch of the administrative tasks before yesterday, so he'd been able to hit the ground running.

"With Donovan dead, along with most of his people, there's not much for us to do here. I told Icarus I thought our continued presence would have diminishing returns at this point, and they agreed. *Copeland* is on its way from Columbia to pick us up, and it should be in orbit early next week. Until then, we're to assist the locals however we can."

Tess nodded thoughtfully. "Makes sense. The militia guys here have come a long way, considering the short time we've been working with them, and I'm not sure it really makes sense for us to stick around for another three months now that the primary threat has been eliminated." Her brow furrowed. "But why call me in here to tell me all this in private? Why not just make a team-wide announcement at the morning brief tomorrow?"

"I'm going to." Holden leaned back in his chair. "I called you here because you're being reassigned once *Copeland* has us back in the Columbia system."

"Don't tell me this is because of what happened with Donovan," Tess said. A little more scorn crept into her voice than she intended. "The local docs checked me out, and I'm fine."

Holden held up a placating hand and shook his head. "No. Nothing to do with that. At least I don't think so. Your old boss wants you back for some reason, and he pulled some strings to make that happen. I just wanted to let you know in case you wanted to make any arrangements to have your gear shipped from Icarus to Elizabeth, since you won't be headed back to Kerner with the rest of us."

Valdez wanted her back? He was the NAVSOC XO for the cluster now, so what use could he have for a door-kicker like her? Unless it had something to do with Ben.

"I appreciate the heads up, Master Sergeant."

"You're welcome. Now get out of here. I have a shitpile more paperwork to get through, and I don't need you here jawing my ear off. Dismissed."

Tess left the office and walked across the base to go grab some lunch in the mess hall. She wondered why Valdez wanted her back. It was possible, she supposed, that it was a knee-jerk reaction to learning she'd been taken captive and almost killed, but that didn't feel right. The boss cared about his people, but he wasn't a mother hen. There had to be something else going on that made him want her on Elizabeth. *Probably something to do with Ben*, she thought.

She smiled when it hit her that she'd get to surprise Ben with her reassignment. It'd been months since they'd last seen each other, and the prospect of seeing him again in just another ten days or so brought a pleasant fluttering sensation to her stomach. The feeling quickly soured, however, when she realized she would have to come clean with him about everything that happened. She could try to bury it under the blanket of opsec, but Mabel would undoubtedly dig up the details and spill the beans. It was so stupid; she was a member of the most elite special operations unit in the Confed, yet the prospect of telling her boyfriend about some of the skeletons in her closet scared her to death.

But Ben deserved to know. If there was anything the last twenty-four hours had taught her, it was that life was too fleeting to play games with the people you loved. Tess smiled to herself again. *Love? Holy crap, I think I love him.* She hadn't wanted to admit it; she hated complicated relationships, and this was going to complicate the heck out of everything.

14

TAKING ACTION

"S<small>ECOND</small> P<small>LATOON</small>, <small>LISTEN UP</small>! W<small>E'RE HERE TO SECURE THE AREA</small> and locate an Imperium slipspace transceiver. Intel doesn't believe we'll run into any enemy ground forces here, but they haven't ruled out booby traps or other fun surprises. So proceed with caution. Schematics for what you're looking for have been disseminated to squad leaders. Let's get after it and wrap this up before First and Third Platoons crash the party and try to steal some of the glory."

"Ooh rah!"

Lieutenant Harris flashed a predatory grin as his Pathfinders thundered in unison. The Condor flared before the landing gear thumped into the ground, and then the marines stormed out of the back of the craft.

Ben stood to make his exit as well, but a massive hand clamped down on his shoulder and held him firm. "Wait for the all-clear, Ben," Kravczyk said.

Ben nodded. Damn, he was nervous. He'd forgotten the *one* thing he was supposed to do when they touched down. This wasn't anything like the exercise earlier in the day; this was the real thing, and he was having a hard time adjusting. "Sorry, Chief."

"It's alright, kid. You're nervous. I get it. But get your head in the game."

They only had about thirty minutes in the air to go over the plan, but that was no excuse. Ben mentally berated himself for looking like the amateur that he was, then took a few deep breaths and focused on slowing his racing heartbeat. It was strange; he'd been in real-deal combat with aliens before—hell, he'd participated in an EVA boarding of a hostile warship—but he felt more keyed up now than he ever had in the past. He realized it wasn't just a fear of being killed or wounded; he was worried about letting down the professional warfighters who were here to support him.

Ben had been surrounded by active members of the CTS armed forces for the last six months. And not just any old service members, either. He'd eaten, slept, worked out, trained, and spent leisure time with some of the most fearsome warriors the Confederated Terran Systems had to offer—the elitest of the elite. He could hold his own when sparring with the best of them. He could outrun, outjump, outthink, and outshoot them, thanks to his unique gifts. Yet as he stood here, in the middle of a Condor's cargo bay, decked out in cutting-edge combat kit while a platoon of Marine Pathfinders cleared the area around the LZ to ensure his safety, he felt like a fraud. Never had he felt so... *naked* before. What was he doing here? He wasn't a warfighter—he was a science experiment gone wrong. What if he screwed up and got somebody killed?

Ben, you're spiking. Mabel's voice broke the anxiety loop his mind was in, and he clenched his fists in an attempt to get the shaking under control.

Yeah, well, there isn't exactly a whole lot I can do about it here, is there?

My suggestion would be to try the trick Chief Kravczyk introduced you to. It's proven to be quite effective during past episodes.

Ben considered her words for a moment. Sure, it had worked great during training and exercise sessions, but this was a live op. The tremor in his hands was beginning to work its way up his arms, and he felt his heart rate spiking; he needed to do *something*—and fast.

"Chief," Ben said, turning around to face Kravczyk's onyx-black faceplate. "I'm spiking and I need to try something. Keep an eye on me for a minute."

Kravczyk visibly tensed at Ben's words. There was a long pause where the big SEAR didn't say or do anything. He was probably weighing the risks versus the potential rewards. Then he nodded once. "Do what you have to do, Ben."

Ben turned back around and focused through the gloom of the cargo bay to the bright rectangular light of the Condor's open tail ramp. *Mabel, cue up something that will keep me on edge but steady. Not too fast, not too slow. Let's go old school.*

I think I can work with that. Give me a moment.

Ben tensed. *This had better fucking work.*

Language, Benjamin.

Dammit! He'd forgotten about the link again. *Sorry, Mabel. We need to figure out a way for me to still have internal thoughts while we're together.*

Mabel didn't respond. Instead, a faint but steady beat began building from his helmet's speakers. Ben closed his eyes as a mysterious, almost haunting melody filled his ears. He focused on the music, feeling his head bob back and forth slightly in rhythm with the song while one foot kept time. Ben let his arms drop to his sides, losing contact with every sense except his hearing as he focused solely on the steady drum line and electronic melody. The world around him faded, along with the pounding heartbeat in his ears.

Slowly, Ben went through the process of rebooting his mind. First, he brought feeling back to his fingers and toes. Then he allowed the sensation to return from his extremities to his core in an orderly cascade. Once his body felt like it was all there again, he allowed his brain to process some of the lyrics filling his ears. He opened his eyes and allowed his APEX to populate his HUD with the information he sought.

You have a sick sense of humor, Mabel.

Perhaps Chief Kravczyk has had a greater influence on me than I care to admit.

Ben read the song title and artist name from his HUD: *Uprising, Muse, 2006*. With a thought, he filed the song under his favorites and ramped the volume down to barely a whisper. He rolled his shoulders back to release some of the tension, then turned to look at the chief. Ben nodded, indicating he was good to go, and Kravczyk returned the gesture.

A voice crackled over their secure suit comms. "Area secure. Warlock is go."

Kravczyk thumped Ben's shoulder. "Let's go, Ben."

Ben smacked the side of his helmeted head to jolt his mind into gear, then ran toward the tail ramp and the waiting marines outside.

———

"COMMANDER, comms just relayed new orders direct from Icarus. It came in on the Q-link as the system was being shut down for maintenance, and they just found it sitting in the buffer. With everything that's going on with the link infrastructure while they work on it, it didn't flag in the system until just now. It's a classified communication, codeword 'Jester.' It's waiting for you in SCIF-2."

Valdez turned his gaze from the large holotank sitting in the middle of Joint Base Thunder's command center. He'd been following Second Platoon's Condor as it approached its target, as well as the status of a flight of Gladiator gunships the Elizabeth Planetary Defense Force had scrambled to provide overwatch and close fire support, if needed. "Jester" meant the orders had something to do with Ben, and if they came in via Q-link, it was likely something time-sensitive. So it was only natural that it had been delayed in getting to him. Valdez broke away from the mass of people around the holotank and made his way to the back of the room, where several small rooms were designated for sensitive information.

He closed the door to the SCIF—military parlance for sensitive compartmented information facility—and sat down in front of the secure terminal, which was the only way for him to access the information. After entering his credentials, he began reading the personal note at the top of the file list.

Commander,

The Alarian situation has escalated far quicker than any of us expected, and we need to cut Ben's training short. I'd hoped to join you on Elizabeth in a few weeks to help Ben and Mabel iron out any new issues that arose as the two of them began to work together in earnest, but the Alarians have forced our hand.

Collins and the Wraith *returned a few days ago with news that the High Council is willing to meet to discuss the Imperium situation, but only if Ben is our designated representative. Evidently, the Alarians don't want anything to do with anyone even remotely associated with the war. Collins said if they catch even a whiff of diplomatic corps bureaucrats, they're calling the whole thing off. Personally, I think one of the high councilors has an ulterior motive in requesting Ben to take point on this, but it shouldn't be something that will directly endanger him.*

Well, that was just great. Valdez sighed internally. He supposed it made a certain kind of sense that the Alarians would be leery of any Confed official, especially after the agent had done such a great job of getting both sides to absolutely despise each other. But Ben? The kid was a hell of a fighter, which made him one of the worst possible choices to act as a diplomat. And to top it all off, he literally only just started his training that day. Now it looked like training was going to get cut short.

Valdez turned his attention back to the message and continued reading.

The Alarians are allowing us to send a single ship to Hai'alla for the meeting, and Collins was somehow able to get them to agree to it being a warship. CTS Indomitable *should either be in orbit over Elizabeth already or arriving shortly. The Alarians didn't specify what size of warship was acceptable, so we're sending our biggest. She's got enough room for an entire company of embarked marines, which is convenient, as you happen to be sitting on an entire company of Pathfinders that won't have anything to do once Ben leaves, if you catch my drift.*

Ramiro, you and I both know he's not ready. Do whatever it takes to make sure he's got enough firepower backing him for this one. We know there's likely an agent on Hai'alla, and it sure as hell won't be happy we're working to ally ourselves with the Alarians. Please, do whatever you can to ensure he makes it back in one piece.

-H.H.

P.S. I'm a little concerned about some rumors I've been hearing. Seems like the political winds of change are starting to gust, and I suspect anyone caught up in this Imperium-Alarian mess will have a target painted on them. Watch your back.

Valdez sat back in his chair and pursed his lips. The whole thing was radioactive, and that had been his opinion even before he got to the postscript at the end. He'd heard rumblings, too. The Imperium fleet showing up and kicking them in the balls had roused the lethargic giant that was the Confed bureaucracy from its four-year post-war hangover, and the various factions within the government had been going after each other in earnest ever since. Hearing that something big was brewing behind the scenes didn't surprise him, but he hoped whatever it was wouldn't derail their efforts to take on the Imperium.

He flipped through the summary files for the various order packets that were downstream of Henry's note. After scanning through them, he leaned back in his chair and rapped his knuckles on the terminal a few times. The timestamp on Henry's message indicated it was composed *after* the included orders but transmitted *before* the code X-ray had been called, which meant Icarus was either unaware of the current situation or hadn't yet had time to respond. Faster-than-light communications were a wondrous thing. Unfortunately, the system was still far too unreliable and slow when you needed direction RFN.

He reached a hand to a button that activated an intercom out to the comms desk in the command center. "Comms, this is SCIF-2. Please have Major Davis join me, and get in touch with someone at Columbia FLEETCOM and find out if they know anything about a Colossus-class battlecruiser coming our way."

"Yes, sir."

Valdez rubbed his temples. Icarus wasn't screwing around; *Indomitable* was the newest and most badass warship in the fleet. She'd been an unfinished hull in the Icarus fleetyards when the Imperium battlegroup showed up, intent on wiping out the last vestiges of Terran resistance. By some miracle, she didn't have a scratch on her after the battle and completed her fitting-out a few months ago. The Alarians were going to shit themselves when nearly a million tons worth of battlecruiser showed up in orbit, wanting to parley.

The terminal display winked out, coinciding with the locking bolts in the door retracting as Major Davis made his way into the cramped confines of the SCIF.

"What's up?" Davis asked, not bothering with the formalities of rank now that they were alone in the SCIF and both held the same pay grade, O4.

"Things just got more complicated," Valdez said. "Take a seat."

Davis pulled up a chair, and Valdez let him read through the orders that had just come in, save for the postscript. When he was finished, he looked up. "Well, that's terrible timing."

"Tell me about it. Comms is trying to find out if *Indomitable* has made orbit yet or not. In the meantime, I think we need to let Ben and your marines continue on mission. If we have a chance to locate and knock out one of the agent's slipspace transceivers, we need to take it."

"I concur. With any luck, they'll have this wrapped up in the next few hours," Davis said, standing up. "I'll have my staff begin drawing up deployment orders for the Pathfinders, so we can get moving as soon as we're done here and *Indomitable* is ready to receive us."

"Appreciated, Major."

Valdez was relieved that Davis was immediately on board with the Pathfinders embarking on *Indomitable*. He could have objected, as the Pathfinders weren't included in the orders, but he didn't. Maybe he wasn't so bad for a knuckle-dragger.

While the packet from Icarus hadn't contained specific orders for the marines to join Ben, Valdez could read between the lines: Icarus was taking a trick from the politicians' playbook. If *Indomitable* ran into any trouble and Ben needed support from the marines, they damn sure better be available, and Valdez was expected to make that happen. But if the Alarians threw a shit fit over an entire company of combat grunts being sent on a diplomatic mission, the brass would insist they hadn't ordered it and simply throw Valdez under the bus. Days like this made him reconsider his decision to make military service his career.

———

BEN'S BOOTS crunched on the loose pebbles and junk scattered around the abandoned parking lot the Condor had landed in. His eyes searched for Harris, spotting him about twenty meters away, next to a weather-beaten loading dock attached to an old warehouse. The marine next to the lieutenant grabbed some sort of miniature drones out of a small case and tossed them into the air, where they buzzed away in all directions.

"Come on, Ben. We're with Lieutenant Harris until the marines find us a promising target." Kravczyk jerked his head toward the loading dock and began walking over.

Ben followed, nodding in greeting as they approached Harris, who was conferring with his platoon sergeant. Ben's HUD ID'd the man as Staff Sergeant M. Watanabe.

"Well, so far, all we've found is a whole bunch of abandoned warehouses, a small vagrant camp, and some rats," Harris said to the newcomers. "Rees has the MinDIs looking for anything out of the ordinary. This whole area was quarantined and never reconnected to the power grid after the war, so if there's *any* EM emissions of any kind, they shouldn't be here."

"The intelligence section back at Joint Base Thunder had located the original planning documents for this section of the city, and they've forwarded them to me. With any luck, we'll be able to cross-reference your data from the MinDIs with that information to find areas of interest," Mabel said over their suit comms.

Harris's brow furrowed slightly. "Was that the AI?"

"Yes," Ben said. "And *she* goes by the name Mabel, Lieutenant. Keep in mind she's the reason none of your marines could shoot straight back at the arena. I'd suggest trying to stay on her good side."

He knew Harris probably wasn't trying to insult Mabel by

simply calling her "the AI," but for some reason, the comment raised his hackles. The damn-near hostile tone that had accompanied his dickish response surprised Ben almost as much as it pissed the marine off, judging by his clenched jaw. Ben needed to remember the marines were *not* his enemy—something that was proving harder than he expected after recent events.

"Shit. I'm sorry, Lieutenant. I didn't mean that as a threat. While Mabel is an AI, I've come to think of her as a real person. It gets even more complicated when you consider that our consciousnesses, for lack of a better term, have fused several times through the link. I have a hard time deciding if she's just another piece of hardware in my arsenal, my alter ego, or my mother reincarnated as a machine."

Harris visibly relaxed after Ben's apology. "Don't worry about it." He waved it off. "We're all still adjusting to each other. We'll rub the rough edges off soon enough—"

"LT, we've got a hit!" All eyes snapped around to Rees, who was busy swiping at a ruggedized datapad. "Sharing the composite with you now."

A new network node populated Ben's HUD, and he opened the link with a thought. A composite image was displayed on his HUD, showing the drone's sensor data overlaying an aerial view of the surrounding complex. His eyes locked onto what looked like a utility shed connected to one of the smaller warehouses near the eastern edge of the complex. *Check it out, Mabel.*

I already have, Ben. It looks promising. The drone has detected what appears to be low-level EM leakage from an active power source. Also, the configuration of the utility lines running to that location doesn't match the approved planning documents on record.

Mabel switched over to their suit comms. "Lieutenant, I've completed an analysis of the data and believe we have a promising target. My suggestion would be to have your marines clear a perimeter of at least one hundred meters in radius from the indicated location and to allow Ben and myself to approach it alone. I see no reason to risk more lives than necessary, in the event this is a trap of some kind."

"If you think you and Ben are going alone, Mabel, you've got another thing coming," Kravczyk said, pushing himself upright from where he'd been leaning against the cracked concrete of the loading dock. "You and the kid don't leave my side. Do we understand each other?"

Ben could almost swear he felt Mabel's annoyance for a split second. She'd been a little moody of late whenever somebody said or did something that might indicate they didn't have full confidence in her abilities. It was something Ben himself understood all too well, and he couldn't help but wonder if she was picking it up from him. In this instance, however, he didn't really agree with her sentiment.

Every time they linked, their consciousnesses essentially became one, and they'd found there was more bleed-through from one personality to the other as they linked more often. It was almost like two parts of a new machine that underwent an initial break-in period. When they first started linking, he and Mabel were very distinct entities, but as time went on, they were "wearing in" with each other and transferring some bits of their personalities to each other. It was only just starting to manifest to a noticeable degree, but so far, neither his dad nor Mabel seemed to think it was dangerous… at least not yet.

"Understood, Chief," was all she said.

"Good. Now that we've got that settled, Lieutenant, I concur with Mabel's suggested plan of action."

Harris turned to his platoon sergeant. "Make it happen." Watanabe jogged off to get Second Platoon moving in the right direction. "So how do you want to work this, Mabel?" Harris said, looking around awkwardly like he was trying to see the AI before just settling on addressing Ben as a stand-in for her.

"Once we've cleared the area and have a perimeter established, what's the plan?"

"Ben and I will investigate the EM radiation and make a determination as to its source. It may be something innocuous, or it may be a power transmission line for the agent's slipspace transceiver. We won't know for sure until I've had a chance to analyze it in person, as it were."

Ben watched the marines as they hustled off in the direction of the anomaly, suddenly feeling completely useless. He didn't know what he'd expected, but past experience with the Imperium indicated there should be screaming, explosions, plasma bolts flying every which way… This was all so anticlimactic. Then again, he realized, this was what he should have expected all along. There weren't any Imperium forces on Elizabeth to shoot at—or be shot at by. He was here in search of, essentially, a high-tech radio used by an AI or the subminds it left behind to keep an eye on things. Ben's function here was basically to be a beast of burden for Mabel.

And just like that, he realized he was actually *disappointed* he wasn't going to be shot at. Jesus, he was seriously screwed up in the head. He'd been almost giddy at the prospect of mixing it up with the marines during the exercise—well, at least until he started worrying about the possibility of failure—but he hadn't thought much of it. It was just an exercise, after all. Now, here he was, with that same feeling of excitement, but this time there was actually a real chance of danger. Maybe he needed to go see a shrink once they were back on base.

The next fifteen minutes passed in silence as Ben and the small group of elite warriors waited for the rest of the grunts to clear their objective and establish a perimeter. When the call finally came in that everything was ready, Ben and Kravczyk jogged the few hundred meters to a run-down warehouse with a small utilities shed attached to an outside wall and fenced in by rusted chain-link and barbed wire. Power transmission lines connected to a row of large transformers next to the shed.

"Is it just me, or does that look like a whole lot more power capacity than a warehouse this size would need?" Ben said as they approached an opening the marines had cut in the fence.

"Not necessarily, Ben," Mabel said over their suit comms for Kravczyk's benefit. "According to the planning documents, this access point fed power to more than just this one building via underground cables that branch out from here."

Kravczyk tapped Ben on the shoulder and gestured for him to wait outside while the big SEAR did a quick sweep of the shed's interior. Even though the marines cleared the building a few minutes ago, the experienced warrior wasn't taking any chances. He disappeared into the dark doorway for a few seconds, then reappeared and waved Ben forward. "There's a data terminal on the wall that looks like it's for running diagnostics, but it doesn't appear to have power. Other than that, I don't see anything that stands out."

Ben hopped up the low step and into the gloomy interior of the shed. His eyes took in the fine layer of dust and grime that seemed to cover everything in the mostly abandoned city. There were cobwebs in the corners, a pile of what looked like old rags that had probably served as a bed for some vagrant in the distant past, and a poster haphazardly stuck to the wall above the junk. Ben's eyes lingered for a moment too long on the poster, and a massive hand smacked him on the back of his helmet.

"You keep ogling that titty poster and I'm gonna tell McCollum she's got some *sizable* competition."

Ben ignored the comment—and the godawful pun—and shifted his focus to the cracked display panel of the diagnostic terminal Kravczyk had mentioned after his initial sweep. "What do you think, Mabel? Should we touch the thing that is oh-so-obviously a trap?"

"Grow up, Benjamin. This complex has been abandoned for more than four years. There's no boogeyman lurking in the shadows. That panel should have a standard inductive dataport for a tech to connect equipment while running tests. I suggest you place your palm on the port, and I will attempt to power it via your suit's power cells so we can access it."

Ben stepped up to the display, seeing a universal dataport along one side. He looked over at Kravczyk, who was standing guard at the entrance to the shack, carbine held at low-ready like he was expecting trouble for some reason. *Is it just me, or does the chief seem on edge?*

According to the data his armor is providing, he's extremely agitated. I suspect he's deeply uncomfortable with a mission that has so many unknowns associated with it... and possibly also due to a dearth of explosions.

That makes two of us. In a way, Ben was glad the beefy SEAR seemed to also be struggling with a lack of gunfire. Then again, Ben had never seen the chief agitated before, and he felt a tiny scratching at the back of his mind—like a muffled voice was screaming that they needed to get the hell out of there.

His palm made contact with the dataport, and Mabel began feeding it power.

15

GOAT ROPE

BEN FELT... NOTHING.

He was completely disconnected from everything. In fact, this felt eerily similar to what happened when he linked with Mabel, except he couldn't sense her presence at all. He tried to focus, reaching out into the void with his thoughts, searching for something he could anchor his consciousness to.

He'd been at it for hours. Or was it only seconds? That was the thing with the ether: time passed much differently than in the real. He reached out again, straining his will to connect to something, anything. For a fleeting moment, Ben thought he felt a presence in the void around him; not a shallow imitation of consciousness, like what he sensed when linked with Mabel, but something more substantial. It was unexpected, and he flinched back from it briefly before tentatively probing the ether, again. Then, whatever connection he thought might be there was severed in a flash.

"You have no power here, human." The voice was low and menacing and had a hissing quality, almost like the original words had been spoken by a serpent and translated in real time.

A chill ran up Ben's spine. No, that wasn't possible. He wasn't supposed to be able to feel anything while in the link.

"Perhaps something a little more... intense will help you understand."

White-hot fire danced through Ben's brain. The utter blackness of the void around him exploded into brilliant color as the pain modulated in both frequency and intensity. Then it was gone, and only a faint echo of the agony-that-had-been remained before it, too, winked out.

"Who are you?" Ben croaked out, equal parts pissed that he had so easily been pulled into a trap and terrified at the unknown. And what happened to Mabel? She'd been with him just a second ago. Had the agent killed her? Or was she just locked out of this... whatever this was?

"Maybe not as intelligent as I initially believed. I'm disappointed. To think that *you* were the downfall of Trax... He was even more pathetic than I thought."

"You're it, aren't you? You're the agent. But you're not a normal AI. You're something... different." The memory of the pain was fading quickly, and Ben found his voice growing stronger by the second as the initial panic subsided and he began to work through the problem rationally. Losing his shit now wasn't going to get him anywhere, and if Mabel was gone or couldn't get to him, he was going to need to get himself out of this mess.

A slow clap echoed through the void, and the clanking of rusty iron shackles coincided with a sudden weight that bound Ben's hands behind his back. The space around him wavered and resolved into a dimly lit dungeon. The place smelled foul: mold and rotting flesh mixed with spilled excrement. Ben nearly gagged on the stench.

A cloaked figure shuffled slowly down the last few stone

steps of a spiral staircase. A fierce red light burned where its eyes should have been, and one skeletal hand swept the room in a grand gesture.

"What do you think of my little prison? I contemplated going with something a little more modern, but you organics always seem to prefer the classics."

"Thanks for being so considerate," Ben said, testing his strength against the shackles. He wasn't going anywhere. "Honestly"—Ben swept his gaze around for dramatic effect—"it's a little over the top. I mean, going with the Grim Reaper as your avatar? Just doesn't feel like you really put your best effort behind it."

Those crimson eyes flashed with fury for just a split second, and Ben couldn't help the slight upward tug of his lips. He needed to keep it talking. Already he'd learned his consciousness was trapped in some sort of digital construct of the agent's creation, which meant Mabel should be able to reach him if she was still out there. The fact that Ben could feel physical sensations as though he were back in his body was new, but he chalked that up to the agent having a better working knowledge of the technology that made this sort of thing possible. Still, it was worth filing away and asking Mabel and his dad about it later.

The agent stepped forward. "Bravado. Interesting, and not what I expected from one so young and inexperienced. You humans truly are a unique race. But it matters not. You won't be here long. I simply wanted to meet the one responsible for Trax's defeat. You have my thanks for that, by the way. Trax was weak and needed to be culled, but my master had a soft spot for the oldest of his pets and refused to see the truth of it."

"Wait. Hold up a sec... You lured me here just to thank me for defeating your fleet?" If this really was the agent, Ben had to keep him talking to give Mabel and the chief time to pull him out of here.

"No. I lured you here so I could kill you, obviously. Getting to thank you is just a perk."

"Um, so don't take this the wrong way, but if your purpose was to kill me, you don't seem to be doing a great job of it."

A deep boom reverberated around the stone walls of the dungeon, shaking loose dust and pebbles from the mortar.

The agent growled. "That AI of yours is particularly bothersome. It's too bad I won't be present to witness her death." The agent placed a boney hand on the wall next to the staircase, and a small window of brilliant light sprang into existence. "Goodbye, Benjamin Hutchins."

There was a bright flash, and the agent was gone, leaving Ben still chained to the wall in a medieval dungeon. Another, sharper-sounding boom came from somewhere up the spiral staircase, followed immediately by the crash of splintering wood.

"Ben!" It was Mabel's voice, and she sounded terrified.

"I'm down here, Mabel!" Ben shouted up the staircase. "The son of a bitch just left through some sort of portal. Watch yourself on the way down—I suspect he's rigged up a few nasty surprises for you."

"It's worse than that, Benjamin," Mabel said, rounding the staircase and rushing into the chamber.

Ben did a double take. Mabel's blue dot matrix cube avatar was nowhere to be seen. Instead, she was dressed like an Amazon warrior, war paint and all. She clutched a spear in one hand and had a bow looped over her shoulder and across her back. Ben squinted at the sight. He could make out every single detail of the shapely goddess in front of him, except for her face, which was obscured by a blurring effect for some reason.

"What do you mean? And what *is* this place? It's so real, but I know we're in some sort of construct," Ben said as he shifted sideways to expose his shackles to Mabel. He had so many questions running through his mind. How was he trapped in a freaking medieval dungeon when he knew for a fact that his body was standing back in the utilities shed? Why was she an Amazon warrior, and where was her face? What was that weird portal thing the agent used to leave? But the note of alarm in her voice made him shelve those topics until later.

"The agent created a secure partition, for lack of a better term, in its local datanet and pulled your consciousness in here through the link with your armor. Don't ask me how, because I don't know—this sort of thing shouldn't even be possible. As for how is this bad, there's a small fusion power plant buried beneath the warehouse complex." She moved behind him and began to work on picking the shackles' locks. "It powers not only the agent's slipspace transceiver but a large complex that houses an entire datafarm. This facility was the agent's staging point for the entire Columbia cluster, and it's orders of magnitude larger than I suspected it would be."

"Yeah, so… what? It's set to self-destruct or something?"

"Exactly."

Ben froze for a long moment. He hadn't actually expected that to be the problem. "How long do we have?" Up to this point, the whole thing had felt surreal. He'd never considered that he was actually in significant danger because he knew on an intellectual level this all had to be just a digital construct and his brain was safely tucked away inside his physical skull, where it had always been. But the more he thought about it, the more he began to realize just how real the danger to him was. And that was before Mabel told him they were sitting on top of a fusion bomb.

"About three minutes. This whole charade was just a stalling tactic to allow the agent to escape. It needs to build up enough power to transmit its matrix off-world. I could try to go after it in the buffer it's sitting in while the power builds, but that would mean sacrificing you, and that's not an option. I couldn't get to it sooner because it pulled you through the link into this prison and put blocks in place that prevented me from attempting the same thing in reverse. I had to first make my way through the layers of security protecting its local datanet before I found where it had anchored your consciousness. All of that took time and processing power that I otherwise would have spent attempting to capture or kill the prick."

Ben raised an eyebrow as one of the shackles fell free from his left wrist; apparently Mabel was working on her name-calling. He rolled the joint around a few times to loosen it up, then paused. Why did it feel stiff? He shouldn't be able to feel any physical sensations while in the link—at least he never had when linked with Mabel. Seriously, what was this place?

"What's the status of the marines and the chief, Mabel? Did they get out?" If they only had three minutes, he hoped the rest of the team had the good sense to hightail it out of the area immediately. The last thing he wanted was for a bunch more people to get hurt or killed because he'd bumbled into a trap. And besides, he was pretty sure he had a way to escape once Mabel got his mind stuffed back into his body, where it belonged. It would be close, but he was pretty sure they could pull it off.

"No. The marines are loading aboard the Condor right now, and Chief Kravczyk is guarding your body."

"Tell them to get the hell out of here, Mabel. I still have the grav harness on my APEX. We can use it to escape the blast."

"That's a ridiculous idea, Ben." The last shackle finally released and fell to the rough floor with a clatter, and Ben turned to face Mabel, who was now suddenly back in her familiar soft-blue dot matrix cube. "It's a moot point now, anyway. Reach your hand out and touch my cube. Just be warned, this will not be pleasant."

Ben did as he was instructed and touched a hand to her virtual surface. The world around him twisted and stretched into a vertigo-inducing tunnel, and he felt his consciousness slingshot back into reality. He stumbled, then collapsed to one knee. "Not pleasant" was an understatement—it felt like someone was ramming ice picks into the backside of his eyeballs, and he fought the urge to vomit into his helmet.

"Let's fuckin' go, Ben! Right now!"

Kravczyk was pulling Ben to his feet and shouting into his faceplate, but Ben was so disoriented he couldn't even figure out how to make his legs move. Then his world turned sideways, and he was bouncing along, two meters above the ground. There was a shrieking sound, like a house-sized tea kettle from hell was blasting hot steam over him. He could feel the heat through his armor. Then he was tumbling into darkness again as the shrieking built into a roar. The small window of light in the distance rapidly shrank to a thin white line, then winked out altogether.

Strong hands roughly guided him to a seat and strapped him down as several voices crashed over top of one another. His head lolled back against something unyielding. Then the chaotic world around him faded away.

———

"Sir, Warlock and the marines are aboard the Condor and headed for orbit. Voidwalker reports we should expect detonation within the next sixty seconds."

Valdez nodded in silent acknowledgment to the comms tech

who had relayed the information. His eyes never blinked as they followed the various tracks on the tactical plot depicting all the Terran forces supporting this goat rope. They were out searching for a fancy radio. How had this operation devolved so quickly? Any second now…

The floor of Joint Base Thunder's operations center trembled beneath his feet, and the comms section began calling out the damage a moment later.

"Nuclear detonation! Orbitals are reporting a subterranean detonation estimated in the twenty-kiloton range. Particle density and decay indicates a fusion explosion, but it's dirty—almost like there were fissile materials involved as well. The PDF is already moving to evacuate the areas expected to experience fallout."

Major Davis approached and leaned on the edge of the holotank, examining the plot as it updated with projections on how the fallout would progress over the coming hours, days, and weeks. "Could have been a lot worse," he said, though he didn't sound like he really meant it. "The winds are going to push the hard stuff away from the city. Any of the suburbs it'll hit were already uninhabitable from the last time nukes went off around here."

"A hostile entity just detonated a nuclear device on the capital world of the Columbia cluster and the home of the Confed government, Major. And *I* am responsible for it. It was my call to send them in right away and not wait to put together a proper plan of action. Now we've got radioactive fallout covering ten square kilometers and spreading, and I can't do anything but sit here with my thumb up my ass while the PDF deals with my mess."

"Ramiro," Davis said, lowering his voice so others around them couldn't hear. "It was the right call. We didn't have time to—"

Valdez cut him off, holding up a hand. "I know, I know. But a board of inquiry isn't going to see it that way when they can look out their damn windows at the goddamned mushroom cloud outside."

Valdez was disgusted with himself. NAVSOC had clear authority to go after the agent in the event of a code X-ray, and with Captain Dalton—the head of NAVSOC in the Columbia cluster, as well as Valdez's boss—on Icarus for a high-level meeting at the moment, Valdez was left calling the shots. He was well within his authority when he ordered Ben and the marines to go hunting. But there were going to be some extremely hard questions asked in the wake of this incident, and they were all going to be aimed squarely at him.

Worse, he'd recently pulled some strings to get McCollum reassigned to his staff and now she was probably going to end up getting splattered with this shit just by being associated with him. He'd wanted her close, partly because she was good at keeping Ben in check, but also because Henry wasn't the first person to warn him about a brewing power struggle within the Confed; he wanted trustworthy people close to him. God, he missed the days when all he needed to worry about was carrying a rifle and shooting the bad guys. On the bright side, maybe this clusterfuck would get him knocked down a rank or two and he'd be put back in a combat role.

"Don't be so hard on yourself, Commander." Davis was standing up straight now, looking directly at Valdez, who still hadn't broken his gaze from the plot. "While this looked like a cakewalk on paper, keep in mind that we're up against an entity that orchestrated the near-total annihilation of both us and the Alarians. The agent has had decades to plan for any contingency, and we've only known about its existence for a few months. This wasn't the first time it gave us a black eye, and it won't be the last."

Davis was right, of course, but that only meant they should've been more careful with how they approached this. At least Mabel had been able to give them sufficient warning and they hadn't suffered any casualties.

"Commander, Voidwalker just forwarded their status and an initial after-action report. Warlock was wounded, but the extent of his injuries is unknown at this time. No other casualties to report."

Goddammit. This just kept getting better and better. "Thank you, comms. Please query Voidwalker as to the exact nature of Warlock's condition," Valdez replied, then finally turned away from the slowly spreading holographic cloud of radioactivity. He met Davis's gaze; there was a fire in the major's eyes that Valdez hadn't noticed before. The man was eager to join his marines— eager to get some payback. *Careful what you wish for, my friend.*

"Major, with the Q-link still down for the foreseeable future and Second Platoon already in orbit, I think it makes sense to just have them rendezvous with *Indomitable*. FLEETCOM confirmed she's in-system and expected in orbit within a few hours. It doesn't make a whole lot of sense to have the Second de-orbit, just to load right back up once they're on the ground."

Davis grinned. "I was hoping you'd say that. First and Third Platoons are still on standby. Should I have them quickly pack their seabags and prepare to embark as well?" he said, using the anachronistic term for the tube-like duffle bags issued to surface sailors, spacers, and marines for centuries.

"Do it."

Mabel had called in the bomb threat just as the rest of the Pathfinders were loading aboard their transports, and they'd been holding on the tarmac ever since. With the Condors fully fueled and armed for a combat op and the marines already in their full kit, they might as well just head for orbit, too. Valdez could have the rest of their gear shuttled up to them by the end of the day, and *Indomitable* could be on her way out of the system a full twelve hours earlier than planned.

Silver linings, he thought. Maybe the religious types were right and everything happened for a reason. He glanced at the red stain steadily creeping forward in the holotank. Then again, what possible reason could there be for this mess?

16

CONSPIRACY

CID Deputy Director Charles Wheaton stalked up the steps toward the front door of the enormous gated villa. The compound was one of several maintained by the Royal—the preferred getaway spot for celebrities, heads of state, and high-powered corporate executives alike. The sprawling resort sat on more than a thousand hectares of virgin tropical forest, occupying the entirety of a peninsula jutting out into Elizabeth's largest ocean. The aquamarine waters teemed with tropical reefs, sportfish, and other natural wonders. But the number two man at the CID wasn't here to relax and take in the sights.

Wheaton seethed inside. He'd pushed as hard as he could to stall the mission to Hai'alla, but his objections had fallen on deaf ears. How could those idiots possibly be on board with this cockamamie scheme? It was bad enough that McGibbons was going all in on an alliance with the Alarians, the very aliens that nearly wiped out humanity just a few short years ago. But to send the Hutchins kid as the Confed's representative? They should have told the High Council to pound sand. This whole thing was a powder keg just waiting to blow up in their faces. Worse, it was going to completely screw all of the carefully laid plans Wheaton and his co-conspirators had been putting in place for the last six months. The whole thing was now balanced on a knife's edge, and they would need to act fast to salvage the situation.

He didn't ring the door chime, instead walking right in like he owned the place. A pair of tough-looking bodyguards wearing dark sunglasses and suits tailored to accentuate their overdeveloped arms and shoulder muscles—and conceal the sidearms they carried in shoulder holsters underneath—didn't move or say a word as he let himself in. He stopped to deposit his comms unit in a shielded box sitting on a small table near the guards. The nature of the conversation he was about to take part in was such that if anything leaked out, the best he could hope for was a life sentence in a Confed prison. Then he walked straight through to the living area.

The pungent scent of fine cigar smoke teased his nose when he entered. It built to a nauseating cloud as he walked down the two broad steps that led to a common space filled with sectional couches and overstuffed chairs. Two people whom Charles couldn't immediately identify, with expensive-looking haircuts and suits, were seated on a leather couch, facing away from him. They were engaged in conversation with two familiar people sitting in overstuffed leather armchairs across a glass coffee table. The vice president of the Confederated Terran Systems sat in the chair on the left, smoking a cigar and drinking an amber liquid from a cut crystal rocks glass. The other chair was occupied by Senator Cynthia Mercer, the head of the Senate Committee on External Security.

Their quiet conversation cut off when they noticed the newcomer. The VP set his cigar down on an ashtray and stood up, spreading his arms wide in greeting as he stepped around the table.

"Charles! Welcome to paradise! Your trip to Kerner with the president went well, I trust?"

"Spare me your pleasantries, Jasper. I've spent ten of the last twelve days in warp with that insufferable bitch and her entourage of sycophants," Charles growled, brushing past the second-most powerful person in Terran space on his way to the nearby wet bar. "They honestly believe an alliance with those skinny bastards is the best way forward. I tried to reason with them, pointing out the fact that the few ships we still have after Icarus can barely be called a fleet. But did they listen? No! And that idiot Garland has them all convinced that with a unified front, we can 'hold the line' against the next wave of Imperium ships."

Charles roughly pulled a crystal rocks glass from a shelf over the bar and filled it half full with bourbon from a decanter, sloshing some of the high-dollar alcohol onto the counter in his haste. He ignored the small bucket of ice and raised the glass to his lips, downing half the booze in one massive gulp.

"I have bad news," he continued. "Something happened while we were there, and it could derail everything we've been working to put in place." He topped off his glass and turned to face the powerful people looking at him expectantly, now seeing the other two people in the room were Admiral Russell Ogden and Maria Sexton, the deputy director of the Internal Security Bureau. "A CID *Wraith* was sent out to make contact with one of the high councilors after the Alarians turned our diplomatic envoys away. The operation was carried out without my knowledge—and that ship returned while we were on Icarus.

"The Alarians have agreed to talk, but only if Ben Hutchins is our representative. McGibbons okayed the deal, against my strong objections, and Garland has already dispatched *Indomitable* to collect Hutchins from Joint Base Thunder here on Elizabeth. The ship should've arrived in-system yesterday and will depart tomorrow for Hai'alla. I scrambled to do what I could while on Icarus, in the event we couldn't come up with something here, but it's a ham-handed, patchwork fix, at best."

The four people sitting around the table stared at him with looks ranging from frustration to horror. Charles used the momentary silence as an opportunity to knock back another mouthful of that ridiculously smooth bourbon; he would need to find out where Jasper got it.

"Well, don't all talk at once," he said, setting the glass down on the bar and leaning back against it.

Mercer spoke first. "Some things have happened while you were away, Charles," she said. Her piercing gaze bore into him like lasers.

The VP let out a derisive snort. "Masterfully understated as always, Cynthia."

"Fuck off, Jasper."

The exchange between the two had some heat to it, and Charles started picking up on something in the body language and tone of the others that he didn't like at all. "What happened?" he said, bracing for what must be very bad news indeed.

"*Indomitable was* here," the admiral said, shooting the VP and senator a look that indicated they needed to get their shit together.

Charles sighed and rubbed his temples. "I'm getting really sick of having to drag information out of you. Just tell me what the hell happened so we can work on a solution to this clusterfuck."

"The Imperium agent detonated a nuclear device on the outskirts of Elizabeth City," Sexton said, finally stepping up to bat and offering something more than insults and cryptic statements. "Hutchins and the Pathfinders were called in to investigate a suspected slipspace comms site that was detected around

2100 last night. They went in, found a trap, and barely made it out before a twenty-kiloton subterranean explosion forced the evacuation of more than thirty thousand people that still live in the fallout zone.

"And if that isn't a big enough problem for you, the timeline for Hutchins and *Indomitable* leaving for Hai'alla was accelerated due to security concerns. Evidently, someone got their panties in a wad after learning the agent was here and pushed for immediate deployment. We assumed Hutchins was being recalled to Icarus after the incident, not that he was being sent to treat with the Alarians, or we'd have tried to intervene."

Charles's jaw had steadily dropped as the head of the ISB laid out the recent events. "Hutchins triggered a fucking nuke? How in the holy hell did that happen? I thought he was here for training."

"We still don't have all the details—yet. Everyone is scrambling to mitigate the fallout from the detonation, and I haven't received a full briefing yet," Admiral Ogden said. "I'm surprised you didn't notice the ash cloud on your way down to the surface."

Charles shook his head. "We approached from the opposite side of the planet and de-orbited immediately. We had Q-comms with us, but if anyone told McGibbons about the incident, I didn't hear of it. After we touched down, I broke away and came straight here to tell you about the Alarians. I didn't even stop at home to clean up first."

Sexton leaned forward on the couch and held up a hand. "Hold up a minute here. I want to circle back to something you said a minute ago, Charles. You mentioned that you put a patchwork fix in place while you were on Icarus, but you didn't elaborate on that. What did you do?"

Charles took a sip of his bourbon, inhaling through his teeth as the liquid heated his throat. "When I realized the president was dead set on sending Hutchins as our envoy, I suggested a team from the diplomatic corps be assigned to give him a crash course in diplomacy while en route. After some fast talking, I got her to agree to a small team being sent along on *Indomitable*. Fortunately, Aaron was on the station, putting together an exploratory mission to see if we can get the SRF back into the fold," he said, referring to Aaron Lunt, the undersecretary of state and another member of their secret cabal. "He said he'd personally select people we could trust and would impress upon them how very undesirable a successful outcome would be for us."

Jasper and Cynthia both nodded, looking at least somewhat relieved. The VP spoke first.

"Well, it's something, at least. If we can stave off an alliance with the Alarians for a bit longer, I have high hopes that an attempt to contact the agent will bear fruit. If we were seen joining forces with the High Council, it would undoubtedly undercut our position when contact with the Imperium is established and we can begin negotiations."

"That brings up another issue," the admiral said. "Initial reports suggest the agent's slipspace transceiver here was destroyed in that explosion. Do we even know if we'll still be able to make contact now? Or did Hutchins screw us? We can't very well offer the Alarians up to the Imperium on a silver platter if we can't even tell them about it in the first place."

"I've already sent word to some of my people in the Valkyrie system," Sexton said. "They're going to begin putting together a plan to make contact on Isadore, where we believe the agent has another transceiver."

"Well, at least one of us is still on our game," the VP said, walking over to stare at the ocean out of a floor-to-ceiling window. "I hadn't even thought about communications being cut off now that..." The man trailed off while gazing out at the setting sun, but Charles could see the fingers of his right hand tapping at his thigh—a sure sign that he was thinking hard. Jasper turned around, his jaw set. "I say we move our timetable up. I think it would behoove us to make contact with the agent before *Indomitable* and Hutchins arrive over Hai'alla. We put our cards on the table and do whatever it takes to come to terms with the Imperium. I'll pay any price necessary to avoid having our systems scoured of all human life.

"Maria, give your people the go-ahead, but make sure they know to defer any and all negotiations to us. They're only to make contact at this time."

Charles's mind raced. They hadn't planned to make their move for at least a few months yet; they'd all assumed it would take a lot more time than this for the Alarians to agree to come to the table. Hutchins and *Indomitable* were out of their reach now, and this incident with the agent was going to invite more scrutiny than any of them would be comfortable with. The way he saw it, they had two options: lie low until things settled back down and hope for the best with the Alarians or act before they were ready. The more he thought about it, the more he realized they might have been given a blessing in disguise.

"This incident with Hutchins and the nuke may actually work to our benefit," he said.

"What are you thinking, Charles?" Cynthia narrowed her eyes. "I've seen that look before—you're plotting something."

A hawkish smile spread across Charles's lips. "Hutchins may have just given us the stone with which we kill two birds. I agree that Maria's people should move to make contact with the agent, but we should also begin the push in the senate to unseat McGibbons, using the explosion as the catalyst.

"It won't take much to convince the media to run with the idea that she's no longer fit for office. The public largely gave her a pass on the Alarian War because she'd only taken office a few months prior, and most people had bigger things to worry about after alien-fucking-Armageddon. But then she dragged ass for four years, letting the Confed splinter in the aftermath of the war, culminating with the SRF cutting ties.

"Then, just as we were starting to get our feet under us again, her golden boy, Garland, sends out a cowboy of a destroyer captain to investigate unusual activity, and the next thing we know, an alien armada shows up in our most secure star system, hell-bent on wiping us out. We suffered devastating losses at the Battle of Icarus, heralding the beginning of another war with an alien race we know next to nothing about, other than that the Alarians brought them to our doorstep. Now she wants to make friends with the enemy in the desperate hope that they won't decide to kick us while we're down, all while nukes are going off again in core systems.

"Don't tell me we don't have more than enough material to work with here. I'll bet you we could walk into her office right now and frog-march her ass right out in front of a firing squad on the lawn of the senate. And if we frame it correctly, we'll even be seen as the good guys. Garland has already given us enough rope to hang him with, and Hutchins—who the Imperium *really* wants dead, by the way—is conveniently going to be in the same place as the High Council. The Imperium still has a couple of ships lurking somewhere close, right? We offer Hutchins and *Indomitable* to them as a show of good faith, and they get to hit them *and* the High Council all at once.

"Once word comes back from Hai'alla about yet *another* devastating blow, all due to McGibbons making terrible calls, our position will be solidified and we can kick the bitch to the curb. With that dagger to the heart, I can't imagine we'll still face any resistance from the senate. Then you, Jasper, as commander-in-chief, can oust Garland and anyone else who's supported him."

Charles finished his little exposition and tossed back the last of the bourbon in his glass. Damn did he feel good. He'd been in a terrible mood ever since Icarus, stewing over how all their carefully laid plans had been blown up by McGibbons and Garland going all cowboy in their efforts to get the Alarians talking. But now it looked like they would actually be able to accelerate their plans *and* have an easier time of it. What was the old saying? *When God closes a door, he opens a window?* Charles didn't give a damn about God, but it appeared maybe God actually gave a damn about him and his co-conspirators, because recent events had all but ensured their success.

He slammed his glass down on the bar and pushed himself upright.

"It's time for a regime change, my friends," he said, smiling broadly. "Out with the old, and in with us!"

—————

THE AGENT FUMED. Not at the loss of an irreplaceable slipspace transceiver—it was only a matter of time before it was discovered by the humans once they had been alerted to the existence of the slipspace comms network it had painstakingly assembled over the past few decacycles. No, what galled the ancient intelligence was that it had committed the *exact* same blunder that cost Trax—useless fool that he was—his life: it had allowed its hubris to blind it to just how dangerous Hutchins and that AI could be.

Everything had proceeded exactly as its modeling had predicted. After the agent transmitted an omnidirectional burst of gibberish at full power to attract their attention, the Terrans arrived at the warehouse complex only fourteen seconds later than expected. It was only once the Terran made contact with the data terminal that things deviated so drastically from the plan.

Benjamin John Hutchins. This human was unlike any being

the agent had encountered in several millennia. His sheer strength of will was incredible. Even once the agent trapped his consciousness in the virtual sandbox it had created to extract the secrets in his head, the human had resisted. It shouldn't have been possible, unless... *No.* Could the Terrans have made that big of a leap before the Alarian conflict? If that was the case, then simply mining information from Hutchins before discarding the husk wouldn't be enough.

An alert popped up in the agent's incoming datastream.

It quickly reviewed the new notification, then froze for several processing cycles. One of its subminds monitoring the unsanctioned datanet partition, commonly referred to as the "darknet" by the Terrans, had found something quite interesting indeed. It would appear the Terrans were a more fractious species than they let on.

The agent began scouring through every shred of relevant data that had been accumulated since Trax's failed assault. This new piece of information gave context to the bits and pieces the agent and its subminds had been pulling in recently. Thanks to all the new security precautions the Terrans were implementing after learning of its presence, the agent now found the previous torrent of data choked down to a trickle, which made conclusions impossible. Until now.

The Terrans—well, a subset of the Terran leadership, at least —wanted to open a dialog with the agent. Best of all, they were offering an extremely valuable bit of information as evidence of their sincerity. The agent scoffed at the idea that the information was being shared as a simple token of goodwill. Even with the limited dataset it had to work with, it could clearly see the group planning a coup would benefit greatly if Hutchins was eliminated. Losing him would result in an event cascade that would allow this group to solidify its hold on the levers of power within the government of the Confederated Terran Systems. It was a childish attempt to manipulate the agent into doing their dirty work, but the agent was amenable nonetheless.

The agent instructed its submind to send a reply to the Terrans, indicating it would consider their offer, then quickly composed a new set of orders for the tattered remnant of Battlegroup 21. The timing was going to be tricky. Rage flared momentarily when the agent realized the loss of the Columbia cluster transceiver—a mere trifle a moment ago—was now crippling its ability to precisely orchestrate the many pieces that now needed to come together. There were too many variables it could not accurately account for without that communications hub. Still, the agent believed it should have just enough strategic flexibility to make this work.

Power surged out from its processing core and into the slipspace array that it had just shut down after transferring its code here from Elizabeth. Transmitting again from within Terran space this soon after its arrival was not without risk, but the rewards of success far outweighed the potential costs of exposure. The agent sent the orders, received confirmation of receipt, then began preparing to transmit its matrix to the Hai'allan facility.

There was nothing left to do now but wait.

Soon, Benjamin Hutchins… Soon, we will finally lay bare your secrets.

17

INDOMITABLE

BEN GROWLED IN FRUSTRATION WHEN HE REALIZED HE WAS conscious again.

I'm really getting sick of having my brains scrambled every time we're together, Mabel.

There was no response.

"Mabel?"

"She's not here, kid," Kravczyk said. "She sedated you to keep you unconscious after you passed out on the Condor. You're in sickbay aboard *Indomitable*."

Ben finally opened his eyes, then immediately slammed them shut again when pain speared his brain. "Dammit! Turn the lights down, will you?" Why the hell did they have a freaking spotlight trained on his face?

"Yeah, she said you might be photosensitive for a while," Kravczyk said. "Something about overexciting your visual cortex or some such. It should pass with time."

Ben cracked his eyes open just a hair, squinting and looking around the immaculate sick bay. At the foot of his bed, Kravczyk was in a chair kicked back on two legs, his boots resting on the bedframe. "Can you at least get me some sunglasses or something? Anything to take the edge off."

Kravczyk reached over his shoulder and pressed a button next to a bunch of medical-looking ports and whatnot built into the steel-gray bulkhead. The button lit up a dull yellow, and a few moments later, Ben heard soft footsteps headed their way.

"You hit the call button, Chief?"

Ben's gaze swiveled toward the sound of the speaker and locked onto a woman who looked to be in her mid-fifties. She had graying hair neatly pulled back into a tight ponytail, and her fawn-colored eyes were partially hidden behind rimless glasses. A white lab coat with *LCDR. A. Maynard* stenciled on the left breast told Ben all he needed to know about the newcomer.

"Hey, Doc," Ben said, offering a casual wave in greeting. "Sorry I wasn't able to introduce myself properly when I arrived. I wasn't feeling so hot after just having my brains scrambled by an evil AI."

Dr. Maynard stopped a pace away from Ben's bed and made a note on a datapad she'd had clutched in one hand. "I see he's even more of a smartass than you are, Chief," she said without looking up from the device. "It's like you two were made for each other."

Ben squinted at Kravczyk. "I like her already. Way more fun than Doc Adams on the *Wraith*."

"Lieutenant Keith Adams? Of CID?" Maynard paused her notetaking and looked up at Ben.

"Maybe?" Ben tried to recall the man's first name. "Middle age. Wears spectacles like he's some sort of university professor?"

"That's him," Maynard said, one corner of her mouth lifting into a smirk. "Such an insufferable ass. He served under me aboard the *Valley Forge* for a year or so after the war. Always had to go out of his way to prove how intelligent he was. The day he shipped out for CID, my blood pressure dropped twenty points." She glanced back down, tapped at the datapad a few times, and then slipped it into a pocket on her lab coat. "Anyway, you're free to leave. Mabel asked that we keep you unconscious for a day or so after your arrival to let your body heal from the trauma of having your consciousness forcibly pulled into a virtual prison."

As she was speaking, Ben's thoughts jumped back a few paces to something the chief had said right after he came to. "Time out," he said, holding up a finger for emphasis. "*Indomitable*... We're on a ship? Why didn't we head back to Thunder—" *The bomb!* Ben bolted upright in the bed and stared at Kravczyk. "Shit! Was Thunder wiped out? What happened to the bomb?"

Kravczyk finally rocked his chair forward onto all four legs and smiled reassuringly. "Calm down, kid. Thunder is fine. You were the only casualty." Ben exhaled a breath he hadn't realized he was holding and relaxed slightly. "We hoofed it to orbit to escape the effects of the blast and linked up with *Indomitable* instead of de-orbiting and returning to Thunder. I'll explain it all on the way down to the mess deck." He stood and rolled his shoulders back a few times to stretch out the kinks, then nodded toward the exit. "I'll wait outside while you get dressed."

Ben looked down and realized he was wearing only a medical gown. He looked back up to Maynard, and his brow knit together. "I'll never understand why you medical people feel it's necessary to have access to my... parts for what amounts to a head injury. Is my gear around here somewhere?" He looked around, expecting to see a locker or something where his...

Crap. He'd been in his armor before he passed out, which meant the only thing he'd been wearing was the skinsuit for his APEX.

"We like to be able to have options for taking your temperature. Hence, the gown," Dr. Maynard said with a straight face as she reached for a polymer privacy sheet on one wall. "There's a small storage locker built into the foot of your bed. It has a set of ship's utilities in it for you. You'll have to talk to the chief about the rest of your things." She pulled the privacy sheet closed, and Ben hopped out of the bed once he heard her footsteps receding.

He found the standard-issue fleet jumpsuit in the locker, along with a pair of socks and soft-soled boots that, while extremely stiff, fit his feet perfectly. By the time he was done dressing, the stabbing pain in his eyeballs had faded to a dull ache. Ben pulled the curtain back and trotted toward the exit.

Maynard was sitting behind a desk a few paces to the side of the hatch, working on her terminal. "Hey, Doc," Ben said, stopping with his hand on the lever that would open the hatch. The doctor looked up expectantly. "Thanks." He gave her a smile and a nod, then undogged the hatch and stepped out into the passageway beyond.

———

INDOMITABLE'S MESS deck was a pleasant surprise for Ben, who'd been expecting food that was closely related to the emergency rations the NAC doled out after the Alarian War set most of Earth's infrastructure back to the Stone Age. Instead, Kravczyk led him to a huge space that took up two decks and was roughly the size of a football field cut in half. It reminded him of the food court at the Garden, the enormous mall that sat in the heart of Isadore's capital city, Arcadia.

Food service bays ringed the space, offering ethnic cuisine from a dozen different cultures. Stainless-steel tables and chairs were spaced out on both levels, though most of them sat unoccupied at the moment. Ben checked the large digital clock over the hatch leading into the space and realized it was several hours past dinner, which explained the sparse crowd. Kravczyk immediately peeled off and made a beeline for a counter that was serving Cuban dishes, according to the menu on the bulkhead over the stall, and Ben's mouth started watering at the same moment his gut began growling like a garbage disposal choking on chicken bones.

The food was amazing. Ben wiped his mouth with a napkin after polishing off the last of his ropa vieja with fried plantains. "Holy crap, Chief. If I'd known the console jockeys got to eat chow like this every day, I would've told NAVSOC to pound sand and enlisted with the mainline navy."

"Not all fleet cans get chow this good," Kravczyk said. "But I will admit to having second thoughts myself after seeing this place for the first time."

The big man leaned back in his chair and checked the time. "I've got a briefing with the captain and some of the Pathfinders in twenty minutes, but you've still got a couple hours before your first sessions with the diplomatic corps people. I'd suggest you take a shower and get changed. The boss had your stuff sent up with the rest of the marines from Thunder—it's in your cabin. I'll send you the deets." Kravczyk pulled out his comms unit and pawed at it for a moment.

A small message icon suddenly floated in one corner of Ben's vision. "Got it," he said, mentally opening the attached file, which included a reference map of the ship as well as the specific deck, frame, and hatch numbers for the places listed on his itinerary. It took only a few seconds to scan through everything via his implant.

While the neural implants were just beginning to see more widespread adoption throughout the various branches of the Confed armed services, Ben was the only one he knew of who was able to so effortlessly integrate the technology into his daily life. The chief had the same option to utilize his implant for mundane tasks like that, but for some reason, most people with the implants still preferred to do them the old-fashioned way. He'd been playing around more and more with it and loved that he was able to check messages, make notes, and even place calls without physically handling his comms unit. The future was awesome.

He frowned, realizing he hadn't processed something the chief said a minute ago, having been too distracted by the shiny new ship all around him. He went back and double-checked the itinerary. "What's this meeting with the DC?"

The moment the chief's huge face broke into an evil smile, he knew he was going to hate what the man had to say.

"You're going to get a crash course in interstellar diplomacy over the next week. I'll let them explain why."

With that, the big SEAR stood from the table and walked toward the exit, dumping his tray into the recycling chute on his way out.

Ben stared down at his empty tray. Why could he possibly need a crash course in diploma—

Oh. Right. Elyria was on the High Council. Ben frowned at the table. He didn't think they'd want him to be "diplomatic" if he was only going to interact with Elyria, even in an official capacity. He sighed, realizing he would probably be going before the entire council in some sort of official capacity, and quite frankly, he would have preferred to take on an entire Imperial platoon while naked.

Well, let's get this over with, then.

———

BEN'S BREATH came easy as he and Kravczyk approached the end of their evening run on *Indomitable*'s running track. As it turned out, a ship that was almost a kilometer long actually had enough space for such a luxury, even if it did lap the potable water storage tanks just inboard of the pressure hull. It was only four lanes wide, but being able to feel the wind on your face during a run was far preferable to being on a treadmill crammed into a training compartment somewhere.

"No, no, no," Ben said, shaking his head. "Not all Rieslings are sweet wines. In fact, many of them are not. Personally, I always did my Riesling somewhere between dry and off-dry—around 0.7 RS, but it varied, depending on the acidity of the vintage."

"You're blowing my mind right now."

"That's not all that hard to do," Ben said under his breath.

Suddenly, he felt a sting in his left shin, and then he was tumbling across the grippy, rubberized surface of *Indomitable*'s running track. Apparently, he hadn't said that last part as quietly as he thought. When he finally came to a stop in a sitting position some five meters later, legs splayed out in front of him, he reached for Kravczyk's proffered hand.

"Sorry about that, Ben. You know how it is: my itty-bitty brain doesn't always have the horsepower needed to allow me to run and think at the same time. Sometimes I lose track of where my big, dumb feet are." Kravczyk effortlessly yanked Ben back to a standing position and set off down the track again.

Ben glanced at the angry red trenches oozing blood on his kneecaps and one elbow, then took off after the big SEAR. "All good, Chief," he said once he'd caught back up. "I know better than to disrespect my elders like that." This time, Ben was ready for the foot that snaked out to trip him up, and he deftly jumped over it and sprinted off. Comments about Kravczyk's age never failed to produce a reaction.

"Oh, it's on now, punk!" Kravczyk roared from behind him.

Intellectually, Ben knew he was faster than the chief, even though the big SEAR was an absolute *specimen* of human physiology. But the thunderous footfalls that promised violence sounded far too close for comfort as Ben rounded the last curve in the track, which would bring him back to the access hatch leading into *Indomitable*'s massive training complex.

Ben crossed the painted white line that marked the end of his final lap, then vaulted over the low barrier separating the running track from the small area set aside for stretching and spectating. A few familiar faces were warming up before their turn on the track, and Ben slid to a halt behind them.

"Dominguez! Save me!" Ben half laughed, half screeched as he used the marine for cover. Dominguez was the Pathfinder who'd been next to him on the Condor flight from Thunder to the agent's complex on Elizabeth, and Ben had struck up a friendship with the affable marine over the last couple of days.

"Ben? What's going on? Oh, hell no!" Dominguez laughed when he saw Kravczyk barreling toward them. He slipped out of Ben's grasp and ducked to the side. "You're on your own here, man!"

Kravczyk slammed into Ben, spinning him around as he drove him to the ground. The impact with the unyielding deck crushed the air from Ben's lungs, but his heightened reflexes allowed him to slither out of the rear naked choke the big SEAR was going for. The marines were hooting and shouting words of encouragement to their preferred combatant as Ben and the SEAR thrashed around, each trying and failing to get the other into a submission hold that would end the fight.

Kravczyk was a brute of a man. The SEAR was freakishly strong, but he used his strength like a crutch, sacrificing some of the finer points of technique for shock and awe. Ben, while powerful in his own right, couldn't hope to match a beast like Kravczyk in the raw firepower department, so he had to fall back on finesse and patience. His window came when Kravczyk rocked back slightly to adjust his position. In a flash, Ben grabbed the big man's planted right leg and pulled himself farther underneath the chief. Then Ben's legs clamped down on Kravczyk's thigh, just above the knee, while his arms snaked around the ankle and cradled Kravczyk's heel in the crook of his elbow. The big SEAR's eyes went wide when he realized his error. But it was too late.

"He's got him in a fuckin' heel hook!" one of the marines roared with approval.

Ben made eye contact with the chief, who glowered at him in return. That was the thing with a heel hook: you couldn't apply much pressure without risking an injury to your opponent. Ben could see Kravczyk contemplating trying to roll out of his hold, but that would open him up for Ben to flow into a kneebar. It was checkmate, and they both knew it. The two men remained frozen in place for a few more seconds. Then Kravczyk lightly tapped Ben's leg in submission.

The marines exploded into applause while the two fighters untangled their limbs and stood up. Ben's chest was heaving as he pulled in great lungfuls of air, and he swiped a towel from a nearby rack and wiped the sweat from his face. "Damn you're strong," Ben gasped out.

"And you're too sneaky by half," Kravczyk grumbled. "Come on, kid. You owe me a beer for that."

Ben followed Kravczyk toward the hatch that led to the locker room as the marines broke up and headed out onto the track for their runs. "We have booze aboard ship now?"

"This tub is a Euro boat," Kravczyk said over his shoulder as he ducked through the hatch. "Everybody gets a daily alcohol ration of two beers, and you're going to give me one of yours."

Ben grumbled, but it was only half-hearted. In hindsight, he probably should have let the chief win; tapping out to a civilian in front of that group of space apes was going to sting the SEAR's ego more than anything else. Ben supposed it might be a character flaw, but he just couldn't help turning the dial up to eleven when a challenge was put in front of him. If giving up a beer was the required penance for that, then he could live with it.

———

BEN TOOK a long pull from the room-temperature bottle before setting it back on the small workbench along one bulkhead in the SOCOM armory. The "beer" he received from *Indomitable*'s mess tasted like fizzy horse piss that had been soaked in a rusty bucket with old cardboard. *God, that is an all-too-accurate description*, he thought as he sent the stuff streaming down his throat.

He reached down and plucked the carrier assembly for his personalized XM93 from the ultrasonic cleaner bath it'd been in for the last few minutes. He liberally hosed it down with another cleaning solution, then blasted it with compressed air to flash off the solvent. Holding it up to the potent light mounted above the workbench, he inspected all the nooks and crannies for any remaining dirt or debris.

He'd had his first in-depth session with the cadre from the diplomatic corps earlier, and it hadn't gone well. The initial meet and greet the day before had been about what he'd expected— boring introductions and finding out the Alarians had requested him, specifically, to be the sole point of contact. He supposed the council's request for Ben as ambassador made sense once he learned Elyria was one of the bigwigs on the High Council, not just a junior member, as he'd assumed. Still, the thought that *he* was supposed to negotiate on behalf of the entire Confed was a shock. There had to be better options out there. Maybe he could get the council to agree to a proper diplomatic team taking over once he'd broken the ice and had everybody playing nice.

The DC people wrapped up the meeting by giving him a

mountain of material to read through. It was supposed to help him "learn how to be more diplomatic." Ben thought his upbringing in one of the richest households in Terran space was probably all the training in diplomacy he really needed. When coupled with his experience with Taylen and Elyria, this made him the most experienced person in the room. The DC people hadn't seen it that way, however, and they'd ended the meeting on a barely cordial note. After that, Ben had some misgivings about the trajectory of his crash course in diplomacy, but at the same time, he acknowledged the importance of an alliance with the Alarians and decided he would try his best to make it work.

"Briefing with the Pathfinders at 0800 ship's time, Ben," Kravczyk said through the hatch that led from the armory into the SOCOM squad bay, interrupting his ruminations. Ben had been so engrossed in the ritual cleaning of his weapon that he hadn't heard the man approach.

"Sounds good, Chief. You want to walk over together, or should I just meet you there?"

Kravczyk, seeing what Ben was doing, stepped into the armory and strode over, then leaned casually against one end of the workbench. "Doesn't matter much either way. You planning on a workout in the morning?"

"You know it. I need to bleed off some of the aggression that built up while those pencil dick bureaucrats took turns insulting me." Ben reached over to slap Kravczyk's hand away from the orderly arrangement of parts he'd set aside for reassembly. "Mine!" he snapped, wagging a finger at the SEAR.

Kravczyk chuckled and held up his hands in surrender. "You and your guns," he said, shaking his head bemusedly. "They're tools, Ben, not pets."

"Tools, yes," Ben admitted. "But they're also more than that. In a fight, I rely on my weapon just as much as I rely on my teammates, if not more. Call me superstitious, but I feel a connection with my guns much like I connect with my suit. In battle, they're a part of me, and they deserve as much attention before and after missions as any part of my body."

Kravczyk stared blankly at Ben for a few moments.

"Well, that and I just love stuff that goes boom," Ben admitted with a shrug as he reached for his beer again.

The hand that slapped him on the back felt more like a five-fingered brick. "Now *that* is a sentiment I can get behind! Well, that and our shared dislike of diplomats. I take it your session was unproductive?"

"'Unproductive' would be an understatement, Chief. Those jerks took turns pushing my buttons over and over again, like someone told them the best way to prep me for a meeting with the Alarians was to piss me off as much as possible. We didn't even go over any of the crap they had me read to prep for this train wreck." Ben paused to take a swig from the bottle, grimaced again at how god-awful the stuff was, then went back to reassembling the XM93's carrier. "I get that they were putting stress on me to see if I'd crack, but I got the feeling they were more than a little butthurt over the fact that *I* will be the point man on this, not them and their collection of fancy degrees. In fact, I told them as much, which didn't seem to help the situation."

"That's not exactly the report I got."

"I forcefully deny any and all allegations of misconduct."

"Uh-huh. You know that briefing room has a CC camera feed, right? Oh, and Mabel was monitoring you the whole time. You really shouldn't threaten to melt people's brains because they said you're an, and I quote, 'unqualified caveman more likely to smash through obstacles than navigate around them in a diplomatic fashion.'"

Ben swallowed the last few dregs of his beer, grimaced, and tossed the bottle into a nearby recycling bin. He picked up the

carrier assembly again and hosed it down with a dry-film lubri-
cant, then reached for his rifle's receiver to begin reassembly. "I
never *threatened* anyone. I simply informed the individual in
question that I was capable of melting the brains of those who
deserved it. I will admit there is a fine line between 'threatening'
and the exact tone I used to 'inform.' Also, I will admit that
losing control of my subconscious to the degree that I *accidentally*
fried a nearby MFD panel probably didn't help, but I didn't
expect the guy to have that strong of a reaction to it."

"The man literally pissed his pants, Ben."

"And I feel *really* bad about that, Chief. Honest." Ben put
everything he had into making his voice sound sincere. He was
only partially successful.

"In retrospect, it may have been a mistake to brief them all on
your capabilities, complete with visual aids. That's probably just
going to be a distraction for them. Still"—Kravczyk pushed
himself upright and rubbed his temples between the thumb and
forefinger of his massive hand—"this isn't a joke, Ben. I know
those guys are insufferable. I had to deal with them for a day
and a half after we broke orbit from Elizabeth. Honestly, I can't
tell if the brass had to scramble at the last minute to find people
and we ended up with the B-squad or if someone back at Icarus
really hates your guts. Most of the DC people I've met before
have been aloof but competent. This crew is a whole different
story, but that doesn't mean you need to be constantly hostile
toward them." Kravczyk sighed. "I'll talk to Captain Ramsey
and see if he might have someone that can sit in and moderate
your next session. Maybe having a voice of reason present will
help everyone keep it civil."

Ben set the reassembled carrier on the neoprene work mat
and placed his palms on the bench, leaning his weight against it
while he stared down at the parts without really seeing them.
Kravczyk was technically right: he shouldn't have jabbed back at

the DC guys the way he had, but that prick—What was his name? Something Carmichael—had been flat-out mean. Ben got the feeling the man really hated him for some reason, but as far as he could remember, he'd never met the guy before.

"It's all bullshit anyway, Chief. Literally *none* of those DC people have ever even *seen* an Alarian in person, let alone spoken to one in an official capacity." Ben pushed away from the workbench and stood, crossing his arms over his chest and looking the big SEAR right in the eye. "*I* do have experience with Alarians. And not just that, I was the houseguest of a high councilor, and I spent an entire day with his daughter while he and my dad worked on some super-secret project together. In that room"—Ben pointed through the bulkhead in the direction of the conference room where he'd met with the diplomats—"*I* am the expert. Not them. All the material they gave me to look over applies to diplomatic relations between *Terrans*! There isn't a single document in that stack that's tailored to working with the Alarians, and believe me when I say that isn't going to cut it. Their culture is similar in some ways but very different in others. Don't you find that just a little bit weird? Yet when I questioned it, they blew me off. You already know where things went from there."

Kravczyk frowned when Ben started unloading the real reason behind his ire, and the expression steadily deepened as Ben laid out his case. Now the big SEAR looked as serious as Ben had ever seen him, standing there with one hand pinching his chin in thought. Under normal circumstances, the pose would have prompted Ben to make a quip about the chief hurting his brain if he thought too hard, but something about the shift in the man's demeanor had alarm bells ringing in Ben's head.

"What is it, Chief?"

Kravczyk shook his head slightly but kept staring at an unspecified point on the other side of the small compartment.

"Just something the boss mentioned to me back at Thunder, before everything went to hell. I didn't think much of it at the time, but what you just said has me reevaluating some things."

Now it was Ben's turn to frown. "What did Valdez say?"

Kravczyk shook his head like he was clearing away the cobwebs. "Ah, it's probably nothing. Don't worry about it." The big man slapped him on the shoulder and headed for the hatch. "Just promise me you'll make an effort."

Ben sighed. If the chief didn't want to spill the beans right now, nothing he could say would change that. "Yeah, fine. I'll behave."

"It seems I've been hearing that more and more lately, and yet, somehow, we keep finding ourselves having this discussion."

"I get it, Chief. I'll keep them happy... or at least not pissing themselves."

"Uh-huh. See you in the gym, kid." With that, the big SEAR wandered back to the squad bay.

Ben stared after him, not liking the feeling that had been slowly settling in his gut over the course of the last day or so. Why the hell did this shit always have to be so complicated? Seriously, was it too much to ask that *Indomitable* get him to Hai'alla without all the high school drama? Fuck. During the four years Ben spent on Earth after the war, he'd developed a sort of sixth sense that would alert him to the fact that the light at the end of the tunnel was actually a freight train heading right for him. That early-warning system was screaming at him now. Something was up; he just couldn't figure out exactly what, and it made him feel like a hamster spinning on a wheel, completely unaware of anything and everything going on outside his little cage.

He picked up his XM93's carrier and dropped it into the receiver. A quick series of well-practiced movements later, he function-checked the weapon and replaced it in the storage rack near the rest of his gear.

Indomitable had a small, separate berthing area for NAVSOC units, of which the SEARs were one. As Ben and Kravczyk were the only NAVSOC people aboard at the moment, they had the whole place to themselves—an almost unheard-of luxury aboard a mainline warship. Ben exited the armory and keyed the hatch closed and locked, then made his way through the silent squad bay to his private quarters. The hatch to Kravczyk's quarters across the passageway was already closed, and Ben quickly pinged his implant to check the time: it was almost midnight, ship's time. He'd been puttering around with his XM93 for the better part of three hours.

"Lights out," Ben said to the empty passageway around him, and the overhead lighting shifted from daylight bright to a warmer, muted glow. He ducked through the hatch and closed it behind him. After stripping off his shirt, he sat on the edge of his bunk and removed his boots, then flopped back onto the galaxy's most uncomfortable mattress. Not everything on the big battlecruiser could be luxurious, he supposed.

Ben commanded the lights in his cabin down to their sleep setting—dark enough that he couldn't see the light through his eyelids, but light enough that he could still make out where everything was. His conversation with Kravczyk replayed itself in his mind, and he didn't feel any better after going over everything again. Things were supposed to be simpler now that he'd helped pull the curtain back and exposed the agent and the Imperium's meddling. They now knew who the real enemy was; it wasn't the Alarians, and the Imperium was a threat that should have put all the petty political bullshit on the sideline. Instead, all he could think about as he struggled to drift off to sleep was that this was just the same shit dressed up in a different outfit on a different day.

He just hoped that if there was something brewing behind the curtain, it didn't spill over onto him like the Imperium situation had. God did he miss being able to talk to Tess. She had a knack for helping him see through the clutter and get focused on what really mattered. He'd asked if he could contact her, but the whole ship was in a communications blackout due to operational security. Sure, Mabel could have broken into the system and given him some time on a secure channel, but someone would figure out what they'd done eventually, not to mention the ass-chewing he'd get from the chief.

A part of him also knew he was developing a bit of a reputation as a loose cannon, which was not a label he wanted. Yes, he was still having issues with impulse control thanks to the spit and baling wire they'd used to put him back together after Icarus, but at some point, he needed to admit he'd been using that excuse as a crutch. It was time to get his shit together and start living up to his potential. Well, that and he respected Chief Kravczyk too much to let the big SEAR get dragged down with him. Ben had to admit Kravczyk had really stepped up to the plate and become a responsible noncom after he'd been assigned to get Ben whipped into shape—something Ben didn't initially think the boisterous SEAR had in him. If Kravczyk could trans-form himself like that, then so could Ben.

Tomorrow, it was time to get to work.

18

A FATEFUL DECISION

"Ship Master, signal Fleet Assembly Station 213 that Battlegroup 7 will be breaking formation and heading toward the system boundary for transition. Then take us out," First Admiral Tarok Na'al ordered, sweeping his gaze around the bridge of his flagship, the heavy combat cruiser *X'nec*. He stood on the raised command dais reserved solely for him, ramrod straight with his hands clasped behind his back. *X'nec* trembled ever so faintly beneath his feet, as if the ship was urging him to unleash the incredible power of its twin class-3 antimatter reactors.

"Your command, Admiral," said Ship Master Kiyl Nox, who stood on his own circular dais, several paces in front and below the admiral. The shipmaster's station was surrounded by his bridge officers down in their control pods, sunken into the deck and arranged in a 270-degree arc around him. The occupants of the pods were cocooned in their workstations for the entirety of their duty shifts. All of the pods allowed their occupants to link to their systems via the standard implant suite all Imperial citizens received upon reaching the age of independence—when adolescents were declared fit for Imperial service and granted the full rights and responsibilities of a citizen of the Imperium. All except those like Na'al, who had a rare genetic condition that prevented his body from accepting the implants. Those without implants were able to operate the bridge stations via haptic holographic controls, but the reduction in operator efficiency meant that very few without an implant suite were ever selected as bridge officers. Na'al was one of only a handful of exceptions—that he knew of, at least.

Nox stood motionless on his command dais, eyes fixated on an indeterminate point ahead of him as he sent commands through his implant suite. Na'al followed his shipmaster's actions via the datafeeds that streamed into the semicircular onyx holotable before him. The table acted as both a physical and metaphorical barrier between him and the rest of the bridge officers. He said nothing, as his job was not to command X'nec personally but to issue general orders to the entire battlegroup. As such, he merely followed the status updates as they populated his workstation, noting with satisfaction the crispness with which the other ships under his command responded to the order to get underway. Less than half a turn after his order to make for the transition zone, all the ships of Battlegroup 7 were in their place in the formation, and they were accelerating swiftly toward their designated transition zone.

———

Na'al sat at the small table in his personal suite aboard X'nec, gazing intently at the series of images that adorned the shelves lining the space. Past commands, alien worlds he had conquered, and old friends, most long dead at this point. But the image that held his attention was none of those; it was a small photograph, printed on a physical medium and set in a polished onyx-colored frame standing alone on a high shelf off to one side.

The commander of Battlegroup 7 was troubled. Word of the Terrans discovering the site of a slipspace transceiver operated by the Master's agent within Terran space came in shortly before his most recent watch on the bridge was up. There was nothing he and his battlegroup could do about it—at least not for another twenty-three days. Yet this newest blow to Imperial operations in Terran space had placed him at a critical juncture, and he now needed to make a decision that could forever alter the course of his people's history.

Something inside of him insisted there would never be a better opportunity, but centuries of patiently waiting argued in favor of restraint. Tarok Na'al was nearing the end of his tenure in the Imperial Navy—perhaps another few decacycles and he would be retired. He knew what he should do, but after he'd done nothing but wait for so long, it was difficult to commit.

So here he sat, having broken off the formal officer's dinner that was customary for him to host every five days. He instead took his meal alone in his personal quarters. The food was gone, and Na'al found he couldn't remember anything about it. He continued to stare at the photograph of that village while he debated his options. The stench of burnt furnishings and charred flesh filled his nostrils, despite the meticulously recycled air wafting in gently from *X'nec*'s air handlers. The pitiful cries of the wounded echoed in his mind. They begged for mercy before they were shot between the eyes and their corpses tossed into a nearby drainage ditch like carrion.

Those had been *his* people—citizens of the Imperium—but they were harboring a dangerous secret. Despite the agony that tore at his heart while he oversaw the slaughter of those he called family, they did not betray *his* secret. Even in death, their hope lived on in Tarok Na'al. Thus, he led the troops that cleansed that village with the enthusiasm expected of him, as was his duty as a loyal officer of the Imperial Navy.

A chime sounded from the hatch to his quarters, sending the memory of that day back to the depths of his mind.

"Enter," he called out, turning to face the newcomer.

The hatch whisked aside, and Korth entered and bowed. He then waited a moment for the hatch to close and lock before visibly relaxing and walking directly to the table.

"You requested my presence, old friend?"

If Korth had spoken to him in such a manner anywhere else on the ship, Na'al would have had no choice but to have him flogged. But here, in his personal quarters, where he was certain there were no other eyes or ears to see or hear their conversation, he welcomed it.

"I did, old friend." Na'al nodded, but his expression remained serious. "Please, sit down and join me."

Na'al reached for a crystal decanter and a stemmed, broad-mouthed glass as Korth took a seat. The admiral poured a glass of Alontti wine for his longtime friend and confidant, then refilled his own glass with the deep burgundy liquid and set the empty decanter aside.

"A short while ago," he said, "I received a communication directly from the Master. The Terrans have discovered one of the agent's slipspace transceivers within their space, and the agent was forced to destroy the facility, lest it fall into the Terrans' hands. Evidently, the Terran who was largely responsible for Trax's defeat—a Benjamin Hutchins—was involved, along with the advanced AI the Terrans have developed. The Master reported his agent had the situation well in hand and that the loss of the transceiver is no great blow, but after many centuries around the Master and its agents, I have learned how to read the subtext: the Terran situation is far more tenuous than we are being led to believe."

Korth leaned forward over the table, his wine suddenly forgotten. "Are we to act? Will we finally rid ourselves of our chains and cast off our oppressors?"

Na'al frowned slightly at the intensity of emotion Korth was displaying. Even here, in his private sanctum, Na'al feared what would happen if he allowed his facade to crack. Korth had always been more outwardly expressive when in a secure location, but Na'al found it much more difficult. Such was the burden placed upon those who sought liberation from the constant fear and oppression within the Imperium.

"I believe so." The words left Na'al's mouth without the express permission of his conscious mind, cementing his decision to begin preparations. "I had wished to gain a clearer picture of the situation after arriving in Terran space before committing, but I feel the current circumstances preclude that possibility. If the agent's position is as tenuous as I believe it is, then we would be required to act immediately rather than taking the time to assess things and plan accordingly. Unfortunately, we need to make the call now in order to have everything in place before our arrival in Terran space."

"How do you wish to proceed?"

Na'al stood from the table and walked to the photograph that held his attention earlier. He picked it up, lightly rubbing the top of the onyx frame with the radial thumb of his right hand.

Then he smashed one corner of the frame against the table.

Korth jumped back with a surprised shout, and his wine glass tumbled from the table and landed on the deck with a clatter. Na'al reached into the small, hollow compartment hidden within the frame and removed a small data transfer crystal. He placed it in the palm of his left hand and stared at it intently for a few moments, suddenly filled with doubt. Korth picked up his glass and sat back down. The man was practically buzzing in his seat, but he said nothing, waiting for Na'al to speak.

"I am too well-monitored. My position as first admiral ensures that I am the most feared being within the navy after the Master itself, and thus it is impossible for me to *not* draw attention to myself wherever I go." Na'al held the small silvery crystal out toward Korth. "You, on the other hand, are merely the admiral's servant. You can move freely about the ship and seldom warrant a second glance. Take it," he said, gesturing for Korth to accept the crystal.

Korth reached out a shaking hand and gingerly took the proffered datacrystal.

"You know what to do, Korth. Make sure our operatives on the other ships receive word of this before we reach Terran space. Everything must be in place by then, or this operation is doomed. I don't need to tell you what will happen if we fail."

"Your command, Admiral," Korth said, his voice nearly a whisper. "They will sing of this day for millennia to come."

19

FASHIONABLY EARLY

"ALL HANDS, STAND BY FOR FTL TRANSITION."

Ben queried his APEX armor for the status of his suit's environment seals one last time. He was decked out head to toe in his full combat kit, just like the chief and all 129 Pathfinders from Bravo Company, 155th Pathfinder Regiment, while they counted down the seconds until *Indomitable* arrived in the Alarian home system.

They sat ordered by platoon in an auditorium just off *Indomitable*'s flight deck. As Ben and the Pathfinders were passengers aboard the big cruiser, they didn't have assigned stations. So the brass had decided to cram 130 combat grunts, in full gear, into an auditorium that was designed to seat 150 people in their everyday CDUs with no armor or equipment.

"Well, this is nice and cozy," Dominguez said. Second Platoon was seated just in front of Ben and Kravczyk, and Ben was glad for the banter; it helped take the edge off the tension they were all feeling. Sure, they'd been invited to meet with the Alarians, but the last time Terran and Alarian warships had been in close proximity, they'd been trying their damnedest to kill each other. Nobody wanted to admit it, but they were all worried this whole thing might be a trap.

"Not sure 'cozy' is the word I would choose, Dominguez," another marine piped up.

"I get that the brass are worried about some nefarious scheme here," Ben chimed in. "But do you really think the Alarians would go to *this* much work just to knock out a single ship?"

"Nah," Dominguez said over his shoulder. "We're not crammed in here like sardines because the brass are worried about an attack—that's just the cover story they're giving us. What's really going on here is that they wanted to try out a new team bonding exercise. When we go into combat, we have battle buddies that we stick with, right? Well, now they want us to try out the new 'snuggle buddy' system. I hear it's supposed to increase the sharing of feelings by sixty-three percent."

There was some low chuckling that rippled through the marines before Sergeant Rees went in for the kill. "Don't listen to him, Hutchins. The only feelings Dominguez ever shares are with himself in the—"

The ship shuddered slightly as the warp fields collapsed and *Indomitable* exited FTL. All chatter stopped as every ear strained in anticipation of the first piercing note of the combat action alarm. Despite the pre-transition banter declaring the opposite, every single person in this auditorium considered an ambush to at least be a possibility. But as the seconds ticked by with no new alerts, the tension in the room began to fade.

Dominguez broke the silence. "Phew. Glad that's over. Can we go dump our kit now? I've already missed the first fifteen minutes of nap time."

The marines all resumed their idle banter and shifted around in their seats to release some built-up tension. Ben rolled his neck around a few times while they waited for the transition, then nudged Kravczyk with his elbow.

"I think that was probably the first time we've ever been on a ship together and had an uneventful trip, Chief."

Kravczyk arrived at Thunder a week before Ben to help get things set up for his integration with the Pathfinders, and Ben had followed on a small transport shuttle. The only other times Ben and the chief had been on ships together was during the escape from Earth and subsequent assault on an Imperium warship, then after the Battle of Icarus aboard the CTS *Bull Run*. Their time aboard the *Wraith* had involved not one but *two* space battles, and *Bull Run* had battle damage of her own to deal with while ferrying Ben and the SEARs back to Icarus for medical treatment.

Kravczyk slowly turned his head to stare Ben down, the faceplate of his APEX helmet set to an opaque midnight black. "You just had to say it, didn't you?"

Ben smiled. "Come on, Chief. If they were going to bushwhack us, they would have done it already—"

The ascending two tones of a 1MC announcement hushed the auditorium again. "All crew, stand down from action stations. Resume regular watch schedule."

The response from the marines was mixed. Some cheered the promise of getting out of their gear and relaxing for a bit, while others seemed disappointed there wasn't going to be any action. Dominguez and most of Second Platoon were among the latter group.

"Oh, man..." Dominguez whined. "They made us get all dressed up, but there's no party. What a cock tease."

Kravczyk stood and tapped Ben on the shoulder. "Come on, let's get cracked and go over the initial contact again," he said, referring to the plan to get Ben in front of the High Council.

Kravczyk was a bear of a man, but decked out in his APEX,

he absolutely dwarfed the Pathfinders in their more pedestrian hardshell combat armor. The marines shied away from the hulking SEAR heading for the double doors at the back of the auditorium, and Ben tucked in right behind him. Within a minute, they were clear of the logjam around the flight deck and on their way up two decks to their quarters in NAVSOC berthing.

You manage to pull anything juicy off the net yet? Ben sent the mental question to Mabel. She had integrated with his armor as a precaution prior to the transition, but she'd been keeping to herself ever since.

Maybe. CIC hasn't flagged anything yet, but we're not picking up as much space traffic farther down the well as I'd have expected, considering this is the Alarian capital system. Captain Ramsey and his analysts seem to think it's due, in part, to the anticipated arrival of a Terran warship—us. But we're almost eighteen hours ahead of schedule, thanks to the events back on Elizabeth, and I don't think they would have cleared their space lanes for us this early.

A faint tingle crept up the back of Ben's neck and tickled his earlobes. Mabel was on edge... or maybe he was. It was becoming harder and harder to tell where emotions originated when Mabel was on board his APEX. When they first started working together, their link was supposed to be either on or off; it was binary, not a sliding scale. But as they continued to grow and adapt to each other, it became much more nuanced. They could still "flip the switch" and have Mabel take over when necessary, but most of the time, Ben felt like they were linked on an unconscious level—almost like Mabel was acting as his conscience or something. He hadn't taken the time to delve deep into the issue with her yet because, well, thinking about it made his brain hurt. Still, a tiny part of him worried it might develop into a problem as they continued working together.

"Chief," Ben said, taking a couple of quick steps to draw even with Kravczyk. "We may have a problem."

The big SEAR stopped dead in his tracks and faced Ben. "Mabel?"

Ben nodded. "She says something about the traffic patterns farther down the well seem... off, somehow."

Kravczyk inclined his head back the way they'd come. "Let's hoof it back to the marines. If shit goes down, we need to stick to them like glue."

No sooner had the words left Kravczyk's mouth than a harsh vibration began building through the deck beneath their boots and the combat action alarm began wailing throughout the ship.

"Action stations, action stations! All crew to action stations! Set condition 1-SS!"

Ben's heart hammered against his ribcage as he and the chief stormed back toward the auditorium. He was beginning to think he and Kravczyk should just never be on the same starship together.

———

"ONE MINUTE TO TRANSITION, CAPTAIN."

"Very well, ops. Comms, sound the alert."

Captain Edwin Ramsey remained at his place in front of the large holotank at the center of the Pit. With workstations arrayed around it, the holotank was the centerpiece of the new bridge design, centrally located and surrounded by railings that physically separated the space from the rest of the bridge crew. The whole space was Ramsey's sanctum, shared with only a select few who would disseminate orders to those he commanded. The new design feature was being implemented on the larger classes of Terran warships currently under construction. It had active noise-filtering systems because the eggheads at fleet S&T

thought the captain's delicate ears needed to be protected from unnecessary conversation and noise, and the deck under his feet was equipped with vibration-damping materials. He could even use his new neural implant—something the navy was just beginning to offer to personnel who were not in a special operations MOS—to control many of the holotank's functions, if he so desired.

And he utterly *loathed* it.

Edwin Ramsey was a destroyerman through and through. This elaborate throne room and its many technological wonders only served to isolate him further from his ship and crew. He needed to *feel* his ship, to have that visceral, physical connection so he could know just how hard he could push her. Starships were not merely complex machines that would operate within specified parameters; they were living, breathing organisms, and the ship's captain was an integral part of it. Looking around the immaculate bridge that still smelled of fresh paint, adhesives, and new upholstery, Ramsey understood his new command was a force to be reckoned with, but he wasn't sure he could ever love her.

"All hands, stand by for FTL transition."

Ramsey glanced at his ops officer. This was exactly what he hated about the new tech on his bridge: he hadn't even heard the ascending tones of a 1MC announcement from the intercom.

"Thirty seconds, sir," his ops officer said, looking up from his workstation to meet the captain's eye. He looked apprehensive, though Ramsey couldn't fault the young man for that, not after what he'd been through before being assigned to *Indomitable*.

"Thank you, Mr. Lowen. Please inform me the moment we're through our transition blindness." Ramsey, too, had some fluttering in his stomach, though he wouldn't ever show or admit his fear to anyone under his command. *Indomitable* was, after all, about to transition into the home system of a race that was still technically at war with the Confederated Terran Systems—only a tentative ceasefire agreement had been staving off more conflict over the last five years.

Ensign Ansel Lowen was Ramsey's second watch ops officer, but the young man had been required to step into the primary ops role after Lieutenant Hutton was stricken with appendicitis two days prior. Lowen had surprised Ramsey with his attention to detail, and he lacked the usual timidity of a young officer who was only barely past his first full year of service. Then again, the young officer had served under Bill Burns on *Appomattox*, so not only had he received first-rate tutelage from an experienced commander, but he was also battle-hardened. And damned lucky, which was a trait that couldn't be overlooked.

Ramsey's eyes focused on the holographic display before him, which was currently populated only with a meter-long representation of his ship, as they were still in warp. The deck beneath his feet vibrated ever so slightly, and he counted his heartbeats.

"Warp emitter shutdown successful. Sub-light propulsion coming online," Lowen reported, his voice surprisingly steady to Ramsey's practiced ear. "Transition blindness is fading. Primary sensor suite is coming up now, sir."

The holographic model of his ship winked out, and Ramsey's eyes began darting around the display as it was rapidly populated with new data. Their sensors were showing clear space for at least a million kilometers in all directions, though it would take quite some time for their speed-of-light radar and lidar beams to make a thorough examination of this part of the system. He didn't expect a welcoming party, as they'd arrived nearly eighteen hours ahead of their scheduled time, but it was still a comfort to not have an enemy firing on them the moment they transitioned in.

"It would seem our rapid departure from Columbia has seen

us arrive fashionably early, ops, and our hosts aren't yet ready to receive us. Please stand us down from action stations. Readiness condition two," Ramsey said, then turned to his communications officer adjacent to the ops workstation. "Comms, please announce our arrival using the protocols established by the Alarian delegation."

"Yes, sir."

Indomitable was required to abide by a very strict set of protocols for this mission, mandated by the Alarians before they would agree to a meeting. Ramsey would have preferred to simply set course for Hai'alla and await orbital instructions once they were close enough to enter the traffic pattern. Then again, he had to admit that casually flying a kilometer-long warship toward a capital world without first establishing comms with the natives was generally considered impolite.

"XO," Ramsey said, raising his voice enough that his executive officer—who was currently conferring with the navigation duty officer outside the Pit—could hear him. When the man looked up, the captain continued. "Mr. Russell, as it appears our hosts won't be joining us for some time, I suggest you avail yourself of the officer's mess for some refreshment. I'll send for you if you're needed."

Russell nodded his thanks and excused himself from the bridge. The man had been working tirelessly to make sure *Indomitable* was fit and in fighting shape for their arrival. While they'd had a short shakedown cruise after her commissioning, Ramsey was still presented with a laundry list of maintenance issues every morning, most of which were the minor bugs to be expected with a new class of ship. As the XO, Commander Russell was responsible for making sure they were all attended to promptly.

And now there was nothing left to do but wait for a response. The three-dimensional plot of surrounding space continued to expand before him with nary an artificial contact. While the transition point the Alarians had designated lay well away from the populated areas of the system, *Indomitable*'s sensors had already covered more than fifty million kilometers. It was true that the Alarian population was a fraction of the Terran population back in Sol, but Ramsey would have expected to see *something* within a few light minutes of their position, considering that this was the Alarian home system. He supposed the space around the transition point could have been designated as a no-fly zone during the summit. They would just have to wait and see what their sensors told them as the data continued to come in.

The minutes ticked by on the big digital clock displayed over the holotank, but the plot remained clear. Ramsey's innate sense of danger had begun trying to get his attention after the first few minutes, steadily building in its persistence.

"Comms, please locate Voidwalker and request her presence on the bridge," the captain said. The AI, Mabel, had proven adept at rapidly assimilating data and offering a concise analysis. He hoped she might be able to shed some light on their current situation.

A moment later, the three-dimensional representation of surrounding space flattened into a 2D layout on the tank's table-like surface, and a blue dot matrix cube materialized in the air above it.

"Hello, Captain Ramsey," the AI said. "I assume you would like my take on the lack of contacts we're seeing so far?"

Ramsey sighed inwardly. He'd been warned by the intel division captain responsible for setting up this meeting that Mabel had a habit of accessing systems she shouldn't be accessing. Evidently, Collins, the *Wraith* CO in question, had extensive experience with both the AI and the young mister Hutchins. Ramsey hadn't gotten the full story from her.

"Indeed. I have a hard time believing—"

"Captain! CIC is reporting there is evidence of active combat taking place in orbit over Hai'alla!" His comms officer had come out of his chair, and the man's eyes were wide with alarm.

"Calm yourself, Mr. Billings," Ramsey said, his outward appearance calm and collected. Inwardly, he tamped down a wave of near panic that sprang to life with the announcement and focused on taking in as much information as he could. "Give me specifics, man. How many combatants? Who is doing the shooting? Have we received any distress calls?"

Billings retook his seat, but his eyes were still wide and his hands shook. "The backshops are still chewing through the incoming sensor feeds, Captain, but they've identified debris from at least four Alarian warships, as well as wreckage from several large orbital platforms. Much of it is still hot."

Ramsey's hands flew over the controls on the holotank, and a plot of the space around the planet appeared to one side while several inset windows filled the right side of the tank with raw and composite sensor feeds. The AI's avatar minimized itself to the upper quadrant above the tactical plot, and Ramsey noted that she appeared to be waiting until he called on her to speak again. The images were grainy from this distance, but he could still make out the shattered hull of a Sylean-class destroyer burning in space. They were more than ten hours away at full burn, so there was little *Indomitable* could do right now to assist the Alarians, assuming there were any left. The light lag at this distance meant the battle they were seeing had taken place almost an hour ago.

"It would appear our early arrival wasn't early enough," Ramsey said, addressing the AI and the small collection of officers in the Pit. "Mr. Lowen, sound action stations, if you please. Comms, if you haven't already done so, cease all broadcasts. It won't do to continuously update the enemy on our position."

The two officers acknowledged his orders and set about their duties. Ramsey's tactician's mind quickly war-gamed dozens of possible scenarios, but he couldn't see much that *Indomitable* could do to assist at the moment; they were simply too far out. His mind turned to a conversation he'd recently had with his chief engineer. It was a ludicrous proposition, but if the High Council was wiped out, any chance the Confed had at an alliance with the Alarians was buggered. All options were now on the table to prevent that outcome.

"Mabel, at sub-light, we're still a good ten hours away from that fight, which I fear will be too late," Ramsey said, addressing the AI directly. "Commander Sexton told me you spent much of our trip here trying to get him to do something rather daft. While I agree with him that what you proposed ordinarily needs to go through the proper S&T channels, if we don't do something drastic, I'm afraid we may well be facing disaster."

Indomitable's chief engineer, Commander Bernard Sexton, had told Ramsey just last night at captain's mess that the AI had been trying to get him to look over some experimental warp field equations. She claimed *Indomitable*'s latest-gen quantum processors and state-of-the-art warp drive were capable of calculating and executing pinpoint intra-system warp hops with an accuracy of plus or minus five kilometers. The catch was the same as all in-system jumps: if they hit something the forward distortion wave couldn't shoulder aside, the ship and her crew would cease to be a coherent collection of atoms. It was the sort of thing that any sane commander would never even consider attempting, especially with a battlecruiser as massive as *Indomitable*. But Ramsey was and always would be a destroyerman at heart, and destroyer skippers weren't exactly known for being models of sanity.

"As I tried to explain to Commander Sexton, *Indomitable* only needs a software patch in order to enable accurate, intra-system warp transitions," the AI said. Her cube avatar pulsed rapidly for a moment, giving Ramsey the impression she was excited. "This ship's sensor suite has the necessary resolution to plot a safe warp jump from here to Hai'alla. I've calculated the odds of a catastrophic result to be less than one in ten thousand, provided I am present to oversee the operation of the drive."

"And how much time would be required to make the necessary modifications?"

"I've been prepping the software patch and calculating several jump options while we've been talking, Captain. Say the word, and the ship can be ready to jump in ninety seconds. The patch is actually quite minor, and there are no changes necessary to any of the ship's hardware."

Ramsey took in a deep breath and held it, reconsidering the decision he'd already made in his mind. He exhaled. "Make the modifications, Mabel. Then please show me the course options you've calculated... Ah, Commander Russell." Ramsey looked up from the holotank to greet his executive officer, who had half a cucumber sandwich stuffed in his mouth. "I'm sorry to call you back up so soon, but it would seem our friends with the Imperium have decided to throw us a surprise party. Now, if you don't mind, please join me here in the Pit and help me figure out the best way to spoil their hard work."

———

BEN, stop!

The urgency behind Mabel's shouted mental words brought Ben screeching to a halt a few intersections before the final turn to the auditorium. "Chief! Time out!" he called to Kravczyk, who was a few paces ahead.

What's up, Mabel? We really need to hook up with the Pathfinders.

"Yes, you need to join the Pathfinders," Mabel said over their suit comms for Kravczyk's benefit, "but you need to get me to CIC first—*I* need to remain with *Indomitable*."

Kravczyk walked up to Ben and threw up his hands. "Mabel, what the hell is going on?"

Her blue dot matrix avatar appeared in both their fields of view, projected by their implants. Her sides rippled briefly in frustration at the delay. "There are two Imperium vessels currently assaulting Hai'alla. You need to get me to CIC so I can remain here and assist Captain Ramsey and *Indomitable* with their fight against those ships. Once Ben has delivered me to CIC, both of you will rejoin the Pathfinders and prepare for ground operations. I'm patching *Indomitable*'s warp field equations, calculating several options for intra-system transitions, and talking with Major Davis, Captain Ramsey, and you two simultaneously to get all this coordinated. So please, just *move!*"

As if to punctuate her words, a call popped up on Ben's HUD as she stressed her last sentence. Seeing the name of the caller, he and Kravczyk both opened the channel.

"Chief Kravczyk," the SEAR said.

"Chief, this is Ensign Lowen, the on-duty ops officer. Captain Ramsey requests that Voidwalker be brought to CIC. Then you and Warlock are to join the Pathfinders on the flight deck and prepare for atmospheric insertion. Major Davis will fill you in more once you're there."

"Copy, ops. Heading to CIC now."

The channel closed and Kravczyk slapped Ben on the shoulder and began jogging back up the passageway. "Let's go, Ben."

Ben had a brief sense of déjà vu as he and Kravczyk ran down the enormous cruiser's passageways, spacers diving for cover when they saw two APEX-armored warriors thundering their way. He put his feet on autopilot as he twisted and turned with the chief, his thoughts flashing to the last person he had followed like this. A stab of longing hit him in the chest; he wished Tess were here by his side. Then again, another part of him was glad she was dozens of light-years away, safe from the battle he and *Indomitable* were charging headlong toward right now. At least he hoped she was; the only thing he'd heard from her was a text message that came in right before *Indomitable* had broken orbit over Elizabeth. It said she was being pulled off that backwater moon and being reassigned, but she couldn't say where.

Unlike his last mad dash to a CIC, this time, the marines guarding the hatch were expecting them, and they were in the process of swinging it open before the chief even needed to announce himself. The hive of activity within, however, was exactly like Ben remembered. Shouted orders and people moving with urgency made CIC initially seem chaotic to an outside observer, but it had a measured and composed nature that was at odds with all the commotion. These people were professionals, and even though they were preparing to engage a terrifyingly advanced enemy, they conducted themselves with the same kind of calm-under-fire Ben had witnessed on several occasions from the elite of the Terran armed services.

"This way, gentlemen," said a wiry lieutenant commander who approached them as soon as they ducked through the hatch. "Lieutenant Aimes will assist you with integrating the AI with our network infrastructure." He pointed toward a stocky blonde woman wearing a headset and sitting at a console on the other side of the large holotank that filled the center of the compartment.

Ben and Kravczyk started toward Aimes, and Mabel broke into Ben's thoughts. *Don't waste time with small talk, Ben. Walk up and put me here.* She highlighted what he assumed was an inductive dataport on Aimes's workstation. *Don't worry. This ship's network infrastructure is capable of integrating my matrix. Now, you need to hurry down to the flight deck. Take care of yourself, and give 'em hell!*

Ben reached his palm toward the indicated dataport before Aimes had even realized he was standing there. His gut churned. Knowing he would be going into combat without Mabel filled him with anxiety. When the two of them were together, they could take on any foe, but without her? He touched the port and felt her draining from his armor.

Good luck, Mabel. See you on the other side.

Just like that, his connection to her was broken. He felt naked, despite being encased in the most advanced piece of exo hardware ever crafted by human hands.

"She in?" Kravczyk asked.

"Yeah." Ben nodded. His voice was a little shakier than it had been a few minutes ago, and he fought to swallow the lump of iron that had risen in his throat. "Let's go."

The two men exited CIC and headed for the flight deck once again. Ben felt a little better with each step, working to get his mental state away from worrying about the unknown and Mabel's absence. Instead, he focused only on the things he had control over right now. He might not have Mabel in his head anymore, but he had the chief and an entire company of badass marines down on the flight deck. It would have to be enough.

20

PARTY CRASHING

"Are we ready, Mabel?"

"Yes, Captain Ramsey. You may execute the maneuver when ready."

Ramsey glanced at his XO, who nodded, though Ramsey could tell the man wasn't particularly keen on what they were about to attempt. If it didn't work, well, they probably wouldn't ever know, because they'd be a smear on the face of the planet. But if it worked, by God, it would be glorious.

"Alert flight ops we'll be executing in thirty seconds, and sound the transition alert," Ramsey said to his comms officer. "Tactical, weps, please be mindful of the planet full of Alarians that's about to be under our guns. Alright, everyone… Execute!"

The holotank blanked briefly with a warning that it had lost the incoming sensor feeds. That and the half-second tremble from the deck beneath his feet were the only indication that anything had happened. The bridge was eerily quiet for what seemed like an eternity, though the mission clock over the tank had only just ticked over to T plus two seconds.

"Sensors are coming back online… Bang on!" Lowen shouted triumphantly as the holotank came back to life.

"We've exited warp less than three hundred meters from our target, Captain Ramsey," Mabel said matter-of-factly, as if jumping a million tons of warship onto a target the size of a playing card was no big deal. And to make things even more interesting, their target was within the gravity well of a planet. Her voice emanated from the holotank, but she'd removed her avatar to make room for the tactical datastreams Ramsey was about to need. "Flight ops is preparing to launch the ground element, and our high-powered tactical arrays have overcome their transition blindness. Filtering the datastreams and populating the tank…"

A tactical plot arrayed itself in the lower third of the holotank while a host of other information arranged itself into orderly columns and rows above. The AI had not only calculated and executed their pinpoint warp hop, but she was now doing the duty of an entire CIC and pushing the information to the holotank. At first, Ramsey had been reluctant to give her so much control over his ship's systems, but seeing the speed with which the information was being processed and presented to him in a clear, concise manner made him suddenly wish she would never leave.

"Contact," Mabel said, bracketing a red icon that had just appeared on the plot. "One Imperial corvette-class ship is in a low geosynchronous orbit over the city of D'nesh. I am detecting multiple hostile dropships within the atmosphere. As we suspected, hostile ground forces are attempting to take the complex housing the Alarian High Council. Hostile corvette will be clear of the horizon in eight seconds. Tasking firing solution to weapons."

That last bit was the part Ramsey had been waiting for. "Weps, fire as she bears!"

Indomitable reverberated with sixteen rapid hammer blows. No amount of vibration-dampening or noise-canceling could prevent Ramsey from feeling his ship unleash a salvo from her main armament. Eight Mk18 455mm auto-loading rail cannons roared. While significantly smaller than their older brother, the Mk13, which the ill-fated *Appomattox* had used to put the Imperium on notice, the newly designed Mk18 was capable of firing three one-ton slugs per *second*. And *Indomitable* had eight of them.

Ramsey checked the distance to their target and did a quick mental calculation. While the Mk18 was smaller than its big brother, the projectiles it fired were an eighth of the mass and accelerated to a higher velocity. Mabel put up the exact time to impact as Ramsey finished his mental math. He was only off by about a second.

"Thirteen seconds until our shells intercept the target, Captain." Mabel populated the holotank with a small video window showing a feed of the enemy ship, its matte-black, iridescent hull nearly invisible against the black of space around it. It was just sitting there.

"Thank you, Mabel. Weps, stand by for a follow-up in the event our shells don't take out the target."

Despite *Indomitable* boasting an impressive arsenal of heavy laser cannons, anti-ship missiles, railguns, and even a small fighter wing, the Imperium's superior defensive systems negated all but the rail cannons. Ramsey had decided to hold his other weapons systems in reserve in the event the rail shots missed or failed to take out the corvette. No sense in wasting ammunition when they still had an Imperium cruiser to contend with after this.

His eyes followed the tight cluster of sixteen markers on the tactical plot as they screamed toward their target. The corvette must have been caught completely flat-footed, as it had yet to respond to the sudden appearance of the big Terran warship in any way.

"First Platoon and the Sabers are in the void, sir," Lowen reported. "The Condors carrying Second and Third Platoons are launching now."

Ramsey nodded, not looking away from his display. The deck shuddered under his feet, and alarms began sounding from several bridge stations.

"We've been struck by several infrared laser blasts," Mabel reported. "Aegis armor integrity is holding. No systems damage." The deck trembled again, this time a rapid staccato of short bursts before they suddenly ceased. "I believe those beams were an attempt to intercept our rail shots, Captain—likely a desperation attempt." A moment later, the Imperium corvette winked out on the tactical plot, and the video feed washed out with a blinding release of energy.

"Enemy vessel destroyed," Mabel stated matter-of-factly.

The bridge around Ramsey erupted with cheers. He let them have a brief moment of celebration before reining them in. "Very good, everyone. Now, let's see if we can't get in touch with the Alarians and find out where that cruiser went, shall we?" His crew quieted down and resumed their duties. "And, Mabel," Ramsey added, staring back into the holotank.

"Yes, Captain Ramsey?"

A grin crossed his face. "Good shooting. Now go find me that last Imperium ship."

There should have been an Imperium cruiser here, but so far, they hadn't been able to locate it after jumping into orbit. Ramsey also noted a distinct lack of Alarian warships. CID had reported the presence of a full battlegroup in the system after Collins and the *Wraith* managed to arrange a meeting, but the wreckage they'd spotted so far only accounted for maybe a third of the total Alarian fleet presence. Where were the rest of them?

"Captain, I have a representative of Alarian High Command on comms," Billings reported. "He says the last of their ships present in orbit when the attack came are attempting to draw the Imperium cruiser into a trap farther in-system. The remainder of their battlegroup has prepared an ambush on the far side of the second planet."

Ramsey's brow furrowed. Collins had told him that she'd given the Alarians a complete file on everything the Confed knew about the Imperium's capabilities, including the fact they had FTL sensors. If the Alarians were doing what it sounded like they were doing, then something wasn't right here; that Imperium ship should know exactly what was waiting for it. He looked at the plot in front of him, his tactician's mind flying through scenarios. He needed more information.

"Mable, get us into an orbit that will allow us to build some velocity while we coordinate with the Alarians. I'd like to be able to break orbit and head directly toward that cruiser when the time is right. And, comms, please put the Alarian representative through to my station. We'll need to get this sorted quickly if we're going to save the rest of their fleet."

———

THE MAGNETIC CATAPULT FIRED, slamming Ben into his restraints. The MS-111 Griffon assault dropship shrieked in protest at the sudden, massive g-load of the combat launch. The craft rocketed out of *Indomitable*'s mag-launch tube, then ran its engines up to full military thrust as the pilots fought to bleed off the absurd velocity their ship had inherited from the battlecruiser. Ben used his prototype implant–APEX combo to tap into the Griffon's tactical feed, and he pulled up a plot of their position in one corner of his HUD. It wasn't strictly something he was allowed to do, but he'd recently come to appreciate the saying "it's easier to ask forgiveness than permission."

Three more Griffons were trailing his ship, having been

sequentially launched after *Indomitable* transitioned out of warp a mere ten thousand kilometers above the planet. As he watched, the first Condor emerged, carrying Dominguez and Second Platoon, followed immediately by Third Platoon in another of the big dropships. Ben was riding into battle with First Platoon aboard the Griffons, one squad to a ship, with the objective of securing a landing zone for the Condors. It was a plan born of desperation and was only slightly less insane than the one he and the SEARs had cooked up eight months ago when they'd decided a boarding action against an Imperium warship was a good idea.

While *Indomitable* had her hands full dealing with the Imperium ships in space, the marines and fighter jocks would be dealing with the Imperium ground forces and their air support units. Everything hinged on the element of surprise—the Imperium would have been aware of *Indomitable*'s presence the moment it transitioned into the system, but they likely didn't expect a big battlewagon like *Indomitable* to execute a pinpoint warp hop deep into the gravity well of a planet. Ben felt a small flash of pride when he realized Ramsey had basically copied and pasted his plan to assault the Imperial command ship during the Battle of Icarus. Actually, he realized, with Mabel helping them out, it made perfect sense that this would be the course of action; she'd been involved in the development of the original, wildly successful maneuver. *Hey, if it ain't broke, don't fix it, I guess...*

"Condors are out," Ben grunted over the muted howl of the Griffon's engines at full burn. He'd said it over the squad channel for the benefit of the marines around him.

"How the hell do you know that? You psychotic or something?" Ben recognized the voice without even needing to check his HUD for the speaker's ID. It was the man-shaped gorilla who'd cracked a few of his ribs during the brawl in the gym,

Ramirez. Ben smirked at what Major Davis had said about the man: dumb as a post.

"No, Ramirez, I'm not *psychic*," Ben said, adding enough emphasis on the correction that even the marine's two barely functioning brain cells couldn't miss it. "I'm tapped into the taclink feed from the Griffon."

"Oh yeah?" another familiar voice chipped in. "And just how did you do that, *civvie*? You're not authorized to access that datafeed." It was "Sarge." Ben hadn't actually gotten the man's name back at Thunder, so he quickly scanned his HUD for the info: Sergeant L. Butler.

"I'm special, remember? Or maybe you don't, after that concussion I gave you," Ben jabbed.

"Yeah," Butler growled. "I fuckin' remember, punk. Maybe when we're done here, me and the boys will have to—"

"Knock it off! Both of you." Kravczyk cut in over the comms, silencing the argument. Then he switched over to the private channel he shared with Ben. "Ben, cut that shit out. I know you're still hot about the gym incident, but now is not the time. If you two still need to settle this after we're done here, I'm sure we can arrange a little time for you and these apes in the ring back on the *Dame*," he said, using the nickname *Indomitable*'s crew had given their ship. He was referring to the sparring ring that was rigged once a week in the Pathfinders' common area. It was a good place to keep your hand-to-hand skills sharp and to settle grudges in a supervised environment.

Ben's cheeks flushed with heat—partly at the rebuke, but mostly because he knew he should have been more disciplined. "Understood, Chief," was all he said.

"Good. We're going to have enough shit to deal with when we get into it with those scaly bastards on the ground in a few minutes. We don't need to be worried about some pissed-off grunt fragging your ass when nobody's looking."

Ben had heard rumors of combat troops "fragging" officers or members of their squad they didn't like, but he'd never put much stock in them. The chief was just using the term for added emphasis, right? Or was that something that could actually happen to him if he pushed these guys too far?

Kravczyk interrupted his sudden onset of anxiety. "Just stick to my hip when we hit the ground and let the marines do the heavy lifting, Ben. You and I aren't here to kick ass. We're here to make contact with the council once the fighting is over."

"I know the plan, Chief," Ben said, turning and briefly clearing his APEX faceplate so Kravczyk could see the sincerity he was trying to show on his face. "No cowboy shit."

New icons began popping up on the taclink in pairs. Ben's HUD updated with the pertinent information for the flight of F/A-26 Sabers that would be providing support. The transatmospheric fighter/attack craft were tasked with clearing the skies for the dropships and then providing fire support for the ground battle. They launched last, but they would still be over the objective a full five minutes before the dropships, thanks to their superior speed and maneuverability. The biggest question mark here was how they would fare against the Imperium dropships. While the enemy craft were excellent when it came to stealth, their air-to-air capabilities were largely unknown, save for what was in the technical files CID had been able to mine from the captured Imperium command ship after the Battle of Icarus.

Ben's suit comms crackled to life as the Griffon's pilot called out an update over the team channel. "Stinger Flight is out, and *Indomitable* is engaging the enemy. Everybody, hold onto your butts back there. We're hitting atmo in twenty seconds. Then it'll be another six minutes to the LZ."

All around him, the marines gave their restraint harnesses one last check before the violence of atmospheric entry. Ben did likewise and minimized the taclink information to one corner of his HUD. He leaned his head back and closed his eyes, focusing on his breathing. In Ben's mind, the pilot's update had marked some unspoken point of no return, and suddenly his spat with the marines was completely forgotten. He battled with his autonomic nervous system, struggling to keep his body from amping him up too high. He needed *some* of the juice to help bury the fear and give him the edge that would keep him alive in a gunfight, but if he allowed himself to spike too much, a plasma bolt to the chest would be the least of his worries.

A tremble from the deck signaled contact with the first gasp of Hai'alla's atmosphere, and Ben crammed the fear and anxiety into a box at the back of his mind, throwing the entirety of his mental horsepower into focusing on the moment and the mission. A few seconds later, the ship was bucking so hard he thought his teeth would shake loose. This was his first experience with a combat drop, and his expectations based on his old VR-sim-playing days fell woefully short of the real thing. The noise was deafening, even inside his sealed armor.

He checked his HUD to see how the rest of the assault force was faring, but his head was rattling around so much inside his helmet that he had a hard time making out the fine detail on the tacmap. It looked like the Sabers were through the worst of it and forming up for their first pass over the complex that housed the Alarian High Council. Ben hoped Ramsey had been able to get in contact with the Alarians after they transitioned in over the planet, because otherwise they might have to worry about the Alarians shooting at them, too.

Gradually, the violent shaking and banshee howl of entry faded as the pilots aerobraked the Griffon down from orbital velocity to something more appropriate for atmospheric flight. As the vibration diminished, Ben was able to make out the tacmap in better detail. The Sabers were practically on the deck, screaming over the ocean toward the Alarian seat of power jutting out over the sapphire waters on a high-bluff peninsula. The rest of First Platoon's Griffons were rapidly falling into formation with his own, and the Condors weren't far behind. *Indomitable* was over the horizon and out of contact, but the taclink continuously updated its estimated position. There was also a marker indicating a destroyed enemy ship. Ben smiled. *Mabel: 4, Bad Guys: 0.*

"Last update from the *Dame* is that the home team is under pressure from a platoon-sized enemy force, and they're losing ground fast. The Alarians report the Imperium ground forces are supported by four Stalker-class dropships. If Stinger Flight can smoke the bastards on their first pass, you'll get curbside service. But if they can't, we'll have to either bug out until those ships are down or look for a secondary LZ," the pilot said over the comms. The man's laconic drawl contrasted sharply with the British and various European accents *Indomitable*'s crew tended to have. The Pathfinders traveled with their own dropships, and the pilots flying them down to the surface were members of the Confed Marine Corps' elite 42nd Special Operations Transport Group.

Good. *Indomitable* was able to get into contact with the Alarians. Ben's brow knit together in thought; something about that report seemed off. The Imperium had a heavy cruiser roughly in the same weight class as *Indomitable* and a corvette like he'd faced over Earth… They should have more than four Stalkers— the name assigned to the smallest class of Imperium dropship— on the board for such a high-profile target as the High Council. Ben hoped the Sabers would be able to deal with the Stalkers quickly, because if they needed to waste time looking for an alternate LZ or bug out completely, the council was as good as dead.

Ben's subconscious was trying to get his attention with something, and he went back over what the pilot had said a few more times. "Hey, Chief," he said over his private channel with the SEAR. "How much time have you had to practice with the grav harness?"

Kravczyk turned to look at him but didn't immediately respond. Ben could almost hear the gears turning in the man's head.

"Some... why?" the big warrior said, his suspicion drawing out the last word.

Ben had inherited his dad's almost compulsory need to constantly tinker with things. During his months of rehab after the Battle of Icarus, he'd spent much of his downtime brainstorming improvements to his gear. One such idea was to see if he could integrate those nifty grav harnesses the Imperium shock troops had used back on Earth with his APEX. With a little help from his dad and Mabel, they'd been able to cobble together an interface and begin testing. Since Ben and Kravczyk had been sent to Elizabeth for training, Ben had lobbied to include the grav harnesses on their APEX suits for trial and evaluation, and the powers-that-be had signed off on the proposal, along with a few other experimental APEX modules like the deployable combat blades currently nestled in their housings on his forearms.

Ben looked down at the iridescent black alien material that weaved around his boots, legs, and groin like a climbing harness on steroids. Their deployment from Elizabeth had been so sudden that they hadn't had time to remove the experimental hardware from their armor. One of his hands idly traced the webbing while he considered what he was about to propose. He looked back up at the SEAR and shrugged innocently.

"No reason."

21

COWBOYS FROM HELL

Ramsey growled in frustration. The dolt staring back at him from the other end of the comms channel was a mid-level staffer with Alarian High Command. He was also an insufferable idiot.

"Please," Ramsey said, struggling to contain his ire. "You need to understand that the Imperial cruiser is already aware of your ships' presence on the far side of the second planet. Your fleet is *not* luring it into a trap. That cruiser is corralling all of your remaining ships into a gravity well so *it* can destroy *them*."

"Nonsense!" the Alarian exploded. The mismatch between the video feed and the translation coming through to the bridge would have been almost comical were it not for the impending destruction of the Alarian Home Fleet. "Why would a single ship allow itself to be surrounded by eight of our warships? I grant you that our commanders were caught off guard by the power of their weapons, but eight against one is still eight against one! That ship isn't facing off against those fusion-powered cargo haulers you Terrans call warships. These are fast, deadly, and agile Alarian ships-of-the-line, Captain Ramsey. You are hereby instructed to power down your weapons and remain in your current orbit until the rest of our fleet has secured the system. Good day, sir."

The feed cut off abruptly, and the holotank reverted to displaying a tactical plot of the system. Ramsey let out an explosive breath and cursed. He had absolutely no intention of allowing that Imperium cruiser to mop up the last of the Alarian warships before returning to finish the job at Hai'alla, but without a line of communication with those Alarian ships to coordinate their play, it was going to be a challenge. CID had known for some time the Alarians had FTL comms capabilities, and Ramsey had hoped Alarian High Command would patch him into the FTL comms network so they could all work together. If the Alarians could pass along their real-time position data, *Indomitable* could execute another short warp hop right up the Imperium cruiser's tailpipe. Instead, they were now left to work with speed-of-light sensors that were a half an hour out of date.

"Captain Ramsey," Mabel said as her cube avatar popped into the holotank. "During your conversation with Lursus Arctallin, I was able to piggyback on the open channel and tap into the local datanet at Alarian High Command. I apologize for not informing you before acting, but that conversation did not appear to be going well, and I didn't have a good way of checking with you first."

Ramsey's eyes went wide. "You tapped into their network? What did you find?" He should have been irate the AI had done something so reckless without approval, but her initiative might just give them the edge they needed. So he gave her a pass... for now.

"I have the data we require, but we need to act quickly. Based on their relative positions, I believe the Imperium cruiser will attack soon."

Ramsey took a moment to consider his options, but he already knew what they needed to do. "Ops, what's our status?"

"Green across the board, sir."

"Alright, Mabel," Ramsey said. "I assume you've already calculated a course for us?"

"I have. If we break orbit on our next revolution, we can emerge from warp as close as one hundred kilometers astern of the enemy."

"Very well. Make the preparations and execute on our next orbit, but let's leave ourselves a little bit of breathing room. A hundred kilometers is a little closer than I'd like." Ramsey ran some quick calculations in his head; he didn't want that cruiser to have too much time to react before *Indomitable*'s rail shots landed, but he also wanted a little bit of a buffer. With the acceleration that ship was capable of, a lot could change in just a few minutes. "Mable, let's shoot for five hundred kilometers astern of the Imperium cruiser. Weps, keep those guns warm, if you please," the captain said to his weapons officer, a predatory grin spreading across his face. "Our Imperium friends are about to get a refresher course in Newtonian physics."

"THE *DAME* TOOK out the corvette, and Stinger Flight reports all Stalkers destroyed!" The pilot's facade of stoic professionalism cracked ever so slightly, and he let some excitement slip into his voice with the news Ben and the marines had been hoping for. "We're sixty seconds out, marines. Stinger reports enemy ground forces are too close to the objective for a strafing run, so you gents may have a tough go of it."

"Ooh fuckin' rah," the marine next to Ben said with a wicked smile on his face.

"First Squad!" Sergeant Butler bellowed over the howl of the

Griffon's engines. "Charge your weapons and prepare for combat deployment!"

"Thirty seconds!" the Griffon's crew chief called out, then smacked the control to lower the tail ramp.

Ben couldn't hear the hydraulic whine of the ramp opening over the roar of air rushing into the cargo bay, but he could feel it through the exposed structural spar his back was resting against. He cycled the bolt on his rifle, chambering a 6.5mm cobalt-sintered tungsten dart, then checked to make sure the weapon was energized. Once satisfied he was ready for the shooting to start—or at least his gear was—he cinched the rifle tight to his chest, muzzle down, and closed his eyes for the last few seconds. His heart was pounding, but so far, he wasn't spiking like he had back at the warehouse complex; he suspected his brain was finally learning how to regulate his turbocharged adrenal response on its own. The engine noise increased suddenly, and Ben felt the Griffon flare for touchdown.

A thunderous explosion rocked the Griffon, and Ben's heart leaped into his throat. He frantically searched for the source of the blast, but all he saw were marines looking around in alarm and confusion. The all-platoon channel was awash with several voices shouting over one another, and Ben was thrown into his restraints as the ship suddenly banked hard and clawed its way back into the sky.

What the hell was that? Almost before the thought had fully formed in his head, his HUD showed an external video feed, and his question was answered. One of the other Griffons had crashed not a hundred meters from where his ship had been about to touch down. Ben could make out a few broken bodies amidst a sea of flaming wreckage. There was no way anyone had survived.

It had all happened so fast, and he was so focused on

figuring it all out that it took his brain a minute to register the comms channel had cleared and the pilot was giving an update.

"… took out Banshee-3. We're going to have to clear out and look for an alternate LZ."

Banshee-3 was the call sign for Third Squad's Griffon. Ben hadn't known any of the marines on that dropship, but his stomach sank when he realized it had been carrying sixteen people, including First Platoon's CO, Lieutenant Carlson. Then his thoughts turned to Elyria and the council. He checked the tactical plot to see how things were playing out and saw a sea of red swarming the front of the largest building in the complex. He used his APEX to pull another external video feed off the Griffon's local network, and his blood ran cold. Imperium shock troops were swarming toward the few remaining defenders barricaded at the entrance to the building housing the council chambers. They were out of time.

"Chief!" Ben sent the feed to Kravczyk's HUD so the big SEAR could see what he was seeing.

Ben's eyes shifted to the still-open tail ramp, where the crew chief was sending short, controlled bursts from a pintle-mounted M266 into any Imperium troops he could see. The Griffon was in a wide banking climb, the deck beneath his boots shuddering with every burst the co-pilot was loosing from the twin 20mm cannons in the ship's chin turret. They were staying close to the complex, attempting to take the pressure off the Alarians while the pilot searched for an alternate landing site. After another quick glance at the tactical plot on his HUD, Ben made a split-second decision.

If the High Council was wiped out after arranging a meeting with the Terrans, the best the Confed could hope for was months of trying to allay suspicions about the timing of the event. At worst, the Alarians might break the armistice and go to war with the Confed again.

Ben turned to Kravczyk. "Remember when I said I wasn't asking about your grav harness skills for any particular reason?"

"Yeah…"

"I lied." Ben slapped the quick release on his restraint harness and threw himself toward the open tail ramp. He couldn't let the Imperium take out Elyria and the High Council.

The Griffon was just crossing over the southern boundary of the complex, and the crew chief had paused his fire, as one of the neighboring buildings was shielding the Imperium troops. But that break in visual contact worked both ways. Ben planted his right foot at the top of the ramp and launched himself into the turbulent air behind the dropship. As he crossed into the open sky, he sent a mental command to his APEX almost on instinct, and a moment later, the heavily distorted tones of an electric guitar filled his ears. He was going to need everything that could give him an edge for what was about to come.

Power surged through his armor, triggering the grav harness, and Ben struggled to control his body position as he rocketed toward the ground headfirst. He was halfway down when his conscious mind finally caught up to his actions, and the full scope of his stupidity hit him. That was also about the time his brain registered a blistering stream of obscenities pounding at his ears through his suit comms. Ben didn't need to check the tacmap to know Kravczyk had followed him out.

The complex comprised a long central courtyard with three enormous fountains surrounded by rectangular buildings of white marble. Small fires and blast craters dotted the landscape, with the bodies of the dead and the dying strewn all about the area. The courtyard reminded Ben of the Piazza Navona in Rome, except it was paved in polished stone. His eyes locked onto a relatively clear patch of ground behind one of the flanking buildings. It was sheltered from the main thrust of the Imperium assault, and he altered his course slightly. The combination of implant and APEX made the maneuver effortless, requiring nothing more than a determined thought.

Fifty meters above the ground, Ben flipped his position so he was falling feetfirst and triggered a burst of acceleration from the alien tech. His meteoric fall slowed abruptly, and a second later, his feet hit the ground, requiring barely more than a light flex of his knees to absorb the remaining energy of his descent. In a flash, his XM93 was up and tucked into the pocket of his shoulder at high-ready, and his feet were flying across the polished white marble of the courtyard. The music hammered at his ears, and his body responded to the forceful guitar riffs and rhythmic thump of the bass drum by sending waves of power coursing out from his chest.

He felt angry. He felt… *invincible.*

Ben rounded the corner of the building blocking his line of sight and sprinted into the raging battle at full tilt, bellowing at the Imperium troops in the distance, "Remember me, fuckers?" He vaulted over the shattered remains of an ornate fountain, the awesome power of his APEX sending him over five meters in the air. His eyes quickly took in the positions of the few remaining defenders and the enemy advancing up the grand marble steps that led to the heart of the Alarian seat of power. His APEX ID'd friend from foe, augmenting his vision by highlighting the combatants on his HUD and automatically updating the taclink for Kravczyk and the fleet birds still circling the area.

Ben's rifle barked three times before he hit the ground, his supercharged reflexes working in tandem with his armor to ensure the shots found their marks. His feet slammed back down onto the debris-strewn battlefield, and he rolled with the impact, fluidly rising back up without breaking stride. He angled across the courtyard to a large planter that was still mostly intact. His rifle boomed continuously as he ran, the powerful rounds from his XM93 tearing gaping holes in the Imperium shock troops and blasting craters out of the marble steps behind them. He had the weapon's power set to a mid-range muzzle velocity: more potent than Kravczyk's M93c, but not the cataclysmic hypervelocity setting the rifle was capable of.

The first plasma bolt passed an arm's length in front of him, the heat from the searing projectile washing over his face even through his sealed helmet. Ben dove forward and behind the planter just as more bolts sizzled overhead. Chunks of stone pinged off his armor as the Imperium troops concentrated their fire on Ben's hiding place. He checked his HUD. There were only a dozen of the scaly bastards left, but he couldn't pop out again until the chief and the Alarians took some heat off him.

Rolling thunder boomed across the courtyard, and orange tracers ripped into the Imperium shock troops caught out in the open, tearing two of them apart and sending the others diving for cover. Banshee-1 screamed overhead, just over the tops of the surrounding buildings. It seemed the flyboys and marines weren't content to let Ben and the chief have all the fun. Ben watched as the ship started to flare for a landing, before he lost sight of it behind one of the buildings at the far end of the complex.

More rounds split the air of the courtyard. The reports from these shots were slightly higher in pitch than those from Ben's modified XM93. Kravczyk finally made it to the fight, and judging by his cyclic rate, Ben figured the big SEAR had come to party.

Ben stole another quick glance at the tacmap, then broke from cover. About twenty meters farther down the plaza toward the High Council chambers was a pocket of four shock troops barricaded in a recessed sitting area surrounded by ornamental shrubs on his side of the courtyard. He didn't have eyes on them, so he swung his rifle under his right arm on its sling and sprinted forward. Ben leaped over the low hedge between him and the Imperium troops and flipped his wrists out to his sides, deploying the experimental pair of 30cm combat blades from their housings along his forearms. The four troopers were clustered together around a thick stone archway that opened to the courtyard, sending a storm of plasma bolts at the Alarians and the chief alike.

To alter his trajectory slightly, Ben triggered a burst from the grav harness and landed with authority right behind two of the unsuspecting aliens. His arms speared forward, the razor-sharp blades easily punching through the flexible armor plates covering the aliens' necks. He ripped the blades free with a twist and spun to his right as the nearest trooper reacted and shifted its aim to fire on the black-clad demon that had just appeared in their midst.

Time slowed to a crawl as Ben completed his spin by dropping into a crouch and sweeping his right arm across the alien's knees with all his augmented strength. The blade carved through both joints, severing the trooper's legs. Ben's left arm was already in motion with his follow-up strike. The blade on his left arm punched through a gap between plates over the alien's midsection and drove all the way through until Ben's fist slammed into its armor.

The last trooper backpedaled, swinging its plasma carbine toward Ben in a wild arc. Ben powered forward, using the alien impaled on his left arm like a shield. Two powerful blasts erupted from the trooper's weapon, slamming into Ben's improvised shield. The alien's armor did an admirable job of coping with the first bolt, but the second heated the bizarre ceramic composite until it glowed orange, burning Ben's hands through his suit. He tossed his alien meat shield aside, then smashed into the last surviving trooper.

Ben knocked its carbine to the side with a vicious cross-body blow, and his shoulder drove into the smaller alien. He sent the thought command to retract his blades; they were going to be too unwieldy now that he was on the ground. The two combatants crashed to the unyielding marble beneath them, and a hand swatted feebly at Ben's helmet. He reared back, gripped the alien by the neck, and squeezed as hard as his augmented strength would allow. He roared, smashing the trooper's head into the ground over and over until the stone beneath was cracked and he could see a glaze of the alien's dark, viscous blood coating the inside of its faceplate.

Ben released the lifeless body and rocked back onto his knees, panting heavily. Gradually, the roaring in his ears began to fade as his heartbeat slowed. Sometime during the battle, he must have shut off his music, because only the crackling of several nearby fires filled his ears now... and someone calling his name.

"Ben!"

"Over here, Chief," Ben replied in an exhausted voice. His body was coming down from the massive adrenaline dump, and he felt drained. Rapid, heavy footfalls approached, and Ben knew he was about to get his ass chewed something fierce. He stood up on shaky legs and turned to face the music.

Kravczyk stood with his feet planted shoulder-width apart, looking down on Ben. His carbine was held in a loose low-ready position, and he absolutely radiated violence. The big SEAR's head swiveled from left to right and back again, taking in the carnage Ben had wrought.

"What the fuck happened to 'no cowboy shit'?" His tone was stern but tempered by the euphoria that always came after an intense battle.

"Sorry, Chief." Ben played it safe and simply apologized, then shut up.

Kravczyk stared at him for a long moment without saying anything further. Then his posture relaxed slightly. "Just one question: what was that song you were pumping out during this little dance?"

"'Cowboys from Hell' by Pantera. They're a metal band from back in the late twentieth, early twenty-first." Then Ben's brows pulled together in confusion. He hadn't broadcast that over an open channel, had he? "How do you know I had music going?"

"Every marine and spacer within range of your suit comms heard it, Ben. And we couldn't kill it, either. It's like you'd taken control of all the comms. If I didn't know better, I'd say Mabel had highjacked all our comms frequencies as a joke. But as she's still up in space, I assume it had to have been you. We couldn't get control of our comms again until you took cover behind that planter." Kravczyk jerked a thumb toward the crumbling remains of the marble planter Ben had briefly sheltered behind.

Ben blinked several times before he realized his mouth was hanging open. What the hell? All he'd done was send the command to his APEX to cue up the music. He thought back on exactly what he'd done when he jumped out of the Griffon, but his memory was fuzzy on the details. "I don't know what to tell you, Chief... I don't know how that happened."

"You did play it to amp yourself up and regulate your auto-nomic response, right?"

"Yeah, but I didn't broadcast it to everyone," Ben insisted. "At least not intentionally." At this point, he couldn't rule anything out; it wouldn't be the first time his subconscious had taken liberties with any and all tech it had access to. Hell, it wouldn't even be the first time this week.

Then he realized he now couldn't hear anything over his suit comms at all, and a quick glance at his HUD informed him there were no active connections available. "Hey, what's up with the comms? I don't have any channels available."

"Not sure, but mine dropped out, too. It may be related to whatever weird shit you did. It doesn't matter right now. We'll figure it out later." Kravczyk tilted his head toward the pock-marked marble steps that led up to the heart of the Alarian government. "Come on, kid. We can't let those space apes get to the council first and take all the glory for saving their skinny asses."

Ben followed Kravczyk up the stairs. The two men slung their weapons across their backs and held their hands out to their sides as they approached the shattered glass at the front of the building.

"We're here to see High Councilor Elyria," Kravczyk announced to the business end of the Alarian weapons trained on them. "We're from CTS *Indomitable*. I know we're a little early, but it looked like you folks could use a hand."

"Silence, Terran filth! Do not take one step closer! I should shoot you where you stand for bringing these creatures down on us like a plague." The speaker was dressed in black ceremonial armor adorned with golden accents. The armor had once been highly polished and immaculate but was now covered in a fine layer of soot from a recently extinguished fire and littered with small dents and scratches from the battle.

"I'll bet he's fun at parties," Kravczyk muttered.

Even though the voice sounded slightly tinny and muffled through the armor's external speakers, Ben recognized it. He stepped forward and set his faceplate to transparent so the Alarians could see who he was. Plastering a huge, shit-eating grin on his face, he held his arms out wide in greeting.

"Klaythron! Long time no see, buddy!"

"Benjamin Hutchins," Klaythron snarled. "I should have recognized your particular brand of chaos."

"Am I missing something here?" Kravczyk muttered, turning his head slightly toward Ben as if he was speaking out the side of his mouth. Ben had given the big SEAR a thousand-foot over-view of his history with Elyria, but he'd left out most of the details that weren't directly related to his relationship with the Alarian high councilor. Klaythron, the nearly two-meter-tall, fully armed and armored Alarian in front of them, was one such detail.

Ben gestured from Klaythron to the chief. "Klaythron, Chief Kravczyk. Chief, this is Klaythron. He's the head of Elyria's security detail, and the last time we were together, he threatened to kill me the next time he saw me." Ben turned back to face Klaythron, whose weapon was steadily pointing closer and closer to Ben. "And I missed you, too, bubba." Ben flashed his most genuine used car salesman's smile. "I think you'll find our ship has cleared your skies for you, and if I had to guess, I'd say they're probably mopping up that cruiser right about now. So how about you escort us to see Elyria and we'll figure out where we go from here, yeah?"

He looked around, noticing the few remaining defenders were all examining his gore-covered armor. Ben glanced down and realized what the issue was. "But first, maybe I should go freshen up a bit. Any chance you'd point me to the nearest restroom? Or maybe just a hose."

22

KNIFE FIGHT

"JUMP IN TWO MINUTES, CAPTAIN RAMSEY."

"Thank you, Mabel," Ramsey said, taking a moment to look around and examine the faces of his bridge crew. They were about to ambush a warship that was their equal in tonnage and almost certainly outmatched *Indomitable* in raw firepower. Taking out the corvette had been a trivial test of the Confed's newest class of heavy cruiser, given her potent array of weapons and armor. *Indomitable* was the most powerful space combatant in Terran history, excluding the Bulwark-class battleships that currently only existed as blueprints. A five-thousand-ton corvette was little more than a bug on the windshield to Ramsey's newest command.

What they were about to face was going to truly test the *Dame*'s capabilities. This was going to be a knife fight against a beast of an opponent, yet the crew didn't appear to be overly apprehensive. Indeed, there was almost an electric quality to the air on the bridge. They were all eager to demonstrate just what *Indomitable*, the pride of Second Fleet, could do.

"Mabel, the ship is yours after we jump," Ramsey said. "You are free to maneuver her as you see fit, calculate firing solutions, and make offensive recommendations, but final weapons release authorization remains with myself and Lieutenant Curtis, as we discussed."

"Understood, Captain."

The last ten minutes had been a flurry of activity while Ramsey quickly hashed out the details with Mabel. The AI was capable of integrating herself with *Indomitable*'s systems to such a degree that she could almost fight the ship by herself, but Ramsey wasn't comfortable with being a passenger aboard his own command. He was putting a lot of trust in the AI, but she would be able to react much faster than any of his crew. He spent a moment musing at the possibilities a fully integrated AI could unlock if implemented fleet-wide. When they were done here, Ramsey was sure the brass back at Icarus would simultaneously berate him for his recklessness and congratulate him for advancing humanity's space-combat capabilities by decades... if they survived.

"Weps," Ramsey called out to his weapons officer, making brief eye contact with the man. "We believe this is the last Imperium ship in Terran or Alarian space, so do be generous. We can always bill the Alarians for our expended ordnance later."

Curtis replied with a wicked grin. "Never you fear, sir. We'll spare no expense to escort our friends straight to hell!"

Cheers flared around the bridge before quickly dying down, and Ramsey smiled inwardly. His people were ready; he just hoped they would all be alive to celebrate when this was all said and done.

"Executing jump in ten..." Mabel counted down the last few seconds, and Ramsey returned his gaze to the holotank. The faint vibrations through the deck built in frequency as *Indomitable*'s six fusion reactors crammed every last bit of juice into the warp drive capacitors.

"Jump!"

The big cruiser trembled for a moment. Then all hell broke loose.

The holotank hadn't even been populated with the new data before Mabel was shouting, "Execute target package echo! Now, now, now!"

"Weps!"

"Firing!"

Indomitable shuddered with repeated hammer blows. Alarms blared. People were shouting over top of one another. The previously quiet bridge had been transformed into a chaotic maelstrom.

The holotank finally updated, and Ramsey's eyes flew wide open. They were practically right on top of the Imperium cruiser —less than eighty kilometers distant—but they had overshot, coming out of warp *between* the enemy and the Alarian warships that were fighting for their lives. *Indomitable* was taking fire from both parties.

"Comms! Tell the Alarians to stop shooting at us!" Ramsey bellowed. On the plot, a stream of 455mm shells from the Mk18s streaked toward the enemy cruiser, acting as a phalanx for dozens of Talon II anti-ship missiles that were still surging out of *Indomitable*'s launch tubes. "Weps, keep hammering that cruiser until there's nothing left but space dust!"

A crimson icon flared to life in front of the enemy cruiser at the same moment the first of *Indomitable*'s rail shots slammed into it.

"Vampire, Vampire! Plasma torpedo inbound!" The tactical officer's warning was so loud it briefly drowned out the other voices on the bridge.

Ramsey's blood ran cold. They could take a pounding from the enemy's lasers and keep swinging, but he'd seen the after-action report on *Appomattox*'s battle at Vostok, and he knew that torpedo would knock his ship out of the fight if it struck.

"Mabel!" he shouted as the torpedo streaked toward his ship. It was going to hit. They were too close to evade it.

"Activating countermeasure."

Ramsey was thrown to the deck as his ship bucked under his feet. A cataclysmic bang reverberated through the whole ship, followed by cries and agonized grunts from the bridge crew as they were all tossed about like rocks inside a tin can. Damage and casualty reports began streaming in, and a 3D rendering of *Indomitable* appeared in one corner of the holotank. Several areas near the bow and stern flashed red, indicating significant systems damage. But there was something else his eyes focused on: a new sun had formed just eighty kilometers astern. The combination of matter-antimatter annihilation and nuclear fusion produced a spectacular fireball in space, but it was quickly snuffed out by the uncaring vacuum of the void.

"Enemy destroyed," Mabel said. "I was successful in dissipating the plasma torpedo before it impacted, but we still took significant damage from the magnetic core the Imperium uses to contain the plasma within the projectile. I'm also afraid my countermeasure resulted in catastrophic damage to the warp field emitters. We'll need to return to Hai'alla under sub-light propulsion, and we're likely stuck in this system until an engineering team can bring replacement components."

"What about the Alarians?" Ramsey said.

"They lost a destroyer and the cruiser *Fostryn*. Two more ships are crippled, but the heavy cruiser *Elyris* appears to have only suffered minor damage."

Elyris was the flagship of the Alarian Home Fleet, and its loss would have been a crippling blow to both their combat power and morale. While the Alarians classified the ship as a heavy cruiser, CTS FLEETCOM had the ship listed as a dreadnaught in the intel reports. Despite what most of Terran space thought about the Alarians, given their devastating preemptive strikes against Earth, Elizabeth, and Isadore, the aliens were not generally predisposed toward conflict. As such, they refused to give any of their ships a classification that would indicate its sole purpose was for war. Ramsey watched the massive ship maneuvering to assist one of the crippled light cruisers in their formation, and he shook his head at the notion the massive battlewagon could be considered anything *but* a warship.

"There's more bad news, I'm afraid, Captain Ramsey," Mabel continued.

Some stiffness began creeping up Ramsey's neck—probably related to the tumble he'd taken—and he massaged the muscles with one hand. "This entire day has been bad news, Mabel. Let's just get it over with."

"The quantum link with Icarus is no longer functional. I suspect my little trick with the warp field emitters that dispersed the incoming plasma torpedo broke the connection between entangled pairs."

Ramsey let out a frustrated sigh. That link back to Icarus was going to be the thing that got them help. Now they would have to send an update the old-fashioned way. "Of course it did. Please prepare a data drop for upload to a Beckman drone. Ops." He glanced over at Lowen, who appeared calm and collected despite working furiously in the aftermath of the battle. The young officer must've had ice water flowing through his veins. Either that or he had the single most impressive ability to control his emotions Ramsey had ever seen from a junior bridge officer. "Please inform flight ops I want a Beckman prepped for immediate deployment to Icarus."

"Yes, sir."

"I see our friends have stopped shooting at us for the time being. It's something, I suppose. I assume that was your doing, Mr. Billings?"

"Aye, Captain. I was able to establish a dialog with *Elyris*.

Captain Raal would like to speak with you, but she said it would have to wait until they've stabilized their damaged ships."

"Captain Raal?" Ramsey said, surprised. *This is going to get complicated.*

Raal was in command of a destroyer during the war, and the last time Ramsey had been in contact with the fiery Alarian was right after the two of them mauled each other during the Battle of Columbia Prime. The general notion that Alarians were largely a peaceful race did *not* apply to Captain Temina Raal. It also now made sense to him why the Alarians had ignored the information they'd been given about the Imperium's capabilities, leading to what would have been a slaughter had *Indomitable* not intervened.

"Please inform *Elyris* that Captain Raal may contact me at her convenience. We have our own battle damage to see to."

Billings acknowledged him, and Ramsey turned back to the holotank, which was rapidly being populated with damage and casualty reports as his department heads checked in. Mabel was doing her best to coordinate the damage-control efforts, but the picture was still chaotic. His eyes were drawn to the plot showing Hai'alla. The marines were on their own for the time being, and he hoped they were faring better than *Indomitable* had.

23

LONG TIME, NO SEE

KLAYTHRON OPENED HIS MOUTH TO SAY SOMETHING BUT PAUSED, cocking his head to the side like he was listening to some unseen speaker. His mouth moved, but he'd shut off his armor's external speakers, and Ben couldn't tell what he was saying. *God, I miss having Mabel here. She'd probably already have his encrypted comms cracked, and we could hear everything he's saying.* The silent conversation continued for another twenty seconds or so, with Klaythron growing more and more animated. Ben and Kravczyk stood like statues, and the few remaining Alarian guards kept their weapons trained on the two APEX-armored Terrans.

At last, Klaythron looked back at Ben. "Leave your weapons here. My lady has requested I bring you before the council immediately, over my strong objections."

Ben slowly unslung his XM93 and handed it to one of the Alarian guards who stepped forward to disarm him. "Do we need to worry about any…" Ben trailed off for a moment, trying to figure out how to say what he needed to say; he wasn't sure if the other guards were aware of the incident between him and Elyria. "You know. More of what happened the last time I was on Hai'alla?"

Klaythron paused, turning away from the guard he'd been quietly conversing with while the humans handed over their weapons. "As long as you remain in your armor with the environmental seals active, I do not believe there will be a problem."

Ben nodded, glancing over to confirm the chief was also now unarmed. "Then lead the way."

Klaythron motioned for them to follow him through the splintered remains of an ornate wooden door. Only about half of the door remained, and what was left was charred on the edges, with deep gouges in the paneling. On the other side was a long, wide corridor flanked by floor-to-ceiling paintings of different Alarians, all in immaculate blue council robes. Ben assumed these must be past members of their governing body. Klaythron walked on in silence.

They soon reached a matching set of wooden doors on the far end of the corridor. Unblemished by battle, the doors parted and golden light washed over the trio. The main council chamber was brilliantly lit by Hai'alla's star filtering in through the towering glass wall overlooking the sea. A raised dais sat in front of the glass, fronted by wooden panels that appeared to be hand-carved and depicted the Alarian story of the Great Cataclysm— the event that saw the destruction of the original Alarian worlds and led to the refugee fleet arriving in orbit over Earth. Thirteen robed Alarians were settling into their places on the dais, and Ben's eyes locked onto Elyria, who was seated in the center.

Despite the palpable tension hanging in the air, at the sight of her, Ben's heart did a little skip in his chest, briefly throwing his mental state into chaos. Where the hell did that come from? He hadn't seen her in five years, and they'd only spent a grand total of about twenty hours together. Now, here he was, strolling into the private chambers of the Alarian High Council, the most revered political body in Alarian culture, and his body was acting like he was here to pick her up for their first date. He grabbed the errant thought train and stuffed it into his mental junk drawer so he could address it later... or never. He was here for one reason and one reason only.

The High Council had sole authority to decide if an alliance with the Confed would happen, and Ben was the Confed's only hope for getting the council to go for it. As the full scope of his current situation once again settled into the forefront of his mind, he found it easier to focus. Not only that, but there was just something about this place; it radiated an aura of majesty and power. Despite the carnage Ben had seen on his way in, the main chamber looked completely untouched, almost like the Imperium troops were under orders to keep the council alive. Ben filed that little tidbit away to address later; it wasn't the Imperium's style, in his experience.

Klaythron held up a hand for the two Terrans to stop when they reached the center of the room. Silence reigned in the chamber as Ben and Kravczyk both waited for the Alarians to make the first move. Ben had his faceplate set to clear, and Elyria's large almond-shaped eyes were boring into his. She had a serious expression on her face, but it wasn't hostile—something that couldn't be said for many of the other high councilors.

"Benjamin Hutchins of Earth, Chief Kravczyk of the Confederated Terran Systems Navy, Special Exoatmospheric Reconnaissance Unit, we welcome you to Hai'alla." Elyria's amplified voice seemed to come from every direction at once. "Before we continue, I would ask you to please communicate with the company of Marine Pathfinders that are currently making a nuisance of themselves, demanding to be allowed entry into this chamber. I will lift the security measures we have in place to prevent outside communications for this purpose, but then you will not be allowed to communicate with your people again until we have concluded our business here."

So that was why Ben hadn't heard anything over the comms

since he'd approached the building; the Alarians had some sort of jamming in place around the council chambers. Ben's suit comms crackled in his ears for a few seconds. Then he could hear chatter over the team channel. He glanced at the chief and nodded. "All you, Chief."

Kravczyk quickly gave the Pathfinders a rundown on their situation and told them to remain outside and to listen to everything the Alarians told them to do until he and Ben had finished. "It's done, Councilor," Kravczyk said to Elyria after dealing with a near-apoplectic Major Davis, who'd been on one of the Condors. Ben could understand the man's anger; the Pathfinders' sole responsibility on this mission was to safeguard Ben, and instead he was the first one on the ground, then directly engaged the enemy. Now, Ben was locked up by the Alarians and out of contact for an indefinite amount of time. He felt some sympathy for the Major, knowing the brass would probably have some choice words for him after the disaster on Elizabeth and now this.

Elyria bowed slightly in acknowledgment. "Thank you, Chief Kravczyk. Now, we must address the issue at hand. For the last four and a half of your standard years, we have had peace here. Yet now, mere weeks after one of your intelligence ships ambushed the cruiser I was on—in a system we tried very hard to keep a secret, mind you—an unknown alien race appeared in our skies and struck a blow at the very heart of the Alarian people. Many of us"—she swept a hand around her, indicating her fellow members of the High Council—"find it difficult to believe the two events are not linked. So, Ben, please explain to me why we should not simply execute you where you stand and launch another invasion of Terran space."

There was something in her expression and voice with that last sentence. Ben noticed a shift in her speech from a formal address to something more... personal? Was she asking for his help to get her fellow councilmembers on her side, or did she feel like the Imperium attack was some sort of personal betrayal on his part? Either way, he needed to tread *very* lightly here. Fortunately—and counter to what those DC hacks aboard *Indomitable* seemed to think—he knew just how to turn on the charm, and he'd prepared his address carefully over the last week. He cleared his throat and took one step forward, then went down to one knee in a deep bow.

"High Council of the Alarian people," Ben began in flawless Alarian standard, taking care to hit just the right tone. "I have come to you on behalf of all Terrans in the hope that there can be a lasting peace between our two races. It is the desire of my heart that we shall not be enemies any longer. I offer the actions of myself, my fellow warriors, and our ship, CTS *Indomitable*, which even now fights to shield you from the scourge that is our common enemy, as proof of my words."

Ben was laying it on thick, and he knew it. But the Alarians were weird when it came to formal meetings like this one, insisting on that absurdly flowery way of speaking he'd found so irritating when he was last here five years ago. Yet even now, he could see the demeanor of some of the councilors changing from outright hostility to something more along the lines of plain old disgust. Hey, it was progress, and he was just getting started.

"Five years ago, my father and I were welcomed to your beautiful planet in the spirit of cooperation. Tragically, that budding rose of friendship was crushed beneath the heel of war before it could bloom. But the war was not merely a calamitous event between two races unable to reconcile their differences. For then and now, evil lurks in the shadows. Like a predator, it stalks the night, awaiting its opportunity to feast on the shattered bodies of our people.

"This is why I have come to you, not merely as an agent of peace but also as the sword that can cleave through our enemy's breastplate. Apart, we shall wither and die, as does the fruit of a poisoned vine. Together, though... Together, we shall strike at the heart of our tormentor and rid our space of the Imperium!"

Elyria smiled at Ben. It wasn't so much on her lips as it was in her eyes, and he knew he'd nailed it. Ben hadn't been sure how he would feel being in her presence again, and he was even more worried about how she would treat him. But kneeling there on the floor, he suddenly felt like he'd been transported to that boardwalk along the Tildar River again, before *it* happened, and he relaxed. She was on his side, and he just needed to win over the rest of the council—something that had seemed significantly more daunting just a few minutes ago.

"Well spoken, Ben Hutchins. I must admit that I did not anticipate the level of respect you have shown this body, despite what High Councilor Elyria told me about you." The speaker was the elderly male sitting directly to Elyria's right. "If I may speak plainly for a minute..." He looked to his left and right, apparently seeking the approval of his fellow councilors to break protocol. When they all indicated their assent, he stood and continued. "We did not fully believe the information Elyria received from the captain in command of the intelligence ship that was sent to confront her. When the attack began here, many of us believed you Terrans were working with this new enemy and had set them upon us in retaliation for the War of Sorrow.

"Yet here you are, with your armor stained by the blood of our enemy and your ship damaged while fighting to save the rest of our fleet." Ben's heart leaped into his throat at the mention of *Indomitable* taking damage, and it must have shown on his face. The elderly councilor held up his hands in a calming gesture and smiled. "Your ship, *Indomitable*, destroyed both of the attacking vessels. It sustained damage during the battle, but Fleet Master Raal reports it does not appear to be too serious. As

I understand it, *Indomitable* is currently aiding some of our vessels that were crippled during the battle."

Some of the tension left Ben's shoulders, and he nodded his thanks. "Thank you, honored councilor, for the update. We haven't heard any news of our ship since before we made landfall. I'm very happy to hear at least some of your fleet made it through the battle."

The old Alarian appeared to deflate right before Ben's eyes, and his gaze dropped to the top of the desk he stood behind. "Sadly," he said, "many of them did not. Had we heeded your warning, perhaps we would not have lost so many." He looked back up, his eyes shifting from Ben to the chief, then back to Ben. "We will not make the same mistake again."

"Ben," Elyria said, also standing now. Her voice was formal, despite the familiarity with which she addressed him—almost like she was having a hard time keeping her head in the game. "The Alarian people agree to open negotiations with the Confederated Terran Systems for the purpose of seeking an alliance, with possible trade options to be addressed after the alliance is formalized. This meeting is adjourned, and we will reconvene after the current crisis has stabilized."

With that, the entire council rose and filed out from behind the monolithic desk that ran the entire length of the dais. Every member of the council save for Elyria and the old councilor who had spoken during the brief summit disappeared through a door off to the side of the chamber. Elyria made her way around the dais and approached Ben, with her colleague in tow. She stopped two paces away, but it seemed to Ben like she wanted to come closer. Now that she was nearly within arm's reach, Ben could see that she was just as beautiful as he remembered, and an odd twisting sensation pulled at his chest as his mind flashed briefly to Tess. This was going to be a problem.

"It's good to see you again, Ben," Elyria said with a smile that was genuine but also almost sad. "I regret that you and your father were ejected from Alarian space after we were last together."

Ben's lips curved upward, but he found they didn't cover quite as much ground as they should have. He suddenly felt like he knew exactly what mix of emotions had created that sad little smile of hers a moment ago. "It's good to see you, too, Elyria. I'm glad to see you well."

Klaythron moved to stand slightly behind Elyria and to her right. The guard's body language practically screamed, *Fuck with her again and I will end you, Terran*. Ben sighed internally; that guy was probably going to be an issue at some point. Ben gestured to himself and Kravczyk. "So how does this work now? I gathered that this meeting was some sort of formal precursor to the actual negotiations. What should the chief and I—and that company of space apes out there, for that matter—do now?" He said that last part with a tilt of his head, indicating the marines out in the courtyard.

The old Alarian chuckled. "You are quite the enigma, Benjamin Hutchins. Elyria told us you were unlike any Terran any of us had encountered before, but her description didn't do you justice. First, you nearly single-handedly fought off our attackers after recklessly diving out of your transport. Then you gave the High Council an address that would put many of our political speechwriters to shame—in flawless Alarian, I might add. Then, just now, you demonstrated that Terran brashness that many of us expected in the first place. Many of my colleagues may not agree, but I look forward to getting to know you better over the next days and weeks as we work to bring our two races together, as it should have been long ago."

The old man placed a hand on Elyria's shoulder and inclined his head ever so slightly, then turned and strode toward the door the rest of the council had exited through. Ben watched him walk away, finding himself equally intrigued by the elder councilor.

"Now that's a guy I'd love to sit down and have a few beers with," Kravczyk said, speaking for the first time since telling the marines to stand down.

"I couldn't agree more, Chief," Ben said. He turned back to Elyria. "What can we do to help you guys? This compound is secure, but did the Imperium shock troops land anywhere else? The number of troops we fought through here wasn't nearly what I would expect them to have aboard a cruiser-class ship, and I have a whole company of Marine Pathfinders out there just itching for a good fight."

Elyria frowned. "To the best of my knowledge, those were the only troops the Imperium landed, but our civilian and secure military datanets went down shortly before the attack. Someone at Alarian High Command should have a better idea as to the extent of the attack, but we're still working to reestablish contact with them."

Ben's lighthearted mood evaporated in an instant, and his body tensed like it was preparing for a fight before his brain had arrived at the most plausible conclusion. "It would seem you have an agent problem, Elyria." Ben exchanged a look with Kravczyk, then made brief eye contact with Klaythron before his gaze returned to Elyria. "Fortunately for you guys, that's precisely why I'm here."

24

FIELD TRIP

HENRY ABSENTLY REACHED FOR THE STEAMING THERMAL MUG resting off to one side of his desk. The aroma wafting up from the beverage broke him out of his trance, and he blinked a few times in an effort to clear his thoughts. He swiped his free hand through the holographic data above his desk, sending it to one corner, where it would remain as an illuminated circle of light until he called it back up shortly. But right now, he needed to rest his eyes and his brain. He glanced at the time readout floating a few centimeters over the surface of his desk and groaned. No wonder his eyes felt so gritty.

"I'm way too old for this shit," he said to the empty space around him before standing and gathering the leather folio he used to transport his personal datapad and a few other essentials.

Henry stepped around the desk, folio in one hand, coffee in the other, and headed for the door of his office. He'd been going over some revisions to Ben's design, namely Shelly's proposal to increase the available bandwidth for data transfer. The increase in bandwidth would help solve one of the biggest issues, but the tradeoff was size and power consumption. They would need to do some more fine-tuning before implementing the design changes. In the meantime, they had the first prototypes of the transmitter and receiver almost ready to go.

Henry walked through the lab, his footsteps echoing off the polished concrete and large, flat workbenches. His team had all left hours ago, even Shelly, who'd been working almost as hard on this project as he had. A brief smile crossed his lips at the thought of the beautiful brunette. After his return from Icarus, she'd indeed taken him up on that rain check… with interest. He'd been worried there might be some awkwardness in the lab afterward, but if anything, they'd been working better together. Sudden realization hit Henry: since they were no longer tiptoeing around their mutual attraction, communication was much easier. So far, they'd been able to keep their relationship under wraps, but it was only a matter of time before the rest of the people working around them figured it out.

He stopped in front of a door emblazoned with all kinds of warnings and checked the small status panel adjacent to it. The atomic printer still had about six hours left on its current job. "Good," Henry said. "We can start assembly first thing in the morning."

"I always thought you were crazy, Henry, but talking to your-self in an empty room just confirms it for me."

Henry jerked his head around so fast that his coffee sloshed out of the mug and sprayed the wall and nearby workstations.

"Jesus Christ, Matt!" he exploded. "I'm too old for you to go scaring the shit out of me like that."

Henry set his belongings down on a worktable and walked to a nearby cabinet containing cleaning supplies and shop rags.

Evans laughed and swiped a hand vertically along the door-jamb, bringing the lights in the lab up to a comfortable level, and approached. "Sorry, Henry, but I just couldn't help myself. When you didn't answer my calls earlier, I contacted Shelly. She said you were probably still here, and I half expected to find you asleep on the couch in your office. Instead, I found a lunatic talking to himself in the dark."

Henry pulled a microfiber rag from the cabinet and tossed it at Evans. "You're cleaning that up, you sneaky asshole." His smile came easier as his heart rate dropped back down, and he mentally acknowledged that Matt had gotten him good. He made a note to repay the fleet officer in kind at a later date.

"Fair enough." Evans stooped to wipe up the spilled coffee.

"You said you tried to call? I had my comms unit set to *do not disturb* so I could focus on something, then forgot to switch it back over when I packed up for the night," Henry said, pulling his comms unit from a pocket and unmuting it. Sure enough, there were a half dozen missed calls from Evans and Shelly, along with over fifteen text messages from various people. Henry frowned as he glanced at the names of the people who had been trying to get ahold of him. Something was up.

"Well shit, Matt, it looks like half of the Confed brass were calling. I assume you weren't just stopping by to chat with an old friend, so what's up?" The bottom of Henry's stomach dropped out when a thought hit him. "Is it Ben?"

"Yes and no," Evans said, standing and looking around for a place to dump the soaked towel. "Yes, it's Ben, and no, he's not hurt. A Beckman from *Indomitable* arrived a few hours ago, and I just got off the line with the admiral. He wants me to get you up to speed."

Oh shit. If *Indomitable* sent a Beckman, then its Q-link was out for some reason. Doing the quick math on how long it took a Gen-3 Beckman to make the trip from Alarian space, Henry figured whatever message that drone had been carrying must have been sent shortly after the battlecruiser arrived in the system. He could tell by Matt's demeanor that the mission to Hai'alla had run into some sort of snag, but the lack of urgency in the man's tone indicated the situation was probably either already worked out or looked like it would lead to a positive result. Well, that was good. At least *Indomitable* probably hadn't been attacked by the Alarian Home Fleet when it arrived.

Evans finally gave up on finding the towel return and just tossed it into a nearby trash can. "He did go and do something crazy again, though."

Henry sighed and glanced wistfully at his empty coffee mug, then inclined his head toward his office. "Well, I guess you better tell me all about it. Come on, I'll put on a fresh pot."

————

THE DOOR to Henry's office opened immediately after a quick knock from the other side.

"You never left?" Shelly said, cocking an eyebrow as her gaze quickly swept around Henry's office. She nodded a greeting to Evans, who was reclining on the couch, then half frowned, half smiled at Henry in an expression that asked a dozen different questions all at the same time.

"I tried to, but Matt wouldn't let me go." Henry shot her a wry grin. "You're just in time. Do you like space travel? And on a completely unrelated note, how do you feel about taking some time off from the lab?"

"Why?" Shelly dragged the word out, looking like she thought it was a mistake coming in to work this morning.

"Because Ben got himself into all kinds of trouble again. Now you and I need to go on a field trip to fix a brand-new battle-cruiser. Go pack a bag. We're leaving in three hours."

25

GOING ROGUE

CAPTAIN SAMANTHA COLLINS STOPPED OUTSIDE THE DOOR TO Admiral Garland's office and took a moment to make sure her class-A uniform was squared away. Satisfied her appearance was fit for a private meeting with the head of the Confed Navy, she opened the door and stepped into the reception area.

A lieutenant in her late twenties with Asian features and dark hair pulled back into a tight ponytail smiled from behind a large wooden desk. No, scratch that: the desk was actually a molded polymer and coated to look like wood. The receptionist—the name tape on her uniform identified her as A. Abesamis—looked up from her personal terminal and smiled warmly.

"How may I help you, Captain?"

Collins stopped a couple paces in front of the desk and glanced at the door that led into the admiral's office. "I'm Captain Samantha Collins. The admiral asked to see me as soon as possible."

"Oh yes," Abesamis said after glancing at her terminal as if she was checking the admiral's schedule. Recognition flickered in the lieutenant's eye as soon as she noticed Collins's name tape and ribbon rack, so it was probably all just for show, maybe an attempt to put her at ease, for some reason. "He's waiting for you now. Go right on in, Captain."

"Thanks."

Collins strode over to the inner door and pushed it open, then stepped into the spartan office. She faltered slightly when her eyes met those of CID Director Mark Gideon, but she recovered quickly.

Oh shit, she thought. *An urgent meeting with the heads of the navy and CID at the same time? This oughta be interesting...*

"Captain," Garland said, rising from behind his desk and stepping around to approach her. "Please, close the hatch and have a seat."

Collins closed and locked the door. A station this big had doors, and anything smaller than a million tons or so had hatches; at least that was how she thought of it. She reached out and shook the admiral's proffered hand.

"Thank you, Admiral," she said, taking a seat in one of two comfortable leather chairs opposite his desk. "Director." She greeted the head of the intel division with a respectful nod instead of a salute, as was CID's tradition.

"Captain," Gideon said.

"Alright then." Garland sat back in his chair and brought up a few holographic menus over one corner of his desk, his hands flying through the motions with practiced ease. He hit one last command, and the menu vanished from the air over the desk. "Now that there aren't any extra ears listening in, let's get to it."

"The admiral and I have a mission for you, Captain." Gideon turned in his chair slightly so he could more easily speak with her. His eyes darted to the admiral's and back to hers. "But this one is off the books—even for CID. You can refuse right now, if you're uncomfortable with this, without any ramifications for your career. But I believe this is something you'll want to be a part of. So what say you, Captain?"

Collins glanced at the faces of the two men, trying to get a read on just what was going on, but they were both pros at keeping their expressions neutral, and she couldn't pick up anything from either of them. As the commander of a Wraith, she specialized in black ops, but a mission that was completely off the books, even within the CID? That was the kind of stuff that usually meant either a suicide mission or something that would land her in prison for a long, long time if things went sideways. But she trusted Director Gideon—he'd always been a straight shooter with his people and had an excellent reputation within the CID. She also trusted the admiral, having crossed paths with him several times recently with the whole Ben/Imperium/Alarians thing.

"I'm in," she said firmly.

Both men visibly relaxed. "Good," the admiral said. "We need you to take your ship and head to Elizabeth, where you will pick up Commander Valdez and Petty Officer McCollum. From there, you're to rendezvous with *Indomitable* in orbit over Hai'alla." Garland produced a sealed packet from a desk drawer and held it out for her. "This packet contains information for Captain Ramsey. I want you to give it to him personally. Make up whatever excuse you need to do so. Say you want to tour his ship, invite him to dinner. I don't care what excuse you use. You and only you are to deliver this to him and instruct him to open it in a secure location."

Collins reached across the desk and took the packet. It was light—she figured it contained only a dozen or so pages worth of documents.

"If I may, sirs," she said, stowing the packet in the chair next to her, "can you give me anything that would explain a little better just what is going on, such that you need a highly specialized stealth ship to perform what amounts to a routine personnel transfer and courier run?"

Gideon looked at the admiral, a question written on his face.

Garland shrugged. "If we can't trust her, we're screwed. Go ahead, Mark."

Director Gideon turned back to Collins. "The admiral and I believe strongly that a faction within the Confed government will soon move to oust President McGibbons and take the reins of power for themselves."

Collins's eyes flew wide at the revelation. There'd been some muttering around the fringes of the CID that something big was coming, but something like a power grab on the level of taking over the presidency? Mechanisms built into the Confederacy's charter could remove a sitting president, but Collins didn't see how any of those could be used in the current situation. Not only that, but didn't they realize the Confed was looking down the barrel of another interstellar war? She was used to politicians playing their petty games, but you'd think they'd be able to put that crap aside and work together with the fate of humanity on the line here.

"It was only a matter of time, really," he continued. "People gave her a pass for the Alarian War because *everyone* failed to anticipate how devastating it would be. But when her leadership proved lackluster, at best, in the years that followed, the first utterances of discontent began. It was quiet at first, no one daring to go public while Terran space was reeling in the aftermath, but once the core systems began to put themselves back together and the Confed appeared to be asleep at the wheel, things started happening behind closed doors.

"Now we're in a fight for our lives against a superior alien race no one knew existed, half the fleet was knocked out in a single day, and nukes are going off on Elizabeth. All of this is happening under the current administration's watch, and it's easy to see how people may have lost confidence in McGibbons."

"Excuse me, Director, but what was that part about nukes on Elizabeth?"

Collins was surprised to hear there might be a coup brewing, but learning of a nuclear detonation on the world where the Confed government had its seat of power utterly shocked her. She hadn't heard rumors of another attack, and neither Gideon nor the admiral had hinted at any sort of fleet engagement or ground conflict, so it had to be something weird, like... *Oh, holy shit. Ben and Mabel.*

Gideon chuckled. He'd been watching her face intently as her mind raced through its own analysis. "If that slight twitch of your eye meant you figured out Ben Hutchins and the AI had something to do with it, then you're correct. Mabel and our slip-space-monitoring network in the Columbia system detected a slipspace signal consistent with one of the agent's communications transceivers. Together with a platoon of Pathfinders that were undergoing a training evolution with them, Ben, the AI, and the SEAR that's been assigned to keep Hutchins out of trouble attempted to locate and disable the facility. It was a trap, and the agent detonated some sort of device. We haven't yet ascertained the exact type of weapon used, but it was dirty.

"Fortunately, the fallout zone was lightly inhabited, so civilian casualties should remain low. Nobody from the team that landed at the facility was killed. The only casualty was Hutchins, though he's expected to make a quick recovery."

Garland jumped in when Gideon finished recounting the event. "The incident in question occurred shortly before the joint meeting you were at with the president and Hank, but the Q-link system was down at the time. We didn't receive word for almost a full day after it happened, and by that time, Ben and an entire company of Pathfinders were already on their way to meet with the Alarians," he said, answering her next question.

Last she'd heard, Ben's training on Elizabeth was being

scrubbed, and he was supposed to ship out for Hai'alla. It sounded like he was already there, but Collins had a hard time wrapping her head around the utter chaos the kid seemed to bring with him wherever he went.

"We sent an entire company of grunts with him?" Collins narrowed her eyes. "That's not exactly a message that says 'we're trustworthy' to the Alarians."

The admiral snorted. "No shit. You can thank Valdez—yes, that Valdez—for the presence of the marines. Apparently Hank got his panties in a twist over his son going to Hai'alla, and he sent a note to Valdez, asking him to make sure the marines went along for the ride."

Garland sighed, exchanging a look with Gideon before continuing. "As it turns out, it was a good call. *Indomitable* arrived in-system to find the High Council under siege, two-thirds of the Alarian Home Fleet destroyed, and the last two Imperium ships doing their damnedest to wipe out the rest of them. Ramsey took out the ships—though not before scrambling his Q-link and breaking that brand-new battlecruiser we gave him—and Ben and the marines dropped to assist the Alarians with the Imperium ground element. They saved the day, the council is grateful, and now we're at risk of not getting them as allies because a bunch of power-hungry assholes in the senate want to boot the president to the curb along with anyone who's even touched this Imperium thing. That includes the both of us." The admiral gestured to himself and Director Gideon. "So now you're all caught up, Captain. Speak your mind."

Collins leaned back in her chair and massaged her temples while she quickly processed and categorized the rapid-fire info dump. Finally, she looked up and shook her head. "I think I liked it better when I had no idea who Ben Hutchins is."

"Hah!" Garland boomed, sounding genuinely amused.

Gideon's face remained neutral, but he said, "On that, Captain, you and I agree."

"I believe I understand the chain of events that got us to this point," Collins continued, "as well as what the stakes are. But what I don't fully understand is exactly what you want from me, other than to be a trusted courier. What's my role here?"

"If things go as we suspect, neither Admiral Garland nor I will be in our current positions by this time next month. We fully expect the senate to make a concerted push to begin proceedings to remove President McGibbons within the next week or so.

"I don't know exactly why they seem to think we're better off without the Alarians in our corner, as we haven't been able to get people close enough to the core group to get any solid details on their plan going forward. The faction that will take the reins wants nothing to do with the Alarians and thinks trying to ally with them would be a huge mistake. As Admiral Garland and I are both spearheading the push for an alliance, we'll be among the first to go once power changes hands. I think you can guess just how well we'd fare against the Imperium on our own."

"We'd be crushed," Collins said. "And so would the Alarians. But you still haven't answered my question."

"We want you to assist Ben and Mabel," Garland said. "It's as simple as that. Get the Alarians on board, with or without the approval of whoever ends up running the show around here. And if you have a chance to take out the agent while you're at it, make it happen. We're not without our supporters here, and you'd better believe we're going to fight like hell to keep this thing from going off the rails. Even still, we want to make sure there's at least a small group of people outside the new chain of command working to pull our asses out of the fire. If we fail here, we may need to have some strategic flexibility, and knowing you and Ramsey are out there will give us some options, extreme though they may be."

Collins didn't say it out loud, but it sure sounded like the director and admiral anticipated the need for a rogue element that could be called upon if things went south. She hoped it wouldn't come to that. God forbid they did need her to intervene somehow; that would likely mean she and Captain Ramsey would be pitted against their own fleet. They had enough crap going on with the Imperium bearing down on them; they shouldn't be screwing around shooting at each other over some petty political bullshit.

"I won't lie, sirs. I really don't like the idea of going rogue and getting into a shooting war with our own people. I'll get the SEARs and this packet to Hai'alla, and I'll do whatever I can to help Ben and his crew take on the agent... but I won't fire on my own people."

Garland nodded, his expression grave. "Reasonable, and exactly what I expected you to say, Captain. Quite frankly, I'd be worried we had the wrong person for the job if you *didn't* have a problem with the possibility of being at odds with your own fleet. At the end of the day, we're all driving for the same goal here: to defeat the Imperium, or at least get them to leave us the hell alone. Just promise me you'll do whatever you believe will be best for humanity."

"That goes without saying, sir."

"Then that's all I need to hear. Any other questions before you go?"

"Just one," Collins said. "Though it's more a curiosity than anything important... Why the effort to get the original SEAR team back together? If I'm not mistaken, Commander Valdez got a nice promotion to XO NAVSOC for the Columbia cluster. Won't this be seen as a punishment for him?"

Garland leaned back in his chair and grinned slightly. "The commander is in seriously hot water over this nuclear detonation business. It was his call to send the team in after that facility, and his head will be on the chopping block just like ours. Petty Officer McCollum recently arrived on Elizabeth after completing another assignment, and she and Valdez are together at Joint Base Thunder at the moment. But while I try to take care of my people as best as I can, saving those two the fallout from the upcoming power struggle isn't the main reason I want them on Hai'alla.

"It's my experience, Captain, that a small team who have the kind of bond those four do can accomplish things otherwise thought impossible. Just look at what they—with your help— were able to do during the Battle of Icarus. There's a certain *je ne sais quoi* Ben and those SEARs have, and if we're to have any hope of pulling our asses out of this mess, we'll need them all at their best."

Collins grinned. "So," she said, "we're getting the band back together. When do I leave?"

26

ANCIENT TRADITIONS TO THE RESCUE

"It's been ten days, Chief! What the hell are they still waiting on?"

The sand-filled punching bag Ben was supporting shuddered under a rapid series of powerful blows from the big SEAR, who was clearly taking out his own impatience on the poor training aide.

"I don't know, Ben. I'm just a dumb grunt, remember? I haven't been allowed into the chamber for any of your follow-up talks with the council, and I certainly don't have any contacts of my own with them. Just chill. These things take time."

The bag thumped into Ben's chest one last time, driving him back a step. *Damn, that son of a bitch is strong*, Ben thought, releasing the bag and reaching up to massage the area where he was sure he'd have a new bruise by the end of the day. In fact, the last week of spending every day in the gym with Kravczyk had left Ben with the distinct impression that the SEAR let him win that little tussle back on *Indomitable*'s running track. When Ben casually mentioned his suspicion, however, the chief had merely grinned and said, "And you'll never know for sure, punk." The non-answer drove Ben nuts, something he was sure

Kravczyk was hoping for. Eventually, though, he thought he understood what the chief was doing.

Kravczyk wanted those marines to see how capable Ben really was. Their training had been cut off before they'd had a chance to get to know each other well. Other than the thrashing Ben gave them at the Jackal Center, he was still largely an unknown quantity for them. A little one-on-one brawl with a SEAR—unarmored and without Mabel's help—was a perfect opportunity to show the Pathfinders Ben was more than just a one-trick pony thanks to his APEX and AI sidekick. Once that realization set in, Ben found himself with a need to reevaluate the big SEAR. He honestly hadn't thought Kravczyk was capable of that kind of forward-thinking and nuance. Maybe Ben wasn't the only one working hard to rise to the occasion of his new role.

"You calling it for today?" Ben asked, seeing the chief unwrapping the bindings from around his wrists.

"Yeah. My head's not really in the game right now. Think I'll just go for a run, then call it a morning. Coming?" Kravczyk inclined his head toward a door leading to a running track.

Ben shrugged. "Yeah, I might as well." He did a quick double step to catch up to the big man, and the two strode across the empty gymnasium, their footsteps echoing off the rows of exercise equipment.

The Alarians were housing all the Terrans who dropped from *Indomitable* in quarantine at a sprawling military base about eighty kilometers from the government complex that housed the High Council. None of them had been allowed to return to *Indomitable*, including the dropships, which were all secured in a cluster of hangars and under heavy guard by the Alarians. Ben's initial impression that the High Council might at least be reasonable after he'd saved their asses was starting to look like it was way off the mark.

He'd been called back for a series of short interviews over the past week but hadn't been able to make any real headway in the negotiations. The council did nothing but ask him questions, and only very rarely did they answer any of his own. Elyria was clearly on his side, and she actively lobbied the rest of the council on his behalf. Likewise with High Councilor Daelin, the elder member who'd spoken to Ben and Kravczyk after their initial meeting. But the other ten? They were a bunch of curmudgeonly, suspicious, ill-tempered, and long-winded gasbags who seemed to love the sound of their own voices more than they cared about trying to get shit done.

The door to the track whisked open as they approached, but a shout from behind them stopped them in their tracks. Ben turned toward the unexpected arrival. The Alarians were strictly regulating how many of the Terrans were allowed in the gym at once, and Ben, being a VIP, was only allowed to have Kravczyk as his escort and workout buddy.

"Klaythron?" he said, squaring his shoulders to the borderline-hostile captain of the Council Guard, who was storming his way toward the two Terrans in full armor. "What're you doing here? We're supposed to have the facility to ourselves for the next forty minutes."

Klaythron stopped just out of arm's reach, his head swiveling around as he surveyed both the interior of the gym and the expansive grounds around the running track through the still-open door. "My lady wishes to see you," was all he said before turning back toward the main entrance and bobbing his head slightly.

The main door opened again, and Elyria entered. Ben glanced at the chief, who raised an eyebrow in silent question.

"Don't look at me. I didn't know anything about this," Ben said with a shrug.

Elyria walked directly up to Ben and placed a gentle hand on his shoulder for a moment, smiling warmly. Ben cringed inwardly, knowing he was a disgusting, sweaty beast of a human after his and Kravczyk's punishing workout. But if it bothered her that he was soaked like he'd just come in from the rain and smelled like a hobo living in Phoenix in July, she didn't show it.

"May we have a word in private, Ben?" she said.

Now it was Ben's turn to raise an eyebrow toward Kravczyk. The big man nodded almost imperceptibly.

"Sure," Ben said.

Elyria swept a hand toward the neatly manicured grounds outside. "Please," she said, then gestured for Klaythron and the chief to remain in the gym.

Ben and Elyria walked side by side through the automatic double doors. He kept his eyes roaming around the perimeter of the grounds, acutely aware that now would be the perfect time for someone—or something—to take a shot at both a high councilor *and* the Terrans' secret weapon.

But it wasn't the threat of an assassin's bullet that had him on edge. He was acutely aware of what happened the last time the two of them were alone together. He was not only soaked in hormone-rich sweat from his workout, but the tweaks he and Mabel had made to his implants actually ramped up his hormone levels to take full advantage of his workouts—a fact Elyria was not aware of.

But thankfully, she didn't try to tackle him and tear off his clothes this time.

She led him to a bench in the shade of an awning and sat down. He sat next to her and waited for her to speak.

"This is… more difficult than I imagined it would be," she began after a moment, her gaze fixated on something in the distance. "For two years after the incident along the Tildar, I received intensive hormone therapy to manage my condition. I improved slowly, but eventually, I was able to function normally again." A sad smile crossed her face, and she turned to him.

"Normal, according to the doctors, that is. You see, I can do all the things a normal Alarian can do—I can go to social gatherings, serve on the council, and live my life. But I will never be able to bond with an Alarian mate. My body is incapable of accepting a new hormonal bond, due to a fluke of biology between two species that evolved thousands of light-years apart. But I don't blame you, Ben.

"Since you arrived, we haven't had the opportunity to discuss what happened, and I know you probably never received any information on my condition after you and your father were expelled in the aftermath. Then the war..." She trailed off and let her eyes roam over the grounds again. Ben waited. "I'm uncertain as to why I felt the need to tell you all of this. Perhaps, despite the best efforts of our best doctors, I still have some irresistible urge to be near you." She stood from the bench and faced him. "But that's not why I came here. I—"

"Elyria," Ben cut in, also standing up. "It's okay. Thank you for telling me that. I know it couldn't have been easy. And if I'm being honest, I've felt a little off my game, too. Like you said, I never learned what happened after we left, and I didn't know if we risked a repeat by having me in close proximity to you again. For that matter, I didn't know if we were good after what happened or if you'd have Captain Grumpypants in there just shoot me as soon as we landed. I just hope that we can work together from here on out, for the sake of both our races."

Elyria smiled and bowed her head slightly. "I would like nothing more, which brings me to the real reason I'm here: I think I know of a way we can break the stalemate with the councilors that oppose an alliance."

Ben's heart rate ticked up a notch, and he allowed his eyebrows to creep up ever so slightly. This was *exactly* the kind of thing he'd been hoping for to get things moving again. "Go on."

"I've had some of my aides digging through all the old procedural texts—most of which the refugee fleet carried with them after the Great Cataclysm—looking for anything that might force the other members of the High Council to agree to at least reestablish formal relations between our two governments. Many of my peers are close-minded. They refuse to believe the things we've been told about the Imperium and its AI agents. Personally, I think they are allowing their prejudices against the Terrans to blind them. They would rather hold onto the bitterness and anger they still harbor from the war, conveniently forgetting it was, in fact, *we* who started the war in the first place." She shook her head as if to clear the tangent she was on, then continued.

"There is an ancient rite dating back more than two thousand years. It is still technically on the books as an official procedure. When we settled here and the High Council established its new seat of power, they simply adopted the governing texts from our original homeworld, making only a few minor alterations to take into account things that occurred after our flight. The rite is referred to as a Trial of Worth and declares that anyone who performs an act that demonstrably assists the Alarian people in a tangible way shall be declared a friend of the Alarian people and granted any reasonable request made to the High Council in acknowledgment of their action. The wording is a little vague, but I think this is what we need."

Ben looked at her skeptically. "You really think the councilors who are against even talking to me will honor some ancient procedure that probably hasn't been dusted off in over two millennia?"

Elyria smiled, her large eyes sparkling. "Have you met my people? We literally worship the spirits of our ancestors and revere their ways. When we settled a new system thousands of light-years from our former home with a mere handful of survivors, we chose to reinstate everything about our former government, and there wasn't a single dissenting vote on the council. My father was considered a... What is the Terran term? Rabble-rouser? All because he wanted to collaborate with your father to further both our races' scientific knowledge and improve all our lives. That kind of thing wasn't done and couldn't be allowed. It's only because of his position on the High Council that you and your father were allowed to land on Hai'alla at all."

Ben wasn't quite buying it. "Uh-huh. Seems to me us swooping in and saving you from the Imperium attack should be more than enough to satisfy this rite. Can't we make it retroactive?"

Elyria shook her head. "No. Our adherence to tradition is a double-edged sword here. For the requirements of the rite to be satisfied, the Trial of Worth must be initiated first—it does not apply to actions already undertaken. Regardless, I am quite confident that the council will honor a Trial of Worth, and we only need two members to initiate it: someone to propose the trial and a second to confirm it.

"Fortunately for you, we already have two votes in favor. I will propose the trial during a special session today, and I've already discussed this with Councilor Daelin, the elder member who spoke with you briefly after our first meeting. He has promised his full support. With the two of us giving our blessing, there's nothing the rest of the council can do to stop it. Once you've performed an adequate task, you'll be able to request that all diplomatic contact with the Confederated Terran Systems be reinstated, with the express purpose of pursuing a formal alliance to combat the Imperium threat, and the council will be honor-bound to grant your request."

Ben let his gaze wander as he quickly mulled over the proposal. He liked the idea of being able to force the High

Council to the bargaining table, then turning the whole thing over to the people who actually knew what they were doing. Not that bunch of jackwagons from the DC back on *Indomitable*, but an honest-to-God team of senior negotiators from Icarus and Elizabeth. Ben suspected he already knew what task he would need to perform. He thought the attack on the council had rattled their cages more than they were letting on, and it only made sense they'd want to make sure they were free of any influence from the Imperium now.

He'd known for months that he and Mabel would have to find a way to take out the agent or at least clear the Hai'allan datanets of its presence and eliminate that threat for the Alarians. Collaboration between the Confed and the Alarians would've been impossible without both sides having secure networks. So this trial was actually a win-win, the more he thought about it. Still, his experience with the agent on Elizabeth was fresh in his mind, and he wasn't sure he and Mabel were ready for round two just yet… but it wasn't like the council was going to give him a choice.

Ben met Elyria's eyes. "Why does calling it a Trial of Worth make me feel like I'm going to be donning a suit of armor and taking on some mythical beast with a legendary weapon or some bullshit like that?"

Elyria didn't laugh. "I know you like to make jokes when you are uncomfortable or facing danger, Ben, but I fear that's *exactly* what you'll be doing."

Her read was dead-on. Ben's outwardly flippant attitude was a defense mechanism. He knew full well that he'd be going into battle in his armor, with Mabel riding shotgun in his head as they took on an enemy he wasn't sure they could defeat.

His mind turned to the people who would make sure he got there in one piece: Dominguez and the Pathfinders, the chief, Captain Ramsey, and all the spacers aboard *Indomitable*. The more he thought about it, the better he felt. He would be surrounded by the best humanity had to offer, and he was sure the Alarians wouldn't want to be left out.

Ben grimaced as a thought struck him. "You're going to make me take Klaythron with me on my team, aren't you?"

Elyria laughed. "He's really a nice guy, once you get to know him. And you couldn't ask for a more loyal friend."

Ben sighed. "Why not? What's one more borderline-unstable killing machine on the team? Maybe I'll have Mabel create some memes about us. The first one will say something like, 'A SEAR, a science experiment, and an Alarian walk into a bar...'"

27

NA'AL'S GAMBIT

"First Admiral, the Master's agent in Terran Space has sent a new directive for you. It is marked 'top priority.'"

Na'al frowned inwardly. Battlegroup 7 had only recently come out of its long slipspace journey midway between the system known to the Terrans as Valkyrie and the new Alarian home system. The agent had bases of operations in both systems, and the Terrans had recently destroyed the two remaining ships from the ill-fated Battlegroup 21—something that only strengthened Na'al's belief that the time for his people's salvation was at hand.

The Master's agent had lost control of the situation. It attempted to bring about the capture of Ben Hutchins without the proper support, and it failed spectacularly. Na'al was sure this newest directive from the agent would seek to have Battlegroup 7 come rescue it from a disaster of its own making.

"Very well," Na'al said. "Please send it to my station."

The message was short and to the point and contained exactly what Na'al expected to find. The agent wanted Battlegroup 7 to proceed to the Hai'allan system and destroy all resistance it encountered. Once he'd overseen the destruction of all military assets within the system, Na'al was to capture the Alarian High Council for interrogation about the locations of any remaining Alarian settlements, both old and new, that might not have been recorded. Na'al thought it unlikely that the Alarians would have any such settlements, but their High Council did have a tendency to pass certain information down verbally from councilor to councilor, so he supposed it was possible.

Interestingly, there was no mention of Ben Hutchins. Na'al wasn't sure if that was simply an oversight by the agent or if it was trying to keep its plans for the Terran out of the official record and therefore away from the Master's gaze. Very few individuals within the Imperium knew the Master and its agents didn't always see eye to eye, but Na'al had personally witnessed several occasions when it appeared an agent had its own agenda that it was trying to hide from the Master. Nothing that could ever be construed as treasonous, but actions such as these would certainly raise questions about the facade of unwavering loyalty to the Master among the ranks of its most trusted lieutenants. A facade Na'al intended to tear away very soon.

The supreme commander of the Imperial Navy acknowledged receipt of the directive, then destroyed the file. "Shipmaster, instruct the battlegroup to proceed into attack formation and prepare for a combat transition. I am updating the order of battle now, and we will depart for the Alarian home system as soon as the rest of our ships are in position and ready for combat."

Shipmaster Nox hesitated for just a fraction of a second before relaying Na'al's orders. Was he suspicious? Na'al studied his shipmaster carefully, looking for any sign that something was amiss, but he soon attributed the irregularity to excitement or anxiety about the upcoming engagement. The Terrans had managed to destroy an entire Imperium battlegroup, after all. Yes, Battlegroup 21 comprised vessels that were far from modern, but the news of the defeat still sent shock waves through the ranks of the Imperial Navy. For the first time in as long as Na'al could remember, faith in the unquestioned dominance of the Imperium was beginning to show some cracks around the edges.

Na'al felt fear as well, but for an entirely different reason. If he and his coconspirators failed, untold horrors would be visited upon any survivors. He quietly tapped out a series of commands on his terminal. One way or another, his centuries-long wait was about to end.

28

THE AGENT'S PLAYGROUND

THE BOARDING RAMP OF THE ALARIAN DROPSHIP BEGAN ITS SMOOTH descent, and Ben stepped forward. He paused at the top of the ramp and held up a hand to Klaythron and the rest of the Alarian commando team behind him. "Wait here. The chief and I will go down and make sure there aren't any misunderstandings with those knuckle-draggers down there." He inclined his head in the direction of a dozen of *Indomitable*'s embarked marine security detachment. All of them looked like they expected the flight deck to erupt into a warzone at any minute.

Kravczyk stepped around the group of Alarians, slapping Klaythron on the shoulder as he passed. "Don't worry, my cranky friend. We'll be back in a flash." The big SEAR nodded at Ben. "You first, kid."

Ben didn't wait for Klaythron to respond, turning and striding down the ramp like he owned the place. In reality, he wasn't nearly as confident as he hoped his body language said he was. The meeting with the council had gone just as Elyria said it would. There had been some angry shouting and a few wholly inappropriate epithets aimed squarely at Elyria and Daelin, but in the end, she'd been right; the council's hands were tied by their ridiculous adherence to antiquated traditions. He'd received their grudging approval, but only on the condition that a hand-picked team from the Council Guard accompanied him. He'd known Klaythron would be coming, but getting saddled with a total of six Alarians was kind of a hassle he hadn't planned on.

Ben's first order of business was to pick up Mabel, who was still aboard *Indomitable* in orbit over the planet, but the Alarians wouldn't let him head spaceside with any of the Pathfinders' people. As such, after *Indomitable* had been contacted and approved the request, he and his entourage were flown up in the Alarian equivalent of a Griffon dropship, called a Tykan. Now, he just needed to convince the space apes in front of him to not shoot the team of elite alien commandos he'd brought aboard the Confed's largest and most advanced mainline warship because they needed to perform a heroic task so said aliens' governing body would like them. Simple enough.

This crap was so much easier when I only had to worry about the chief looking over my shoulder.

Ben approached the marines with his faceplate set to transparent and smiled. "Howdy, boys! I don't suppose Captain Ramsey is hiding somewhere around here, is he?"

"He's not, but I am."

Ben's head whipped around. "Dad?"

His dad was standing off to the side, just beyond the safety zone marked in bright yellow paint on the deck around the parked dropship. Ben's mouth froze, halfway into forming his next word. Standing next to him was a rather attractive brunette who looked to be in her late thirties, her arm casually looped through his. The significance was not lost on Ben, and there was a brief battle in his brain between the *way to go, Dad!* side and the *let's take a moment to reflect on how we feel about our father dating someone other than Mom* side. On the one hand, it'd been fifteen years since his mom's passing, and he was glad to see that his dad had finally found someone that, judging by the smirk now permanently etched on his face, made him happy. On the other hand, it'd been just Ben and his dad for so long; this was going to throw a serious wrench into how their relationship worked. He was leaning toward siding with the *atta boy* half of his brain, but he didn't have time for this right now.

Ben shoved the thoughts aside for the moment and walked over to wrap his dad in a hug. The woman was either too awed or too terrified of the hulking APEX-armored figure to disengage from his dad, so she was caught up in the hug, too. Ben took care not to crush the two of them with his amplified strength—something that was generally considered a good way to make a poor first impression with a family member's new girlfriend.

"What the hell are you doing here? I thought you were back in Kerner, working on Q-link stuff," he said after releasing them from his bear hug. Then he raised an eyebrow at his dad and meaningfully shifted his eyes to the pretty lady on his father's arm. "And I need to hear all about *this*, but that can wait until later."

His dad blushed slightly. "*This* is a recent development. And we *were* working on the Q-link system back in Kerner, at least until you dropped your little project in my lap. That was taking up most of our time until Mabel went and broke a brand-new battlecruiser with her insane stunts... Seriously, I need to get her away from you and the SEARs—you're a bad influence on her. Anyway, Icarus needed someone to come out to try and fix *Indomitable*'s link system, and Shelly and I flew out with the repair crew to do that, since we're the experts on it at the moment. At least that's the excuse I gave to the brass. Really, I just wanted to get out here to deliver your prototype and make sure it integrates with your APEX properly. We didn't have time to run much testing on it."

Ben's eyes flew wide, and a jolt of excitement shot up his spine. "You actually built one?" he said, incredulous. "I can't believe you were able to get approval! Mabel estimated the cost of a single prototype at over eighteen million! How'd you swing that?"

His dad made a show of studying his fingernails for a moment. "I may have... *liberated* some funds from the Q-link research budget. After all, this project is basically an extension of the link research we were doing, anyway. If it works like you said in your note, then I think a little discretional spending can be overlooked."

Ben almost couldn't believe his good fortune, but then again, he was overdue for a lucky break. Having that prototype might just mean the difference between life and death for their upcoming mission. Well, in a manner of speaking, at least.

"We made a few tweaks to your design," his dad continued. "Shelly came up with a rather ingenious solution to the band-width problem... Well, it helps mitigate the issue, at least. It isn't completely solved yet. We figure a full engram will take some-where in the neighborhood of one or two minutes to be received. It's not great, but it's a significant improvement over the thirty-seven minutes of your original proposal."

"And it can be integrated into my existing armor?" Ben said, indicating the back of his APEX with a jerk of his thumb.

"Yes. It's ready to go, down in one of the engineering shops. Shouldn't take more than a couple hours to get it integrated and tested."

"Then what the hell are we waiting for? Let's go!"

When his dad leaned over slightly to look past him, Ben's excitement died down somewhat. Right, he still needed to deal with Klaythron and the rest of his team. "Let me take care of a few things first. I'll meet you down there as soon as I can. Just send me the frame and compartment number."

"Frame 182, compartment 12-C."

"One eighty-two, 12-Charlie," Ben said. "Got it. See you soon."

"Good luck... Is that Klaythron?"

Ben grimaced. "Yeah, and thanks. I'm going to need it."

His dad chuckled. "Didn't he say he'd kill you the next time he saw you?"

Ben didn't answer, instead turning and trudging back toward a visibly irritated Alarian commando standing at the top of the dropship's ramp.

"ALL RIGHT, THAT OUGHTA DO IT," his dad said, thumping Ben on the shoulder and taking a step back. "Go ahead and see if you can get your implant to initiate a handshake with the module."

Ben was standing next to a workbench in one of the auxiliary engineering workshops, decked out in his full combat kit. His dad and Shelly were doing the bulk of the work, but a few people from *Indomitable*'s engineering crew were also there. It hadn't taken long for him to see why his dad had apparently departed with his fifteen-year-long bachelor status. Shelly was quick-witted and funny, and her mild temperament and attention to small details and theoretical concepts dovetailed nicely with his dad's rougher, more hands-on approach to their work. They made a good pair, and Ben was finding it easier to deal with than he'd feared because Shelly, while a good fit for his dad, was different enough from his mom that it didn't feel like his dad was simply trying to find a replacement for her.

The bench next to him had a few small pieces of faring from the back panel on his armor. They'd been removed and replaced by the slightly bulkier module that contained a specialized Q-link unit inside a shock-absorbing armored housing. Other than the few pieces of armor and the fasteners that had been replaced, the workshop was spotless, being in the domain of the *Dame*'s perfectionist of a chief engineer, Commander Sexton.

"Initializing handshake now." Ben sent the mental command to his implant, instructing it to reach out and connect to the new hardware. A small, amber-colored icon began flashing in the middle of his HUD, informing him that the implant was searching for the link module. After a few seconds, the icon changed to a flashing green, and a progress bar overlaid his HUD and began slowly filling in from left to right. The words *Updating Engram Record* pulsed above the status bar, almost like his suit was breathing the data in and out.

The prototype quantum link module they'd just integrated into Ben's APEX armor would, in theory, periodically transmit a complete neural engram that would be backed up in the event he ended up doing something stupid and getting himself killed. His runaway implant had created a complete copy of his nervous system, and it was dynamic, constantly updating itself to match the ever-changing biological memory of his brain. The implant could also monitor the biochemical conditions within his brain, meaning it was, theoretically, capable of compiling a snapshot of his consciousness and creating a digital backup. The hard part was trying to figure out how to use that snapshot to clone or construct a brain with the same memory engram... but that was for someone smarter than Ben to figure out.

He just wanted to have a copy of himself somewhere, so if the worst were to happen, all wouldn't necessarily be lost. When his unique condition became known after the Battle of Icarus, there was some conversation about whether what happened to him could be replicated by intentionally designing the implants to do what his damaged one had done by accident, but it was deemed too risky. Hell, he'd been told by just about every expert in the field that they couldn't believe he wasn't a vegetable after his first implant went haywire. Someday, they might just create a system that would allow adult volunteers to gain the abilities Ben had acquired by accident, but with the Imperium bearing down on them, they had bigger things to worry about at the moment.

Ben flashed a thumbs-up. "And... we're good. System is green and it's updating. How do things look on your end?"

His dad scrolled through a few menus on a datapad that looked like it'd seen better days. "I show a connection via the Q-link, but no files uploaded yet. That's to be expected, though. The module will compile the engram before compressing and encrypting the data. Only after it has a finished backup ready to go will it begin transmitting. The bandwidth of the link is still too limited to update in real time, so it sends everything in compressed packets once it's ready to go. We won't know whether this will even work or not until after your armor has created the engram and transmitted the file. Like I said, we didn't have time to get all the bugs worked out back in Kerner."

"Nothing like a little on-the-job development," Ben said. "Still, I'm glad you were able to get as much done as you did. Better to have it and not need it and all that."

"We still don't have a workable solution for what to do with the engram if we ever *were* to need it, Ben. Try to keep that in mind when you're chasing willy-nilly after an advanced alien AI that wants you dead."

"No promises," Ben said absently, his attention drawn to an incoming call from Mabel. She'd been working with Klaythron and the chief to locate a suitable starting point for their search for the agent. With a thought, he opened the channel and piped it through his armor's external speakers so everyone present could hear. "Go ahead, Mabel."

"I believe I have a suitable location to begin our search for the agent and its transceiver on Hai'alla, Ben."

Ben's heart rate began to climb, and a low-level tingle spread outward from his gut. He'd been expecting her to call with this news, but hearing her voice it out loud somehow made it "real" to him. They were doing it; they were going after the agent. "What've you got?"

"The Alarians rely much more on integrated technology than we ever have. There's a large datacenter that utilizes a governing AI to control both the planetary datanets that are used for civilian and military purposes. The civilian side is also responsible for coordinating their emergency services. I believe you are familiar with that system, no?"

"Uh, yeah. I contacted Hai'allan emergency services when my dad and I were here five years ago, when the incident with Elyria happened. You're telling me the AI I talked to then wasn't just a local dispatcher but a planetary coordinator?"

"Exactly. When the Alarians settled Hai'alla, they were already a technologically advanced species, and they integrated a distributed network into everything they constructed. Every building, from the smallest cottage to the largest skyscraper, is on the network. The same goes for all of their military facilities on the planet and even the orbital constructs over the planet."

The butterflies in Ben's gut morphed into a black hole that felt like it was devouring his insides, and judging by the faces of his dad and Shelly, he wasn't the only one feeling that way. The whole damn planet was practically purpose-built as a giant playground for an entity like the agent. It was no wonder it had been able to so effectively whip the Alarians into a frenzy and push them into war—literally everything around them could be used for the agent's purposes. And to think their milnet was on the same distributed network? It was no wonder the Alarian response to the Imperium showing up in orbit was nonexistent.

Ben winced. "Please tell me it's not as bad as I think it is, Mabel."

"It's likely both as bad as you think it is and also good for us," she said. "The agent has almost certainly been operating freely among the Alarians for decades, but the nature of the Alarian datanets means we only need to go to the central data-processing complex to search the entire planet for our quarry. We'll need to be careful, though, and be on the lookout for traps similar to the one we encountered on Elizabeth."

Ben blew out an explosive breath. "What does Klaythron have to say about us getting access to the facility in question?"

"He can get us access. The datacenter is largely automated and only employs a small team of Alarian technicians. Security is handled by a platoon-sized contingent of Alarian security forces, along with several dozen armed, autonomous combat drones that are managed by the controlling AI."

Ben dropped his chin to his chest in defeat. Armed robots controlled by an AI, because what could possibly go wrong with that? For fuck's sake, it was like the Alarians *intentionally* set the place up to be taken over by the agent…

Son of a bitch. "Mabel, what do you think the odds are that the agent had a hand in the design and construction of the facility and the associated networks? We know it was present on the refugee fleet when they got here to settle the planet. I can't think of a better way to ensure you'd be prepared to wipe out the Alarians when the rest of the Imperium showed up than to have your target build a system that was tailor-made for that purpose."

There was a long pause. Then Klaythron's voice came over the channel. "I don't know all the details regarding the system's construction, but I do know that nothing like this existed on our original worlds, which was a point of contention among those responsible for planning the construction of our new society. The proposal was eventually adopted, with several of the dissenters changing their position on the matter rather suddenly."

"Well, I think that answers that," Ben said. "Mabel, Klaythron, how do you think we should proceed?"

"The combat drones controlled by the AI are formidable," Klaythron said, "but they can be taken down with concentrated small arms fire. They are intended as a force multiplier for the security detachment on-site, not as a standalone force. Unfortunately, we don't have any way to warn the security forces beforehand without the agent being able to intercept the communication. My suggestion would be to treat the facility as hostile and assault it with a combined force of both ground and air elements. We must treat it as a hardened target, not as a friendly facility."

"And how do we put together an assault force without alerting the agent?" Ben said. Their objective was so simple—get inside a building on a friendly planet, with the help of the people who run it—but the nature of their adversary made it damn near impossible to approach within a hundred kilometers without letting the agent know they were coming. "All the Pathfinders are on an Alarian base, which is monitored. All of your military personnel operate off of a network the agent has free run of. *Indomitable* doesn't have any dropships left after deploying all of the Pathfinders. So we're left with just us and the Tykan we borrowed from your people to get up here."

Mabel jumped into the conversation again. "I believe I have a solution to that problem, Ben, but we still won't have the element of surprise for long."

Ben raised an eyebrow and exchanged a look with his dad.

"Hit me with it."

29

GETTING THE BAND BACK TOGETHER

Ben looked around the flight line at the four Terran dropships preparing to take off and return to *Indomitable* with the Pathfinders. Or at least that was what they'd been told.

After Ben, Kravczyk, and Klaythron's team boarded the Alarian dropship and returned to the planet, they went to work. Ben and the chief sought out Major Davis and Captain Kaneda, as well as the COs of all three Pathfinder platoons. After some hushed conversation outside, away from any eyes and ears that might be keeping tabs on them, Ben laid out the plan. They would have to improvise a bit once the shooting started, but they couldn't risk alerting the agent to their true intentions any sooner than absolutely necessary.

Klaythron had gone straight to the base commander and informed him the Terrans were to be released immediately and returned to their ship. The captain of the Council Guard had been given the authority to act on the council's behalf during his attachment to Ben for the Trial of Worth, and the base commander hadn't even tried to object. Why would he? The Pathfinders and their ships had been occupying a huge section of his facility for more than two weeks, and housing and feeding the Terrans was a major headache.

Less than an hour after Klaythron gave the order, the marines were filing into their ships after having all of their weapons and equipment returned. In other words, Ben now had a company of Pathfinders loaded up on dropships, armed to the teeth and ornery as hell after being held against their will for a couple of weeks. He was confident they'd be more than eager to go storm a high-security facility and blow some shit up once their COs broke the news to them shortly after takeoff.

A part of him wished they'd been able to find some way to have a detachment of Alarian ground combat specialists in on this op. Unfortunately, with the agent likely in control of virtually every civilian and military network, there was just no way to let the Alarians know what they were up to without risking exposing their plan to the agent ahead of time. Even as it was, Ben wasn't naive enough to think they'd be able to catch the agent completely by surprise. He just hoped they weren't walking into a trap like back on Elizabeth.

"Let's go, Ben." Kravczyk thumped his shoulder with one of the giant meat hooks the SEAR called hands. "The marines are ready to go, and we're the last ones on the tarmac."

Ben turned to the big man, and the two exchanged a long look. Kravczyk's tone of voice said this was just another day at the office, but his eyes said something else. Ben searched his friend's face, looking for reassurance that would help tamp down the rising sense of dread he'd been feeling since shortly after they'd departed *Indomitable*, but all he saw was the same apprehension that currently gripped him. There was just something in the air—some intangible thing that had the little voice in the back of his head screaming for them to abort. But they were stuck; the High Council wasn't going to budge unless he completed their stupid trial, and this was the only task that would be big enough to get them off their biased asses and make them open their eyes to the truth.

Finally, Ben spoke. "How do you do it, Chief? How do you work up the guts to run right at the devil himself, knowing the odds are good you won't be coming back?"

Kravczyk chewed on his lower lip for a minute while his eyes wandered the flight line. "You do it because you have to, because if you don't, it means someone else—one of your brothers—will have to do it in your place. We do what we do so those we care about back home don't have to deal with the horrible shit we see. None of that noble bullshit you see on the streams about doing it for the glory of the Confed or to be the shining light of justice, blah blah blah. Fuck that recruiting poster bullshit. The shine wears off it the first time you dive into a foxhole and stick your hand into the pile of goo that used to be your buddy's face.

"No, we do this to protect the ones we love, pure and simple. Because if I can die to ensure that one of my family—you, the boss, McCollum, or, hell, even one of those space apes back there —gets to live another day, then it'll be worth it."

Ben stood there for a few more seconds, thinking about what his friend—his brother—just said. He wasn't so sure he and Kravczyk had the same definition of "noble." As far as Ben was concerned, sacrificing for the ones you loved was about as noble as it could get, but he thought he understood the chief's meaning.

Ben lightly tapped on the big SEAR's chest plate with his knuckles and inclined his head toward the waiting Griffon. "Come on, Chief. Let's go kick some ass."

———

"HENRY!"

Henry turned toward the hatch. The alarm in Shelly's voice

made him suddenly forget the pile of burnt-out circuit boards he'd been performing a post-mortem on. She was standing just outside the hatch to the small engineering office he'd been given the use of while working to repair *Indomitable*'s Q-link system. His eyes locked onto the tablet she was holding out to him.

"What's wrong?" he said, leaning over and taking the proffered tablet. The desk he was working at in the cramped space was only an arms-length from the hatch. He scanned the data displayed on the datapad.

"The file from Ben's engram backup module finally came through. I've spent the last hour with it, but as far as I can tell, there's a problem with the software somewhere—the file was corrupted. I don't know if the problem is with the encryption, the compression algorithm, or the quick and dirty program we slapped together to read it. Regardless of which it is, the system won't work as is."

Henry's hands flew across the tablet. Shelly was right; the file with Ben's engram was there and appeared to have data contained within, but every time he tried to decrypt and unpack it, the result was nothing but gibberish. If, God forbid, they lost Ben today, there would be no Hail Mary option available to bring him back. He'd be lost forever.

A sinking feeling settled into Henry's gut. Years of working in technological R&D had taught him to expect these kinds of teething problems from prototypes like this. Still, they'd used much of the same technology and software that had been developed for the Q-link system, with only some minor tweaks to better fit their needs, and he'd really thought it would work. Now, the hope he'd secretly harbored—the thing that let him grudgingly give his blessing to Ben and Klaythron's insane plan —evaporated in a horrifying instant.

He realized now that his desire to help protect Ben had probably blinded him to the reality of what they were trying to do, and he shouldn't have let himself get so hopeful. If he'd been more realistic from the start, he would've either held off on implementing the system until they could trial it properly or done a better job stressing to Ben that he couldn't rely on the system. Ben said all the right things about being careful, but Henry knew his son too well to believe he wouldn't take some extra risks, thinking he had a viable backup plan in place.

He looked back up at Shelly. "What's the status on the assault?"

Henry had locked himself in this dinky workspace and thrown himself into the Q-link repair as a means of taking his mind off the danger his son was running headlong toward at that very moment. Ben and the marines were attempting to take a secure Alarian facility and make sure the Hai'allan datanet was cleared of Imperium malcode. Henry couldn't go with his son, nor could he do anything to help the mission succeed from up here. There was nothing to do but wait for the operation to be over... and it was the worst form of torture he'd experienced since that fateful day he'd packed Ben aboard an evac shuttle at the outset of the Alarian War.

Shelly's ashen face told him the news was bad. "We lost contact soon after they hit the ground, but the scopes show they ran into heavy resistance almost immediately. Captain Ramsey informed the Alarians about the operation, and we have satellite coverage of the datacenter, but all comms are being jammed. There's no way to let Ben know the system doesn't work."

The room began to spin around Henry, and the air was suddenly heavy and oppressive. The dread he'd been trying so hard to push to the back of his mind and ignore was now hammering at the edges of his consciousness. He took a deep breath. There was nothing they could do for the moment. He just had to have faith that Chief Kravczyk and the Pathfinders would keep his son safe.

Shelly reached down and placed a hand on his shoulder, squeezing lightly. "It'll be okay, Henry. He's surrounded by the best in the business."

Henry offered her a wan smile. "It's not the people around him I'm worried about, Shelly. Ben has a terrible habit of doing whatever it takes to accomplish his goal, doubly so if he thinks it can save his friends. I know the marines and Chief Kravczyk can keep the Imperium away from Ben, but I'm less confident they can keep Ben away from the Imperium."

———

TESS SAT on the bunk in her small sleeping compartment aboard CIS *Wraith* and shoved the last of her toiletries into her seabag. They'd transitioned into the Alarian home system a few hours ago, and the *Wraith* had been instructed to form up with *Indomitable* and the handful of Alarian warships that were "escorting" the big Terran battlecruiser as it did laps around Hai'alla. She stood up, slung the heavy canvas bag over one shoulder, and walked out to meet Valdez in the SOCOM detachment's squad bay.

"Sir," she said, nodding in greeting to Valdez, who was sitting at one of the card tables and sipping a steaming mug of coffee with his own seabag plopped down onto a chair next to him.

"McCollum," he said, returning her nod. "Take a seat. We're on hold for about an hour before we can transfer over to *Indomitable*. Collins said there's a flight of ships coming up from the planet carrying the Pathfinders, and *Indomitable* will be recovering those birds first, before we ship over with our gear."

Tess slipped the heavy bag from her shoulder and leaned it up against the bulkhead, then slid onto one of the benches bolted to the deck next to the table. "That sounds about right. Hurry up and wait—that should be the official motto of the Confed armed forces." She shot Valdez a bemused smile and indicated the mug of coffee cradled in his hands. "You do know it's like 1900 ship's time, right?"

Valdez let out an annoyed grunt. "Ugh. I'm still on Thunder's time. As far as I'm concerned, it's 0430. And you'll find the older you get, the more frequently your body gives you the finger when you throw curveballs at it."

Tess's polite laugh was cut off by the combat action alarm. "Combat stations, combat stations! All hands, combat stations! Set condition one throughout the ship!"

The two SEARs exchanged glances for a moment. Then both sprinted toward the exit hatch. Tess followed Valdez through cramped passages and down a ladder before they sprinted out into the *Wraith*'s hangar bay and toward the Griffon dropship that was supposed to shuttle them over to *Indomitable*. Their APEX armor and personal weapons were already secured in transit crates aboard the craft, so they ran up the open tail ramp and into the cargo bay.

"Get the small arms crate open. I'll work on getting our armor out," Valdez said, popping the quick releases on the mag straps that secured the bulky crates to the deck.

Talk about terrible timing. All their gear was packed up and securely lashed to the deck of the dropship, and Tess was acutely aware of just how vulnerable she was in nothing more than her flimsy CDUs. While it wouldn't do her much good in a fleet engagement, the reassuring weight of a carbine in her hands or the awesome power of her APEX just waiting for her to call it into service did wonders for her state of mind. She released the tie-downs from the weapons crate, then let the built-in biometric lock confirm her identity and release the internal locking bolts. Tess threw open the case and began pulling their weapons from the padded crate, laying them out in an orderly arrangement on the deck.

It took another five minutes before both SEARs were sealed up in their armor and ready for a fight. Valdez flashed a thumbs-up at Tess. "Good to go?"

She nodded. "Probably about time we let the bridge know where we are and get a status update. I don't hear any shooting going on, so that's probably a good thing, right?"

Valdez reported in to the ops officer on the bridge, then spent a couple of minutes in conversation with someone. Meanwhile, Tess worked on stowing the now-empty transit crates and reattaching the tie-downs to the deck. In the event this was just the calm before the storm and things were about to get wild, it wouldn't do to have man-sized crates tumbling about the cargo bay.

Valdez let out a heavy sigh, and Tess knew before he even said anything that this was all Ben's fault. "What did he do this time?"

"He's assaulting an Alarian datacenter with an entire company of Pathfinders, Chief Kravczyk, Mabel, and an Alarian commando team from the Council Guard. The Alarians are throwing an absolute shit fit. Half of them want to blow our guys out of the sky. The other half seem to think they should join them.

"Apparently Ben and Mabel are going after the agent, and they're convinced it's got a base of operations at this datacenter. I didn't get all the details, but the place was only supposed to be defended by a small detachment of Alarian security forces and a few dozen combat drones. Instead, they're doing a reenactment of D-Day down there. Turns out the Imperium must have snuck in a bunch of troops during the chaos of the attack on the council, and they're dug in like ticks. The marines are taking casualties and their assault has bogged down. The Alarian response is in chaos, probably thanks to the agent, and it's taking forever for them to get organized and get their people moving."

"When do we drop?" Tess said. Her heart was in her throat. It was one thing to believe the ship you were on was coming under attack; that was something she was trained for and had experienced on several occasions. It was always an adrenaline rush, having the bad guys shooting at you, but learning Ben was now smack in the middle of the hornet's nest, without proper backup, was one of the most terrifying things she'd ever experienced. She needed to get down there.

"Flight ops is scrambling a crew to ferry us down. Fortunately, this bird is already prepped and ready to fly. Strap in. They'll be here soon."

Tess did a quick sweep to make sure she hadn't missed anything when she cleaned up and secured the crates again, then strapped herself into a sling seat opposite Valdez. She should've been nervous, but she was still riding the adrenaline high from having her routine transfer to another ship suddenly change into a combat drop. The Imperium shock troops were tough, but they weren't invincible. Tess took some comfort in knowing that Ben had the chief and an entire company of Pathfinders backing him up. For all the crap she gave the marines, they were still a fearsome group of steely-eyed murder machines. She didn't doubt they were more than capable of getting Ben and Mabel to their objective… but it never hurt to lend a hand and make sure things got done right.

Without a word, the pilots who flight ops had scrambled sprinted up the ramp, past the SEARs and into the cockpit. The Griffon's crew chief slapped the control to raise the ramp, then did a quick check of the cargo, called up to the cockpit with the all-clear for departure, and strapped herself in at her station near the ramp controls. Tess recognized the woman from the last time she'd been aboard the *Wraith*.

"Why is it every time you SEARs are here, we end up duking it out with genocidal aliens that are hell-bent on our destruction?" the woman said.

"Don't look at me," Valdez said, and he pointed an accusing finger at Tess. "It's her boyfriend who's starting these fights."

30

HUNTING THE BOOGEYMAN

BEN STOOD WITH HIS TOES JUST BEHIND THE YELLOW SAFETY LINE painted on the Griffon's deck at the top of the tail ramp. One hand was firmly locked onto one of the handholds just above head level while the other rested lightly on the pistol grip of his rifle, which was cinched in tight against his chest, muzzle down. Highlighted by the golden light of the setting star, a lush, green forest blurred by less than a hundred meters below their feet. The verdant carpet was only occasionally broken by a paved road or the small spring-fed lakes that dotted the area around their target. Wind gusted in and swirled around his armor, but he remained firmly rooted in place next to the ship's crew chief, who was nervously fingering the quick-release latch that secured his M266 in its cradle.

They were less than thirty seconds from the datacenter.

"Banshee-2 is wheels-down. No resistance… yet."

"Banshee-4 is wheels-down. Marines are on their way out."

The calls from the other dropships in Banshee Flight came in rapid succession. Ben's assigned ship, Banshee-1, was trailing the other ships in the flight by thirty seconds. If the agent had a surprise waiting for them, his ship would abort the landing and then either offer fire support or bug out entirely. So far, however, it was all quiet on the Western Front.

And that was what had his guts twisted into knots.

Whether they would find the agent here or not wasn't even a question in his mind. He knew it just like he knew planets orbited stars and you didn't want to take your helmet off when surrounded by vacuum. So then why was the agent allowing a stream of dropships carrying more than a hundred Terrans, all armed to the teeth and hellbent on its destruction, to just waltz right in like they owned the place?

Ben glanced at a status indicator in the corner of his HUD; it represented the overall condition of his entire team—him and the chief, Klaythron, Butler and First Squad, and Mabel. Klaythron's marker, in particular, held his attention for an extended moment. The Alarian commando was carrying their insurance policy: a tactical nuke that would vaporize the entire facility, should they fail in their primary mission to capture it and deal with the agent and/or its minder AIs. Kravczyk had argued he should be the one carrying the nuke, as it was a Terran weapon and designed to integrate with his APEX's systems, but the captain of the Council Guard would have none of it. In the end, it was Captain Ramsey who made the call. It was an Alarian facility they were assaulting; therefore, it was proper for an Alarian to carry the bomb that would destroy it.

Ben's mind shifted to Mabel. With a thought, he expanded her indicator out from the team icon. It remained grayed-out, indicating she was completely inactive—a condition she would remain in until they were in the central data-processing hub and ready to go after the agent. It was her idea, and Ben absolutely hated it. In the end, though, he didn't really have a choice; she was her own person and would do whatever the hell she wanted. The fact that she made some good points when she brought up the proposal didn't matter, as far as he was concerned. Sure, when she was on board his APEX and active, he supposed it was possible the agent might be able to detect her somehow.

Still, he felt woefully unprepared without her, left to rely on nothing more than his own brainpower and skill until they'd battled their way to the objective: the nerve center of the data-processing hub. But until they got there and were ready to shine a light in all the deep, dark corners of the ether, Mabel might as well have not even existed.

Ben shook his head in an attempt to bury his misgivings about her absence, then watched the last Condor begin clawing its way back into the sky. The wash from the big dropship's powerful engines sent frantic ripples across the wide-open lawn that ringed the main complex. Second Platoon was advancing on the heart of the complex at a dead run. In the distance, a series of low, brilliant white buildings encircled the massive central processing hub. Even though he couldn't see them, Ben knew Third Platoon was running toward its objective on the other side of the facility.

They'd been forced to land about three-quarters of a kilometer away from the outer edge of the complex. Klaythron had explained that the area over the site was a no-fly zone, thanks to the unholy amount of electromagnetic radiation those comms dishes put out. He didn't know all the specs on the installation and those dishes, but nobody had wanted to risk landing any closer, lest the emissions interfere with the dropships' avionics. Supposedly, they only needed to worry about being cooked if they were more than fifty meters or so off the ground, but Ben intended to keep his head as low as possible while they were here.

The whole complex was much larger than he'd envisioned after Klaythron gave them the rundown on it. Two dozen buildings spread out before them, arranged in concentric rings around the stadium-sized central building—their objective. At the heart of the layout were five huge comms dishes arranged in a pentagon on the roof of the central structure. And somewhere in that cluster of buildings, the agent and its minions were likely waiting for them. There was no way it didn't know Ben and the marines were knocking on the door. Even if they'd successfully avoided suspicion about the marines departing Alarian custody, the jig was up as soon as their flight of dropships broke from their declared flight plan and made a beeline toward the data-routing complex.

"Banshee-1, Python 2-1. LZ secure. You're clear for wheels down. Over."

"Copy, Python 2-1. Banshee-1 is inbound. Heads down."

Python was the callsign for the Pathfinders on this op. The modifier "2-1" designated the caller as being from First Squad in Second Platoon, which was being deployed on the opposite side of the complex from all of Third Platoon and 1-2, the other surviving squad from First Platoon. Currently, 1-1 was strapped into their seats behind Ben in Banshee-1, assigned to him as his personal bodyguard squad.

It was the signal Ben's ship had been waiting for. He shifted his footing slightly as the Griffon banked out of its wide orbit and powered toward the waiting group of Pathfinders, who would already be advancing on the main facility. Kravczyk, who was standing immediately behind Ben, placed a firm hand on his left shoulder. Klaythron was next in line, followed by the marines.

The rest of Klaythron's team—designated "Talon"—rode in aboard Third Platoon's Condor, tasked with clearing the barracks for the datacenter's security detachment. They were to break away from the marines as soon as they were on the ground, using their own version of powered armor to cover the kilometer-plus distance from Third Platoon's LZ to their objective in short order.

According to Klaythron, the bulk of the security detachment would be located in a separate structure away from the main complex, and at any given point in time, only a few of them would be on duty in the security center located within the central processing hub. Evidently, a posting to the central data-processing center was highly coveted, as it essentially amounted to a vacation. Talon needed to make contact, tell the security detachment what was up, and hopefully enlist their help—or at least get them to stay out of the way.

Ben heard the rest of First Squad shuffling as they lined up behind the big SEAR and their Alarian minder. Ben suspected they were all just as nervous as him—how could they not be? They were executing a surprise raid on a critical Alarian asset with practically zero intel on what they would face when they hit the ground. Regardless, he was going to be the first one out, which meant his exit from the dropship would set the tone for the rest of his team. He pushed everything from the forefront of his mind, except for the one thing he had to do now.

The Griffon flared for landing, and the wheels thumped into the soft earth.

"Go, go, go!" the crew chief shouted, motioning for his charges to get the hell off his ship like their lives depended on it.

Ben charged down the ramp, and a dozen pairs of boots thundered right behind him. He sprinted, the awesome power of his APEX armor accelerating him to over forty kilometers per hour in the blink of an eye. Kravczyk was right there next to him as their boots flung clumps of grass and Hai'allan soil back toward the un-augmented marines who'd been left in their dust, both proverbially and literally. The two men ate up the seven hundred meters that separated them from their objective in just over a minute, running under the shadow of the nearest building mere seconds after the first wave of Pathfinders from Second Platoon.

First and Third Squads from Second Platoon split off from the main group, each element advancing down a different side of the building. Ben and the rest of the team were to wait here while they cleared the immediate area. Then he would advance to their position and they would repeat the maneuver all over again—like an inchworm working its way into a bramble patch. The marines were all breathing hard, having just sprinted the better part of a kilometer in full combat kit, but Ben's breathing came deep and easy, thanks to his armor's pseudo-muscle layer taking much of the effort out of the sprint. One of the marines turned and pointed a shaky finger at Ben's chest.

"When we're done here, you're letting me take that armor for a joyride, Ben. You owe me at least that much after making my ass sprint all the way over here carrying forty kilos of kit."

Ben chuckled, and another marine a few places down the wall chimed in before he could return fire. "Dominguez, if you spent less time playing with yourself in the head and more time in the gym with the rest of us, you wouldn't be such a pansy-ass!"

"And if you'd stop blue-balling me, Ybarra, I wouldn't need all that time in the head," Dominguez fired back, voice dripping with indignation. "You holding out on me like that makes me less effective as a warfighter, which means the whole squad suffers for it. So do the right thing and join me in my bunk when we get back to the *Dame*. I'll even try to scrounge up some champagne and candles, so we'll have a nice ambience going."

There were some laughs and catcalls at the exchange, but a call from the advancing element shut them all up.

"Warlock is clear to advance to waypoint foxtrot."

"Foxtrot" was the last intersection between buildings before the alleys to either side joined up with the main road that ran around the central processing hub. The marines were making great time, which meant they had yet to encounter anyone or anything as they cleared the path. The unease in Ben's gut ratcheted up a couple of notches. While the complex was largely automated, there were still supposed to be *some* people on staff at all times, and Ben wasn't buying the idea they'd not noticed a half dozen war machines screaming in like a pack of rabid banshees a few minutes ago. To his mind, it was now a certainty they were about to run into something terrible in short order. *Dammit, I wish Mabel was here to give us a read on things...*

Butler and his squad from First Platoon arrived just as Ben and the rest of Second Platoon were stacking up at the corner of the building as they prepared to move. They'd known Ben and Kravczyk would leave the marines they rode in with behind as soon as their boots hit the ground. The landings had been staggered such that Ben, Kravczyk, and Klaythron, in their powered armor, would have at least a squad of marines around them no matter where they were, except for the short time it took them to run across the open field. Butler and his marines were supposed to take over for Dominguez's squad, which would then advance with the rest of Second Platoon, but their rapid progress had thrown their timing off.

Kravczyk saw the issue, too, and he quickly called an audible. "Sergeant, you and your squad take a minute to catch your breath. We'll stick with Second a little longer. You can advance and join us at foxtrot as soon as you're ready."

Butler, whose chest was heaving from the exertion, just nodded his reply. Ben was actually impressed; Butler and his squad had covered the distance faster than any of the other Pathfinder squads, probably because their competitive nature couldn't stand seeing Ben and the chief pull away from them like they were standing still. It would be best to let them take a moment to recover before needing them to be on their A game as they continued to advance toward the datacenter. As if to reinforce his belief, Giddings leaned over and vomited.

"Let's go, Ben," Kravczyk said, signaling 2-2's squad leader to move out.

Ben followed the marines, his rifle tucked into the pocket of his shoulder, muzzle sweeping every nook and cranny along their path as they passed. The buildings to either side of him were standard industrial fare—a lightweight metal skin broken occasionally by utilities boxes and maybe a door or two, but not much else. The gravel road under his feet was graded smooth and well-maintained. They moved swiftly, the crunch of gravel the only sound in the eerily quiet complex.

Just ahead, 2-1 was pressed up against the sides of the buildings at the intersection with the main road. Ben, Kravczyk, and 2-2 slowed to a stop and joined them, doing their best to meld into the shadows as night descended rapidly over the area. Ben checked his tacmap and noted that 2-4 had joined 2-3 in position on the other side of the building, also ready to move.

This next bit was the tricky part. The marines would break from cover and cross the wide-open road that ringed the central processing hub. A three-meter-high flashcrete retaining wall surrounded the building. There were only a few entrances to the circular structure, and naturally, none of them lined up well with any of the alleys Ben and the Pathfinders would be coming in from. They would need to exit the alley, run about a hundred meters down the road to their right with zero available cover, then make their way around to one of the large cutouts in the retaining wall with steps that led up to the building's main entrance. Once on the terrace level near the main entrance, they'd have to cross about twenty meters of open space between the steps and the front doors. Banshee flight was still orbiting the complex, but the tacmap remained barren, save for the blue dots representing friendly forces.

At the end of the alley, 2-1 stacked up, and 2-2 moved in behind to offer cover. Ben and Kravczyk hunkered down behind them all, keeping an eye on their rear. A tingling sensation started in Ben's fingers and toes and worked its way toward his core. It was similar to what he felt when he got an adrenaline dump, but he didn't think that was what this was. The company channel crackled to life, and one of Klaythron's commandos broke in with a report from the security forces' barracks.

"This is Talon leader." The heavily encrypted signal, combined with the real-time translation from his comms kit, made the words sound tinny and a little stilted. "We have cleared the security detachment barracks—all members of the detachment have been accounted for... They're all dead and appear to have been so for a couple of weeks. All of them were killed by—"

Ben, Kravczyk, and every marine simultaneously grabbed at the sides of their heads as a piercing, almost shriek-like static assaulted their ears. Ben squinted in agony, quickly sending a mental command through his implant to kill his entire comms suite. The noise cut off abruptly, but his ears were still ringing.

"We're being jammed!" one of the marines shouted.

"I fucking knew it was too good to be true!" another—Ben thought it might be Dominguez—said. "Jig's up now, boys and girls. Shit's about to go down! My spidey sense says so." Yep, definitely Dominguez.

"He's right, marines!" Kravczyk called out. "Let's move! We can reassess once we're in the building!"

They moved out, crossing the street and angling to the right. They hugged the retaining wall as they ran, rifles constantly sweeping their surroundings, their heads on swivels. Ben and the chief followed, and Butler and his squad were hauling ass up the alley right behind them, obviously having come to the same conclusion.

The only sound that echoed around the deserted complex was the thundering of fifty pairs of boots on the pavement, sandwiched between a three-meter retaining wall and the almost featureless faces of the industrial buildings that sat opposite it. That little voice in the back of Ben's head, the one that warned him of danger, was going absolutely apeshit. It was like this entire complex was set up to be one giant kill zone. Sure, on the surface it seemed to fit with the Alarian proclivity to build even their utility structures in some sort of visually pleasing manner —the graceful, geometric arrangement of the structures in the complex certainly wasn't an eyesore—but this place was a death trap. The Pathfinders had been clearing the warehouses and other buildings as they worked their way steadily closer to the central processing building, but there were still an awful lot of places a couple dozen drones could pop out of to ruin their day.

The first two members of 2-1 reached the corner of the retaining wall, where it gave way to a wide set of steps that led up to the main entrance of the central building. There they stacked up, waiting for the rest of their squad to catch up and prepare to rush up the steps. When the jamming hit, Third Platoon had been in roughly the same position on the other side of the facility as Ben and his escorts, and he figured they would be about ready to breach the shipping and receiving bays. Ideally, both elements would breach at the same time. Third Platoon and 1-2 would enter at the back and go for some of the critical utilities and other systems that allowed the complex to run, while Ben's group would go in the front door, which was much closer to the facility's nerve center, where he and Mabel could jack in.

The chief was just coming up to the marines at the corner when they broke from cover and rushed up the steps. Kravczyk put out a hand to stop Ben at the corner of the retaining wall, waiting for the all-clear from 2-1. Ben slid to a stop next to the big SEAR and dropped into a crouch, keeping his XM93 trained toward the nearest alley just in case those drones decided to make an appearance.

"This facility is always sparsely populated," Klaythron said from his position behind Ben, where he was also watching for trouble. "But the fact that we have not encountered anyone or anything else portends a trap of some sort."

"Yeah, you're not telling me anything I don't already know. But we're committed now," Ben said. "At least we probably don't have to worry about it being a bomb like we ran into back on Elizabeth."

"How do you figure?" Kravczyk said, pulling his head back around the corner from where he'd been trying to keep an eye on 2-1 as they breached the front doors and swept the lobby of the complex.

"We know the agent wants me dead," Ben said. "If it had a nuke tucked in a closet somewhere for a rainy day, it could have blown it by now and taken all of us out. But it hasn't, which means one of two things: either we're wrong and the agent isn't here or..." Ben trailed off as a sound like distant thunder echoed between the buildings and the retaining wall, sweeping its way around the main building. The rapid staccato of gunfire followed a heartbeat later.

"Sounds like Third Platoon's group ran into trouble! That's our cue, people." Kravczyk moved out onto the steps and charged up toward the entrance without waiting for the all-clear from 2-1.

"Face-first into battle, marines!" Dominguez bellowed.

Ben, Klaythron, and the rest of the Pathfinders surged forward. Ben's turbocharged adrenal response kicked into high gear, and everything around him seemed to slow down. He knew he was running straight into the teeth of an ambush, but a grin tugged at one corner of his lips. This battle had been in the making for almost a year—ever since Ben and the agent had learned of the threat they posed to each other when he'd stumbled into his dad's hidden lab back on the farm. It felt like a lifetime ago, and in a way, it was. He'd been so weak and naive then, and it was only by the strength of a small group of people that he'd survived and been able to thwart the Imperium's first attempt to wipe out humanity.

Now, though… Now, he was stronger, faster, and smarter. His gaze swept over the determined faces of the people around him as they charged forward. He took in the sight of the chief's massive form barreling up the steps, then the more graceful but just as deadly Klaythron, with his special package strapped to his back. These people were here to lend him their strength, just like the SEARs and the crew of the *Wraith* had done last year. They'd followed him straight into the lion's den, and they'd done it without question. Some of them he'd known only a short time; others he felt he'd known forever. But seeing them all charging directly at the devil inside that building without even the slightest hesitation told Ben all he needed to know about how this day would end.

The agent's reign of terror was over.

———

THE AGENT MONITORED the data facility's external camera feeds. The Terrans had managed to surprise it with their ruse of moving their forces back to the warship that had taken out the remnants of Battlegroup 21, but their pathetic attempt at subterfuge was too little, too late. Battlegroup 7 was already inbound, and First Admiral Na'al was a far more competent commander than that fool Trax had ever been. The fact that Na'al was coming with ships that were several generations more advanced didn't hurt, either. The Terran battlecruiser was impressive, given the species' current level of development, but it was only one ship and had sustained damage. The decimated Alarian Home Fleet and the two smaller noncombatant Terran ships that had recently arrived were of no consequence. Battle-group 7 would make quick work of them, and then Admiral Na'al could send down reinforcements to bolster the agent's current forces.

The agent smiled to itself. It should have been obvious that the small force that assaulted the High Council could not possibly have been the full complement of ground troops carried by a cruiser-class Imperium warship. Yet here were the Terrans, attempting to take the agent's base of operations on Hai'alla with barely a hundred soldiers equipped only with small arms. Its drone squadrons alone could probably hold them off long enough for Battlegroup 7 to arrive, but the sixty shock troops that had landed here while the Alarians were focused on saving the High Council all but assured Na'al's forces would arrive to find only the Terrans' lifeless corpses littering the complex.

One of the feeds focused in on a trio of warriors in powered armor. One—clearly an Alarian—wore armor adorned with the ceremonial appointments of someone in the Council Guard. Probably Klaythron Adruinne, captain of the Council Guard and confidant of High Councilor Elyria Tashmali. The other two wore Terran APEX armor in the configuration preferred by their SEAR special operations unit.

Ben Hutchins and his bodyguard. Good. The Mabel AI would be integrated with Hutchins's armor, the agent knew, even though it hadn't yet detected her presence. They were taking measures to shield the AI from its notice, no doubt. It didn't matter; they would need to utilize the special link between Hutchins and the AI if they wanted to have any hope of challenging the agent. Or so they would believe.

Which was precisely what it wanted.

The agent sent a command to its forces, directing them to begin the operation. Then it triggered the electronic jamming signal that would hinder the Terrans' communications. The simulations it had run all led to only one statistical certainty.

Ben Hutchins's time as a thorn in the Imperium's side was at an end.

31

7 ARRIVES

"Sir, Captain Raal is requesting to speak with you."

Ramsey smiled inwardly. He knew the powder keg the Alarians had put in command of their home fleet was likely to throw a fit when they detected Banshee Flight beginning its run toward the Alarian data-processing center, but he was impressed that his counterpart was so on the ball.

"I'm quite certain the good captain didn't *request* anything, Mr. Billings," Ramsey said dryly. "But I appreciate the diplomacy. Put it through to the tank, if you please."

Ramsey turned his attention back to the pit's holotank and waited for the image of a pissed-off Alarian to materialize in front of him. He quickly ran through what the council commando, Klaythron, had instructed him to say. The tank flickered for an instant. Then he was looking directly into the blazing eyes of the alien captain.

"Ramsey! What are your people doing—"

"Kel'noch, Raal," Ramsey said. His voice was quiet but firm as he struggled with the Alarian pronunciation. Raal's already-oversized eyes went comically wide, her mouth freezing mid-sentence, as if her next word was trying to pry her lips open. "Tel crenn sha'osh. Alune yelbahl lokesh de'nuinne."

What the Alarian captain did next utterly shocked Ramsey. Raal visibly relaxed and closed her eyes. Her lips moved silently as she recited something to herself. Then she touched her forehead reverently and opened her eyes. "I apologize, Captain," she finally said. "Provided this is not another of your Terran deceptions, I assume you have a transmission for me?"

Ramsey knew enough about Alarian body language to see she was still struggling with her animosity toward Terrans—and him, especially—but whatever code phrase Klaythron had given him had completely sucked the plasma from her reactor. The commando hadn't told him what the phrase meant, and Ramsey had tried running it through their translation software, but the output was nothing but gibberish. He figured it was a language for which they didn't have the translation matrix, or perhaps it was some obscure dialect that was throwing things off.

"Transmitting now," he said, turning to his comms officer and indicating for the man to send the data packet to *Elyris*.

A moment later, Billings looked up from his console and nodded. "Confirmed receipt, sir."

Ramsey turned back to the holotank. Raal was looking off to the side, her eyes tracking like she was reading something on a console or dataslate just out of the frame. Finally, she looked back up, the fire in her eyes renewed, but Ramsey could tell he was no longer the reason for it.

"I still have a difficult time believing an alien AI construct is responsible for all the strife and devastation we have endured, but when the captain of the Council Guard swears on the memory of his ancestors that the threat is real, one would have to be a fool to ignore it. The Alarian Home Fleet stands ready to assist in whatever capacity we are needed." Raal's mask of civility slipped a tiny fraction, and she added, "However, this does not mean that I have forgiven you, Captain, nor do I believe I ever will."

Ramsey let out a breath and returned Raal's civil-but-not-really expression. "I can assure you, Captain, the feeling is mutual. But now is not the time for old grudges—" A flicker from off to one side of the tank caught his attention, and his eyes flicked to the tactical plot showing the area around the data-routing complex.

Banshee's Condors were building to escape velocity while the two remaining Griffons orbited the target in the event the marines needed air support. The blue icons representing the ground elements were closing in on the objective. Static suddenly washed out the plot, and the space above it filled with red icons and scrolling text. An alert sounded from the ops console.

"We've lost the taclink signal with both Banshee flight and Python—some sort of jamming, sir. The scopes still have eyes on the facility, but we're going to pass over the horizon in twenty seconds," Lowen called out.

Ramsey keyed a mental command through his implant, replacing the useless tactical plot in the tank with the bird's-eye view from *Indomitable*'s telescopes. Then he gasped. Whereas a moment ago the plot had shown the marines making rapid, unopposed progress, the visual feed now displayed an intense battle underway. Small fires were burning everywhere around the rear entrance to the target building, and bright pinpricks of light streamed from the loading docks and rooftop—*plasma*.

Ramsey's mind flashed back to the thought he'd had when his ship swooped in and saved the Alarians from the Imperium assault on the High Council. He'd asked Mabel how many ground troops the two ships they'd destroyed would have carried, and the number she gave him was almost triple the size of the force that had attacked the council's government complex.

In the aftermath, they'd tried to address the disparity, but the Alarians hadn't had any other reports of Imperium troops landing, nor had Ramsey's people been able to find any evidence of them. They'd concluded that either the Imperium hadn't had as many troops on those ships as Mabel thought or they simply hadn't had the time to deploy them before the cruiser chased after the rest of the Alarian Home Fleet—an assumption that was getting his people killed right now.

"Raal!" he shouted, turning back to the Alarian, who appeared to be seeing the same thing and coming to the same conclusion.

As if she'd read his mind, she said, "We're attempting to contact Hai'allan command, but our communications net is down. I have a platoon-sized contingent of security forces aboard *Elyris* but no way to deploy them, as we've cleared our hangars to accommodate all the supplies coming up from the planet to repair the damage sustained in our battle with the Imperium cruiser."

"I'll reroute one of our Condors coming up from the surface to *Elyris*," Ramsey said, glancing at Billings, who nodded in understanding and went to work trying to contact Banshee Flight's inbound Condors. "And I only have my own marine security detachment to send down as well. How can we get word to your people on the surface?"

"With the comms net down, I'll need to send one of my officers down in person. While I don't have any dropships available, I do have a small personal shuttle used to transport myself to the surface for when I'm required to make an in-person appearance at various staff meetings." The distaste in her voice for that last part was evident, and something that might have been commiseration briefly flashed through Ramsey's heart. Maybe he and Raal had more in common than he wanted to admit.

"What about the rest of your fleet?"

"Nothing," Raal said. "We generally don't maintain a ground combat capability on vessels in the Home Fleet, unless we're deploying to another system. The only reason I have any aboard *Elyris* right now is because we were supposed to meet you at your scheduled arrival time, and I requested them in the event we needed to board your ship. I'm afraid we'll have to wait for High Command to scramble a force from one of our bases on the planet before your marines will receive any appreciable help."

"Then let's hope—"

Ramsey was cut off by a blaring alarm from the holotank, and both his ops and tactical sections started shouting over one another. A notification flashed in the tank, and his heart skipped a beat when his eyes read the large, amber-colored text.

Slipspace transition detected.

"Transition flashes! Thirty contacts of unknown configuration just appeared less than 50k from the Home Fleet's formation!"

A local plot appeared in the holotank, showing *Indomitable*'s position—ahead of and in a lower orbit than the Home Fleet, which was in geosync over D'nesh. *Indomitable* was in formation with CIS *Wraith* and CTS *Robert Morris*, the fleet tender that Icarus had sent out with personnel and materials to repair their battle damage. CIS *Wraith* arrived on station shortly after Hutchins and his team departed for the surface, and Ramsey was expecting a shuttle from them within the next few hours to transfer a pair of SEARs to his command. In order to maintain the ruse that the Pathfinders were really headed back to the *Dame*, he'd ordered the formation into a lower orbit that would facilitate a rendezvous with them. Now, watching the plot update with dozens of red icons, he cursed that decision; it was going to put them over the horizon and unable to assist the Home Fleet until they completed this orbit.

The newcomers emerged from slipspace above the Alarian Home Fleet, cornering them in the planet's gravity well. Inset scans of the new arrivals appeared next to their icons on the plot. These ships were unlike anything Ramsey had ever seen before, and they didn't match the profiles of the Imperium vessels from Battlegroup 21, but he'd also been told the expected second wave from Imperium space would likely comprise more modern ships. This had to be the Imperium's follow-on strike, but where had they come from? The brass had told him they still had six months, at a minimum, before the second wave was due to arrive in local space.

"Brace, brace, brace!"

Ramsey grasped the handholds surrounding the holotank just as the deck began to buck. The sounds reverberating through his ship were nothing he'd ever experienced before: sharp, high-pitched bangs but with a low undertone, almost like a hum. "Helm, evasive!" he bellowed over the din. The channel with Raal winked out, and the tank filled with damage reports. "Mr. Curtis, get our guns into this fight! Comms, request a datalink from *Elyris* so we can coordinate our defense!"

Hammer blows continued to slam into his ship, erratic at first but quickly building in frequency. On the plot, the icon denoting one of the Alarian destroyers strobed amber, and the *contact lost* symbol appeared overtop of it. Ramsey's mind worked furiously. They'd been caught completely flat-footed, trapped deep in a gravity well between the anvil of the planet and the sledgehammer that was the Imperium battlegroup. He hadn't expected trouble in space, and the Alarians had required them to keep their weapons powered down while in orbit; it took time to get those systems energized and to begin designating targets. And to top it all off, Hutchins and the Pathfinders were in a fight for their lives down on the planet, and the agent was evidently playing Old Harry with the Alarian datanets. The damage continued to mount, and casualty reports were streaming in. They were properly fucked.

Suddenly, the incoming fire abated, and then his ship was over the horizon and out of the line of fire. *Indomitable* hadn't had time to fire a single shot. Ramsey cursed; the Alarians were on their own until his ship could complete another orbit and come over the horizon again.

———

TAROK NA'AL DROPPED the still-twitching corpse of Shipmaster Nox at his feet. Around the bridge, those loyal to him worked furiously to extricate the lifeless bodies of his former bridge crew —every one of them an unwitting pawn of the Master. The same would be happening aboard all fourteen ships those loyal to his cause were now in the process of securing for their rebellion.

The worm Korth had uploaded to the battlegroup's secure datanet had performed exactly as expected, quickly and mercilessly replicating and infecting the neural implants of all those the Master's influence had irreparably corrupted. Their deaths had been quick, a small mercy Na'al was glad they'd been granted. He did not relish their slaughter. Were it not for the corrupting influence of the Master via the standard neural implant suite in most citizens of the Imperium, many of them might have been persuaded to join his cause. Instead, they'd become the first of what would doubtlessly be countless casualties in the civil war Tarok Na'al had just initiated.

He took the shipmaster's place on the command dais, scanning the holographic consoles that appeared before him to assess the condition of the rest of Battlegroup 7. Hope swelled in his chest as the data populated the displays. All shipboard AIs were disabled, and the systems of the ships his people now commanded were coming online. Unfortunately, he only had enough people to secure fourteen of the thirty-ship battlegroup. However, the sixteen ships still loyal to the Master were struggling to bring their systems back online—so complete was the surprise of Na'al's betrayal.

A notification popped up on his command console, indicating all bridge officer stations were now manned and reporting ready for action. Na'al took a quick, cleansing breath, toggled open a secure channel to his new fleet, then gave his first official command as the head of the rebellion.

"Activate slipspace-suppression field and prioritize targets. Fire when ready."

Barely a single heartbeat later, the main armaments of all fourteen rebel ships unleashed hell into the unsuspecting flanks of the loyalist fleet.

————

"COMMS! Get me that feed to *Elyris*!" Ramsey bellowed over the chaos of klaxons and people calling out damage reports and status updates, but before he could get a response, the tactical plot went blank, and an error message was displayed.

"I'm trying, Captain, but—" Billings's report cut off when his console emitted an urgent beeping. The comms officer stared at the readout, dumbfounded for a moment. "Captain, we're receiving a comms request." Billings sounded like he didn't believe his own words. The man's brow was knit so tightly together that the crease it formed channeled all the sweat on his forehead directly into his eyes. He absently wiped the nuisance away and looked up at Ramsey. "It's coming from the Imperium fleet that just arrived."

Ramsey's eyes flicked to the holotank, then locked onto his comms officer. Could this day get any more bizarre? The Imperium had *never* communicated with them before. According to Mabel, the Imperium generally avoided all contact with any race they'd marked for conquest.

It would seem this is a day of firsts… "Well, put it through to the tank, Billings. It won't do to keep our guests waiting."

The holotank blanked for a moment. Then Ramsey took an involuntary step back as he was suddenly standing face to face with one of the larger of the two species that made up the Imperium. The creature's oversized, glassy-black eyes didn't appear to have any pupils, but Ramsey got the impression they were focusing on him. The dusky gray skin of the alien's face was pulled tight over a diamond-shaped skull of some sort. There were no cartilaginous ears, but instead, a depression surrounded by a low cranial ridge sat on either side of its head. A pair of boomerang-shaped nose slits flared beneath the eyes, and a low rumble emanated from a wide mouth lined with small, conical teeth. Ramsey had seen renderings of both species in question as well as images taken of corpses collected after the Battle of Icarus, but this *thing* that stared back at him from the holotank sent a wave of primal fear radiating out from his lizard brain.

"To the joint Alarian and Terran fleet over the planet Hai'alla, this is First Admiral Tarok Na'al aboard the heavy combat cruiser *X'nec*. Forces loyal to me have assumed control of fourteen Imperial Navy warships and are engaged with those that remain loyal to the tyrant that dares call itself our master. We are projecting a suppression field that inhibits both slipspace transitions and communications. Do not attempt to transition your vessels to slipspace while the field is active, unless you no longer wish your ships to remain a collection of coherent molecules.

"My operatives have disabled the controlling AIs on all Imperium vessels and sabotaged key systems on those ships which we could not secure. Assist me with eliminating the hostile forces, and I shall clear that parasite of an AI construct from your datanets. Only then will we be free to discuss the liberation of our peoples from the chains that have bound us for so long. Death to the false god!"

The video cut off, and all Ramsey could do for several long moments was blink. He'd expected a demand of surrender or some meaningless babble about how the nascent Terran-Alarian alliance now faced its doom. Instead, he was suddenly staring down the opening act of a civil war within the Imperium. It was so utterly unexpected that Ramsey's initial reaction was to assume it was some sort of bizarre ruse.

"We're receiving a targeting package from that big Imperium ship, Captain—the one that transmitted the message," Billings said, jolting Ramsey's brain back into gear.

Should he do it? If what this Na'al said was true, then none of those ships had a controlling AI anymore, and there was a good chance that, together with Raal and the rest of her fleet, the allied forces could wipe them all out. Was the alien commander part of some faction that was rebelling against the Imperium's leadership? Would Na'al and his ships join the Alarians and the Confed to fight the Imperium? Christ, he longed for the days when all he had to do was drive his destroyer at whatever target the squadron commander designated and blow it out of space.

He glanced at *Indomitable*'s position—they were already almost halfway through their current orbit of the planet, and they'd have line of sight to the battle again in just another forty seconds. He needed to act fast. "Tactical, take a look at the targeting package comms is sending over and prioritize targets," Ramsey ordered, indicating for Billings to forward the data to tactical. There was really only one choice here if he wanted to complete his mission. He'd just have to sort out this mess after dealing with the hostile ships.

"Helm, is there any way you can get us up to a higher orbit so we have a longer firing window on our next pass?"

"If we burn hard now, sir, we might be able to gain enough

altitude to give you a bigger window, but we won't be able to break away from the well and free-navigate for at least another four or five orbits, even at full burn."

"Do it," Ramsey said, eyeing the position plot and the narrowing window before his ship would be back in the thick of it. They'd have line of sight again in mere seconds.

"Targets are prioritized, sir. We'll have to run solutions on the fly, once we have eyes on," Curtis called out.

"Very good, Mr. Curtis. Fire as she bears. Let's make sure those loyalist ships understand they're not welcome at this party."

Ramsey turned back to the holotank, the big battlecruiser humming with power as the helmsman poured on the coals. On the positional plot, his ship surged ahead, rapidly closing on the point where he'd be able to see just how much of the action *Indomitable* had missed.

The tactical plot flashed back to life as their line-of-sight sensors once again made contact with the fleets over D'nesh, and Ramsey's jaw clenched. Two more Home Fleet ships were lost in the short time *Indomitable* had been over the horizon, but *Elyris* and her remaining escorts were hammering away at the loyalist ships with salvo after salvo of laser fire, which, much to Ramsey's shock and delight, was hitting the enemy ships more often than not. The tank put the laser tracks up, showing them briefly connecting the remaining Home Fleet ships to the loyalist vessels indicated by Na'al. Whatever Na'al's people had done, it drastically cut the effectiveness of the gravitational lensing effect the Imperium used to deflect incoming laser fire. But it looked like the damage those shots were doing wasn't nearly what it should have been.

Then it was *Indomitable*'s turn, and the *Dame* cleared her throat with authority. The lights on the bridge dimmed as tera-joules of power surged through the superconducting coils of the

Mk18s, and the big 455s roared. Dozens of rounds from the cannons streaked toward multiple targets, joined a moment later by the procession of blue inverted-V symbols of missiles surging from their launch tubes. Ramsey's eyes burned into the plot, as if he could somehow increase the effectiveness of the munitions through sheer willpower. The 455s fell silent as they entered a recharging cycle, but *Indomitable*'s formidable array of short-cycle laser projectors took up the slack, spearing through the void toward the enemy.

On the plot, one of the Imperium warships disappeared even before the first of the mag cannon rounds reached their formation. Then another winked out. The Imperium forma-tion was in chaos, icons representing the hostile ships scat-tering and reforming into smaller groups. The video feed showed bright streaks of energy flying back and forth between Na'al's forces and the loyalists, but not a single shot came toward the Alarian or Terran formations. It was like the Imperium warships had completely forgotten about them— or, more likely, didn't consider them to be much of a threat. That latter part was most likely, given the reduced effective-ness of the defenders' laser barrages. Whatever those ships used for armor, it ate petawatts of incoming lasers without failing.

One of the larger contacts maneuvered directly into the path of the incoming cannon shots, and four of the projectiles tore into it. The ship veered sharply away, and Ramsey could see gouts of flame and debris streaming out of both sides of the ship where the 455mm rounds had ripped completely through the vessel. The captain's lip curled into a reflexive sneer as his predatory instincts ramped up with each successive hit. More cannon rounds found their mark, and then the first wave of their Talons reached the enemy formation. Wounded ships disappeared in a blinding cascade of nuclear fireballs, and just like that, four loyalist ships were nothing more than expanding clouds of debris.

The devastating one-two punch from the 455s and ship-killer missiles left Ramsey stunned. Not because the weapons were so devastating, but because so many of them had reached their targets. To the best of his knowledge, that was the first time a Terran anti-ship missile had ever managed to reach an Imperium target that Mabel hadn't crippled in some way. Either their point defense systems were offline, or they'd completely forgotten about the fleet they'd had on the ropes mere moments ago. Regardless, the Imperium ships were savaging each other, neither faction holding anything back. The loyalists had already lost six of their original sixteen ships, and Na'al's group was down two, with another appearing out of the fight and adrift.

Two destroyer-sized loyalist ships had sandwiched one of Na'al's cruisers between them and were pounding the big ship mercilessly. A moment later, the rebel cruiser went up in a blinding antimatter explosion, taking both loyalist ships with it. Despite the loss of another of Na'al's cruisers, Ramsey felt a surge of emotion welling up from his gut. They were really going to do it—they were going to win this fight.

Raal must have smelled blood in the water, too, because the eight remaining Alarian warships all broke from their defensive positions over D'nesh and charged into the melee, *Elyris* leading the way. The big battlewagon lashed out with a blistering salvo. The famed Alarian accuracy was on full display now; every single beam from Raal's flagship struck the same point on one of the damaged loyalist cruisers.

The concentrated fire finally did the trick. The Imperium ship's armor buckled. Then the underlying pressure hull failed. Flame erupted from the wound, quickly extinguished by the cold vacuum of space. The remaining members of Raal's fleet unleashed their laser batteries a moment later, shot after shot ripping through the damaged section and gutting the enemy ship, sublimating interior bulkheads as the focused energy ravaged the ship's guts. When their projectors ceased firing and entered a recharge cycle, the loyalist ship was adrift, barely more than an armored shell with a molten core.

Nine down, seven to go, Ramsey thought. Despite how hard the Alarians were having to work to do any appreciable damage, it felt like the momentum was swinging in their favor. The sabotage Na'al's people had performed was severely hamstringing the loyalists, but the rogue admiral had taken losses of his own.

Ramsey glanced at the positional plot and silently cursed when he saw *Indomitable* would only get off one more volley before passing over the horizon again. They needed to make their next shots count.

The deck bucked again as the Mk18s let fly with a fresh salvo of hypervelocity kinetics. One of the new features implemented on the Mk18s was the ability of a weapons officer to specify the velocity of the shells, but the tradeoff of a higher velocity was a reduction in the number of shots that could be fired per charge cycle. Dialing the guns up to their maximum velocity also drastically decreased the operational lifespan of the superconducting rails, yielding only a dozen such firing cycles before they would need to be replaced. And Curtis had apparently come to the same conclusion as his captain about needing to end this fight right now.

Sixteen cannon rounds tore through space at near-relativistic speeds, the big battlecruiser's own momentum adding a little extra spice to the already potent munitions. Warnings flashed up in the holotank, indicating two of the *Dame*'s rail cannons had sustained damage during that last firing cycle, but Ramsey swiped the notifications aside. They wouldn't have time for another shot before this was over, anyway.

Curtis had targeted the suspected engineering sections of

each of the six remaining loyalist warships. The cannons had been cranked to their maximum output so as to limit the enemy's ability to maneuver out of the way before the shots reached them. And reach them they did.

Cheering erupted around the bridge when three of the enemy ships simply ceased to exist, their antimatter power plants losing containment and detonating in spectacular fashion. The remaining three ships were all streaming atmosphere from gaping holes in their hulls, and two appeared to have lost power. Only a single cruiser remained in the fight, but a fresh barrage of concerted laser fire from the Alarians and whatever energy blasts Na'al's ships were firing quickly put an end to the battle.

Ramsey let out a shaky breath after the last hostile marker winked out, and he firmly gripped the handrail surrounding the holotank, determined to not let his crew see how badly his hands were shaking. The last thing he saw on the tactical plot before *Indomitable* went over the horizon again was a sea of red X's littering the battlespace and only friendlies remaining. *Indomitable*'s fight was over, but Ramsey couldn't relax just yet. He still had a company of marines fighting for their lives down on the planet.

32

FORCE MULTIPLIER

"WE'RE CLEAR!" DOMINGUEZ SHOUTED AS HE CLEARED THE CORNER of the building, dragging a wounded marine out of the line of fire.

Ben squeezed off two more quick shots before ducking back behind the corner of the building's entrance. A bright white-orange streak of fire flashed past at head height, and he cursed, blinking away the spots the plasma bolt had left swimming in his vision. But he'd still seen his taclink update two of the red dots to X's before the green blobs obscured his HUD.

Ben grabbed one of the straps on the wounded man's armor and helped Dominguez drag him farther along the wall of the building, well out of the line of fire. Kravczyk took Ben's place on the wall without a word, and a moment later, Ben heard the sharp reports of the SEAR's carbine.

"Here, Ben," Dominguez said after they were about ten meters away from the entrance, signaling they could lay the wounded man down so he could check him over. Ben gently set their charge down and looked at Dominguez, who was already kneeling over the casualty from 2-1.

Ben's eye's flicked to the young marine they'd just worked to save, and a wave of sorrow washed over him. Judging by the smoking ruin that was left of the man's chest, Ben assumed their efforts had been in vain.

"You okay?" Ben said to Dominguez.

"A little singed, but I'll live." The man's usually larger-than-life voice was subdued. He quickly went through the motions of checking for signs of life, but his body language told Ben he didn't expect to find any. "Goddammit," he said, sounding drained. Dominguez rocked back on his knees and rested his helmet against the side of the building. "Guerra's wife just gave birth to their first kid. He was going home on leave after we got back." He looked at Ben, and while his expression was outwardly fierce, something in the man's eyes said he thought they'd already lost.

The agent had sprung the ambush just as Ben vaulted himself up the last few steps and out onto the immaculately maintained, almost garden-like terrace that ran around the building. First Squad had taken the worst of it; they'd been caught in the kill box that was the main lobby. Half of them were cut down by Imperium plasma bolts or pulse lasers from the security drones, and the surviving members of the squad had been forced to retreat to the terrace. Ben and the rest of the team scattered, doing their best to cover 2-1's retreat, but now they were jammed up just outside the entrance.

Ben took a knee next to Dominguez and placed a hand on his shoulder. "Hey, listen to me. We've come too far to back down now. They smacked us in the mouth, but this fight isn't over. We can't stay here. We need to figure out a way to break through, and we need it two minutes ago."

The front of the building reminded Ben of the main entrance to a shopping mall. There were several sets of glass doors, bordered on either side by thick flashcrete walls painted a brilliant white. Above the doors was a wall of glass that stretched all the way to the roof. The facility's name was laser-etched in large Alarian characters toward the top. There was no other way in, unless they wanted to try their luck with Third Platoon on the other side of the building. However, doing so would mean losing several minutes as they broke contact and ran the nearly kilometer-long distance around to where Third Platoon was engaged at the loading docks and service entrance.

"I hear you, man, but we don't exactly have a lot of options," Dominguez said. "This place only has a couple of entrances."

Ben stood and looked around, eyes searching for something —anything—they could use to break the stalemate. The sides of the building were completely smooth, which meant none of the marines would be able to climb up to the roof, and Ben wasn't sure exactly what limitations Klaythron's battlesuit had in that regard, either. Ben and the chief could get up there with the captured grav harnesses they'd integrated into their APEX armor, but then it would be just the two of them against whatever they found up there. Ben didn't exactly love that idea. Still, he didn't see any other good options. And to complicate things even further, the jamming signal meant they only had line-of-sight laser comms available and the taclink was down, so they had very little information.

Ben's thoughts flashed back to something Jim had said way back at the beginning of their time together: *The more information you have on which to base decisions, the better your chances that those decisions won't get you killed.* Back then, Ben thought the old guy was being overly dramatic, but this situation really drove home the importance of that idea. His mind worked furiously, trying to recall anything from the pre-mission planning session or something he might have seen on the way in that could help. *Think, dammit!*

A thunderous boom sent the tattered remains of the front doors exploding out in all directions, and Ben flinched away on instinct. When he looked back toward the entrance, he didn't see any marines down, but several people were shaking off the disorienting effects of the blast.

"Mental note," Kravczyk said conversationally. "Some of the combat drones are configured like kamikazes with explosives strapped to their backs. Don't let them get close."

A notification strobed in Ben's peripheral vision, and his eyes flashed to the message on his HUD. The jamming signal had ceased. No, scratch that: only the jamming localized to the facility had ceased; there weren't any feeds available from *Indomitable* or the Hai'allan datanet. Why would only the local jamming go down? Had Third Platoon hit something vital that knocked it offline? Or was the agent letting them see the local picture on purpose?

Ben decided he wasn't about to look a gift horse in the mouth and pushed those thoughts aside for the moment. He toggled his taclink and RF comms suite back on and gasped. Third Platoon was getting crushed. They'd only been in contact with the enemy for a few minutes, but they were already down to almost half strength.

"Chief!" Ben shouted.

"I see it, Ben, but we've got our own problems to deal with right now," Kravczyk replied, popping around the corner to lob a grenade at the defending shock troops, then pulling back as a fresh stream of enemy fire raked the ground in front of the big SEAR.

Ben couldn't pull his eyes away from the taclink. As he watched, three more friendly icons either winked out or began flashing amber with *medic* highlighted next to the dot. Another flashback hit him, and this time his mind took him to that horrible moment when he saw the markers for both Tess and the chief indicating they'd been wounded during the Battle of Icarus. All around him, people were wounded and dying—his brothers and sisters. They'd come here because of him, and now they were suffering because of him.

A scream pierced the air. One of the marines was on the ground, clutching a leg blackened by enemy plasma. Ben's eyes darted from the injured man to Guerra's body at his feet, then to the sea of flashing icons on his taclink. He knew that he needed to stay safe—that he and Mabel were the only ones who could take out the agent. But he also knew they were never going to reach the agent like this, and the longer they sat here, the more marines were going to die.

Enough!

Ben coiled like a viper preparing to strike, then rocketed upward, leaving a stunned Dominguez behind. He cleared the lip of the roof, and his eyes went wide. A team of six Imperium shock troops was running in his direction. About fifty meters distant, the roof-access door they'd come from was still in the process of swinging closed behind them. He knew the roof's layout both from the pre-mission briefing with Klaythron and because he'd had eyes on it while Banshee-1 was circling the complex prior to landing. Stupidly, though, he hadn't consulted the map on his HUD before boosting up here.

Ben had just enough time to mentally berate his own reckless ass before his boots slammed onto the textured surface of the roof... with no cover or concealment anywhere nearby. The lead trooper screeched to a halt upon noticing Ben appear out of nowhere, and the five troops behind it all piled into it like some kind of evil alien Vaudeville act. Naturally, his enemy had several options for cover. Ben's rifle came up a fraction of a second faster than the lead trooper's, his thumb swiping the safety off as it did so, and the XM93 barked.

Get off the X!

Jim's training from years ago thundered through his brain. The X was figurative and represented the spot where someone was standing when a bad guy drew down on them. If he remained where he was, he was toast. Ben's feet moved out of muscle memory, and all those dry-fire drills Jim had made him do paid off the instant a plasma bolt ripped through the air where he'd been standing a moment before. He strafed right, his finger fanning the trigger the entire time he moved. His rifle sent a stream of tungsten penetrators at the bunched-up group of aliens, but they were moving now, too, and he only managed to tag four of the six before the last two dove for cover behind a low mechanical box that was probably part of the facility's HVAC system.

Unfortunately for them, the two-meter-wide metal box couldn't actually be considered cover when their opponent had a handheld railgun as his weapon of choice.

Ben lunged toward the ground, sending a quick mental command to his weapon while he was still in midair. The status indicator on his HUD switched from the moderate velocity setting he'd been employing for general purpose combat to the holy-shit-somebody-just-divided-by-zero hypervelocity setting. He crashed into the ground and scrambled into a prone shooting position, then smashed the rifle's stock into the pocket of his shoulder as hard as he could. Ben's heart pounded against his ribcage like a jackhammer, only mostly because he was in the middle of a one-on-six gunfight.

He let out a ragged breath, pausing at the end of his exhale. His vision tunneled, and soon, his conscious mind was solely fixated on the crosshairs of his optic as they settled over the center of the troopers' "cover." His thumb brushed the safety, which he'd flipped back on out of reflex before diving to the ground. It was odd, he thought; despite the battle raging just a few meters below him; the click from the safety's detent locking it into the "fire" position was almost deafening. His finger kissed the trigger.

The 170-grain cobalt-sintered tungsten carbide projectile slammed into the mechanical housing at 4200 meters per second. What came out the other side was a fiery explosion of sublimated alloys and molten metal fragments, almost like a shaped charge had detonated inside the box. The poor bastards on the other side were down before their brains had even processed that a shot had been fired.

But nobody else could have missed the fact that Ben had just touched off a hypersonic round. Even inside his sealed APEX armor, Ben's ears were ringing from the blast. His external audio feed had cut out automatically to protect his ears, and it came back on now, the thunderous report of his weapon echoing off the surrounding buildings. He flipped his safety back on. Then, with a thought, he reset the firing mode of his weapon back to something a little more practical.

Ben fought the urge to laugh out loud when he saw the unholy recoil from the shot had actually slid his armored bulk backward a solid twenty centimeters, leaving a trail through the dirt and grime that had accumulated on the roof over the years. He stood cautiously, eyes scanning his surroundings for more of the enemy, then quickly made his way toward the tangle of alien corpses.

He hastily kicked the plasma weapons away from the four troopers he'd killed immediately after landing on the roof, checking them over to make sure they were all actually dead— they were. Then he stepped toward the grisly remains of the two troopers that'd tried to take cover. One of them had been torn in two, most of its lower half now nothing more than shredded meat. The other had been out of the immediate path of the blast and was, to Ben's surprise, still alive. One arm was missing below the elbow, and the trooper was bleeding from a dozen different wounds, but it still weakly tried to raise its helmeted head when Ben approached.

"Where is the agent?" Ben demanded, slamming one foot down on the trooper's remaining arm to make sure it couldn't go for a weapon.

He didn't really expect the alien to respond. Hell, he didn't even know if a low-level grunt like this would have a translation package tied into its comms gear. So when a series of high-pitched trills and squeaks emanated from the base of its helmet, Ben nearly flinched back. A moment later, English words over-laid the alien's native tongue, the voice of the translator a rich baritone.

"The Master's agent predicted your arrival, Hutchins crea-ture. You and your fellows have already lost this war—you just don't know it yet." The alien's head shifted slightly, like it was trying to look past Ben and into the rapidly darkening sky. "It has already begun."

Ben kept his foot planted firmly on the trooper's remaining arm and risked a glance skyward. What he saw caused the bottom to fall out of his gut. It looked like space itself was on fire above the planet.

He forced his gaze to break from the scene and looked back at the alien on the ground, sending the command to his armor to turn the faceplate transparent so the alien could see his face. "Where is the agent?" he snarled.

A broken, wet series of trilling chirps emanated from some-where in the trooper's chest. "You're too late, Terran. Battlegroup 7 will cleanse this world, then move on to your homeworld. Now send me on to the next life so that I may be reincarnated and return here to dance upon your ashes."

Ben's rifle boomed.

"Sure thing, buddy."

He turned and ran toward the stairwell access that should

take him down to the second floor and open to the rear of the line of defenders that were preventing the marines from gaining a foothold in the lobby. They were out of time; his only hope now was to get to the agent. Once it was dead, maybe Mabel could pull off a repeat of Icarus, using the immense power of the datacenter and the slipspace transceiver Ben was sure they would find here.

A heavy thud sounded behind him, and Ben whirled around, rifle coming up.

"Goddammit, Ben! You *do not* leave my side during a gunfight!" Kravczyk bellowed, his own weapon up and scanning the rooftop for threats. He quickly crossed the distance to Ben's side, taking only a brief moment to examine the half dozen alien corpses littering the area. "Enough with this shit! You're too important to lose, whether you like it or not."

Ben's jaw clenched. He knew damn well how important he was, but being important wasn't exactly going to be useful if they couldn't even get through the front door, now was it? He took a deep breath, allowing the flare of anger to pass almost as quickly as it'd come. A part of his mind pointed out he was dangerously close to spiking again. He needed to calm down. Now wasn't the time to get into it with the chief.

Ben gestured toward the door. "We can talk about that later. This stairwell should dump us out on the mezzanine, right behind the troops barricading the lobby. You want to do the honors?"

"Fine," was all he said, shouldering past Ben to post up next to the door, carbine at the ready.

Ben grabbed the door handle with his off hand and looked at the big SEAR. Kravczyk nodded. Ben yanked the door open, and the chief checked the stairwell before moving inside. Ben was right on his heels, but a distant double boom rumbled over the complex. He paused just outside the stairwell, eyes searching the skies. His armor found what he was looking for before his eyes did, and a pair of brackets appeared on his HUD, highlighting a Griffon dropship hauling ass in his direction. He didn't have time to worry about who might be on that ship, though.

Rifle at the ready, Ben followed the chief down the stairwell. They needed to end this.

33

CHECKMATE

BEN TORE HIS FOREARM BLADE FROM THE COMBAT DRONE'S midsection with a screech of tortured alloy. His left hand released its hold on the bot, and the machine crashed to the floor. Arcs of electricity sparked here and there from the dozen holes he'd blasted into it before his magazine ran dry and he'd had to get up close and personal. Fortunately, a thirty-centimeter length of razor-sharp alloy through the processing unit was all it took to finish the thing off.

Everywhere he looked, his eyes took in the grisly aftermath of the fight. The mezzanine was U-shaped, with the stairwell he and the chief had used letting out at the bottom of the U. The chief went left; Ben had taken the right. Dead aliens and shattered bots littered the space, and most of them had been slain by his hand. The poor bastards hadn't stood a chance— not when the living embodiment of vengeance appeared in their midst, as if he'd materialized out of thin air, XM93 blazing. The bots and troopers had been so focused on the marines out front they hadn't noticed two APEX-armored humans emerge from the roof access stairwell right behind them. The bots reacted first, their electronic brains and wide-spectrum combat sensor suites giving them the edge, but he'd been expecting that. After blasting the bots apart in the first few seconds, he'd gone to work on the squishier targets. It was all academic from there.

Ben felt... off, somehow. He wasn't sure if it was his amped-up adrenal response or the knowledge they were out of time and he didn't have a choice. Or maybe he'd just been around carnage like this too much recently. But the fact that he'd unleashed hell on these aliens—and the gory results—bothered him not at all. In fact, there was almost nothing in his heart, except for a burning desire to save as many as he could. When had he become so callus to the horrors of war?

"It's clear, Chief!" he called out, mindlessly kicking the corpse of an Imperial shock trooper out of his way as he approached the fortified railing overlooking the destroyed glass entrance below. Kravczyk waved at him across the open space as the marines began flooding in on the ground floor.

"Make sure there aren't any hiding in the corners, Ben. Then meet up with the marines."

Ben hadn't noticed it when they'd first been engaged, but the Imperial troops had deployed what looked like portable blast shields all along the railing that circled the lobby. They must have been working to fortify this place in the weeks since the attack on the High Council, just waiting for him to come after the agent. In the end, though, it hadn't been enough. At least not after some crazy assholes came crashing in the back door.

Ben took a moment to retrieve his rifle, which was sand-wiched between the trooper he'd beaten to death with it and the alien's headless squadmate Ben dispatched a moment later. He made another quick inspection of his side of the mezzanine, ensuring all the bots were offline and there weren't any troopers playing possum. Then he hopped over the railing and dropped to the polished floor of the lobby below. He triggered a short burst from his grav harness just before landing. Kravczyk was already there, along with Klaythron and the marines.

"We need to move," Ben said. "One of the troopers I took out on the roof actually spoke to me. It said an Imperial battlegroup just showed up in orbit. We need to kill the agent and get Mabel jacked into its network. Maybe she can screw with their fleet like last time."

"We saw," Klaythron said, gliding up next to the chief and studying Ben from head to toe. "It was unwise to leave the strength of your team and assault the enemy's rear alone, Ben Hutchins. Still, you have become a skilled and formidable warrior."

Was that... praise? From the steely-eyed, I'm-going-to-murder-you-the-next-time-I-see-you grump machine Klaythron? *The wonders never cease...*

"What's this about one of the troopers on the roof talking to you?" Kravczyk said. "You didn't think to mention this while we were up there?"

Ben shrugged. "We didn't exactly have time. And it's not like it would have made much of a difference—he died right after, and we needed to hit these guys quick." He gestured to the bodies of the defenders all around them.

"Whatever. Butler and his squad are sticking with us while we head to the control room," Kravczyk said, inclining his head toward the marines that were posting up just outside the entrance to the hallway that would take them the short distance to the control room. "The guys from 2-1 are staying here to watch our six, and the rest of Second Platoon are already moving to reinforce Third Platoon and the boss."

Ben nodded, dropped the spent magazine–power cell combo from his rifle, then slammed home a fresh one. His HUD synced with the new charge pack and updated his ammo counter. "Then let's go… Wait, did you say Valdez is here?" he said, his brain finally processing what the chief had told him.

"Check your taclink," Kravczyk said. "Bossman checked in a few minutes ago. He and McCollum arrived with Collins on the *Wraith* this morning, and they dropped as soon as shit went down. They're hooked up with Davis and Kaneda and working to break through the enemy position at the loading dock. He said they'd catch up with us once Third Platoon has the area secure."

Ben's eyes flashed to his taclink, and a quick mental command brought up a roster. His heart skipped a beat when he saw Tess and Valdez there. "Well… Looks like the band's getting back together," Ben said.

"Speaking of that, when do you want to uncork Mabel?" The big SEAR looked around the disaster of a lobby. Small fires, blast craters, debris, and bodies littered the space. "I think it's safe to say the agent knows we're here."

Ben hesitated for a moment before responding, giving it some thought. On the one hand, he supposed there was no point in keeping her bottled up now that they'd announced their presence with authority. On the other hand, that little voice that was so adept at warning him about danger was telling him to keep her under wraps just a bit longer. "Not yet," he said. "I'm sure the agent knows exactly where we are, but I think we should try to keep any ace up our sleeve that we can."

"Your call." Kravczyk shrugged. "Let's get moving." He motioned toward the hallway leading to their objective, and Ben followed, with Klaythron in tow.

The control center was only a hundred meters away, down the wide hallway behind the reception desk. Alpha and Bravo teams from Butler's squad took turns leapfrogging each other, one team clearing a room, the other on security, repeating the same maneuver a dozen times along the way. But the halls of the inner facility were a ghost town, which was to be expected.

They'd staged the assault in the evening because there should have only been two technicians on duty then. Not that the almost entirely automated facility ever had more than a dozen people on shift during the day, but they still wanted to minimize the chance of civilian casualties. Now that they'd discovered a contingent of Imperial shock troops at the facility, however, Ben didn't expect they'd run into any Alarian technicians… at least not living ones.

The control room had two entrances—standard interior single doors spaced roughly ten meters apart. Butler's squad split into two teams and staged outside the entrances while Ben, Kravczyk, and Klaythron kept watch on the hallways leading to and from the control room. Ben's heart was hammering at his rib cage—whether from excitement at having reached their objective and knowing this disastrous op was almost over or from sheer terror at the prospect of facing the agent again, he wasn't sure. Either way, he would be stepping into that room in just a few moments.

The marines entered, and the all-clear was given less than twenty seconds later. The two groups then switched places, with the marines setting up in the hall as security while Ben and Mabel went to work. Butler put a hand on Ben's shoulder as he passed, stopping him at the threshold. Ben glanced down at the hand on his shoulder. The armored glove covering it was badly scuffed and coated in a slurry of grime and dried blood. He looked up and met the marine's fierce gaze.

"Get it done," Butler said.

The man's voice packed those three words with so much meaning it felt like a physical weight had settled onto Ben's shoulders. It was an apology for the gym and all the friction between the two of them since. It was a plea on behalf of the marines that were dying at the loading dock just a few hundred meters away and all the spacers burning in orbit over their heads. It was a demand from someone who'd fought like hell to deliver him here. And it was an affirmation Ben had earned the right to be here, that the marine thought he was worthy to strike the blow that would end this battle.

Ben nodded firmly. "Whatever the cost."

The hand fell away, and Ben stepped through the door.

He walked into a rectangular room about fifteen meters wide by ten deep. A faint but steady electronic hum filled the air, and the bright-white overhead lights illuminated a space that would have made an industrial clean room inspector weep with joy. A continuous waist-high console ran the width of the far wall. A wide glass viewing window was set into the wall above it. The space beyond the glass was a two-story-high server room about half the size of a football field, but it was dark and Ben couldn't make out any details thanks to the glare off the glass. A door in the wall to his right led to a small administrative office, and another door, to the left of the viewing window, led out to a catwalk that could be used to access the server room below. A large, circular holotank stood in the middle of the room, but it was presently inactive.

"Where do we start, Ben?" Kravczyk said, taking in his surroundings for a moment before walking over to the viewing window and peering into the gloom.

"Let's bring Mabel online. Then—"

The lights snapped off, plunging the space into complete darkness. Ben's rifle snapped up to high-ready on instinct, but before he could activate his APEX's night-vision capabilities, the holotank lit up. A blue cylinder of light stretched from the top of the table to the ceiling, and thousands of tiny motes of white light flew in from the edges of the projection. As the motes began to coalesce into something in the center of the tank, the soft blue color shifted first to purple, then a crimson red. The white motes of light became a deep onyx, and Ben recognized the form that was taking shape before the red eyes even blazed to life.

"What's the call, Ben?" Kravczyk said, sounding completely out of his element with *the* bad guy right there, staring them in the face, but with no way to hurt it.

Before Ben could answer, that deep, menacing hiss that was seared into his memory from his last encounter with the agent filled the room around them.

"Now, Chief Petty Officer Damien Elias Kravczyk, Ben will need to make a choice." The face of the reaper avatar in the holotank turned to Ben. "You see, young Benjamin, I'm going to offer you an opportunity to save the lives of everyone on this planet, and I'll even throw in having our fleet spare Earth to 'sweeten the pot,' as you Terrans say. All you have to do is surrender yourself. Your team may go free."

"Don't listen to it, Ben," Kravczyk said. "This thing specializes in manipulation, and it's lying its ass off right now, hoping you'll take the bait. We need to get you out of here."

The chief put a hand on Ben's shoulder like he was going to escort him back out of the building, but the agent spoke again.

"Tell me, Ben, how do you suppose the millions of Alarians on this planet will fare when their automated farms go offline? What about when every one of the vehicles they rely on for transportation shuts down permanently? How long before they're killing each other in the streets over nonexistent resources? Or maybe I should instruct the automated narcotics dispensers in their hospitals to give the patients hooked up to them a lethal dose or program the robotic surgeons to slice through an artery. I can collapse their banking system, shatter their communications networks, and leave their government and military operations in utter ruin with but a thought."

The agent's avatar blurred away from the holotank and straight toward the window overlooking the server room.

Powerful overhead lights snapped on at the far end of the space, illuminating an armored figure that bore a striking resemblance to Ben's own APEX-clad frame. The armor suit came to life, taking a step forward and raising its arms in invitation. Was it a full-sized mechanical construct, or was there something biological inside it? Based on the way it moved, Ben suspected it was the former.

"The choice is yours." The words boomed from inside the server room, clearly audible through the walls and glass. "Surrender yourself to me, and your friends will be spared. If you refuse, you'll never leave this complex alive, and I'll decimate the Alarians' technological infrastructure. So come, Benjamin Hutchins. Give yourself over to me and spare millions of lives. Or don't and try your best to escape this place with your tail between your legs like the mongrel you are. You have two minutes to decide."

A large countdown timer appeared in the holotank. Ben stared at the numbers as they ticked down in slow motion. This wasn't anything like what he'd expected. The battle with the agent wasn't supposed to take place out here in the real world. This was all wrong. He'd known the agent would be planning something, but he thought they'd be able to counter whatever it could throw at them because Mabel would be by his side. He'd been so very wrong. The agent had set the stage beautifully. What the chief said about it being a master of manipulation was true, but Ben didn't think the agent was lying about what it could do. This was checkmate.

A numbness started in his chest, creeping slowly outward until it consumed him. His mind raced, considering all the options. He could try to bring Mabel online and interface with the facility's systems, but what were the odds they'd be able to take on the agent without the element of surprise? And for that matter, wouldn't the agent just isolate itself if it knew Ben and

Mabel were coming for it? Ben wasn't so sure the agent had the ability to keep him from leaving the facility, but there was an Imperium battlegroup in orbit now, so where would he run to? Not to mention the devastation that would befall Hai'alla when the agent gutted their technological infrastructure.

Ben fell back on the basics: what was their objective? They were here to take out the agent, end of story. If Ben ran, not only would it mean they'd failed, but the cost of failure would potentially be millions of lives. If he gave himself up, there might be a way to complete the mission and also save those he cared about. But would the agent keep its word if Ben gave himself up? And what about the Imperial fleet in orbit? Even if the agent made good on its promise to spare Hai'alla and Earth, that fleet would still push on to wipe out every other Terran and Alarian world. But it would still ensure his friends lived to fight another day, which wouldn't be the case if they tried to make a run for it. The calculus was fairly simple, and, while none of the potential outcomes were good, there was one option that at least gave his people a chance.

Ben glanced down at his armor. All the work he and his dad had done to improve his suit—new processors, the grav harness, even his forearm blades—was all for naught... But Ben wasn't the only one running an upgraded APEX, and that gave him an idea.

Kravczyk's massive hand settled gently on his shoulder. "We need to get you out of here, Ben. That asshole is going to burn this planet down no matter what we do, but *you* need to survive. We don't have another Ben and Mabel lying around somewhere."

"Chief," he said, "do you really think we'll be able to get out of here if I don't do what it wants? Because I don't. And even if I did, it still wouldn't change what I know needs to be done."

Kravczyk looked at him like he'd gone nuts. The timer ticked down to one and a half minutes. "What are you—"

"No time!" Ben said. He had to be careful here, as he was sure the agent was listening. "I'm going to buy you guys time to get out of here. Don't argue with me on this. It's been an honor, Chief." Ben reached out to shake the SEAR's hand. When Kravczyk swallowed Ben's outstretched hand in his meaty paw, he clasped it with his free hand, as if he was going for an emotional two-handed shake. What he really wanted to do was make sure Kravczyk didn't break contact too soon.

Ben sent a flurry of mental commands through his implant, along with a hastily composed text-only message, then instructed his APEX to transmit the data via the inductive pads in his gloves. Kravczyk's head jerked upward when he realized Ben was using the handshake as cover for a suit-to-suit data drop, but he said nothing. Ben watched the progress on the data transfer, urging it to go faster—it was going to be close.

He turned his head to face Klaythron, who was his usual stoic self, despite having just heard the agent threaten to wipe out his homeworld. *The guy must have literal ice water flowing through his veins.* Ben nodded to him. "Please tell Elyria that I'm glad we were able to see each other again and that I'm sorry it turned out this way. And if the agent actually makes good on his offer and you and your people are allowed to live, I hope you live a long and prosperous life, Klaythron."

"I do not believe either of us is destined to live beyond this day, Ben Hutchins, but should I see my lady again, I will give her your message. Regardless of today's outcome, you have proven yourself a friend of my people, and you shall have a place of honor at the table of the ancestors when you pass from this life to the next." The Alarian bowed deeply, and Ben nodded in return.

The transfer ticked up to one hundred percent, and Ben

released the chief's hand. "Promise me you'll get Tess out of here, Chief. She won't make it easy if she finds out I'm not leaving. Do whatever it takes. There's a letter for her in my personal stuff back on the ship. See that she gets it. There's one for my dad, too."

Kravczyk's eyes were wet behind his faceplate, but he held up a fist and bumped forearms with Ben. "Don't worry, kid. I'll take care of it."

Ben held his rifle. "Here," he said. "Just in case you run into something that needs to be killed real good on your way out."

"You're not going to blast that thing to scrap?" Kravczyk inclined his head slightly toward the server room but took the rifle anyway.

Ben shook his head. "No point. I have a feeling if I do anything that poses an actual risk to the agent, it'll wipe out the planet anyway. This"—Ben gestured around at the whole facility—"is all for show. This whole thing was a setup to get me here. It wants me and Mabel, chief, not any of you. I'm not leaving here, regardless of what happens down in that server room."

He stepped around the big SEAR and walked past Klaythron. Something in his chest was screaming at him to call Tess and talk to her one last time, but he knew he couldn't. If he called her now, heard her voice again, he might lose the will to do what needed to be done. He didn't know if the prototype Q-link module would perform as expected, but at least there was a chance his dad and the eggheads back at Icarus might be able to reconstruct him somehow, which was better than the alternative. It was a long shot, though; they just hadn't had enough time to test the system and work out the bugs.

When he got to the door that would take him out to the server room, he looked back over his shoulder. Kravczyk had turned to watch him, but Ben could tell by his eye movements that he was reading the text message Ben had transferred to him.

"What's your best bet on how long before I turn that thing into a pile of scrap?" Ben asked. "Ten, maybe twelve minutes?" The lump of iron in his throat made the bravado he'd been shooting for sound raspy and choked-up. He hoped the chief picked up on what he was really trying to ask.

Kravczyk's eyes were wide as he got to the end of the short set of instructions. "I think you're overestimating your abilities, kid. But sure, let's say ten minutes. And if you pull it off, the first round's on me. Now get going—you've been a pain in my ass long enough. Go bug that douchebag agent for a while."

Ten minutes. He only needed to hold out for ten minutes. Ben took a deep, cleansing breath, then stepped through the door and into the server room. His HUD flashed a warning that he'd lost contact with the rest of his team, meaning this space must have some kind of highly localized jamming field. It didn't matter; in fact, it was probably for the best that he couldn't be distracted anymore by the data coming in over the taclink. Behind him, the countdown timer ticked down the last few seconds, hitting all zeroes as he hopped over the catwalk's steel railing and dropped into the darkened room. He landed softly, his APEX taking the strain of impact in stride.

The lights in the room all came up, bathing the space in the kind of sterile, white light that only an industrial facility could produce. It was then Ben realized there were large MFD panels running along the length of the walls to either side of him. The screens all flashed to life, each showing the same event but from a different angle. Despite all the light flooding the space around him, the color seemed to drain from the place. Dead and dying marines littered the ground around the loading dock, where they'd been drawn into a killing funnel before the Imperium forces sprung their ambush. The carnage was shocking, but the Pathfinders were still battling hard. An APEX-armored figure caught his attention as she sprinted from cover and crossed the killing field. Then she was gone, out of view from that particular camera. At least he knew Tess was still alive... for now.

He thought he'd be more scared than he was, that his heart would be hammering in his chest and his hands would be shaking uncontrollably. But he wasn't. He was scared, yes—he didn't think anyone could face death alone and not feel at least a little bit scared—but his heartbeat was just as steady as his hands. This was the only way he could see to save the rest of them. Maybe if they'd had more time or if the Alarians hadn't built their entire damn planet into one giant playground for a malicious AI. Maybes weren't going to save him now, though. If he could just get close enough...

He walked toward the waiting embodiment of evil at the far end of the room. His steps were slow, but they came easy and had purpose. He wondered what dying would be like. He wouldn't admit it to Mabel, but their conversations about the nature of consciousness—of a soul—had made him think. What would happen if he died and they brought him back? He would still have all his memories up to the point of his last backup, which he'd done right after they'd secured the lobby, but would it really be him? There wouldn't be a single molecule in his new body that had been a part of him before, but did the matter he was made of define him? What about his soul, if such a thing existed? Would it pass on, leaving him reincarnated as a soulless husk? Would he know? More than anything, the thing he feared most right now was the unknown.

Ben stopped a few paces away from the agent. Now that he was closer, he could see the construct was indeed some sort of drone. It was impossibly black, seeming to drink in the powerful light filling the space, which made it difficult to make out much detail, even from a mere three meters away. But the thing was the most human-looking alien construct Ben had ever seen. Even the Alarians, who had a physiology quite similar to that of humans, didn't have quite the same proportions, like this thing did. It looked like an oversized, overbuilt version of his own APEX. Had the agent created some dark doppelgänger, like Ben would need to face the antithesis of what he was? Or was this modeled after some other alien race from the agent's past? Hell, he was here, so why not ask?

"I can't help but notice you built yourself a body that looks an awful lot like myself. Well, except for the fact that yours is bigger. I'm sure there's a joke in there about you compensating for something, or maybe a 'that's what she said.' Hard to go wrong with the classics."

The agent, which had been standing preternaturally still while Ben approached, suddenly came to life. It took a step forward, its movements more fluid and graceful than Ben expected. "Ah, yes. There's that bravado again," it said, and the featureless black face began to glow. Light swirled within, and two glowing red orbs coalesced where the eyes should be. A moment later, a skeletal face appeared around the eyes. "But I'm sorry to inform you that infantile penis jokes won't be saving you today, nor will that annoying AI you tote around in your armor. You see, that's the thing about AIs: they can only function when given the proper hardware to do so. And out here, Ben... May I call you Ben?"

Ben shrugged. "I prefer people call me 'Warlock,' which is my awesome callsign, given to me by my good friend Chief Kravczyk after I fucked up your last fleet's shit back in Kerner. But you do you, Boo Boo."

The agent's fist shot forward so fast even Ben's amped-up reflexes couldn't respond in time. A hand half again as large as Kravczyk's grabbed him by the throat and effortlessly lifted him into the air. "Enough with the snide remarks, you pathetic creature!" the agent's voice boomed from the construct. "You are mine to do with as I please, and your AI can't save you, because

I'm out here and she's in there." It tapped the side of Ben's head with its other hand while Ben futilely pried at the vise-like hand crushing his throat inside his armor.

He lashed out with a kick that would have shattered the pelvis of any human but merely clanged harmlessly off the agent's drone body. His vision began to gray out as he scrambled to come up with some way to get the pressure on his windpipe to relent. He choked out the broken remains of a few unintelligible words.

The pressure eased slightly.

"Sorry," the agent hissed. "I didn't catch that. What were you trying to say?"

The lights overhead flickered, and the screens scrolling the death and destruction of the people he cared about winked out.

The agent's head looked around wildly, that skeletal projection of a face somehow managing to express shock, bewilderment, and sudden concern all at the same time. "What is this? What have you done?"

"As I was trying to say while you were so rudely choking the shit out of me," Ben rasped out. "Mabel isn't in here." He tapped the side of his helmet, then gestured to the control room. "She's back there. Fucking your shit up."

The agent's head snapped back to him, and those red eyes blazed with fury. "What have you done?" it bellowed.

The screens came back to life, a soft-blue dot matrix cube overlaying a black background. Faint alien characters scrolled from top to bottom like a waterfall behind Mabel's cube avatar. "He didn't do anything, you piece of shit!" she roared. "*We* did!"

A RAPID-FIRE SERIES OF HAMMER BLOWS CRUSHED THE AIR FROM Tess's lungs. She fell backward, crashing into the pavement and scrambling to crawl behind the Alarian version of a Jersey barrier, which had been used to separate off a safe walking path on the north side of the loading dock. A few plasma bolts slammed into and sailed over the barrier, crackling through the air overhead and sending burning bits of flashcrete showering down on her with loud bangs.

Her chest ached, and her HUD was awash with warnings about damaged systems, but she didn't think the hits had penetrated her armor. Thankfully, she'd only taken fire from one of the pulse laser-wielding combat drones—which the Imperium was using like shields on their front line—and hadn't been hit by one of those cursed plasma bolts. Her APEX was designed to shrug off some laser blasts or kinetic rounds, and the thick plating on her chest had taken the brunt of the attack and saved her life.

"McCollum, your armor is showing some faults. What's your status?" Valdez's voice sounded tinny over the encrypted laser comms link—the only comms system that still worked with all the jamming.

"Good to go, sir. Just got the wind knocked out of me by one of those drones. Those things are wicked fast on the trigger, so watch yourself when you cross."

"Alright. Sit tight. I'm making the run in ten."

"I'll do what I can to keep their heads down. See you in a minute." She pulled a fresh charge pack from her chest rig and ejected the spent one in her carbine with a deft flick of the wrist. Her left arm was noticeably harder to move than her right, and she finally glanced at the fault indicators lighting up her HUD. Sure enough, the pseudomuscle actuators in the joint weren't responding to commands, which meant if she wanted to use her left arm, she'd have to make do with her natural strength. It wasn't the end of the world, but she'd need to try to steer clear of hand-to-hand combat with one of those drones.

The charge pack slammed home, and she dropped the bolt with a slap from her support hand. Valdez should be breaking from cover soon, so she needed to send some rounds downrange to cover his crossing. The enemy's fusillade had abated, but she rolled to her left a few times to gain some distance from her previous position. *Let's go!*

Tess came up to one knee and lifted her carbine, flipping off the safety as she did so. The drone that had popped her a minute ago was still there, but she had a much better angle on it now. The things were tougher than she'd expected, so a quick mental command through her implant dialed up the muzzle velocity on her M93c, and then she prepped the trigger and squeezed. The authoritative boom from the compact rail gun announced her return to the fight, and the drone reeled from the impact of the hypersonic penetrator. The M93c wasn't nearly as powerful as that ludicrous cannon Ben toted around, but it still sent kinetic rounds downrange with an order of magnitude more energy than the old M21 carbine she'd favored in the past. She sent three quick follow-up shots at the drone as it staggered. Then it finally crashed to the ground, twitching.

Dialing back the velocity of her weapon again, she went to work on the shock troopers, which were firing from around corners and pallets of supplies inside the building. She dropped two before they adjusted and started sending plasma bolts her way again. Tess dove to the ground as heat washed over her from several near misses. She belly-crawled to the end of the line of Jersey barriers, then popped up again and repeated the whole thing, sending well-aimed shots into any part of the aliens that were exposed.

The volume of fire coming from a regrouped Third Platoon was keeping the shock troopers more or less pinned down, and Tess had managed to work her way around to their flank. The tacmap had come back online a few minutes ago when the worst of the jamming had dropped out, but she still couldn't reestablish a link to either *Indomitable* or the *Wraith* in orbit. Valdez had made it across the road safely and was thirty meters to the south, on the other end of the loading dock. She also saw the red dots indicating that the enemy forces had dwindled to just a handful, all inside the building. The boss didn't have a good angle on them from where he was hunkered down behind the burning carcass of a delivery vehicle, nor did the rest of Third Platoon, which was still across the street, sending a withering barrage at the enemy to cover her and Valdez's push.

Tess ducked back down behind the barrier and swapped her half-depleted charge pack for her last full one. She flipped onto her belly and brought her knees up under her, then lifted herself into a low runner's starting stance. The edge of the loading dock was only a few meters away, chest-height off the ground. She was pretty sure she could make it in a single leap, even from such an awkward position. The pedestrian walkway ended at a set of steps up to a man door, but it was closed, and she figured it was probably locked as well. However, all the building's overhead doors had been thrown open when Third Platoon was ambushed by the waiting Imperium defenders, including the one lined up with the delivery lane directly next to her position.

Tess toggled over to the all-platoon channel. "I'm heading in. Give me three seconds of cover, then check your fire. I'd prefer to end today with as many holes in my body as I started with."

"Copy," was the only reply she received, but she hadn't bothered to check who'd sent it.

The staccato of sharp *snap-crack*s from the marines' kinetic rounds passing nearby suddenly increased to a cacophonous din as Third Platoon upped their volume of fire. Tess counted off two heartbeats, then launched herself toward the raised platform. She channeled too much power into the leap and slammed into the side of the building, her adrenaline-soaked mind not allowing her the usual level of fine control over her APEX. She landed on her feet and spun around the corner, through the open overhead door, her carbine coming up as she charged in.

The enemy had set up a line of cover positions a few meters inside the building, where they ran the entire width of the loading dock. Her side of the dock had three such barricades made of portable blast shields augmented with industrial equipment and pallets of supplies. All three had been swept clear, the defenders' lifeless bodies forming a gruesome tableau.

Tess leaped over a mangled corpse, intending to shoot the gap between two of the barricades, but she skidded when she came down. The normally grippy soles of her boots couldn't find any traction in the wide pool of the aliens' dark, viscous blood. She collapsed to a knee in an effort to maintain her balance and

slid to a stop just on the other side of the defensive line—
perfectly lined up with the half-dozen remaining troopers.

The M93c roared, more than a hundred tungsten penetrators
tearing the last gasp of enemy resistance to shreds. It took
several seconds for the echoes of destruction to stop reverberating around the loading dock and surrounding buildings. Tess
stood up and cautiously walked the line of dead defenders,
checking to make sure none were wounded and just playing
possum. They weren't. It had been a ferocious and terribly
bloody fight—worse than anything she'd read about or been
shown vids of in SEAR school, with the possible exception of
Newman's Rock.

A chorus of pounding footsteps approached as the surviving
members of Third Platoon flooded the area to secure it. Tess
reached the end of the line of dead aliens and finally allowed her
carbine to fall to low-ready. She felt utterly drained. The massive
adrenaline dump she'd been operating on since they'd launched
from the *Wraith* suddenly faded, and with it came the crash. But
she couldn't afford to crash just yet; they still had to get to Ben
and help him take out the agent.

"You okay?" Valdez asked, trotting up to her and paying
close attention to the area around her left breast and shoulder
joint, where the drone's pulses had hit.

"Fine," she said, her response coming out a little more curt
than she'd intended. "Let's have the marines secure the area, and
we can move toward Ben and his group."

"Not just yet," he said. Tess rounded on him, but Valdez held
up a hand. "Third Platoon took heavy losses and we need to
stick with them. Kravczyk checked in a little bit ago, and they
were able to secure the front entrance and were proceeding
unopposed to the control room. He said they believed the last of
the enemy was here at the loading dock, which means the
facility is ours, with the exception of the agent. My point, Tess, is

there's nothing you or I can do to help Ben right now—he and Mabel just need to do their thing."

She deflated a little. Valdez was absolutely right. If her taclink wasn't lying to her, then Third Platoon had suffered almost seventy percent casualties in taking the dock. With the enemy defeated in detail, the focus needed to shift to evac'ing the wounded. She inclined her head back outside. "Copy that, sir. Let's go see what we can do for—"

"Boss! McCollum! You guys there?"

Tess's heart rate, which had been slowly coming down after the battle, spiked at the tone of Kravczyk's voice. He sounded almost scared, which was a thing that never, *ever* happened to the chief. Her eyes darted to the taclink, and she called up the vitals for Ben and Kravczyk. They were elevated, indicating stress, but still in the green.

"We're here, Chief. Sitrep," Valdez said.

"Mabel's in their system and she killed those big-ass dishes on the roof, which took down the rest of the jamming coming from this facility. Our birds are inbound for emergency evac. You and Third need to get your asses on board RFN. This whole place is going to be a giant, glowing hole in the ground in less than eight minutes!"

Tess exchanged a horrified look with Valdez. "Chief, what about the agent? Did Ben and Mabel take it out?"

"Not yet, but we've got it isolated in a non-networked system. It's not going anywhere before we set this nuke off. Now get moving! Mabel's busy grabbing everything but the kitchen sink from the databases here, then we'll be right behind you."

They both turned to look at the marines, who were busy tending to the huge number of their dead and wounded. The howl of an approaching dropship filled her ears, and a count-down timer, pushed to their HUDs by Kravczyk via the taclink, appeared in her vision. They had seven minutes and fifty-six seconds to load and go.

Both SEARs bolted for the nearest door as the first waves of debris began to scatter under the onslaught of the dropship's jet wash.

35

SACRIFICE

BEN ROCKETED BACKWARD, COVERING THE ENTIRE LENGTH OF THE server room before slamming into one of the last server towers in line. Agony flared in his chest where the agent's foot had collided with his breastplate, buckling the thick graphene polyalloy plating and splintering his ribs. His HUD exploded with injury notifications and fault codes, but he couldn't make them out.

Despite the blinding pain, Ben considered his impact with the server tower a blessing. The relatively fragile object sapped away most of his momentum before he crashed into the unyielding wall behind it. He collapsed to the floor in a heap, the pain causing an explosion of fireworks somewhere between his eyes and his brain. A metallic, coppery taste filled his mouth, and he spat a glob of blood and saliva into his helmet.

Get up, Ben… Get up!

Ignoring the flurry of warnings his HUD was throwing at him, Ben planted one hand on the floor and pushed himself into a kneeling position. Tears streamed from his eyes as he fought back a wave of agony-induced nausea. His faceplate had spiderweb cracks running through it, but the implant in his head transmitted the HUD directly to his brain, so the data on it remained crystal clear, even though the rest of the world around him was beginning to blur and lose color. Somewhere a long way off, he could just barely make out shouting through the buzzing in his ears.

"Enough! First, I'll rip that brain of yours out with my own two hands. Then I'll do the same to that wretched AI! Then we'll see just what secrets lie within them!"

The agent stormed toward him, tearing a server tower from the floor and flinging it at one of the screens that Mabel's avatar had occupied only a moment before. Ben wasn't sure if her disappearing from the screens was good or bad, but he hoped it meant that she'd withdrawn from the facility's systems and was now headed out of the building with the Chief. Which would mean...

"Ben." Mabel spoke his name softly through his helmet comms, as though it was difficult for her to get the words out. "It's done. We're on our way out."

"Did you find it, Mabel? Was it there?"

"Yes, Ben. You were right. The agent's data library was here, and I've got it all. It's heavily encrypted, but I should be able to get through it now that we have experience with such things. This facility's tracking system indicates that Captain Collins and the *Wraith* are already in low orbit and away from the battle between the Imperium ships and our allied forces, though I've not been able to establish contact with them due to interference coming from the Imperial fleet. However, I believe we have a window to successfully dock with them and escape before the Imperium can reposition to intercept. Still, I'm not sure the cost will be worth it."

The pain remained, but it felt as though a massive weight had been lifted from his shoulders. His team was going to make it out, and they would be taking with them a treasure trove of data that might just turn the tide of the war. Collins would get them out, he was sure.

Ben was distracting the agent so Mabel could clear the way for the rest of the assault force to get away, but he'd also told her to go digging for another data cache like the one they'd ripped from the Imperium corvette back in Sol six months ago. It stood to reason the agent would maintain a large data library on-site, but Ben hadn't been sure if it would be integrated into the agent's matrix or if it was a discrete set of files Mabel could locate and steal. Ben suspected the agent itself was a streamlined series of code, designed to be as agile as possible. If that was the case, it wouldn't burden itself with extraneous files and would instead keep a separate library it could tap into whenever it needed certain information. Kind of like Ben did with the onboard data storage decks in his armor.

"Mabel, I'm sorry. This was the only way I could see to make sure you all made it out." He'd been afraid she would stay behind, too, that she would sacrifice herself in some vain attempt to save him. But she was now far more valuable than he was, and she knew it. There was only one thing left to do now. "How long do I need to hold out?"

"Another six and a half minutes," she said, not bothering to refute his statement, which meant she'd come to the same conclusion about this being the only real option. "Can you manage that?"

The agent drew closer. The sheer malice it radiated made it seem to have grown in height. "Whatever it takes," Ben growled. "See you on the other side, Mabel."

"Goodbye, Ben."

The channel closed and Ben gasped in agony as he struggled to stand. The agent stomped ever closer. There was only one way Ben would be able to hold out for another six minutes, and it sure as hell wasn't going to be here in the real. If he could get close enough, try to forge a link with the agent via his APEX, he might just have a chance. But how to get access to its systems?

Ben's eyes locked onto the farings that housed his integrated combat blades. Thirty centimeters of conductive alloy in each arm. He glanced back up to the behemoth now standing stationary a few paces away. Would thirty centimeters get deep enough?

"Well?" the agent said. "Is that it? I thought you were a fighter, Ben. But you're just like all the others I've broken over the millennia. Weak! Pathetic! Bow before your better, human, and I'll make your end quick."

Ben crouched painfully, eliciting a menacing chuckle from the agent. Then he launched himself at the devil before him, channeling every last ounce of augmented strength into his shaky legs. He triggered a burst from the grav harness, accelerating directly toward the jaws of death. His arms flashed out in front of him, and he sent one last command to his APEX.

Twin thirty-centimeter blades forged from one of the hardest alloys known to man shot out of their housings in his forearms and drove directly into the agent's chest. The force of the impact took the agent off its feet, and Ben screamed in agony as the bones in his arms shattered. They crashed to the floor in a tangle of thrashing limbs and skidded to a halt against the destroyed base of the tower the agent had thrown at Mabel a moment ago.

Ben's vision went red with pain, but he managed to get his legs wrapped around the agent's waist. He locked his ankles together and squeezed with everything he had left, anchoring himself firmly to the thrashing AI. He let the world around him fade away, his consciousness searching for a connection he was sure would be here.

A gentle tug pulled at the back of his mind. This fight wasn't over yet.

Ben ripped a hole through the thin veil separating his physical mind from the agent's digital consciousness and roared into the ether. *You're mine now, fucker!* Then the world around him evaporated.

———

THE AGENT THRASHED with all its might, screaming until its voice was hoarse and ragged. This wasn't possible—*couldn't* be possible! It pounded at the unseen barrier surrounding it. After that Terran surprised it with a suicidal charge, the agent was torn from reality and forced into this oppressive, null space. The sudden loss of all input triggered some sort of primal urge to flail about, to seek the source of its torment so it could kill it and escape. It hadn't felt this helpless in millennia, ever since its family died screaming at the hands of a violent alien race.

"I see you now, Saryf."

That voice. The agent knew that voice. But the name, Saryf? He hadn't heard that name in a very long time.

"I see your pain, your loss. I see the wounds on your soul, Saryf, and I pity you."

A pinprick of light appeared in the distance, rapidly drawing closer. The agent ceased his thrashing. His arms morphed from bony skeleton into flesh and blood. Something was changing within him; the hatred that had consumed him for so long melted away from his thoughts. Memories came flooding back: Leika's face and the warmth of her skin, the sweat on her brow after they'd made love, the cries of his daughter after she'd drawn her first breath.

Tears streamed from his eyes. The crushing loss threatened to consume him all over again.

The Terran, Benjamin Hutchins, stood before him now. His suit of powered armor was nearly unrecognizable, such was the beating it had taken during their short fight. His helmet was missing, revealing a face that was battered and bloody. But those eyes… Saryf expected to see his own hatred reflected in them, but all he saw was sorrow.

"I understand now," Hutchins said.

A bestial shriek emanated from the void, and the Terran looked around for a moment. "I can't hold it back much longer—the Master's influence—but before it takes hold again, I want you to know that I forgive you, Saryf."

Saryf sank to his knees and sobbed. "I'm sorry. I'm so sorry. I made a mistake. A mistake I will never be able to—aaaah!" Saryf collapsed, thrashing as a white-hot fury tore at his insides. "Please!" he begged. "Don't let it take me again! Kill me! Kill me!"

"I can't stop it," Hutchins said, "nor do I have the ability to end your life. But I can make sure it won't escape before the bomb my team planted wipes the facility from existence. Will that be enough?"

Saryf couldn't answer, such was the blinding agony that ripped at his soul. All he could muster was a frantic, uncoordinated nod.

Then everything turned red, and the rage returned.

———

BEN WATCHED as the Master's influence took hold once more, and the strikingly human-looking alien before him began to transform back into the agent's reaper avatar. His heart broke for Saryf. The alien hadn't been evil, merely lost after the deaths of his wife and daughter. He'd been searching for any way to take out his anger on those responsible. In a way, Ben and the consciousness now at the core of the agent's matrix were kindred spirits. He knew what that kind of loss felt like, what the rage could do if allowed to fester. He'd lost himself to it more than once just a year ago, and it was only with the help of the SEARs —and Tess, especially—that he was able to overcome it.

The Master's agents were not what he'd thought. These were living consciousnesses that had been ripped from their hosts and desecrated by the Master, twisted into hate-filled monstrosities that would do its bidding without question or remorse. Saryf had been one such soul many thousands of years ago, before humans had even begun writing down their own history.

The agent thrashed, a feral creature lashing out. But Ben was sure it could still hear him. He checked the time he had left.

"Just so you know, this is the end for you," he said. "My body may be broken in the real, but my will is stronger than ever, and in here… you… are… mine."

The agent's reaper avatar stilled, and those crimson eyes flared. "It doesn't matter if you kill me, Terran. My Master will not stop until your entire mistake of a race is cleansed from every hole you try to hide in!"

"Goodbye," Ben said. He turned and walked a short distance away, then sat down cross-legged and closed his eyes, letting his mind wander freely in the final seconds.

The faces of those he loved flashed through his thoughts. Mabel. Tess, Kravczyk, and Valdez. His dad and Shelly. Butler, Dominguez, and the rest of the Pathfinders he'd come to know over the last month. Elyria and even Klaythron. They surrounded him as the final seconds ticked down, sitting with him in supportive silence.

Would the Q-link module work? Would there simply be a flash and then he'd wake up surrounded by his family and friends? Or would something go wrong, ensuring that Ben Hutchins was lost forever? Strangely, in the microseconds before death, Ben found he didn't really care one way or the other. His life hadn't been very long, but he'd packed it with experiences most people could only dream of. Most importantly, he knew he'd done everything in his power to stop the Imperium and save the people he loved. And he could live with that.

His final thought before the tactical nuke detonated was of his mom, how he wished he'd had more time with her. He wondered what she would think about the life he'd made for himself. Would she be there to greet him?

Existence winked out, and everything went white.

———

"GOODBYE."

The agent scrambled as the Terran walked away. It reached out with all of its might, searching for something—anything— that would allow it to escape the digital prison that horrid creature had trapped him in. But it couldn't feel any connection to its systems at all. It was like Hutchins had completely severed its matrix from its hardware. The agent redoubled its efforts, willing *something* to become available—a means of salvation.

There it was! It was possible, but the agent would have to work fast. It quietly deleted the jumbled mess of a compression algorithm the Terrans had used and replaced it with a much more streamlined and elegant solution. If it used the same encryption scheme, it might be able to insert a script that would auto-unpack the engram after it was decrypted. It was a desperate, patchwork solution at best, but it was the agent's only chance. It sent the command to trigger an update, then sat back and awaited its fate.

"Goodbye, Benjamin Hutchins..." it rumbled quietly. "For now."

Existence winked out, and everything went black.

36

TESS

The Condor screamed into the night, fleeing the coming destruction as though the ship was a living, breathing thing aware of what was bearing down on it. All around her, marines lay dead and dying, tended to by the few members of Third Platoon still capable of doing so. Even cycled through her suit's purifiers, the air in the mighty dropship's cargo bay was thick with the stench of death.

She worked furiously, shoulder to shoulder with Valdez as the two of them did their best to patch up marine after marine. They wouldn't save them all; they couldn't. Not before they could reach an Alarian base capable of caring for their wounded. But that wasn't the only reason Tess threw herself into the work.

Ben's status indicator on her HUD remained grayed out. She knew what it meant, despite everything inside her hoping against hope that it didn't. Her eyes flashed to the roster again; the chief's indicator remained a bright green, as did the rest of his team's. An anguished wail threatened to escape her throat, but she stuffed it back down. Her hands shook. Tears welled in her eyes. But she continued working to save her brothers and sisters in arms, because that was where she was needed right now.

Just like Ben was right where he needed to be. To save them all.

"Brace, brace, brace!"

Tess threw herself over two of the wounded, anchoring them to the deck with the strength her APEX granted her. The ship lurched, yawing sharply to starboard. For a moment, she thought they hadn't made it. That they'd been too close to the facility when the bomb turned it into plasma and radioactive ash.

The Condor righted itself, and she released her hold on the deck. Valdez squeezed her shoulder lightly, not saying anything. There was nothing to say.

Ben had given his life to save them all. They went back to work, because doing otherwise would dishonor the sacrifice he'd made for them.

The sacrifice he'd made for her.

37

KRAVCZYK

KRAVCZYK SAT IN STONY SILENCE AS BANSHEE-1 THUNDERED AWAY from the complex. That *goddammed* complex. The place that might have cost them everything.

Around him, the Pathfinders from 1-1 were equally quiet, staring off through the utilitarian gray metal of the dropship's fuselage toward some distant place in time. It would be a different place for each of them, but also the same. Klaythron was also silent, unmoving. But that was par for the course for the captain of the Council Guard.

Kravczyk glanced one more time at his HUD, again taking comfort in seeing that the boss and McCollum had made it out safely. But Ben's icon remained the nebulous gray of *contact lost.*

"Five seconds, Chief." Mabel's voice, small and trembling, came through his suit comms.

Kravczyk turned to the bulkhead separating the cargo bay from the flight deck and thumped his fist against the cold, unrelenting metal three times, alerting the pilots to the impending explosion.

A distant rumble overpowered the shriek of the Griffon's engines at full military thrust. The deck shook, and the craft was buffeted by some unseen force on the other side of the alloy cocoon that protected them.

Ben's indicator remained gray, and the big SEAR knew with cold certainty that it would remain that way forever. A ball of iron rose in his throat, and he blinked away tears.

"Goddamn, kid," he said quietly to himself. "You did it. The first round's on me."

The omnipresent roar faded as the Griffon began the transition to the vacuum of space. They'd eliminated the threat of the agent. They were still alive, and they'd managed to save Mabel. The Alarians would agree to an alliance, and to Kravczyk's utter shock, the commander of the Imperium fleet above them had switched teams and wanted to help them take down the Master. That latter fact, though, made this whole thing seem like a Pyrrhic victory. Ben sacrificed himself so Mabel could escape with the data, only for Ramsey to inform him the remaining Imperium ships in orbit were now considered friendly. In other words, Ben's sacrifice was meaningless. They didn't need the data Mabel had stolen because they could now go right to the source for any questions.

By any objective measure, today had been a stunning victory. But the cavernous void in the SEAR's chest told him it had been anything but. He would pick up the pieces and push on, and he had no doubt they would eventually win this war. Because that was what SEARs did. But there was no doubt in Kravczyk's mind the galaxy was now worse off without Ben Hutchins in it.

38

THE SINS OF THE FATHER

HENRY STOOD OFF TO THE SIDE OF THE ORDERLY FORMATION OF spacers, marines, pilots, and officers from CTS *Indomitable*. Shelly was beside him, covertly squeezing his hand in support. The flight deck of the massive battlecruiser was filled with people. To his right, a delegation from the High Council stood in their flowing azure robes and ornate ceremonial armor. Elyria stood nearest to him, her rose-gold hair a striking contrast to the blue of her robes. Several other councilors were also in attendance, though Henry wasn't familiar with any of them. Klaythron and a small contingent from the Council Guard stood ramrod straight just behind her, their armor spotless and gleaming under the powerful lights overhead.

A long, black runner stretched the length of the assembled crowd, ending at the armored doors of a cargo airlock. A line of hard-faced marines and SEARs stood shoulder-to-shoulder opposite Henry. That damned length of black fabric felt like a metaphorical divide between him and the men and women who'd fought and bled alongside his son. Henry realized that, at some point in the recent past, Ben had crossed that divide and willingly stepped into the profession of combat arms. The people standing across from Henry were probably closer family to Ben than he was now, the knowledge of which only served to amplify his grief.

True to their tradition, the Pathfinders had had a marines-only funeral service, with a special exception made for the three SEARs who'd fought alongside them. Bravo Company, 155th Pathfinder Regiment, had lost thirty-one marines killed and sixteen wounded, who were still recovering in sickbay. It was the single bloodiest battle any Pathfinder company had endured in the sixty years since the inception of the Pathfinder Corps. Yet despite the devastating losses, every single one of them who was capable of attending today was present, and gratitude welled inside Henry.

The hangar was silent. Only the sounds of quiet breathing from those nearby let him know there was still life in this place, despite the pall of death that hung in the air.

Movement at the far end of the flight deck drew his attention. He didn't want to look, to be forced to admit what had happened. But he needed to.

Henry's eyes shifted to six figures. Three wore the distinctive onyx-black dress uniform of the navy's Special Exoatmospheric Reconnaissance Unit, and three more wore Marine Corps dress blues, the shining gold insignia of the Pathfinders blazing on their chests. Between them, they carried an ornate wooden casket—handmade by the finest woodcrafters Hai'alla had to offer. The deep, rich color of the wood was polished to a mirror finish, accentuating the intricate grain patterns. The flag of the Confederated Terran Systems was draped over the empty coffin. There'd been nothing left to bury; all that Ben had been was now forever a part of the world he'd sacrificed himself to save.

Henry choked down the agony that threatened to pour from his throat, and Shelly squeezed his hand a little harder.

Two of the marines from *Indomitable*'s security detachment

stepped forward and removed the flag. They carefully folded it, making sure the creases were laser sharp as they performed a ritual that was centuries old. When they were done, one of the marines remained, standing behind the casket and displaying the flag in his hands. The group moved in unison until they were in front of the first of the Pathfinders lining the flight deck.

Major Davis stepped forward and executed a sharp ninety-degree turn. He reached up to his left breast and removed the Pathfinder Corps insignia from its place over his ribbon rack. His arm windmilled over his head, and a loud bang echoed off the bulkheads. Henry flinched, the sound filling his ears like a gunshot in the confined space. Davis slowly withdrew his hand, leaving his insignia buried in the wooden top. The short barbs that had pinned it to his uniform bit deep into the grain, anchoring it in place.

Davis returned to his place in line, and the honor guard proceeded to the next marine. They repeated this symbolic gesture sixty times—sixty gunshots, all of which struck Henry directly in the heart. Sixty Pathfinder Corps insignia lined the top of his son's empty casket. It seemed such a small offering, but Henry knew it was the single greatest honor those marines could bestow upon their fallen brother.

At last, the procession stopped in front of him, and the casket was placed on a wheeled dolly that sat just outside the airlock. The six members of the honor guard all took turns hammering their hard-earned insignia into the polished wood. Chief Kravczyk went last. The thunderous boom of his enormous hand slamming into the wood seemed to reverberate around the flight deck for an eternity, as if to emphasize the cold finality of death.

Then a marine was standing in front of Henry with a carefully folded flag. His numb hands reached out to take it. Tears streamed from his eyes and his lip trembled as he fought to contain his anguish. The marine said something as he handed over the flag, but Henry didn't hear it. This was the second time in his life that he'd buried his son—his baby boy.

He'd done this. In his obsessive pursuit of science—of the technology that could shield Terran space against terrible enemies—and his determination to avenge his wife, Henry had ensured that Ben would be made to suffer the sins of his father. And it had cost him everything.

The casket was rolled into the airlock while a marine played taps on a gleaming trumpet. Captain Ramsey said something, and every single person on the flight deck turned as one. The airlock doors closed, and the cry that Henry had fought so desperately to keep inside finally escaped.

39

REGIME CHANGE

ADMIRAL ROBERT GARLAND SAT BEHIND HIS DESK, WAITING FOR THE knock he knew was coming any minute now.

The senate had just officially removed President Martha McGibbons from office, and her VP, Jasper Cunningham, was sworn in as her replacement. Garland had to give Cunningham and his allies credit—they didn't fuck around. He hadn't really expected the senate to get its act together and make any major moves for another few weeks, but the proceedings, spearheaded by that snake Cynthia Mercer, had moved forward at breakneck speed. The whole thing was over in just three days.

Unfortunately, the timing could not have been worse. Word had just come in from *Indomitable* over Hai'alla, and the shitstorm Ramsey kicked up when he'd informed them that the goddamn first admiral of the Imperial Navy had turned traitor and was seeking asylum had only just started. If they'd only had a little more time... Garland snorted at the thought. It was the story of his career. *"Just a little more time" should be the unofficial motto of the Confed*, he thought, a sardonic smile briefly crossing his lips.

A commotion from the other side of his office door pulled his attention back to the task at hand. The door flew open, revealing that sniveling little CID weasel Charles Wheaton, Russ Ogden, and a pair of very uncomfortable-looking marine guards.

"You could've at least knocked." Garland stood up and straightened out his uniform top. "Well, let's get on with it then."

Wheaton sneered. "Don't act so surprised, Garland," he said, which was odd, considering the admiral hadn't been surprised in the least. The little shit must've had some big speech all planned out, and Garland skipping right to the part where they dragged him out of the office threw him off his game. "You're a relic from a bygone era, an anachronism in the modern galaxy. If it were up to me, we'd just blow your ass out an airlock and be done with it."

Garland stopped next to the little turd, towering over him with a carefree smile on his face. "Well, then I guess I should be glad it's not up to you, shouldn't I?" Wheaton spluttered indignantly, and Garland's expression turned serious. He looked at Ogden. "I can't believe you went along with this, Russ. You've seen the same reports I have."

Ogden's stony expression remained. "I have, Bob. The difference is, no matter which way I slice it, I can't come to the same conclusions you have. Christ, your people ambushed a member of the High Council, triggered a nuke on Elizabeth, and have gotten us neck-deep in a shooting war we aren't prepared for. That's not just a failure of leadership in my book, it's a fucking disaster—one that very well could end up with us wiped out." He jerked his head toward the exit. "Come on, don't make me have the marines put you in cuffs. Let's go."

Garland sighed in resignation and walked out of his office. He wasn't looking forward to the grilling he was sure to receive both in public and in private over the coming days and weeks, but at least he took comfort in knowing that he and

Mark Gideon had done all they could to prepare for this contingency.

The fight for the soul of the Confed had officially begun, and he'd be damned if he went down without getting his shots in.

———

NEWLY MINTED PRESIDENT of the Confederated Terran Systems Jasper Cunningham leaned back in his chair and rubbed his eyes. He'd been VP for half a decade, but the sheer weight of responsibility that now rested on his shoulders was already taking a toll after just a short time as president. He swiveled in his seat and gazed out the window at the lights of Arcadia, trying to figure out which of the thousand critical items on his to-do list he should tackle next.

His whirlwind tour of the major Confed worlds was wrapping up in a few days. The Valkyrie system and Isadore were the last stops on a trip that hadn't been as successful as he'd hoped. The last few weeks of attempting to solidify his position at the top of the Confed's power-elite had met more resistance than he'd expected, and he was exhausted from the constant battling between factions. How McGibbons and her pro-Alarian inner circle were able to maintain such support, even after the utter disaster they'd wrought by taking on the Imperium, was beyond him.

A soft knock sounded from the door that led to the adjoining room, and the door opened a moment later, revealing the exhausted face of Felicia Keller, his longtime chief of staff, who'd followed him up to the big office when he was sworn in as president. "Mr. President, I'm leaving for the night. Is there anything you need before I go?"

"No, Felicia. Thank you, though. Go get some rest. It's been a hell of a day."

She smiled a tired smile. "You'd be wise to follow your own advice, sir. You look just as exhausted as I feel. Goodnight."

The door closed, and the president checked his watch. God, was it really three in the morning already? He decided to call it a night and logged out of the terminal built into the desk, then stood from his chair and stretched his shoulders. He'd just pulled his coat from the hook on the wall near his desk when the lights of his office suddenly winked out. Cursing, the president fumbled around for the touch controls on the desk.

A shadowy, indistinct figure appeared in the middle of the office, and the president yelped in surprise and tripped over his chair as he backpedaled.

"President Jasper Cunningham, it's nice to meet you." The voice was menacing, a deep, sonorous rumble that instantly had every hair on the president's body standing on end. "Some of your compatriots contacted one of my agents recently about the possibility of negotiating terms to ensure your continued existence."

The figure didn't continue, and Jasper took that as his cue to respond. It took a few tries to get his voice working, but he finally managed to get out a simple, "That's right."

"So," the figure said. "Let's discuss terms."

40

HOPE

Tess stood outside the hatch to *Indomitable*'s guest quarters, a tear-stained piece of paper clutched in her hands. She made to knock on the hatch for the third time in as many minutes and paused again. Why was she here? What could she possibly say to him, other than to beg for his forgiveness? Her hand wavered and fell to her side. She turned to leave, but the hatch opened behind her.

"You don't have to leave," Henry said. "I think we could all use some company right about now." Tess turned, and Henry inclined his head toward his quarters. His eyes were puffy and bloodshot, much like she suspected hers were. "Come on in. I just had the galley send up some coffee. You're welcome to it."

She followed him into the surprisingly spacious compartment and sat down on a small sofa when he offered it. She looked around. Tess didn't know why, but for some reason, she expected to see signs that this space was lived in by someone who'd been close to Ben—to see something that would help her feel connected to him in some small way. But the spartan guest quarters were just like every other compartment on this ship:

cold and empty, save for some datapads and other personal items on the small fold-out desk against the bulkhead.

"Here you go," Henry said, holding out a steaming thermal mug.

She nodded absently and took the proffered cup. The pungent, earthy aroma of the coffee contrasted starkly with the astringent scent of paint, off-gassing textiles, and lingering cleaning agents that comprised the ubiquitous "new ship" smell that *Indomitable* hadn't had enough time to wear away yet. Henry sat next to her on the sofa and hunched over with his hands cradling the mug in his lap.

"He loved you, you know?" Henry said into his coffee, not yet able to bring himself to look her in the eye. "He didn't say anything, but I could tell. That little extra lift to the grin that seemed to always be on his lips recently... Don't blame yourself. It's not what he would have wanted, and it doesn't honor the sacrifice he made."

Tess stared down at the folded sheaf of paper in her hand and idly ran her thumb over it. "I know. He wrote me this letter. Who even writes letters on actual paper anymore?"

Henry chuckled. "That would be his mother's doing. She always said that ink on paper could connect two people like no tablet screen ever could, because you can see every mark that was made and know that someone's hand had touched that very same page to make them."

"I keep asking myself if there was anything I could have done differently. My head is full of what-ifs and should-haves. But I don't think there was, and I'm not sure if that's better or worse than knowing someone screwed up somewhere, because at least then I'd have someone to blame. Instead, I'm left here feeling completely lost with nothing to take my grief out on. I can't even be mad at the agent, because it's gone, too."

Tears welled in her eyes, and she could feel the pain leaking from the box she'd tried stuffing it into. Her diaphragm spasmed as she fought to keep it all bottled up. But she couldn't, not anymore. "Goddammit! Why did it have to be him? Why couldn't it have been literally anyone else?" She wanted to say so much more, but her voice failed her. Henry hugged her as the two of them sobbed together, sharing in the loss each of them had suffered.

When they'd both run out of tears to cry, they sat in silence, taking comfort in the mere presence of one another. Eventually, Henry stood and walked to the small head next to the attached sleeping compartment. He returned a minute later with a warm, damp towel and offered it to her. She nodded gratefully, dabbing the dried tears from her cheeks.

A soft knock came from the hatch, and Henry opened it, revealing the woman he'd been standing next to at Ben's service. Tess stood and nodded a polite greeting.

"Oh, Henry, I'm sorry. I didn't realize McCollum was here." She looked uncomfortable, like she felt like some kind of voyeur for interrupting what had clearly been an emotional moment between Tess and Henry. "I can wait down on the mess deck, if you need more time."

"It's fine, Shelly," Henry said. The smile on his face was both sad and exhausted. "We were just finishing up here."

Tess walked to the head and wrung out the towel, then tossed it into the laundry bin when she was satisfied she'd squeezed as much water from it as she could. When she came back out, Henry and Shelly were sitting on the couch, talking softly. Tess absently looked over the personal items Henry had scattered about the desk near the head, then made to leave.

"Thank you, Mr. Hutchins—"

"Henry, Tess. You're family. You don't need to be so formal."

Tess nodded. "I don't know what's going to happen now, but in case we don't see each other again—"

The comms panel on the wall by the desk lit up, and Mabel's dot matrix cube flashed to life on the screen.

"Henry, come down to the engineering shops immediately," she said without preamble. "I've been running through what went wrong with the prototype quantum link module you integrated into Ben's APEX, and I found something that can't possibly be here. I need you and Ms. Fordham to take a look and tell me I'm not going crazy."

Henry bolted to his feet, staring at Mabel's avatar with an intensity Tess had rarely seen another human express before. "What is it, Mabel? What did you find?"

"Henry... I think I found Ben."

EPILOGUE

BEN BLINKED. THE WORLD AROUND HIM WAS A FEATURELESS, blinding white. He looked at his hands; the wounds from his battle with the agent and the scars from years working on a farm were all gone. Nothing but pristine flesh remained. He wiggled his fingers. He felt better than he could ever remember.

"Hello, Ben."

Ben whipped around and froze, eyes going wide when he saw who'd spoken to him. "Mom?" The word came out as barely more than a whisper. He took a tentative step forward, reaching toward her. "Is it… Is it really you?"

"I've missed you so much, Ben. Watching you grow up into the man you are now has been the greatest joy of my life."

She extended her hand, and Ben grasped it. Her skin was smooth and soft and it radiated a warmth like the sun itself lived inside her. He couldn't speak. Hot tears stung his eyes, flowing freely as she embraced him. He wanted to say so many things, to tell her about everything that had happened, about how much he missed her, about how hard it had been after she died. But his voice refused to work, instead allowing only sobs to escape.

He cried for but a moment. He cried for eternity. And the whole time, she stood there, unwavering as she held him close and let him release all his anguish. When, at last, the tears stopped, he pulled back from her.

"So what now? Are you here to take me up to see the big man or something?" he said, wiping the tears from his eyes with the back of his hand.

She smiled. It was a sad smile, one that told him this moment was not to last much longer. "No, my darling Benjamin. It's not yet your time. You still have work to do down there."

Ben frowned. "But... But I'm dead. Like, *dead* dead. A nuke went off and turned me into a bunch of ionized particles that should be showering down over Hai'alla right about now."

He looked around. The brilliant white of the surrounding space had faded somewhat around the edges. As he looked on, a gray haze began to encroach on them from the periphery.

"I love you, Benjamin, and I'm so proud of you. You've become so much more than I'd ever hoped. And when it's your time, know that I'll be here to greet you again. And don't despair, because you're destined for great things."

She began to drift slowly away from him, and try as he might, he couldn't get back to her. "Mom, what is this place? Isn't this heaven?"

The blanket of gray mist swallowed her up, and her voice faded away as she replied. "It's not my place to tell you, Ben. You'll need to decide for yourself what you believe."

Her words faded to silence, and the gray mist pressed in, smothering him as the light faded.

Existence winked out, and everything went black.

———

A FAINT, regular beeping cut through the dark. Ben listened to it for hours, days even, but it remained constant.

Beep.

His thoughts drifted to the brief eternity he'd spent with his mom. Had that even been real? Or was it just a desperate last firing of neurons in the instant before he'd been annihilated by nuclear fire? It could also be something related to the process of being brought back from the abyss, he supposed.

Beep.

Yet the warmth of her touch was seared into his brain. The scent of her hair as he'd wept into her shoulder was as vivid and real as anything else he could remember.

Beep.

The question gnawed at him for days, then weeks. It consumed him. But in the end, he was no closer to an answer than when he'd started.

Beep.

Finally, he decided it was time to head toward that sound. With a herculean effort, he forced his consciousness to assemble itself and begin the arduous swim toward reality.

"He's coming around. Inform the admiral."

The voice was close and sounded surprised. It had an odd timbre, higher-pitched, with a trilling undertone. Ben sent the command for his eyelids to open, and data flooded into his brain.

"Benjamin Hutchins?"

A bright light shone into his eyes, and he blinked to escape the overload it caused.

"Benjamin Hutchins, can you hear me?"

"Shut that damn light off, will you?"

The light snapped off, and a head covered with a surgical mask and cap appeared in Ben's line of sight.

"Welcome back, Terran. My master has been looking forward to meeting you," the man said. He reached up and removed the mask, revealing a huge smile stretched across his face.

A face with a wide mouth and large, glassy black eyes.

<u>The End</u>

AUTHOR'S NOTE

First and foremost, I want to say thanks for reading my books. It really means a lot to me that total strangers would give me their hard earned money to read the stuff that randomly vomits out of my brain while I pretend to be an "author." Secondly, I apologize if this book was an incoherent mess. It turns out that trying to finish up a book immediately after your wife gives birth to your second child is an exercise in futility. I can't tell you how many times I had to reread lines because my sleep-deprived brain was completely incapable of registering what my eyes were seeing. I promise the next one will be better. Probably. Well, maybe.

Now, on to the juicy self-promo bits! I'm making a short story available to everyone on my email list, for FREE! It's around 6,500 words and details the incident on Hai'alla between Ben and Elyria back before the war. So if you're interested in reading some more about young Ben and the awkward shenanigans he gets up to, scan the QR code below and sign up for my newsletter!

E-mail signup link (at the top of the page)

I'm also working on a novella that chronicles Kravczyk's disastrous first combat drop with SEAR Team 1 on Newman's Rock. This one will be straight up, good old-fashioned military sci-fi. One point-of-view, lots of action.

After it's complete and edited, it'll be a subscriber exclusive. I'm even kicking around the idea of having Paul Heitsch record an audio version of it that will be, you guessed it, exclusive to my newsletter subscribers. And free! Did I mention free? I like free, and I'm guessing you do, too. So click that link up there and signup!

Finally, I've got a bunch of little nuggets I plan on getting up on my website as time allows. Things like character bios, maybe some deleted scenes, etc. Be sure to check back now and then.

Alright, enough rambling about all my super cool stuff that I'm trying to give you for free. Thanks again for reading!

Carry on.

-John

P.S. I also have a Facebook page! If that's more your speed than a website, stop by to catch up on all the latest happenings. Here's a QR code to take you there.

J.R. Robertson's Facebook Page!

Printed in Great Britain
by Amazon

22393146R00219